TOM DEITZ

"A MASTER"
Brad Strickland, co-author of *Crisis on Vulcan*

"A MAJOR FANTASY AUTHOR"
Booklist

"ONE OF THE BEST"
OtherRealms

"DEITZ KNOWS HOW TO SPIN A GOOD
YARN . . . HE DOESN'T STINT ON
ATMOSPHERE AND PLOT . . . AND
TRANSMITS A STRONG SENSE OF DREAD."
Publishers Weekly

"DEITZ HAS THE ENVIABLE ABILITY TO
MAKE CLEARLY FANTASTIC INCIDENTS
SEEM REALISTIC AND SUPERIMPOSE THEM
ON A STORY OF GENUINE CHARACTERS
DEALING WITH GENUINE PROBLEMS."
Science Fiction Chronicle

"TOM DEITZ IS WRITING
BETTER THAN EVER."
Mercedes Lackey, author of *Friends of Valdemar*

LANDSLAYER'S LAW

TOM DEITZ

AVON BOOKS • NEW YORK

This is a work of fiction. Names, characters, places, and incidents either are the product of the author's imagination or are used fictitiously. Any resemblance to actual events, locales, organizations, or persons, living or dead, is entirely coincidental and beyond the intent of either the author or the publisher.

AVON BOOKS
A division of
The Hearst Corporation
1350 Avenue of the Americas
New York, New York 10019

First AvoNova Printing: July 1997

AVONOVA TRADEMARK REG. U.S. PAT. OFF. AND IN OTHER COUNTRIES, MARCA REGISTRADA, HECHO EN U.S.A.

Printed in the U.S.A.

WCD   10   9   8   7   6   5   4   3   2   1

In memory of River

ACKNOWLEDGMENTS

Soren Andersen
Jennifer Brehl
Beulah N. Deitz
John Douglas
Amy Goldschlager
Tom Jeffery
Virginia Martin
Deena McKinney
Howard Morhaim
Wilda Quarantino
Jeff Smith
B.J. Steinhaus
Hollis Townsend

And a special thanks to
Buck Marchinton for
lending me John Devlin

Prelude:
The Splendor Falls

(Sullivan Cove, Georgia—
Wednesday, April 23—midafternoon)

"Where does *that* 'un go?" Ralph Mims demanded from the passenger seat of Ben Carl's black Grand Cherokee. He pointed ahead and to the left for emphasis—straight under Ben's stubby nose, which irked the hell out of that feature's rather more attenuated owner. Not for the first time did Carl wonder what he'd got himself into: agreeing to show this flatland resort developer around the wilds of Enotah County. Though technically a flatlander himself, he'd lived up here in the north Georgia mountains for over thirty years and sold real estate for twenty of 'em: more than long enough to know every pig trail, logging road, and mile-long gravel driveway in half a dozen counties.

He'd just not expected to play tour guide down all of 'em in three days. Shoot, the Cherokee showed more mud than paint now; he'd had one flat, chipped an expensive aluminum rim, and this dratted picky money-monger *still* hadn't found a piece of property that suited him. Of course it'd help if Mr. Fat-ass'd explain what he actually wanted!

The finger hovered in place, though Ben had a strong urge to swat it halfway back to Athens, whence Mims had emerged like a grumpy rattler with the coming of spring. "Sullivan Cove," he supplied instead—because he had to. "Private property—or Forest Service."

"So?"

"So what?"

1

"So was every other piece you've shown me the last two days. Why should this be any different?"

Ben ground his teeth and accelerated gently—pointedly—along the long straight that had uncoiled at the tail of the tortuous curves, grades, and switchbacks that marked the descent from Franks Gap and the White County border. Mountains rose to either side, lush with spring hardwoods spiced with evergreens: a frame of wilderness bracketing the cultivated river bottoms ahead and mostly to the right. "It's different," he sighed through his teeth (still not slowing), "because the Sullivans've been there two hundred years and haven't sold an acre they haven't been forced to. Shoot, the REA had to march the old man out with shotguns when they built the lake, and even then—"

"Lake?" Mims removed the finger, but effectively replaced it with the rest of his stocky body, as though he would climb through the grimy windshield if he could. "Turn! Now!"

"Waste of time," Ben countered, even as he complied. After all, he was charging by the hour—and charging a lot. Maybe he should think about overtime—or, given the Sullivans, hazard pay. *Please God, don't let's meet old Dale*, he prayed, with an audible sigh, as he swung the Cherokee hard left across a culvert and down a gravel road.

To the right, a low wooded ridge loomed close upon a few acres of freshly plowed farmland, facing an old, if much-augmented, clapboard house perched atop a bare hill an eighth-mile across the way, with the mountain they'd just descended lurking protectively above the splintery gray rampart of decrepit outbuildings behind it. A slim blond woman in jeans sat on the front porch drinking something from a glass that sparked in the sunlight; a newish Ford F-150 and an oldish Crown Vic marked the terminus of a steep, rocky driveway just past the dwelling. "Sullivan number one," Ben announced. "Bill and JoAnne. I'd mess with him 'fore I'd mess with her, but I wouldn't recommend messin' with either."

"Farmers?"

"Technically. She works in a plant once in a while; he

fools around with sorghum, and I think there's family money.''

Mims (blessedly back in his seat) eyed the house speculatively—likely equating its patchwork shabbiness with lack of prosperity, which was a mistake in this case, and a big one. ''Reckon they'd sell?'' he queried, right on cue.

''Not for a million bucks.''

''Any kids?''

Ben started at that, which he reckoned a non sequitur, except that maybe Mims figured setting their kids up right might make a difference. He knew better. Still . . . ''Two boys. Little 'un's still at home—must be 'bout ten or eleven now; older 'un's down at the University. 'Bout to graduate, I reckon. Smart kid, that 'un is: smartest boy in the county, I'd say—maybe the smartest person, period.''

Mims merely grunted. They passed a small church and graveyard to the right, a series of steep rolling pastures to the left. Matching arcs of woodland angled in further on, reducing the roadside fields to cramped strips no more than fifty yards wide, before opening out to the left on another farm even more run down than the first. An ancient, tin-roofed frame house stood there, abandoned behind a range of ragged cedars, looking for all the world as though some enormous constrictor had coiled about the structure and squeezed. A newer trailer further back and across the drive appeared well-kept and occupied. ''Sullivan number two,'' Ben observed. ''Dale. Bill's uncle.''

''Age?''

''Seventy—maybe? Who knows?''

''Kids?''

''Nope.''

''Heirs?''

''Bill's boy David, I reckon.''

''The smart 'un?''

''Yep.'' And by then they had entered the wilder land that marked the last half of Sullivan Cove Road. Mims had perked up, Ben noted sourly, as though he'd finally found something that interested him. Just his luck, too: for him to get the hots for the one chunk of real estate he'd never pry loose from its masters.

"Where's this lake?"

"Road dead-ends there," Ben replied, grimacing as they crunched into an unexpected rut. "Old Sullivan place is underwater beyond."

Ralph nodded smugly. Ben masked his irritation with a yawn. The land had opened up again, fallow fields alternating with patches of woods, alternating with serious forest. Ahead was a glitter that could only be water. Blue sky rose above: cloudless, save for a vague troubling in the air, like wind made manifest.

The road petered out in a turnaround ringed by the pale, worn-out stalks of last year's broom sedge and pockmarked by the darker detritus of countless campfires. Without asking, Ben parked the Jeep and switched off the ignition. "Wanta get out?"

"Wouldn't miss it," Ralph replied smartly, fumbling with the door lock. "I'm real impressed so far."

You would be, Ben nearly blurted out, even as he schooled his expression to careful blandness. A pause to steel himself, and he joined Mims on the scraggly grass at the end of the road. Mims inhaled deeply. "Looks good!" he enthused, striding toward the fringe of pines that screened all but the merest shimmer of the lake. Ben followed doggedly. The larger man's ample bulk blocked most of the view ahead.

"This is it," Mims proclaimed, hands on hips. "Why didn't you tell me about that mountain?"

"What mountain?" Ben wondered, easing up beside his client. But then he saw.

The land sloped down before him in a series of bare shelves, equal parts red clay and yellow rock until they disappeared beneath the glassy waters of a wide, mysterious-looking lake. But straight ahead—no more than half a mile offshore—a small mountain reared a near-perfect cone above the surface: a cone whose summit was faced with raw cliffs of some white stone—quartzite, probably—that glittered so brightly in the sunlight it hurt to look upon.

"*That* mountain," Mims snapped, pointing.

"Oh . . . right," Ben choked. "I forgot about that."

Mims stared at him incredulously. "You *forgot*? How

could you forget something like that? Hell, it's perfect! We'll put a lodge on top, with a cable-car to it, and a marina here, and cabins, and—''

Ben wasn't listening, absorbed as he was with pondering how he could possibly have failed to recall a view as spectacular as this. It wasn't like he hadn't seen it before, though not often since high school, it being a popular parking and skinny-dipping spot—if the Sullivans didn't catch you. Yet the image he'd retained in his mind as he'd turned down the road had included the lake but not the mountain. Funny that was; *real* funny. And even odder now he thought of it, was the fact that this had happened before. More than once, in fact, he'd trundled down this very road, come to the lake, and been amazed to find a perfectly good mountain there. It was as if he forgot about the place as soon as he left it. Or, he realized with a shudder, as if the peak didn't *want* to be remembered.

''Who owns this?'' Mims bellowed, gesturing broadly to either hand.

''I'll . . . have to check,'' Ben managed, desperately glad to confront something comprehensible, however stressful, in lieu of what seemed to be tricks of the mind. ''Doubt it's the Sullivans, though. REA condemned it for the lake, so it's either them or the state.''

''In either case, money talks,'' Mims boomed. ''Leave the state to me. You find out who holds the deed.''

''Right,'' Ben murmured absently, rubbing his eyes. Maybe *this* time he'd remember.

PART ONE

Part One

Prologue I:
There . . .

(near Sylva, North Carolina—
Thursday, June 19—late afternoon)

". . . and stay where you can hear me!" Jamie's ma hollered from the open door of the run down pink-and-white trailer that perched precariously on the steep hillside. Dark pines loomed behind it: the Pisgah National Forest. Jamie tried not to feel ashamed as he looked back. It was no fun being poor, no fun having a redneck daddy and a sometime whore for a mom (though he wasn't supposed to know that word, or what it meant), no fun living in a place that looked like the woods had kicked it out like so much trash piled on its doorstep but not collected.

No fun having to keep tabs on a tomfool dickhead of a younger brother.

Still, the park beckoned: the nice clean streamside picnic area down the hill and to the right, where the government land ran up against 441, with only his folks' washed-out gravel drive dividing all that neatness from their place, with its—what was that word he'd learned in school last week? Squalor?

(Eight-year-old Alvin running on ahead like a banty rooster didn't count, 'cause he was actually a fairly sharp kid most of the time, good-hearted when Ma and Pa let him, and cleaned up decent well in the bargain.)

No! He wouldn't think about that; he'd think about good things. Pretty country everywhere but straight behind. A sweet, clear stream to play in: collecting rocks, or chasing crawdads, or looking for raccoon tracks; or even, sometimes, and not always in vain, panning for gold.

And the tourists. Most folks hereabout didn't care for 'em, but Jamie kinda liked 'em, 'cause they mostly drove cool new cars or (increasingly) pickups, and wore new clothes, and had good food and lots of it, and sported fresh haircuts and—and even smelled good. (And when was the last time Ma or Pa smelled good?) And often as not, they had kids him and Alvin could play with, who didn't know his folks were Poor White Trash.

Jamie kicked at a pine cone, venting a rush of anger that had risen, maxed out, and faded all in a dozen strides. And by then he'd reached the road—no need to check before dashing across the gravel drive—and was dogging Alvin's shadow into the fringe of pines that hid the park from his folks' ugly lot. Quiet enclosed him there in that borderland, if not true peace. He inhaled deeply, relishing the scent of evergreens in lieu of the all too familiar sweat, beer, and burned grease that clogged the air back home.

"Come on, slowpoke!" Alvin chided up ahead, his Appalachian twang softened by the million dark green needles that filled the yards between. Impulsively, Jamie darted forward—and emerged into dazzling light.

It could've been another country: the clean, bright land of his dreams. But it was only a parking lot, recently paved, newly marked and painted—and empty. Jamie felt a pang of regret at that. No new kids to hang out with today and pretend he was a savvy and sophisticated city boy. No one to let him try their electronic toys, no town talk to listen to, so he could copy it—and maybe, someday, work the hick out of his own voice.

Empty.

"Damn!" he muttered, and jogged off to where Alvin was already disappearing down the trail to the creek. He joined him a moment later—and was shocked to discover that his brother was not alone. Two other boys crouched on the rocks there—or were they boys? They had *really* long hair, for one thing, and were awfully smooth-faced and slender, but they had wide shoulders too, and strong jawlines. It was hard to tell their ages—fourteen or fifteen, maybe: a little older than himself. There was also a girl, which might be good or might not. You had to be careful of city girls.

And these were clearly not country folk—not in clothes like that: new leather jeans and bright silk shirts, and with their hair dyed shimmery green and blue like those guys in Green Day, only darker, and with their ears and eyebrows pierced, but—there was no other word, in spite of two of 'em being boys—beautiful all the same.

"They're from the mountain," Alvin announced, as he sat down on a flat rock and commenced dabbling in the water. "They're musicians."

The girl's eyes twinkled with mystery, even as she laughed; and the sound was like harmony sung with the tinkling water. She was also carrying a small drum. "You found that out already?" Jamie gaped. "Boy, you're fast!"

"We told him," the smaller outlander admitted. "We knew he wanted to know and was afraid to ask—so we told him."

"You stayin' over at the lodge?" Jamie wondered, feeling even smaller, dirtier, and uglier than usual.

"Near there," the taller boy acknowledged. "We became bored and decided to . . . see what we could find."

"Well, you found us," Jamie grinned. "That's about it. Not much goin' on 'round here."

"I do not think I would agree with that," the girl retorted, flashing a smile so dazzling it almost hurt to look at. She shook her head so that the rings—six at least—in each ear jingled. There was something else funny about her ears too, but Jamie didn't dare look too close, 'cause that would be staring, which was rude—and he suddenly wanted, very badly, for these strange, neat folks to like him.

"So what shall we play?" the smaller visitor inquired, rising.

"Tag?" From his larger companion.

"Follow-the-leader?" Alvin countered—because he was good at it, quick and nimble and fearless as he was.

The girl bit her perfect lips, then shook her head. "Hide-and-seek," she proclaimed, staring at Alvin curiously. Then: "Jamie, I think *you* ought to be it."

Jamie started to protest, but decided these folks might

choose not to play with him if he did, so he nodded. "How high you want me to count?"

"Nine times nine," the girl replied, taking Alvin's hand. "Now come away, child; you can hide with me."

Jamie clamped his hands over his eyes, leaned into the rough bark of a nearby pine, and began: "One—two—three—" He'd reached twenty before he recalled that it wasn't like Alvin to agree to hide with *anyone*, much less a girl. And he'd reached seventy-four before he realized he had never once mentioned his name.

Prologue II:
. . . and Back Again

(Gargyn's Hold—Tir-Nan-Og—high summer)

"Da's comin'!" The Littl'un crowed from the cottage's open door, eyes round as the bottom of one of those all-too-perfect bottles the Quick Folks discarded so carelessly— and as green as some of them, too. He was fidgeting like a hop-toad on a griddle: bouncing from foot to bare foot almost too quick to see. *Dirty* feet, Borbin noted. Torn shirt. Mud on the hem of his kilt, and the Lord Lugh knew what kind of leaves stuck in that impossible thatch of crimson hair, which more than hinted that the lad had been where he oughtn't—like the feathery woods visible across the melon patch behind him.

Borbin sighed wearily—tolerantly, though she hid that lapse at once—and wiped her pudgy hands on the snowy apron that encircled her ample girth: ample for a bodach, anyway. "An' where, a worried mother might inquire, did you *do* this seein', my child?"

The Littl'un braced himself on the doorjamb, which stabilized his upper half somewhat, though his lower part kept right on twitching. "Out by the—" His face fell. His eyes grew even rounder.

"By the *Hole*, perhaps?" Borbin snapped, suddenly all steel.

The boy turned pale—and stilled as far down as the knees, likely from raw terror. "I didn't *mean* to! Me an' Urgo was playin', an' all at once we were just there, an'—"

"Urgo's gonna be the death o' you," Borbin grumbled—

13

"an' it's *hard* to kill one o' us, as well you know!" A pause for breath, and to take an ominous step closer, then: "Don't let me tell you again! Them Holes is dangerous. They're eatin' through everywhere 'round here now! Why, one could gnaw through right here 'tween us, 'fore we knew it! Lugh knows one opened up under poor old Maddy MacOrpins t'other day, an' she ain't been seen since! I oughta—"

She paused abruptly. "What did you say?"

The Littl'un looked puzzled. "When?"

"When you came in!"

"That Da's home—"

"Gargyn!" Borbin shrieked, and forgot her youngest entirely until she was ten strides out the door—and only recalled him then because she tripped over the mechanical manticore Gargyn had carved him before his voyage. And by the time she'd picked herself up, Gargyn himself was running through the melon patch toward her. She winced, even as she laughed, certain she'd heard at least two 'loupes split beneath that reckless tread. Markon, the eldest old'un, wasn't far behind: any excuse to get out of work, though she supposed she'd forgive him this time. Wasn't every day your sire returned from a voyage to Ys. Wasn't *every* day a voyager to Ys made it back safe and sound, not anymore; not with the Holes nibbling away on the Seas Between as much as on land, so she'd heard.

"Sweet wife!" Gargyn yelled.

"Darlin' husband!" Borbin hollered back. And a moment later they were entwined like newlyweds among the pumpkin vines.

Eventually Gargyn released her, but she knew the news wasn't good long before then, by the way his embrace had seemed impatient and tired, dull eyes had capped what she knew from centuries of wedlock was not a sincere smile, never mind the preoccupation hiding in his kiss.

"Any news?" she prompted softly, even as she drew him toward the piled stone wall between the patch and the cottage proper. Gargyn's shoulders slumped as he collapsed against her. His feet were dirty too, just like the Littl'un's, and raw and blistered, as though he'd run most of the way from the haven at the coast. He smelled of sweat and weariness. But all that was for later, for now he needed peace—as much as she needed to know.

Finally Gargyn spoke, voice thin as his shanks, his shoulders, and his sides. "*Bad* news," he agreed. "Herself's withdrawn her offer. Says Ys is bustin' at the seams now; says she can't take no more refugees, an' may have t' send some of the ones is there now back. Says Lugh's let the trouble go on too long, and it's for him to fix—which I've been sayin' all along."

"But the gate? I thought—"

Gargyn shook his shaggy head. "Gate's got to be too dangerous—*she* says. Says even she don't dare poke through the World Walls no more—not since Lugh cheated her out of the Openin' Stone."

Borbin snorted. "Wouldn't o' worked no better"—an old argument. "First off, it weren't his to give or hold back; it belonged to one of the Quick Folks—though how that 'un got such a thing, I have no idea. An' second, a Hole in the Walls is a Hole in the Walls, far as I can see."

" 'Cept she said she thought the Walls might heal 'round a permanent one," Gargyn countered. "If it was made with Power, I mean."

"Fuck they would!" Markon grumbled, stomping up to join them, sweat streaking the dust on his bare chest and legs. He peered at his parents sullenly from beneath the wide brim of an intricate purple velvet hat one of the Seelie Lords had lost last time they rode by. He sat down without asking—breathing, Borbin thought, a little *too* hard for the amount of hoeing he'd actually accomplished. Concern made her ignore the Quick Folks curse she'd had no luck eradicating.

"What're the World Walls?" the Littl'un blurted, out of nowhere. "An' who's *she*?"

"The Queen of Ys," Markon hissed. "Rhiannon—'less Rigantana's took over like folks was sayin' she might, on account of how she's better at dealin' with the Quick Folks—"

"She hasn't—yet—that I know of," Gargyn broke in, fondling the Littl'un's head. "As for the World Walls . . .

they're whatever separates this World from the Lands of Men, or the Quick Folks Land, or whatever you want t' call it. Don't you remember *nothin'*, lad?''

''I forgot,'' the Littl'un mumbled, turning red.

''They've got Holes all through 'em now,'' Markon inserted. ''Like them places where Quick Folks iron has burned through. But there's even worse Holes where a couple o' Quick Folks boys got hold o' some kinda stone from another World an' started usin' it to jump from World to World, only those Holes had Power mixed up in 'em, an—''

''An' the Queen of Ys tried to steal that stone to make a gate to that other World she'd found beyond Ys, where nobody lived, that she was gonna open up to us bodachs and other small folk what feels like the Seelie Lords give us short shrift.''

''And now she won't,'' Borbin finished for him. ''Which is a damned fine how-de-do.''

''So wha'cha gonna do?'' Markon inquired, scratching his scrawny bottom through his threadbare kilt.

''Gonna go see Lugh himself,'' Gargyn sighed.

''Again,'' Borbin sighed, more loudly, in turn.

''Again!'' Markon spat, and rose, kicking at a convenient cantaloupe. ''Blood an' iron, but I hate Quick Folks!''

''Yeah,'' Gargyn agreed with a final sigh. ''I do too.''

Chapter I:
Changing Shifts

(Athens, Georgia—
Thursday, June 19—sunset)

"Marlboro-Lights-in-a-box," snapped the girl with the Maori tattoos binding her thin wrists like tight black handcuffs wrought of some odd lace. Scott Gresham spared her face the briefest glance—she *looked* of age to buy smokes—and reached up reflexively to snare the requisite white-and-gold pack from the eight-foot rack suspended above the newsstand's checkout counter. Free Camel matches joined the box on the flat plexiglass sheet beside the register, beneath which an array of Zippo lighters gleamed like metal ice. To his left, Byron was already ringing in the purchase. Meanwhile, Scott's gaze had meandered from the girl's nondescript visage to her more intriguing waist, where was displayed the first bare midriff—with attendant pierced belly button—of the evening.

Transaction completed, Scott caught Byron's gaze and winked. Byron grinned back enigmatically from beneath his trademark *X-Files* cap. They were an unlikely pair at best. Byron was a citizen of the world: erudite, witty, and charming; muscularly compact, short-haired—and black (one of Scott's two friends of that persuasion). Himself: born-and-bred in Tellico Plains, Tennessee, bright but not brilliant, sarcastic rather than clever, likeable in lieu of charismatic; and lankily tall, curly-topped, and Nordically caucasian. They got along famously. Or perhaps it was merely the camaraderie of shared combat in the behind-the-scenes trenches of Barnett's Newsstand. God knew it was damned hard work, much of that resisting the ongoing urge to tell the terminally brain-fried to fuck off. Or to tell the fatally lottery-addicted to find their own fortunes. Not that he was any example, he hastened to add; what with a still-incomplete geology dissertation hanging over him like the geode of Damocles.

Speaking of which, it was almost 9:30, which was when the Money Talks numbers were drawn, which was also when (because of reduced demand on the lottery machine) he got off.

Got off job *numero uno*, rather. He still had *numero dos* to attend: his quasi-assistantship over at UGA's cartography lab.

"Quick pick on Lotto," a new arrival coughed. Scott shifted toward the machine, but Byron was there before him, dusky fingers dancing across the keypad. Scott grimaced and leaned back against the shelf behind him, head barely clearing the assortment of rolling tobaccos kept there. He ignored the short businessman (by his dress) even now receiving the requested random numbers, for his gaze had been snared by a pair of figures pounding up the sidewalk beyond the glass windows up front. And before his weary brain could do more than catalog the set, they had yanked the door open and burst inside, tumbling to a breathless halt beyond the counter.

Alec McLean and Aikin "Mighty Hunter" Daniels; at twenty-twoish, a fair bit younger than Scott's own pushing-thirty, and more friends-of-his-friends than actual friends themselves—had not the three of them been party to certain extraordinary secrets. Secrets *so* extraordinary, in fact, that they'd make Mr. X-phile here abandon his little cap in the despair of the utterly outclassed if he even suspected.

Otherwise—basically they were typical UGA seniors. Aik was shortish, with close-cropped dark hair, silver-framed specs, and a tendency (as now) to dress in black T-shirts and cammo fatigues—which made sense, given he was a forestry jock. Alec—whom Scott knew better because the lad had been in a geology lab he'd TAd—was almost depressingly average: average major (computer science), average height, average weight, mouse-brown hair above blandly handsome features. True, he sported the obligatory loop earring, subtly spiked hair, and carefully trendy clothes, but the overall effect was too contrived, too—there was no other word for it—neat.

Well, except for the moment, when he was flushed, panting, and had his shirttail half undone.

He was also lugging a beige plastic pet cage of a size to contain an average (of course, it being Alec's) feline. Which, to judge by the caterwauling issuing from behind the chrome steel bars, the cage, at least at present, did.

Alec, having now regained his wind (and Scott's assessment having expended less than a second), managed to compose himself sufficiently to blurt out a desperate, "Whew, Scotto, thank God you're here; I need a major favor *now*!"

"Oh?" Scott drawled back, with the deliberate languour of someone who'd had to contain himself with too many people for too long and now found an opportunity to push someone else's buttons for a change.

Alec's eyes were wild, almost panicked. A glance at Aikin showed much the same, with a fair bit of resigned irritation thrown in. "We need to borrow the back room! I mean, it's an emergency, okay?"

"Sure," Scott agreed amiably, having concluded (in part from certain suspicious about the cage) that perhaps this wasn't the time to prod the proletariat after all. Byron was looking bemused—and relieved, the Lotto Machine having, for the ten minutes of the draw break, shut down.

"Oh wow, thanks, man!" Alec gasped, already scooting past a twelve-foot rack of cigars toward the door to the Staff-Only storeroom-cum-office.

"Back in a sec," Scott told his compatriot. "Sorry."

Byron shrugged and proceeded to sell a stubble-haired kid in an REM T-shirt a pouch of American Spirit.

Scott joined the two invaders in a cramped and cluttered cubby walled on two sides by shelves bearing an assortment of spare-stock magazines and newspapers, as well as several boxes of returned publications sporting such evocative titles as *Busty, Manshots,* and *Shaved Orientals.*

"So what's the deal?" he demanded, even as Alec

plopped the cage on the relatively uncluttered surface of the owner's desk and fumbled with the latch. Then: "Hey, you're not gonna let *that* loose in here, are you?"

"No choice," Alec countered, as wired as Scott had ever seen him. Evidently the occupant of the cage was clawing him through the barred front, thereby complicating its own release. A release it apparently craved in no uncertain terms, to judge by the screeches and very unfeline whistles issuing from within, which sounded like a bobcat trying to mate with a bagpipe and a flute.

"Thank God!" Alec sighed, as the door finally opened.

"You may thank *me* instead," Scott shot back, then, in spite of the fact he'd seen it numerous times before, gaped at what had just stepped onto Midge Lee's green felt desk pad.

Not a cat—entirely—at the moment. Or more precisely, it seemed to have begun as your basic orange tabby—the head had clearly been short-muzzled and green-eyed when it emerged. But already the nose was growing longer, the fur assuming a ruddy tinge, the eyes shifting to yellow-gold. And the forelegs—well, they'd started out standard old *Felis domesticus* issue: round, soft, and furry; only now they were bare and scaled from the elbow joint down (and feathered for another joint above it), ending in what closely resembled the claws of a good-sized raptor. An eagle perhaps, or something more exotic, like an African secretary bird.

As for the tail (which had now joined the rest of the beast in the cold electric light of not-quite-day), it was exactly like that of a small red fox—as indeed (save the front limbs), was everything else.

Scott exhaled a breath he didn't recall holding, and as if on cue, so did his accomplices. "Well," he began preemptorially, "which of you lads would like to explain why you felt compelled to bring the fuckin' *enfield* in here, right at shape-shiftin' time?"

"Not 'the fucking enfield,'" Alec corrected. "*Aife*, since that's her name. And we brought her here because— well, basically, we had no choice."

"Would you like to *explain*?" Scott repeated, leaning back with his arms folded expectantly.

"Shouldn't have to," Aikin grumbled from the corner.

"You don't have to explain the critter," Scott conceded wearily. "I've *seen* it a time or two, even in that shape. What I wanta know is how two bright lads like you happen to be luggin' a patently magical animal around downtown Athens, when you *know* the damned thing changes from Aife-the-housecat back to its enfield secret identity at dusk and dawn. I still don't understand that," he added. "Why it *has* to change, I mean."

"Don't ask *me*!" Alec spat. "That was Mr. Lugh's bright idea!"

"It has to do with keepin' brain patterns imprinted, or something," Aikin supplied. "And with keepin' McLean on his toes by remindin' him this is a magical beast he's got custody of."

"*Don't* remind me," Alec groaned. "Doesn't help that she's also my girlfriend."

"*Was* your girlfriend," Aikin amended. "Lover, anyway."

Alec bared his teeth and shot Aikin a warning look which took even Scott (who knew how wimpy Alec usually was) aback.

"Sorry," Aikin grunted. "As to what we're doin' here—uh, actually, it was an accident."

"A *stupid* accident, okay?" Alec admitted. "See, Aik's been bugging me forever to let him do some before-and-after X-rays of our furry friend here"—he patted the now complacent enfield encouragingly—"so anyway, a bud of his who's in vet school finally found a slot when he could zap her with the nukes off the record, and—"

"You told somebody *else*?" Scott yipped, aghast.

Alec shook his head. "Favor for favor. Guy showed Aik how to work the gizmo; Aik promised him two packs of venison."

"It's addictive," Aikin explained helpfully.

"Right. So anyway, the plan was to sneak in at sunset in a forestry van we'd got hold of, and do the deed—except that somebody showed up who wasn't supposed to, which means we had to boogie before we even got the first round done.''

"And then we had to explain ourselves," Aikin added, rolling his eyes. "Which cost a bunch of time, which meant we had to get Miss Aife here home before she shifted."

"So guess what?" Alec took up again—to Scott's amusement; it was like watching a comedy relay team, which concept would have chagrined the hell out of either nominally sober boy. "Guess whose van died in the middle of downtown Athens?"

Scott lifted an eyebrow.

Aikin nodded sourly. "Piece of shit. More to the point, piece of shit with no upholstery in back, which means Our Lady of the Iron Phobia looked set to do her thing in the worst place you can imagine."

"But being the quick thinking lads we are," Alec went on, "we abandoned our wheels and beat feet to the nearest safe haven. Actually, we tried Myra's place first, but she wasn't home."

"Right."

"And we thank you for it," Alec concluded, then turned to inspecting the enfield, which was quietly combing its elegant vulpine tail with one not-so-elegant claw. It trilled happily.

Scott eyed the door with alarm. "Please don't let it do that again. I'd hate to have Mr. *X-Files* barge in."

Alec turned pale. "Sorry. Like I said, it was the only place we could think of to let her out to change."

"I still don't understand why you couldn't just leave her in the cage."

Alec scowled. " 'Cause she would've been too close to the iron bars, which really freaks her when she changes. It's Aik's famous imprinted conditioning, I think; when the change kicks in all that runs is instinct. Last time something like that happened, she yowled for three days solid."

"Yeah," Scott nodded. "I heard about that."

"Made me wonder what'd happen if you tried to kill a double-cursed Faery woman who's wearing the substance of this World."

"I don't wanta know," Scott sighed, checking his watch,

then sighed once more—from relief—as he noted that the enfield was reverting to its more conventional form. Which was still damned disconcerting, even when it only wore its magical shape for roughly five minutes twice a day. "Must be a pill," he told Alec.

Alec nodded sagely. "I hate magic."

"Yeah," Scott murmured. "I know."

A quick check to confirm that the enfield had fully lapsed back to cat shape, and Alec shooed his nominal pet back into the carrier. "Sorry," he repeated. "Any port in a storm."

"And speakin' of storms," Scott noted. "It's supposed to rain tonight, and I've still gotta put in some grunt time down at the lab."

"At least there's no magic there," Alec retorted with a smirk. "Just good old high tech-no-lo-gee."

"Right," Scott snorted as he ushered his callers out, to the curious regard of his partner-in-crime at the register. "Thank God."

Interlude I:
A Time Between

(near Sylva, North Carolina—
Thursday, June 19—early evening)

"You say they had *green* hair?" the Macon County Sheriff rumbled incredulously, his voice an uncanny echo of the thunder brawling among the mountains behind Jamie's folks' trailer, on the warped front deck of which they were presently ensconced.

Jamie didn't reply. Terror had caught him again—that cold, sick tightening in his gut that arose whenever something *bad* happened and he was forced to confront it with neither mercy, grace, nor warning—and sent him off to that dreamy distant place where he only lived in *now*. And for the moment, *now* consisted of contemplating his own scrawny reflection in the sheriff's mirrorshades. Unconsciously he stretched up on tiptoes, which made his glassy twin's tummy go as fat as his flesh-and-blood ma's really was.

"Pay attention!" that ma hissed. He wished she'd go away and leave him alone. Or maybe that she was as little as her reflection, where it showed in a second set of mirrorshades belonging to a deputy Jamie strongly suspected by his black hair, rusty skin, and the name Bushyhead emblazoned on his plastic name tag, was a for-real local Indian, which was to say Cherokee. It was too bad, Jamie reckoned, that it wasn't Ma who'd vanished, 'stead of Alvin. Pa might've complained some, but Alv wouldn't have protested at all, and certainly not had hysterics all over the mountainside the way Ma had. What was she worrying about anyway? Sure, Alv was her kid, but Jamie was the one who mostly took care of him, or at least made sure he was loved and happy, which was the most important thing.

The sheriff cleared his throat. Jamie's gaze drifted back to his own silver doppelganger, then down to the man's name tag. *Smith*, it read. Which was why he'd forgotten it. Twice.

"Green hair," Smith prompted, more irritably than before.

"One of 'em," Jamie acknowledged at last, and it took him a moment to realize that it was his own voice that had spoken. "I said *one* of 'em had green hair."

"Jamie, don't lie!" Ma snapped.

"I'm not! I—"

The sheriff silenced her with a glance. "Might be so, ma'am," he conceded. "Kids nowadays dye their hair a lot. Even little 'uns. They use Jello or Kool-aid."

"This wasn't like that," Jamie protested before he could stop himself. "This looked . . . I dunno, it just looked real. It was kinda dark, for one thing. Metally-lookin'—almost."

"Anything else?" Bushyhead urged. "Any detail at all?"

Jamie shifted his weight, wishing he could sit down. His gaze had gone wandering again, to the trailer's glass front door, which had likewise assumed the quality of a mirror. Unfortunately, it revealed a vista of the trees at the foot of the hill: the trees and the park. The park where Alvin had—

". . . vanished." The sheriff was saying.

Jamie shook himself, trying really hard to concentrate and be grown-up and cooperative, which was hard when your ma wasn't being any of those things, and you were scared to death of what your pa would do when he came home, and it really was your fault that you'd disobeyed both your folks' warnings about playing with strangers and as a consequence misplaced your only brother. Yeah, that's what it was: *misplaced*. Better that than lost, or abandoned. And darn sight better than that word everybody was avoiding, which was kidnapping. Alvin had been kidnapped.

"Now let's go over that last part again," Sheriff Smith

said through a yawn. "You were playin' hide-and-seek . . . ?"

Jamie nodded. "And the girl said that Alvin could hide with her, and she told me to count to 'nine-times-nine.' And—"

Bushyhead scowled. "That's what she said? How she put it, I mean? Nine-times-nine?"

Another nod.

The scowl deepened. Bushyhead puffed his cheeks. "Did you get that far?"

"Huh?"

"How far did you actually count? See, the longer you counted, the longer they had to do . . . whatever they did. Or to go wherever they went—you *did* say you didn't see a car, right?"

A third nod. "Right. But they said they were from near the lodge, 'cause I asked 'em."

"But we've already checked there, and all the houses 'round there, and nobody remembers seein' three"—Smith consulted his notes—"' 'good-lookin' teenagers with fancy clothes, rings in their ears, and colored hair.' "

Jamie could think of no reply.

"So basically they were there when you arrived, and when you stopped counting, they were gone?" Bushyhead concluded.

Jamie stared at his feet. "Yeah, I guess. I mean, I tried to track 'em, and all—I guess I forgot to tell you that— but all I found was prints goin' into the creek but not comin' out."

The sheriff sighed wearily. "I wish you'd told us that before."

"Sorry," Jamie mumbled. "I forgot."

"What else you forget?" his ma spat. He glared at her reflexively, and suddenly realized that her anger was only a disguise, a flimsy veneer over fear as deep as that he felt gnawing away his whole insides.

"Nothin'—I hope," he whispered. "I mean, I might remember something else if something makes me remember, but . . . I mean, shit, Ma, I was scared, okay? I was scared for Alvin, and scared to tell you about Alvin, and . . . and scared whatever happened to Alvin might happen to me!''

"Hush," his ma sobbed, as the requisite tears appeared all in a rush. Then, to the sheriff, as she dabbed at her eyes with a paper towel, "What you reckon happened?"

The sheriff shrugged and exchanged glances with his deputy. For his part, Bushyhead scratched his head and peered at Jamie with curious sympathy. "What about *drums*?" he asked softly.

Jamie felt a chill dance down his spine, even as he spoke. "Drums?"

"Drums—or music. Any kind of music. Music where you wouldn't expect it. Or odd music."

The sheriff frowned. "What you gettin' at, 'Head?"

The deputy ignored him. "Let the boy answer."

Jamie took a deep breath and squared his shoulders, at once more grateful than he could say that the deputy seemed inclined to cut him some slack, and scared to death of what he'd just dredged up from another dark place in his memory. "Yeah," he began, swallowing hard. "It's like I told you: sometimes stuff makes me remember stuff, and all. So yeah, there was drums. I forgot about 'em. Well, no, not really, I just . . . I just got scared by 'em. See, it was gettin' late, and I'd lost Alvin and I was lookin' for 'im, only I couldn't find 'im, 'cept that once I thought I heard voices—voices laughin'—only they were scary kinda voices, and then I heard somebody hit a drum three times real fast, and . . . and the voices stopped."

"Voices in the wind," Bushyhead breathed, to no one in particular.

The sheriff regarded him sharply. "What was that?"

Bushyhead shook himself, as though he too had become lost in some odd dream. "Nothing—not that'd do any good. I was just remembering a movie I saw on TV one time, based on a legend of my people. And two things come to mind right off. One is that it was about a tribe being warned about a threat from outside that it would be very bad for them to face. And the other thing"—his face went suddenly strange and distant—"the other thing was that there was a subplot about two little girls who got lost in the woods—*these* woods—and nobody could find 'em, but then they turned up safe.''

''H-how?'' Jamie's ma choked, intrigued in spite of herself.

''They said they weren't lost at all,'' Bushyhead replied. ''They said some folks had took care of 'em.''

''Oh,'' Jamie's ma grunted dully, into a suddenly ominous silence, punctuated by more and closer thunder.

''Yeah,'' Bushyhead finished. ''Some beautiful spirit people my folks call the *nunnehi*.''

The sheriff studied his deputy for a long, worried moment, then sighed. ''Reckon I best call in a search.''

Jamie watched him trudge to the waiting cruiser. But his mind was already speeding elsewhere: following that tiny new spark of wonder Deputy Bushyhead had unwittingly awakened in his dull, drab world, in the form of one soft spoken word.

Nunnehi.

Interlude II:
Spying

*(near Sylva, North Carolina—
Thursday, June 19—early evening)*

"What could be keeping Elvrin?" Fionn grumbled, from where he crouched on the fringe of the forest—as close as he dared approach to the Quick Folks hold he and Rallyn had lately discovered.

Sprawled in the leaf-mould beside him, Rallyn twisted around to face him, oblivious to the muddy detritus that clung to the tight sleeves of his gray velvet tunic. "Likely he saw a rock or a tree or a butterfly he had not seen before. You know how he is in this World. Just like Silver: cannot do his task for looking."

Fionn wiped a lock of coppery hair out of his eyes. "One would have thought Silver would send someone less easily distracted."

"He sent someone interested in this World, and Elvrin knows as much as anyone—about *that* problem, anyway."

"Yet he is not here when we need him—of course."

"We therefore rely on orders."

"Perhaps."

"Why not?"

In reply, Fionn eased away from a sunbeam lest it bestir the glamour that hid him from human eyes—and promptly flinched as his hand came down on something burning hot. He squinted at the small round object embedded in the mould. A thumbbone's length across, the object was—*an inch*, to use the Quick Folks term Silver had drilled into them—and fluted along the edge like a crown. A perfect circle. He flipped it over cautiously, with a twig. Letters showed on top: white on red. *Coke* it read, in the script Silver had also made them learn. "Top of one of their bottles," he growled. "Amusing, if you think of it: how they leave such dangers about, not knowing."

"Iron is not hot in this World," Rallyn hissed back. "Lest you forget," he added. "Nor does your discovery offer any clue regarding what is to be done about *her*."

Fionn scooted closer to the edge of the bluff, where the Quick Folks had hacked away a slice of the earth—a portion of woods and wild—to make space for a mountainside dwelling. The house was not unappealing, for one of *theirs*: made mostly of wood and stone that still looked like wood and stone, which was what houses *ought* to look like, palaces being another thing entirely.

The woman was also acceptably attractive—for a human. Taller than some, and slim; blue-eyed and sandy-blond— nothing remarkable there; that description fit easily half the *Sidhe*. But there was a fire of knowledge in her eyes, confidence in her stride, and joy in her wide white smile that made her seem far more alive than most human women he had seen, with their painted faces; hard, dead clothes; and narrow, selfish minds.

Trouble was, she *knew*. He had known that as soon as he saw her; had indeed sensed a tug of Power long before he and Rallyn had come to this place. Why, even now, as she loaded bundle after bundle into the back of one of those metal carriages the Quick Folks used (*Explorer*, read the words on this one's shiny, dark green flanks), he could hear her pondering things no human should be able to contemplate—like Faerie, like the World Walls, like the Rade itself, which was due to depart a day hence; and which she not only knew about, but was actually anticipating. (And cursed be all that iron, which made a clearer read impossible.)

But orders were specific about such things. Any human who knew *anything* about other Worlds was to be dealt with: any human who had heard rumors or seen anything odd, or had light-paintings or sound-shadows or any of those Quick Folks memory tools. It had sounded amusing when he had volunteered to help scour the Lands of Men of such like. But it had been hard work—cursed hard. And that was with much of it already finished when he joined— like changing the master copies of printed works to blur references to unexplained occurrences (mostly in the north of a realm called Georgia, away to the south and west), then using Power to extend that change to all known replicas. Rigantana had been especially good at that, before she had returned to Ys to try to resolve *that* situation. And Rigantana had recruited him.

But that did not tell him what to do now, when a routine scouting expedition in search of a band of the Sons of Ailill who had been stirring up trouble nearby had produced a "knower" along the way.

Orders said to deal with such humans whenever they were encountered; but Silver also said final action must be confirmed by the cadre commander—who was not to hand just now.

But if the woman entered the steel carriage and departed (as was surely the intent of all that packing), they would lose her, and who know when—or if—she could be found again. Even if she did not leave right away; even if she entered the house and stayed, they would still have a problem, because this house had steel mesh on both its windows and doors, and Power could not reach through such things and yet perform such delicate tasks as clouding memories. And of course clumsiness might cloud too much and rouse even more suspicions, when the less humans knew about or thought about or speculated about Faerie the better. Even Silver agreed with that. Humans had caused too much grief already.

But what was the woman doing? Fumbling around at the door with a key and jingling others; and she had a pouch now—no, a *purse*, they were called. Which meant she was leaving, so they had to act fast.

Rallyn eyed his accomplice narrowly. "Do you wish to do it or shall I?"

Fionn sighed. "I will. And if I err, be it on my head."

"It matters not," a third voice murmured from the woods behind them: a voice that a human would have heard as a sighing on the wind had they noted it at all. Fionn did not need to look around to recognize his commander, the missing Elvrin. He exhaled his relief—a human thing to do, some would have said.

"Why—?"

"She is one of the Safe Ones," Elvrin replied, easing up to join them, his green-black cloak indistinguishable from leafy shadows, even to Faery eyes. "Her name is Sandy Fairfax. She knows, and Silver knows she knows, and approves."

"And the Ard Rhi?"

"He knows as well. She is a friend of the boy."

"Oh," Fionn nodded through a frown, "I see."

Chapter II:
Maps and Legends

*(University of Georgia, Athens, Georgia—
Thursday, June 19—late evening)*

Fifteen minutes and a halfhearted rain-squall after fleeing
Barnett's Newsstand, Scott was a good chunk of a mile
south of there, trudging up the wide marble stairs in the
foyer of GGS—the Geography-Geology Building—in the
approximate center of campus. A Vendo ham-and-cheese
filled one hand, an unopened Mello Yello the other. It was
dinner on the fly, in spades, all because he'd elected to
indulge a couple of far too irresponsible . . . associates, or
whatever the hell McLean and Daniels were.

No, that wasn't fair. Or if it was, he had no right to
complain, given that he wasn't exactly a model of responsibility himself, what with his dissertation so long unfinished he'd start losing credits in one more quarter. Never
mind that his assistantship would likewise go bye-bye then,
leaving him degreeless, destitute, and directionless: a failure
at even professional studenting, all at twenty-nine. He wondered how the job market was for traveling map salesmen.
Or maybe Dr. Green, his major professor, needed a yard
man. Scott knew more than enough about dirt.

"Hey, Scotto!" a female voice sang out behind him:
cheerfully familiar, if distorted almost past recognition by
the glass display cases that lined the upper landing. "So
what brings you here this time of night?"

Scott forced himself to stop and turn around, in no mood
for small talk when what he needed was a beer and a good
night's sleep, and what he had to do was analyze two years'

worth of Landsat photos of Georgia's northeast corner by tomorrow morning. Which basically meant checking each version of each photograph in a (usually) vain attempt at determining what kind of vegetation overlay what kind of strata, and whether there'd been any significant patterns of change. It was a weird cross-discipline thing he'd more or less lucked into during a brief interlude as a geography major a couple of years back. Trouble was, that major had required him to unthink some things, which was hard, given his personal chaos of the time. And faced with the choice between a hard place he didn't know, and a rock (rocks, rather) he did, he'd sided with the latter.

"Scotto?" the speaker repeated, sounding a little concerned this time. In spite of his irritation, Scott squinted at the shape who had just appeared from behind the six-foot globe that dominated the stair head. It was Liz Hughes: another of that corps of underclassmen he seemed to have become a sort of older adjunct to—or mascot for. *Trackers*, they sometimes styled themselves, because they'd all had adventures on those odd roads between the Worlds that McLean's friend David Sullivan called Straight Tracks. Shoot, he'd effectively been on one himself, in one of the stranger episodes in his life, and the mental fallout from that was the source of half his grief. At least *this* Tracker was more levelheaded than most—and damned nice to look at: middle height for a girl, slim, pertly pointy-faced, and with a cap of feathery red hair. At the moment she wore jeans and a green T-shirt proclaiming something vaguely ecological he couldn't quite read. She also carried a sheaf of flyers, one of which she'd clearly been applying to a nearby bulletin board.

"Liz," he acknowledged tiredly, as she sauntered toward him, looking genuinely glad to see him. He tried to appear as pleased. "Uh, one might better ask what *you're* doin'" here, given that this isn't exactly your end of campus, never mind your building."

Liz flourished the sheaf of flyers. "Putting up posters for the concert Saturday night."

"Concert?" Scott echoed. "Oh, right. Forgot about that."

Liz eyed him askance, with a bit more amused mockery than he really felt like enduring. "You *forgot* that half the people you know are getting together to play at the Earth Rights Festival?"

"Time flies when you're not havin' fun," Scott drawled. "But actually, I did forget. Forgot what day it was, if you wanta get technical. Hard to keep up with, if you work weird hours and don't have TV."

Liz spared him a sympathetic smile. "Yeah, well, it oughta be fun. 'Least I'm looking forward to it. Haven't heard some of these folks in a couple of years, or seen some of 'em perform in longer than that. And of course there's the Tracking party . . . *tomorrow* night."

"Right," Scott muttered, turning away.

"Catch you!" Liz called brightly.

"Right." And with that Scott fled down the hall, at once angry at himself for being grumpy with someone who'd done him no harm, and irked at yet another person who seemed bent on reminding him that the reality of scientific rationalism, which had been the foundation of his world-view until a few years back, was effectively built on sand. Yeah, the last thing he needed was to have to confront enchanted mythical beasts, then be reminded of Straight Tracks all in thirty minutes. And the worst part was that he'd have to soak in the whole mess major league tomorrow, because his sometime girlfriend, Myra (who was also a Tracker), would make him.

Sigh.

At which point he finally reached the sanctity of the local tributary of the cartography lab. As he slipped from the deserted hallway into the unlit space, he breathed another sigh—this one of relief. The place was deserted, which meant he might actually accomplish something for a change. Make that *had* to accomplish something. Green wanted hardcopy tomorrow. Scott had until then to contrive some.

Depositing his make-do dinner on one of the long Formica-topped tables that divided the room, he moved to the right, where a series of floor-to-ceiling cabinets contained sheaf upon sheaf of Landsat photographs of most of the

state of Georgia. A quick shuffling secured the ones he
needed: the extreme northeast corner; notably, from west
to east, Welch, Fannin, Union, Towns, Enotah, and Rabun
counties. These particular photos were long and narrow,
reflecting the satellites' orbit, and there were several ver-
sions of each, shot in various wavelengths, including infra-
red. He paused to double-check them, then laid them on
the table beside his food. Another pause for a bite and a
sip, and he rifled another cabinet, from whence he retrieved
the appropriate standard geological survey maps for the ter-
rain encompassed by the pics. A third cabinet provided one
final set of Landsats—these so squeaky clean he hadn't
seen them before—nor had Green, though he knew what
data they ought to contain. In any event, this might actually
prove mildly interesting, given that they represented exactly
the same locale he was already working on, shot from exactly the same height and angle, but precisely a year apart.
The only difference, so far as he could tell, was that the
older set had been taken at midday, the new one at dawn.
Hopefully that would produce some patterns distinctive
enough to ease his work.

So it was, that he actually found himself marginally ex-
cited (then again, this *was* his field) as he settled himself
for a long evening identifying the telltale markers of certain
types of ground cover on one of the older photos, corrob-
orating it on two others, using a set of proportional dividers
to transfer those limits to the survey map in red pencil—
and then repeating the process with the new batch of pics.
It was fun, in an odd way, though also depressing. New
maps almost always showed more open country and less
woods than their predecessors. It was a good thing a big
hunk of north Georgia was national forest, else it'd be just
like Atlanta in ten years' time. Well, Atlanta, only hillier;
no way anyone could put serious hurt on those kind of
mountains, Myra's rants about overdevelopment notwithstanding.

Time passed. No one disturbed him. The sandwich was
eaten, the Mello Yello (chosen for its high caffeine content)
consumed and replaced with another. His eyes were getting tired. Another hour and he'd retreat to his little

apartment on Toombs Avenue and turn in. He'd done all of Welch, Fannin, Union, and Towns. Enotah remained, and Rabun. No, forget Rabun; he'd have to seek forgiveness for that one. Shoot, if it weren't for the fact that Myra was (functionally, if not by birth) from Enotah, he'd give up on it too. At least this way they'd have one more thing to talk about when she returned from her latest round of gallery hopping. He grinned at that—in anticipation. Then scowled, having once again recalled the unresolved ambiguity of their relationship.

Cool it, man, he chided himself. *Focus on the matter at hand.* Idly his gaze swept over the photos. It was mostly familiar turf, though he'd never studied that specific area from the satellites' view before. Without really intending to, he found himself locating places Myra had talked about or taken him to. Like the rest of the northern tier of counties, Enotah was mainly forest, with a splatter of manmade lakes filling many of the valleys, and those that remained largely cleared for farmland. It looked a lot like Ireland, Myra had told him. He wouldn't know, he'd never been out of the States.

But there it was: Enotah County—MacTyrie in the southwest, from which Myra and her troublesome brother, Darrell, hailed (and Alec and Aikin as well). MacTyrie had a junior college and—that was about it. From MacTyrie, he traced a route northeast, to where it joined US 76 in Enotah, the county seat. Continuing east, the road plunged into some serious elevations over on the border with Rabun. South . . . He found the one major artery that snaked in from that direction: White County via Franks Gap, and straight through the land where yet another of Myra's young cronies lived. Sullivan Cove, it was called. He wondered if he could find it from the air. Yeah, right: there it was: a sliver of gravel road leading west from the main north–south trunk. He tracked it curiously, magnifier in hand. Houses showed as dark spots. More river bottoms, some pasturage, but with the mountains looming close, and an arm of one of those lakes at the end of the road.

He started, staring. Blinking. Knuckled his eyes and stared again. It was as if a flash of brilliant insight had just exploded in his brain, only to vanish into nothingness before he could fix on it. Like Coleridge's "Kublai Khan," perhaps, which the great poet had composed while zoned-out in an opium fugue, only to lose almost entirely when an interruption soon after waking jerked him from that heightened sensibility and back into his everyday world. This was like that: a precious memory surfaced, then drowned again, as though someone had thrown a heavy velvet shroud across a whole generation of synapses.

A pause for a deep breath, and he stared at the map once more. Yep, definitely something odd there, a little ways out in the lake at the end of the Sullivan Cove road: a strange sort of blot distorting a portion of the water, like . . . like a flat mirror floating on choppy waves. Both reflected the same sky, but differently. A check showed this was the daytime photo, so probably that was just some sort of sun-on-the-water effect. Or something. (*Something he* ought *to know, if only he could recall.*) Maybe if he checked the survey map. (*For what? Oh, right: the weird water effect.*) He did. Nothing there. (*What could've been there, anyway?*) Nothing but the lake and contour lines around it as flat as a desert—which, now he thought about it, was pretty weird too, given how steep that country was, and how many folks lived up in the mountains now, who'd have to have their places surveyed to get their deeds. Yeah, all in all, it was a damned odd phenomenon, and one he didn't recall having seen before, though he hadn't spent that much time assessing bodies of water. So maybe he'd check the new pics, just in case. He had to regardless, and this was as good a place as any to begin.

It took a moment to find the newer shots of the area in question: the ones done at dawn. And it took a moment longer to locate the precise section that had roused his interest. But when he did find it, a chill raced across his body, even as memories flicked and faded through his brain, like a strobe light: alive one instant, dead the next—and finally gone for good.

For there, clearly visible maybe half a mile offshore, surrounded completely by the lake, in precisely the location

where he'd seen the blot, was, unmistakably, a small, but
perfectly cone-shaped mountain!

A mountain that did not appear on the geological survey
map.

Which was impossible.

Another chill, as memory stirred again but wouldn't quite
coalesce.

But it was sure as hell disturbing. *Damned* disturbing.
No way a mountain could possibly be present in one photo
and not the next. No way two centuries of surveyors could
ever have missed an entire peak, certainly not when they'd
built the lake. Absolutely not when it rose so blatantly from
an otherwise flat sheet of water. (*And he knew why, too;
only he also didn't.*)

A third chill, and he thrust himself back from the table.
A fourth found him on the threshold of the the storeroom
where the older Landsats were stored. It took almost an
hour (a very quick, nervewracking hour), but in the end,
Scott had proof—or at least he'd unearthed enough sweeps
of the target zone to establish a viable hypothesis.

Which was essentially that there was some sort of visual
aberration in the south end of Enotah County. More precisely, that there seemed to be a mountain there, surrounded
by the waters of what he'd discovered in passing was called
Langford Lake. A mountain, however, that seemed to register on film only at dusk, dawn, and (erratically), noon and
midnight.

All of which were what the Trackers called "between
times," and two of which were also when Alec McLean's
damned magical enfield changed from cat to its far less
likely alter ego. Which was not the kind of coincidence he
needed.

(*Part of him knew why, too, but that part wasn't saying.*)

Chapter III:
Out of the Night

(Athens, Georgia—
Friday, June 20—morning)

. . . Plink . . .
. . . plink . . . plink . . .
. . . plink . . . plink . . . plink . . .
. . . Plinkplinkplinkplinkplink . . .

It began as a tremor in the silence that wrapped David Sullivan's sleep. It waxed amid the half-sounds of breathing and the soft hum of electronic toys. It manifested fully in a smothered, mumbled "Shit!" as he gained precisely enough groggy awareness to curse yet another day's rain.

Rain on the plain tin roof an attic's height above the antique pressed-tin ceiling of the second-floor studio apartment in which, nestled within the heirloom-quilted snugness of a Murphy bed, he lay.

He held his breath, listening; relaxing finally, as anger at another day potentially ruined by the latest of far-too-many summer showers gave way to a languorous appreciation of how neat it actually was to lie here on a warm June night, in one of the scores of turn-of-the century walk-ups that walled the streets of downtown Athens, and know how few folk even suspected the magic that went on there.

It wasn't the magic of chants, spells, or divination he had in mind, however, but the more basic, earthy, and primal wizardry of the best woman in the world curled warm and pretty and naked by his side. A woman who had loved him when the rain had fallen not on the roofs of a trendy, sophisticated mini-city, but on that of the isolated mountain

40

farmhouse in which, until college, he had spent his youth. The rain had soothed him then. It soothed him now, urging him back to slumber. Something about moving water releasing oxygen ions—he *thought* that was how Alec had explained it.

A yawn ambushed him; he stifled it with a strong, tanned hand. The movement awoke an itch, which provoked a scratch, which prompted him to roll over. His hair slid into his eyes: thick, blond, and shoulder-long when (as now) it wasn't bound back in a stubby tail. He raked it aside—and could see her. Liz. *His* Liz. A smooth shoulder frosted into eerie blue by the streetlamps outside; a feathery cap of red hair fallen into a coxcomb upon the embroidered pillow. The gentle S-curve of her spine as it slid from the nape of her neck into shadows lower down, beneath the coverlet.

Shadows.

Curves and shadows.

A smile bent David's full, merry lips as he considered that, where he reclined on his elbow, watching. And then remembering: a fair chunk of the previous evening spent exploring those curves, shadows, and hollows, with eyes and hands, mouth and tongue alike; and of his own harder, more angular (though almost as smooth—she said) body being as thoroughly investigated.

. . . *plink* . . .

. . . *plinkplinkplink* . . .

. . . *plinkplinkplinkplink* . . . *PLUNK.*

David grimaced at that discord, for he knew without doubt that it signaled a leak in that otherwise excellent antique pressed-tin ceiling; and a leak, so Myra Buchanan (who owned this particular studio apartment in which he and his lady were house-sitting) had said, was not to be endured—not with a small fortune of expensive *objects d'art* filling every conceivable corner, cove, and cubby, save only the oasis beneath the skylight where her easel took pride of place like a skeletal walnut altar.

Grunting softly, he rolled back over, slid the cover aside and rose, buck naked, to pad away on his quest. It wasn't dark—it never was, what with the skylight and the streetlamps outside, that were only partly barred by the slatted

wooden blinds of the studio's single streetside window.
Even so, it took a moment to locate the drip—near the
fireplace and directly atop the legless department store
dummy whose rusty, steel-helmed skull and chain mail–
shrouded shoulders testified to a boyfriend of Myra's who
once (and occasionally still) dallied with a medieval re-
creation group called the Society for Creative Anachronism.

David winced as a drop caught the helmet's visor and
splattered across his face. A frown followed, as he confronted a conundrum. By rights he ought to move the armor, but that would be impossible to accomplish quietly,
and too much noise (he had little confidence in his dexter-
ity, all sleep befuddled as he was) would surely rouse pret-
tily dozing Liz, and that would be a crime. Unfortunately,
it was something over twice his height (five-seven-and-a-
half) to the ceiling, so plugging the drip was not an option.
The only alternative was therefore to shift the sound of
impact to some more pleasing tone. Sighing, he glanced
around in search of a suitable muffler. Fabric would be
ideal—whatever this was underfoot, say, which was blatantly *not* thrift store oriental carpet. He glanced down, saw
a swath of white, picked it up with his toes and squinted
at it in the gloom. His underwear: size 30 Hanes tightie-
whities. Not a good choice. A towel would be better. A
moment later he'd procured one from the bath and wound
it around the helmet's peaked crown, then waited with arms
folded across his chest to assess his handiwork.

Something between a thud and a splat, as it evolved, but
in any case more pleasing than the causal *plunk*. And so,
mission accomplished, David moved to renew his slumbers.
The clock by the bed read 5:30 in bright red LED that
would've been easier to decipher had it not been entombed
in the gaping maw of a yard-high papier-mâché dragon's
head Myra had made as a prop for one of her paintings.

But did he really want to return to bed now?

Well, he could definitely stand more shuteye, but he
feared that rejoining Liz would only rouse (that was the
operative word, too) his interest in activities he would have
to awaken her to properly pursue. And while he doubted
she'd complain, he also knew they both had finals the fol-

lowing afternoon and really needed to catch whatever Zs they could. A shower was out, because of the noise. But maybe he could relax (or at least distract himself) in the rain-cooled breezes by the window.

Moving as silently as he did when hunting in the woods of his native Enotah County (which was pretty damned quiet, even Calvin McIntosh, who was authentic Cherokee, admitted), he threaded his way between stacks of paintings to the velvet-draped square of striated light that filled most of the streetside end of the long narrow room. A pair of love seats faced each other there, avalanched with brocade pillows. A glass of zinfandel he'd abandoned the previous evening gleamed on the windowsill. He snared it as he sank down and sipped it absently, even as the other hand sought the cord that would raise the blinds. They rustled softly, and he found himself holding his breath as he lifted them just high enough to permit him to gaze out on College Square. Actually, the view was mostly of treetops and two lanes of one-way street flanked by parking. The buildings across the way were largely obscured: China Express on the corner of College and Broad, The Thirsty Scholar next door, and adjoining that, Barnett's Newsstand, where various of his friends worked, and one door down from that, the Grill, which in spite of being open all night, seemed as lifeless as everything else.

Probably it was the rain, a steady patter that made the pavement gleam like charcoal silk and the branches glitter with a fey shimmer that reminded him far too much of realms where a much more malignant magic than love or rain on a tin roof was alive, well, and perhaps growing stronger.

But it was certainly deserted out there now. Not a single Goth girl or townie boy lingered beneath those dripping boughs. Not one of the scruffy, rootless young urchins he'd heard called street elves (*Ha!*), who often hung out all night in front of Barnett's playing hackey sack, bumming cigarettes, and braiding each other's Kool-aid-toned hair. And certainly not one of the older, uglier (odd, if you thought about it: how that seemed to be a given) derelicts whom that same anonymous taxonomist had christened sidewalk trolls.

Another sip of wine found David staring dully at the shining tarmac, listening to the pattering susurration of the rain—hovering on the ragged fringe of slumber. Almost he returned to bed, for the breeze had taken a colder tack that made him shiver, as though someone had opened a door on the arctic north and admitted a blast of December.

He did shiver when he thought of that, for sometimes that actually happened—almost literally. Sometimes doors *did* open to other places, other worlds—Worlds, rather—that overlay his own. He'd seen them. Been there. Walked their meads and meadows with a fair number of his friends, and made friends of a sort there as well. Tomorrow was Midsummer's Day, too; a day born in part to celebrate those other folk.

But a door to *there* shouldn't have opened now. Not here, not in downtown Athens. Not if all was right with the World Walls. The last time that had occurred was two autumns back, when he, Alec, and Aikin were engaged in their annual ritual hunt. That had precipitated yet another in a seemingly endless series of adventures among those other Worlds.

This was Athens. *Downtown* Athens. Athens of concrete and steel. An Athens which, if anything, should be burning holes into that other place.

The breeze grew colder, and with it came a spicy scent, as of exotic flowers. But with it also came a too familiar, too ominous burning in his eyes. He stiffened abruptly, combing the striated shadows with his gaze, seeking . . . what? Movement, probably, or mass where there had been none. And then he saw. A figure—young, by its slightness; male, by the width of the shoulders—emerging from the recessed doorway next to Barnett's. A figure inhumanly pale, clad in a preposterously dagged cloak the color of a stormy night. The figure glanced around furtively, then froze as though startled and lifted his head to stare straight across the street to where David sat sag-mouthed at an open window. Teeth flashed in a scornful smile, and then the youth raised one hand in a mocking salute, turned, and was gone: a swirl of darkness in a deeper gloom.

David simply gaped, too stunned to react more overtly. And was still sitting there seconds—or minutes—later, when that same darkness that had received the figure suddenly fractured again, to spit out a small, pale shape who stumbled a half-dozen paces before coming to a shivering stop on the empty, sodden walk.

Boy, David guessed tentatively, from the clothes: jeans, sneakers, T-shirt, and baseball cap worn backward. Eight or nine, by the size.

And dry, he realized an instant later, shuddering all over again, the more so because the boy was simply standing there, shaking and getting soaked. Obviously the kid was in shock.

David's first impulse was to call someone—but that would disturb Liz, nevermind the quizzing he might have to endure. His second was to go down himself, retrieve the kid, and try to get someone in the Grill to take charge.

He was spared either action by an Athens Police cruiser, which eased around the corner from Clayton to turn down College. Fortunately (or maybe not, depending on what it portended), the boy didn't run, even when the Crown Vic angled toward him. Nor did he react when the car stopped, a uniformed woman got out, spoke briefly (and apparently inconclusively) to the lad, then whisked him into the back seat and drove away.

David exhaled his anxiety in one long hiss, and drank the remainder of the wine to the dregs. One crisis averted—he hoped. If he was lucky, it might not even have been a crisis, not of the sort he'd dreaded. Optimally, he'd read about it in the *Banner Herald* the following afternoon. No way, though, any article could reveal more than a shadow of the truth; no way it would—or could—say that the nameless figure who had left that very human child standing shocked and shivering on a city sidewalk was not what most folks would have called human.

Another half-glass of wine killed the bottle, and that plus fatigue and the ungodliness of the hour made him sleepy all over again. Liz's body warm against his back, he drifted off, pondering how he'd spend the next few days distrusting shadows.

Chapter IV:
Rude Awakening

(Athens, Georgia—
Friday, June 20—early morning)

Something was gnawing Scott's nose.

Something with very sharp teeth, a musty odor, and which, though it weighed almost nothing at all, still managed to muster sufficient mass to be annoying when that mass pressed untrimmed claws into the bare skin of his hairless belly. He batted at it drowsily, provoking a scratchy arc of pain across his chest. Another swat—which connected more firmly—prompted those teeth to snare a nostril and dig in.

"Goddamn, Marsh! What the fuck is *with* you?" he grumbled, as he brought both hands to bear on the normally placid ferret that had elected to play surrogate alarm clock. One hand lifted the aft end of the persistent creature, the other pried ever so gently at the offended orifice.

Oh well, he thought grimly, as the critter proved tenacious, *maybe it's time to get a nose ring.*

A final squeeze, and Marsh let go. Scott resisted the urge to instruct the critter on teleportation, and dumped him on the floor instead—which maneuver caused the remaining cover to slide off his legs. Somewhere in the chaos near his head, the for-real alarm clock produced a steady, piercing chime. He fumbled at it—just as the backup arrived with the cavalry, in the form of very loud radio: something especially raucous by Pearl Jam, if his ears were still functioning right. A well-aimed swat silenced the first. A trip across the cluttered bedroom in the Toombs Avenue apartment would likewise have negated the latter, had his feet not become ensnarled in an unlikely combination of rumpled sheets and irate, leg-climbing mustelid, and sprawled him lengthwise on the floor. The Pearl Jam succumbed to an incredibly irritating local Mitsubishi commercial, and that did it.

Regaining his feet by the expedient of climbing up the front of a bookcase, Scott finally found the radio, thwacked the OFF button hard enough to rattle the dishes in the adjoining kitchen, and managed to secure the ferret just before it invaded the no-man's-land inside the more occupied leg of his purple satin boxer shorts.

Scott paused for a moment, winded from the fall and subsequent exertions, and no more than one-third awake in spite of all that, raised the ferret scruffwise to eye level, and regarded it speculatively. "I have a garbage disposal," he hissed through fine white teeth. "*And* a flush toilet. Hear my words, O beast, and amend thy ways!"

The ferret twitched its nose; then, as if bored, yawned and closed its eyes.

"Beast!" Scott growled again in disgust, and set it on the bed, then stumbled through the crockery chaos of the kitchen into the bath.

Fifteen minutes later he was clean if not quite dry, and fifteen after that, was bageled once, coffeed twice, but still unshod.

At exactly eight o'clock, he slumped out the front door of the old blue-and-white house, half the upstairs of which he rented, and climbed into the black Mercury Monarch his one-time roommate, Jay Madison, had entrusted to him on that same roommate's wedding day. Where Jay was now, he had no idea, save that it was clearly not Athens and he almost certainly wasn't having to endure either nose-piercing alarm clocks or persnickety major professors.

The Monarch, alas, failed to start, and though Scott had a backup ten-speed, he feared for the second time that day, that he was doomed.

Doomed, because, though he'd worked a good chunk of the night on the latest batch of Landsats, and had actual hard copy as proof, he had not, in fact, completed all he'd promised, courtesy of that distractingly screwy anomaly in Sullivan Cove.

And though slighting Rabun County had seemed a viable option at somewhere between one and two AM, the reason for that omission did not seem as workable in the brighter light of day. Even worse, he'd crashed (around three—having stopped at Jittery Joe's for a cappuccino) intending to arise early, finish Rabun before anyone else arrived, and leave the results on Green's desk before the Great Man sailed in. That way, they wouldn't have to actually meet. That way, too, Green would neither be in a position to chide him about his unfinished dissertation, nor present him with more time-consuming tasks.

Trouble was, he'd forgotten to reset the alarms—and had just lost another crucial fifteen minutes fiddling with the stupid car.

Which in no way got him off the hook with Dr. Green, who always showed up spot-on at 8:30.

His only hope now, was to reach the lab ASAP, avoid observation if possible, unearth last night's efforts, and drape his head and arms atop them, as though feigning sleep. If he was lucky—luckier than he'd been so far today—Green himself would find him there when he didn't show for his scheduled audience, and he could pretend to have just awakened. That way he could appear to be super-conscientious, while still having an excuse for botching the assignment.

Of course it still meant he'd have to deal with Green, but that was unavoidable.

"Bloody hell!" he spat, as he turned the bike down College Avenue, aiming toward East Broad. And then, as though awakened by that sincere, if ineffective, curse, another phrase popped into his mind.

A name rather: one he'd heard Myra toss around now and then, and most of the so-called MacTyrie Gang as well.

Bloody Bald.

That mountain which showed on some Landsats but not others, and on no geological chart whatever, was called Bloody Bald. Which meant that the locals, at least, knew it existed; otherwise, it would still be unnamed.

Well, maybe. Sasquatches had names—terms, at any rate—as did unicorns and yetis, but he hadn't seen George Page expounding on either on *Nature.*

All of which, in spite of a temperature already in the low eighties, gave him a chill.

At which point a pouty-looking brunette in a white BMW convertible changed lanes *right* in front of him, and the resulting adrenaline surge and subsequent shout of anger washed all other concerns clean away—

—Until five minutes later, when he found himself confronting the gray, magnolia-fronted slab of the GGS Building.

Please God, I will go to church for the rest of the year if You will make me invisible for fifteen seconds now, he prayed, as he dashed up the granite steps.

And I promise to be nice to every Jehovah's Witness who ventures by, he added, as he achieved the lower foyer still unmarked.

If his sudden change of luck (or divine intervention) persisted, he might even make it up the central stairs, around the globe at the top, and down to the lab as planned.

Holding his breath and trying to look neither furtive nor five years older than the surrounding underclass crew, he ascended to Foyer, Level Two. Miraculously, the coast was still clear: no one in sight with even vaguely gray hair, never mind as much as Green sported.

Around the globe now, and right down the hall (ducking below window level of Green's office in transit), and he'd attain the Promised Land.

"Thank you again, Lord," he breathed, as, beyond hope, he scored the door to the lab, already fishing in his pocket for his key. The lights were on. He wondered if he'd left them that way.

"Ah, Mr. Gresham!" a voice drawled as he eased in. "I was *wondering* when you'd happen by. How would you like to join me for breakfast?"

"Uh . . . uh, sure . . . sir," Scott mumbled helplessly, as his major professor unfolded all six-plus feet of his lanky, Texas-bred frame from the lab stool on which he'd been sitting, and ushered his white-faced acolyte out the door.

Chapter V:
Reunion 101

(Athens, Georgia—
Friday, June 20—early morning)

"God, I hate makin' decisions," David mumbled from beneath the pillow he'd moments before crammed over his eyes to shut out the morning light. He punctuated the complaint with a yawn and a languid stretch, then mashed the floppy mass deeper into his sockets with one hand, while the other roamed down between the sheet and his own bare skin to scratch an itch that had awakened along his side.

Another hand met his there: softer and smaller-boned. It twined with his for a moment, then reached lower still. His breath caught as it found a certain something. "And what decision might that be, lad, that you'd be havin' to make?" Liz murmured in a bogus, but very . . . arousing brogue.

"Whether to drag my butt off to study or pass the mornin' in more pleasant pursuits."

"Acing our finals is all we'd *better* pursue right now, growing boy!" And with that the hand withdrew, to linger at pouncing distance on his thigh.

"It's not the pursuit I'm concerned about, it's the arrival."

At which point memory overtook reality and David recalled that he had, in fact, witnessed something fairly disturbing during the wee hours, which demanded further investigation; and that said experience was, by implication, downright sobering. He was trying to school his smug, sleepy grin into a scowl (having his balls stalked by a

50

creeping hand didn't help), when he noticed two things together.

First, it was daylight, and more to the point, bright daylight of the kind that proclaimed cloudless heavens—a notion he confirmed by a squinting glance toward the skylight.

Second, someone had just rapped sufficiently hard on the door to rattle the stained glass pane.

"Shit!" he spat, as he his brain filled with visions of uniformed men come to grill him about shell-shocked kids who appeared from nowhere in the middle of the night. Then, as his gaze sought frantically for his clothes: "Who is it?"

Nothing.

Nothing. . . .

Another round of knocks, followed by—no other way to describe it—a sort of raspy moan.

"Somebody looking for Myra," Liz yawned. "Go see."

"Land shark," David muttered back, and rose—to discover to his dismay that Liz had claimed squatter's rights on the sheet, the coverlet had gone AWOL entirely, the towel on the helm was soaked, and that both his skivvies *and* his jeans (which had wound up under the armored armature) had played sponge to the ensuing puddle.

Another knock—raspier than before—and a muffled thump.

"Great! David grumbled. "Just great!" He grabbed a fringed silk scarf from the back of a cut-velvet chair and whipped it around his hips sarongwise as he stumbled toward the door. Unfortunately, it didn't meet, and he had to hold the gap closed with one hand. "Who is it?" he demanded.

No reply. But he could certainly hear breathing. *Odd* breathing, actually. He considered retrieving a sword from the remarkable stash of edged weapons stuffed into a nail keg by the entrance, and greeting the persistent visitor armed. Only that would either require three hands or abandoning his sketchy modesty. He settled for visually marking the likeliest candidate, then shooting the dead bolt and cracking the door just enough to peer around, while lurking discreetly behind it.

He came face to face with an alligator.

An honest-to-god *Alligator mississipiensis* standing clumsily erect on its little hind legs to stare him (at foot-long nose length) straight in the eye.

Not stuffed, plastic, cardboard, nor papier mâché.

A for real and true, living, breathing alligator!

Which had just sort of . . . leered at him.

It was difficult to say which happened first. He screeched in a most unmanly manner and tried to slam the door. Liz (who had line of sight to observe both him and portal) screamed with unrestrained enthusiasm. His hands went numb. The scarf dropped—and the 'gator slumped forward against the door.

Since the critter was at least as tall as David and had physics (and hinges that flexed inward) on its side, the door flew open. David staggered back. Liz clutched the sheet to her chin and whimpered. And the 'gator (now supine on the antique prayer rug before the door) rolled onto its back, kicked its legs in the air—and appeared to be trying to giggle.

David—stark naked again, courtesy of his own clumsiness—stared at it aghast from behind the cut-velvet chair where he had taken shelter. And then he noticed something glittering in one half-closed paw, and his eyes narrowed suspiciously.

The 'gator regarded him with one slit-pupiled yellow eye—and winked.

David frowned. A surge of anger pulsed through him—and *not* at being awakened—even as a certain doubt fought it down. "You perhaps think this is funny?" he growled, eyeing the supine reptile.

The reptile winked again.

David emerged from behind the chair, drew himself up to his full height, and fumbled one of the swords from the nail keg, with which he prodded the unwelcome visitor in its leathery solar plexus. "Shall we try for crocodile tears?"

The alligator suddenly looked very contrite, then closed its eyes. The paw-with-shiny-object slowly curled closed.

Abruptly, the tail retracted. The limbs lengthened, the snout grew stubbier, the skin smoothed. Black hair sprouted on the skull and groin as the beast acquired shoulders, hips, and a waist. And then everything seemed to twist upon itself, and David suddenly found himself confronting a handsome young Native American exactly as bare-assed as he, save that he was standing, and the visitor sitting neatly (and modestly) at his feet.

"Fargo, you asshole!" he roared.

"White 'Possum, ditto!" the other snickered through what was possibly the silliest grin David had ever seen. David found the scarf, rewrapped it, and sank down on the arm of the chair. The visitor smirked. David smirked too. Then giggled. Then guffawed. A pillow sailed in his direction from the bed. Then another. A glance that way showed Liz, still sheet-clad, fishing around on the floor for the T-shirt they had so happily abandoned the previous night. She found his instead (it was larger anyway), pulled it on, located her panties, and thus arrayed joined them by the door, pausing only to retrieve something from the landing outside. A pile of clothing, a backpack, and a drum case as it evolved, the former of which she deposited atop the visitor's feet imperiously. "Nekkid savages are only slightly more welcome than nekkid crocodilians."

The visitor managed to stop sniggering long enough to cock an inky brow. "So what bugs you most? The nekkid part, or the savage?"

"The early morning part!" Liz snapped, gazing carefully away as the visitor located a pair of well-used jeans and inserted his feet. "So, Calvin MacIntosh, what brings you here this time of day?"

While David continued to alternately smirk, snort, and giggle, Calvin rose to secure his pants, casually shoving David off his precarious perch in the process. David toppled backward into the chair, feet in the air. Calvin ignored him. "I thought I'd cook you two breakfast in bed," he answered brightly.

"Unlikely," David challenged, righting himself.

"Shelter from the storm?"

David shook his head. "Storm's over."

Calvin looked appealingly at Liz. "I suppose unbridled desire to see two of my very best friends won't fly either?"

Another shaken head.

"How 'bout—"

"—Unbridled desire to scare the livin' shit out of two people who may, at present, be having difficulty remembering they *are* your friends?" Liz supplied with a haughty sniff.

"How 'bout embarrassin' the livin' shit out of at least one of those folks?" David chimed in, helping himself to a dry pair of Levis from Calvin's pack.

"You know," Liz took up once more, eyeing Calvin speculatively. "I kinda like the breakfast in bed part."

"Yeah," David agreed. "Since we're awake anyway."

"But you're already up!"

"That," David observed sweetly, "can be changed."

"You can blame this on McLean," Calvin announced over his shoulder, peering intently into the aging refrigerator that occupied one fifth of the studio's kitchen wall. It was likely the only appliance in the world with a carpet page from the Book of Kells reproduced in metallic auto enamel on the door. The fluorescent light inside washed Calvin's face with an eerie glow that turned his rusty skin a sickly shade of pink and made the palm-sized wire-bound object dangling from a thong at his throat seem to glow. Which, for all David knew, it could. The blinds were up now, admitting the morning light and the sound of traffic building out on College.

"What?" David called back from the bed into which he and Liz had retucked themselves, the better to observe the creation of their impending meal.

Calvin emerged from his delving with a jug of milk in one hand and a carton of eggs in the other. "I said, 'You can blame this on McLean.' " He brandished the jug for emphasis. "My untimely arrival, I mean."

David raised a brow. "I'm listening."

Calvin broke eggs into a frying pan. "Short form: I was doin' graveyard shift up in the Great Northern Place. Didn't get off 'til three. Didn't get away until four, and thanks to our friend the storm and a recalcitrant motorcycle, didn't get here until seven—soakin' wet. Bein' the gentleman that

I am, and knowin' that you two were stayin' here, and also bein' a lad who blushes easily, I chose to seek shelter at *Casa McLean Y Sullivan*, which is also conveniently north of here. Imagine my surprise when I pull up there to discover the door locked, no secret key, and no friendly computer geek to let me in. I become pissed. I ride away in a huff. I find a pay phone. I use it to melt yours down with verbal heat. I then call Aikie-boy on account of the fact that I didn't want to intrude on you guys. Get him—pissed as hell. He says him and McLean have been gamin' late, so Alec's stayed over 'stead of drivin' back home in the rain. I ask about the key. He wakes up Alec. Alec says it should be where it always is. Then he says, 'Oops,' no it's not, 'cause he'd locked himself out earlier, used it, and not replaced it, but that I'm welcome to crash over there—over there bein' further than over *here*. I become more pissed. I say 'screw it, the worst I can do is catch you guys in the sack'—which I seem to have done. It's not like I haven't seen you *en flagrante* before.''

"The 'gator was an interesting flourish," David noted, but with a troubled glint in his eye.

Calvin grinned. "Glad you liked it."

"I didn't say that."

"You didn't give me shit about it either, which I appreciate. Suffice to say some things have . . . changed."

"Changed?"

"It's a long story, and they're best told on a full stomach."

David rolled his eyes, but said nothing. Politeness required it; and Calvin was no fool. He had to trust him. Still. . . .

Calvin plundered the refrigerator again. "So, does this make me the first arrival?" he inquired, when he re-emerged.

Liz pleated the coverlet absently. "You want the body count?"

"Shoot me."

"I've considered it," she advised. "But as far as *I* know, you are in fact *numero uno*—not counting those of us who live here, which is to say me, David, Alec, Aik, and Scott—if you want to count Scott as one of us.''

"Depends on which us," Calvin gave back. "Performers or Trackers."

"Scotto's definitely no musician," David chortled. "If he ever starts singin', head for the hills, for your sanity's sake.''

"I'll remember that," Calvin replied. "But you were sayin'. . . .''

"As for out-of-towners—well, from my old crowd, there's Darrell, who's a solo—fortunately, since he's also a Tracker, and havin' to give a band the slip would be a bitch—and probably beyond him, him bein' kind of a space cadet. Gary might come Tracking if the wife'll let him, but only for that part, and he said to look for him when we saw him comin'. Myra's definitely comin' Tracking, but won't be in until this afternoon at the soonest—said she might have to come straight to rehearsal.''

"Which leaves Piper and LaWanda," Liz concluded. "Who'll probably show at rehearsal too. I mean, we know 'em, but they're not exactly friends. And as far as Tracking—well, they have, but it kinda freaks 'em. Piper, especially.''

"So that's it, musician wise? Me, Darrell, Piper, and LaWanda?''

"Think so. What about your lady?''

"Sandy? She headed out yesterday, but she had some kind of mysterious errand down south she wanted to tend to before she checked in with you guys. Said she'd show up at rehearsal.''

"Just like everybody else," David groaned. "I was hopin' folks'd space themselves out so I could spend some one-on-one time with 'em, 'stead of everybody showin' up in a clump.''

"You've still got me," Calvin pointed out, then busied himself at the stove. The odor of frying bacon and herbed omelettes filled the air. As if on cue, the programmable coffeemaker turned itself on and began to add its own enticing aroma.

"As for Trackers," David went on, "since you asked.

There should be the three of us, plus Alec, Aikin, Darrell, and maybe Gary; Sandy, Myra, Scott, Piper, and LaWanda, if we can talk 'em into it, and—I guess that's it.''

"Aife," Liz appended. "If enchanted critters that *used* to be people count.''

"How's McLean handlin' that?" Calvin queried.

David shrugged. "Who knows? Sometimes he's fine; sometimes he's not. But shoot, man, how'd you like havin' a former girlfriend who'd shafted you *livin'* with you? Plus havin' to be her de facto jailor 'cause the King of the Faeries asked you to, and you can't refuse 'cause of who and what he is; only you hate anything to do with Faerie.''

Liz nodded sagely. "Never mind that most of the time she's a cat, which can be either good or bad depending, except that twice a day she turns red and grows a fox's head and tail and eagle talons, at which time you have to be sure there's no steel close by, or anybody who doesn't know, and—''

"Stress for the McLean boy," Calvin broke in. "I see.''

"I'm kinda worried about him, actually," David admitted.

"We're also worried about Scott," Liz added.

"Uh-uh," Calvin cautioned. "That's it. No serious stuff before breakfast.''

"Suits me," David agreed. "I'll hold off on the other thing.''

Liz's eyed him narrowly. "*What* other thing?''

"Things that go bump in the night. That's as much as I'm gonna say.''

Fifteen minutes later, the three of them were neatly ensconced in the bed, with Calvin leaning against the foot, legs folded beneath him, precisely between David's and Liz's feet. A pair of lacquered bed trays balanced precariously between them. "So," Calvin prompted, between crunchings of bacon (he hadn't eaten either), "what gives?''

David chugged the remainder of his orange juice, wiped his mouth, and flopped back appreciatively. "Which do you want first?''

"Search me. McLean's stuff, I guess, since I know him better."

David sighed. "Actually, the main problem is that Alec's just not cut out for the kind of stuff he gets into—or that we get him into, rather—not that we've been tryin' lately. Trouble is, he's always been the rational one of the Gang: the voice of reason when the rest of us wanted to get wild and crazy."

"Except that he also uses you guys as an excuse to get wild and crazy," Liz countered. "He always wanted to grow up to be you."

"Even though we're the same age, and he's taller'n me—and looks older now."

"Age has nothing to do with it. He's as much a kid at heart as the rest of us. Trouble is . . . I dunno, he just doesn't seem to learn from his mistakes."

David shook his head. "No, it's more that he lives in Camelots."

"Camelots?" asked Calvin.

"Brief shining moments. He's enshrined certain periods of his life in his mind as golden ages and won't let 'em go. Like the summer he and I got to be friends. Like the first summer after me and him and Aik all hit puberty—which he beat us to, incidentally. Like the summer G-Man and Darrell moved up, and we started the MacTyrie Gang."

"Ah," Calvin yawned, "I see."

"Possibly," David yawned back. "But most of 'em were before we got involved with Faerie and the Worlds and all—back when magic was just fun, 'cause it was mental masturbation out of a gaming manual. But anyway, the last golden age lasted about two days, which was back when I first met you, and Liz and me finally got together, and he got jealous of all that, and Aife used his jealousy to get to us through him. She also popped his cherry, which was something he'd romanticized: doin' it under perfect conditions with the perfect woman."

"And then findin' it was all a cheat," Calvin finished for him. "Poor guy."

"Except that he can't seem to let go and get on with his life. I mean, he really has been hurt, but there're a lot a people in the world, and surely somewhere there's somebody he can love who'll love him back."

"Unfortunately," Liz said quietly, "he's *nobody's* number one—not even his folks', 'cause they've got each other. I mean, it really isn't fair: that some of us are the most important person in the world to two or three people, and poor Alec, who is absolutely not a bad guy, isn't to even one."

Calvin gnawed his lip. "I don't suppose we could boil this down to something as crude as the fact that—'scuse me Liz—his first piece of ass was a Faery woman? I mean, no offense, but everything I've heard leads me to believe that any mortal woman would be an . . . an anticlimax after that."

David grimaced at the probable pun. Liz scowled. "Even if the woman proved to be an ice-hearted bitch?"

"—Who finally admitted that she really did love him," David shot back. "Who suffered imprisonment for him. Who risked Lugh's wrath to be with him. Who's stuck by him even with cat instincts ruling her mind most of the time, and you know how fickle even normal cats can be."

"So we all agree that what Master McLean needs most is somebody to love him as much as he loves . . . the memory of Aife?"

David nodded. "We have to be honest: the boy can certainly love. I've felt that love and it's wonderful. Trouble is, he fell in love with the wrong person. God knows it's hard enough for two *regular* folks who love each other to keep things straight, as I'm sure you know, considering how different you and Sandy are."

Calvin rolled his eyes. "Tell me about it."

"Speaking of which," Liz inserted. "Everything okay with you guys?"

"Fine as frog hair," Calvin replied, with a wink. "So that's it with McLean, then?"

David shrugged again. "Basically. Well, except that I guess things are a little worse with him right now, given that we're going Tracking tonight and he doesn't like doin' that. Plus, it's gotten to be kind of a couple-thing, and he's often odd-man out. I could probably think of some more if I tried.''

Liz checked her watch. ''Not if we're gonna get through Scott's woes and whatever's bugging you before you have to head out for your final.''

''What *about* Scott's woes?''

''Simply stated,'' Liz began, ''he's been in grad school so long he's about to start losing credits.''

''Faerie, again,'' David appended. ''His crowd had their own little interface with the dark side of the Sidhe a few years back—before I knew any of 'em but Myra, and her only 'cause she was Darrell's sister. But anyway, I eventually found out about it, and, again to make a long story short, it had much the same effect on Scott it had on Alec. Freaked him out, made him withdraw into himself, turned him distrustful and paranoid. Even worse, made him dump most of his old friends, includin' the ones in the SCA, 'cause they reminded him too much of Faerie.''

Calvin rubbed his chin. ''So what happened to him there, exactly?''

David sighed. ''Best I can tell, he spent most of his time captive in a tree, but he also got to see . . . let's see: a maze of mirrors, a wizard's tower, and a bunch of gryphons. Oh, and all that dissolved by some kind of screwy Track.''

''Not a lot there to base an opinion on.''

David lifted a brow. ''*You* ever see a gryphon?''

''Can't say I have.''

''Neither have I, but we've both seen equivalent wonders—the uktena, for instance—and we both know that while things like that can scare the livin' shit out of you, they've also got this . . . this terrible power of fascination. See one once, and you're changed forever. Trouble is, *we* both got to ease into it gradually—relatively speaking. Scott got it out of the clear blue without warning.''

''Right. . . . So where you headed with all this?''

David chuckled grimly. ''I'm not sure myself, but one of the keys to Scott is that me and Liz and him and Myra got drunk one night and he told us that in spite of all the crap that went down on him there, he actually *loved* that tiny taste of Faerie, and that nothing in this World had any

flavor afterwards; that life in this World was just goin'
through the motions.''

"Sounds like McLean again: him and Aife.''

"Yeah—and like Alec, that World scared him to death,
'cause he's a scientist and it didn't fit with what he knew.
The difference is, that he *admits* that it also attracts him;
Alec *denies* that it does.''

"So he missed a lot of school trying to get his head
straight,'' Liz continued. "Did a lot of drugs trying to re-
capture Faerie, got straightened out by Myra, swapped ma-
jors once, swapped back, then discovered that he's about
to start losing credits. And since he already owes a fortune
in student loans and isn't very employable to start with,
he's under a lot of pressure to finish his degree and get a
job before the ceiling caves in and he's doomed to the late
shift at Barnett's.''

Calvin looked at David. "Which brings us to whatever's
buggin' you.''

David took a deep breath and closed his eyes. "Maybe
it's nothing,'' he began finally. "I *hope* it's just a minor
aberration and doesn't mean anything. Only I've come to
doubt that kind of thing, when it comes to . . . *that* stuff.''

Liz lifted a brow. "We hadn't established it involved *that*
stuff.''

David snorted softly. "Does anything else really bug me
except that stuff?''

"When I'm late,'' Liz retorted. "But go on.''

Another deep breath. "Well, I don't want to sound like
Scotto or Alec, but when anything weird happens anymore,
it always makes me nervous, 'specially when we're right
on the doorstep of the longest day of the year.''

"When the Faery good-guys ought to be strongest,'' Liz
emphasized. "And you really do need to head out, so do
you think you could get to the point?''

"It started,'' David sighed, "when I woke up last night
to the sound of rain.''

"Whew,'' Calvin whistled five minutes later. "I can see
why that might put the wind up you.''

David gnawed his lip. "Seein' how our last run-in with

Faerie began with weak spots in the World Walls."

Calvin scratched his chin. "That screwy deer that came through while we were huntin' back fall two years ago, right? Or has there been somethin' since then?"

"I hope not!"

Liz puffed her cheeks. "But how do you know this was a World Wall thing? Lugh's supposed to have banned any fooling with them."

David counted on his fingers. " 'Cause, number one, I felt a blast of chill, which seems to be a side effect of someone stepping straight through; and number two, 'cause we know for absolute fact that the only Track around here's the one out at Whitehall."

"Which implies," Calvin mused, "that whoever brought that kid through was either breakin' Lugh's law or actin' on his specific authority."

"Yeah," David agreed. "That's what I figured too. Unfortunately, I suspect the former. For one reason, 'cause this was clearly a human kid, and dumpin' him out on the street like that's exactly the sort of petty, risky thing Ailill's faction—the anti-human faction—would do. And for another reason, 'cause it was a young guy that did it— younger lookin' than most of 'em, anyway, say early teens, human standard—and the young ones seem to be the big movers of the anti-human bunch, which is odd, knowin' how much they like to slip into this World to raise hell and get their jollies—"

"Like some of us go to the zoo, or hike, or go hunting— any place that's different from home," Liz observed.

"Right. But what really spooks me," David went on, "was the way the guy looked at me. He knew I was there, and he knew I'd caught him doin' something he shouldn't—it was like he was defyin' me *and* what I represented by my implicit connection with the old-line Faery hierarchy. Like he was thumbin' his nose at Lugh through me."

"At authority, in other words," Liz concluded.

A shrug. "I guess. Never thought of myself as an authority figure."

Calvin leaned back and gnawed his lip. "So what I'm

readin' between the lines here is more trouble in Tir-Nan-Og.''

Another shrug. ''We've known for a while that things aren't right there. There's the human/anti-human faction for one thing: those who acknowledge that we're stronger than the Sidhe in some ways, and that since we control the World whose gravity maintains *their* World, we need to be cultivated and trusted; versus those who think we're a threat to them, and that our World would do as good a job supportin' their World if it was a glowin' mass of slag.''

''Wrong word,'' Calvin cautioned. ''Slag's often iron residue—and iron melts through the World Walls, if I recall.''

''If they're thin enough where iron is in our World,'' David acknowledged. ''But to get back to Tir-Nan-Og, there's also the problem of the small Faeries—bodachs, leprechauns, and so on—feelin' ignored and dispossessed by the Seelie Lords, as they call 'em. A lot of 'em have emigrated to Ys, which is another Faery realm that, best I can tell, overlaps our World underwater, but which also has access to another, empty World, where the small guys would have nothing to fear from us.''

''All of which I knew,'' Calvin yawned.

''Sorry,'' David grunted. ''I forget who knows what anymore. Need to do a chart, I reckon.''

''Comes of keeping secrets,'' Liz muttered.

''Of *havin'* to keep secrets,'' David amended.

''Whatever.''

''Anyway,'' David continued, ''the bottom line is that Faerie, which was always fairly factionalized, has become more so since—forgive my ego here—I found out the Sidhe were trompin' around my pa's back forty. Basically, I've given both big factions a rallyin' point, and—'cause of the effects of all the Gating we've wound up doin'—helped polarize all kinds of minor factions and grievances as well.''

''My man, the revolutionary figurehead,'' Liz drawled.

David grimaced. ''Very unwilling figurehead. Frankly, it still feels unreal, 'specially when I think back to when I first heard music and sneaked out of my folks house, and met the Faeries riding in the woods one summer night. *That* all seems like a dream now.''

"Good dream, too," Calvin assured him. "Oh, sure it changed your life—it changed all our lives, and I didn't even know you then. But look me straight in the eye, David Kevin Sullivan, and tell me you'd undo it if you had the chance."

"I'd undo the *damage* I've done those folks in a minute!" David replied hotly.

"But not the experience itself. If Lugh, or Nuada, or any of 'em told you they'd wipe your memory if you wanted— which we know they can do—you wouldn't let 'em."

David shrugged a third time. "I dunno. Probably not."

"No," Calvin echoed firmly. "Because we both know there can never be too much wonder in the world."

Silence, for a moment, then, from Liz: "Well, the main thing *I* wonder right now, is whether I oughta take a bath or a shower." And with that she uncoiled herself from the bed, gave both David and Calvin perfunctory smooches, and pranced into the bathroom. As the patter of water began, David likewise rose and crossed to the window, to stare down at the thronging street. Calvin joined him. "I have a terrible feeling," David whispered, "that something may be starting. I—What the fuck?"

He spun around in place, saw Calvin caught between confusion and alarm. Someone had just rattled the lock. And voices sounded outside: the barely audible whispers of at least two people.

David relaxed, even as Calvin cocked a brow. "God, I'm jumpy," he griped, and strode toward the door. He twisted the knob exactly as the recalcitrant key performed its intended function, and the result was a brief tug of war that ended only when Calvin calmly removed David's hand from the knob and dragged him back.

"Liz!" David yelled. "We got company."

"Company indeed!" the first arrival snorted as she stalked into the room, so laden with parcels she was visible mostly as a fluffy topknot of wheat-blond hair. "I *live* here, David Sullivan! Nor do I recall giving permission to entertain!"

"Cal's family," David protested, as he helped Myra Buchanan, the studio's actual owner, disencumber herself.

"I know," Myra retorted, nodding over her shoulder. "So're these guys."

"Literally," one snickered: a tall, lanky lad with hair as blond as Myra's, and much the same cast of feature, save that his were younger, more angular, and foolish, rather than savvy. "Runnerman!" David yelped, snaring his startled friend in a hearty embrace. "Look what the cat dragged in!—Shoot, an hour ago, it could've been a 'gator!"

"Ahem!" Myra warned, cocking a curious and rather resigned brow that assumed there was story behind that remark which would have to be related in due time. Darrell merely gaped. David reached up to knuckle his friend's head: one of their ancient MacTyrie Gang rituals—at which point he caught the merest shadow of movement from the darkened landing and found both himself and his childhood pal embraced as a set and lifted a foot off the ground. *"Gary?"* he gasped, trying to twist around so as to confirm his assailant. "Better be, 'cause nobody else that strong's entitled to this kind of foolishness."

One arm relinquished its hold, though the other was still sufficient to bind David and Darrell together in a stifling bond, with David playing principal entree in a sort of buddy sandwich. Meanwhile, the newly freed hand had found his sensitive (and still bare) ribs, and had begun to tickle. David squirmed but couldn't escape, and began first to giggle, then to cackle helplessly. At some point Darrell joined the attack, and for a moment the studio echoed with curses, laughter, and the dire threats of young men who'd known each other forever and loved each other like the brothers none, save David, possessed.

"Ahem," Myra warned again, whereupon she grasped her younger sibling's waist-length ponytail with one hand and dragged him away.

David availed himself of that lull to hook a leg around one of Gary's, twist, and wrest him to the floor, where he straddled the larger boy and began his own quest for vulnerable body parts. It was, given Gary's cast of features, a little like assailing a larger and less buffed Tom Cruise.

"God, Sullivan," Gary panted. "Get off me, man! I've got, like, *kids*."

David paused in mid assault. "Kids?"

"*A* kid, anyway."

"In that case, we'd best take pictures for the little tyke," David crowed, and dived in again—whereupon something wet inundated him from above. He whipped around to see Myra standing calmly beside him with an empty plastic pitcher in her hand. "I take it," she intoned archly, "that you *boys* are glad to see each other?"

David disentangled himself from his friend, and rose, reaching down to give his beefy buddy a hand up—and immediately regretted it. Gary had always been the largest of the Gang, or at least the strongest and most muscular, if not actually the tallest, which honor went to six-foot Darrell.

"Well, Myra," David wheezed, when they'd resumed reasonable, if soggy, decorum, "I thought you weren't coming till tonight—and that this guy"—he elbowed the grinning Gary—"wasn't comin' at all."

"I promised his lady he'd be good," Myra confided. "A little girl-talk goes a long way!"

"I'll say it does!" Liz agreed, emerging from the bath toweling her hair but otherwise fully dressed. "Welcome back. Uh, good to see you guys, too."

Gary and Darrell immediately leapt to their feet and took turns hugging her—then repeated the process—several times. "Hey," David called after the sixth round, "how many times you gonna do that, anyway?"

"One each for every month since we've seen her," Gary shot back with another grin. "What you guys get for playin' hermit down here in Bulldog Land and forgettin' your domesticated pals."

"I'm not domestic," Darrell objected. "Speak for yourself, G-Man!"

Myra wrinkled her nose. "Is that bacon and omelettes I smell?"

Calvin, who'd remained by the window during the chaos of greetings, sauntered forward at that, to give Myra a hug of his own, which he repeated solemnly with the two guys.

"Red Man lurk in shadows," he grunted theatrically. "Red Man hear compliment to cooking. Red Man willing to trade cook-breakfast for blankets, beads, and gossip."

Myra eyed the much-rumpled bed, then her assorted companions. "Well, guys, what do you say?"

"White Man hungry," Gary acknowledged, rubbing his tummy—which, David noted, seemed to overlap his belt a bit more than the last time they'd got together.

"Hungry," Darrell echoed, from where he was already sorting through the head-high CD tower between the fireplace and the kitchen corner.

A moment later they were all—save Calvin, who was back at the stove, and Liz, who'd volunteered to help—ensconced in Myra's bed, waiting expectantly. "So," David inquired, "what brings you back so soon?"

"That's our David," Darrell sighed. "Got grown-up and serious on us."

"Just 'cause I'm not a vagabond of the road," David retorted, cuffing him on the shoulder.

Myra regarded him curiously. "Actually it *is* serious—kind of—maybe."

David lifted a brow.

Myra handed him a rolled-up newspaper. David spread it open across his lap. It was a copy of the *Mouth of the Mountains*, the weekly rag of his home county: the newest edition, which he hadn't seen, nor would've been likely to, since he didn't subscribe nor get back home all that often. He scanned the headlines, finding nothing more than usual small town trivia, until Myra drew his attention to a mid-length article tucked away on page two.

Amnesia Rampant in County

David started to skim the column, but Myra preempted him. "Basically what it says is that there's been an upsurge in folks in our old stomping ground showing up with gaps in their memories. No big deal at first; but then a couple of the doctors got to comparing notes, and folks to talking, and all of a sudden everybody's coming forward."

"So?"

"That's what *I* said," Myra replied. "Folks do forget, and a lot of those are old folks, 'cause there are a lot of old folks up there. But the thing is, one of the doctors got to looking for common elements, and he found a couple—"

"Which are?" From David.

A sigh. "That the bulk of them are either members of the MacTyrie Fire Department, or else they live in or near Sullivan Cove or go to church there. *Not* your folks, though!" she added hastily. "Nor any of ours."

David's eyes grew large, and a cold, hard knot formed in his gut. "And you think. . . ."

"Yeah, I do," Myra finished. "And there's more. See, somebody bothered to check the dates that those folks have forgotten—they've lost specific events, apparently—and guess what? They're the dates of . . . certain occurrences we all know about, and that you, in particular, Dave, have been party to."

David swallowed. "Like—let me guess: a certain fire in a certain campground in MacTyrie? A certain storm during a certain graduation? A certain white stag freakin' out traffic umpteen years back?"

Myra nodded grimly. "See?"

Calvin wandered over to join them, with a pile of ome-lettes and bacon. Liz followed with coffee. "Red Man eavesdrop," Calvin rumbled. "Red Man think these all be times *that* place impact *this* place."

"Whew," David breathed. "Wow! I mean, this is really weird. Like, we knew Nuada had spin doctors in this World moppin' up hard data about Faery incursions and all. But it sounds like he's been foolin' with folks' minds—which isn't cool."

"No," Myra agreed, "it isn't, not from an ethical point of view. Which is why I took one look at this, rounded up these dudes, and came on down. Figured you'd want to know posthaste, and since we were coming anyway. . . ."

"Damn!" David gritted. "And the trouble is—well, there may be trouble brewin' down here too."

"And the *real* trouble," Liz observed, "is that there's nothing we can do right now—if there's anything we either *can* do or are *supposed* to do at all"—she eyed David speculatively—'' 'cause me and this gaping lout here have dueling finals today.''

Myra's brow wrinkled. ''Yeah, I know, and maybe I should've waited, but I kind of had to strike while the iron was hot, Garywise—catch him before the little woman could think of reasons not to bring him along. And—'' she paused. ''See, it's like this. I've got a bit of the Sight, as you know, and . . . I've got a feeling about tonight. No more than that, so don't ask, but it *has* been six years since all this began for you guys, never mind mine and Scott's little adventure, and Midsummer's coming on, and we all know what that means.''

''It gets worse,'' David growled, checking his watch. ''Maybe, it does,'' he amended. ''But Liz is right: I really do have to boogie, and she does too, though she won't admit it. So, Cal, my man, you get to be the one to tell 'em.''

''After breakfast,'' Calvin said flatly. ''Angst is bad for the digestion.''

''Fair enough,'' Myra conceded, eyeing him speculatively. ''By the way, what's that nice buff bod of yours doing this afternoon?''

''Anything you want it to,'' Calvin shot back sweetly, with a warning glare at David. ''You want smooth, scaled, furred, or feathered?''

Interlude III:
Debriefing

(Tir-Nan-Og—high summer—midday)

"Will My Lord wear silver tonight or gold?"

Nuada Airgetlam, sometime warlord to Lugh Samildinach, High King of the Daoine Sidhe in Tir-Nan-Og, ignored the handsome young man who had posed that question: Taran O'Neill, his valet—his half *human* valet, in fact, which appointment had scandalized his household when he'd given the lad that post, though the baser part of the boy's heritage showed only in a more robust frame than most men of the Sidhe, and in hairier limbs and body, which Taran had the sense to keep concealed.

But Nuada had no time for pondering clothes at the moment, intent as he was on events in his sovereign's audience hall, which he observed in his quarters via a small table mirror that reflected whatever transpired before a certain tourmaline in a carved zoomorph in the base of the High King's throne. Just now it provided a splendid view of the hem of that High King's robe: gold velvet edged with black, along which sun-circles worked in topaz and tiger eye rolled in endless file. Beyond that, it showed the front curve of a carpeted dais, with, further on, a vast, high-arched hall thundering off to vagueness and haze. A hall through which Lugh's courtiers, most of whom Nuada outranked, and most of whom were also, to some degree, his friends, strolled and gawked and gossiped.

Law older than any of the Faery realms required that the High King sit his throne once in every quarter of this World's moon, and hear whoever had nerve enough to de-

70

mand a say. And so it was that Nuada chanced to attend this latest petitioner.

It was one of the small folk—a bodach, it appeared, one of many who'd dared Lugh's court the last few seasons. All of them had the same complaint: that their voices be heard, that Lugh be advised that their lands, which most often lay on the fringe of Tir-Nan-Og, were likewise most subject to the predations of the Lands of Men; that their fields, farms, and houses were ever more likely to be plagued with those Holes into nothingness where the World Walls dissolved, typically (as seemed the case now), where iron had lain longest in the Lands of Men and worn those barriers (which were thinnest there anyway) through.

Yes, that was the most common charge, and this complainant—a particularly knotty example in a threadbare kilt and clean white shirt, worn beneath a handsome velvet hat he now, however, kneaded in nervous, gnarled hands, revealing a head of crimson hair—was no different, save that he seemed also to have fallen victim to a less common human incursion, namely that a carriage from the Lands of Men had burst through the Walls completely, to terrorize his clan a few seasons back. Nuada couldn't help but smile at the man's impassioned description of the red dragon his wife had told him was called a shev-ro-lay. He knew better. Having spent a fair bit of time in the Lands of Men himself, and having made it his study for time untallied, he knew that had been no dragon, but what the humans called a *car* or an *automobile*. Indeed, he'd even ridden in one, when he put on human substance so he might tarry among that folk at length and not suffer the pain of iron.

He paused for a languid sip of the spiced pomegranate wine that filled his cup of gold-bound amber—amber in which paired scorpions lay locked in a frozen embrace that could have been either battle or sex.

And frowned.

He'd heard it all before, too many times; had his own opinions on what ought to be done, and had given Lugh his advice, solicited and not. Almost he stopped watching; almost he heeded his anxiously scowling valet. But then the bodach raised another matter, and Nuada found himself paying closer mind.

This bodach—Gargyn was his name—had been one of many similar supplicants who had sailed west the last few seasons seeking sanctuary with Rhiannon of Ys, whose willingness to accept them (for whatever reason) was widely known. This one had evidently reached her realm and been refused. Nuada had known part of this before, of course. But Gargyn was the first of those failed refugees who had actually conjured sufficient gall to plead his case in court. He was unlikely to be the last. It was also unlikely to make much difference.

"My Lord—" Taran prompted behind him.

"In a moment!" Nuada snapped, more irritably than was his wont. Still, immortality conferred a certain patience that half-bloods (who might live forever and might not) were sometimes late in learning, and so he twisted around to fix the man with an icy glare. Just as a knock sounded on the door: a knock in a certain cadence he had no choice but to acknowledge.

"Gold," he told his servant, who fled at a run, narrowly avoiding a younger man who neatly sidestepped him as he entered: graceful and lithe even in what were clearly travel-stained cloak, tunic, boots, and hose. An odor rode with that man: the pungent richness of forest loam from the Lands of Men. Leaves clung in his hair. He was panting hard.

Nuada passed the newcomer his own goblet as he strode down the two crescent steps from the door, and filled the vessel's twin as the youth drained the first goblet to the dregs. Nuada refilled it, and motioned the youth to a seat across the table, pausing only to extinguish the mirror with a pass of his hand.

"My Lord," the man breathed finally. "My thanks to you for your courtesy."

"Those who serve me deserve to be served in turn, El-vrin," Nuada replied. "Do I take it you have some *need* for haste?"

Elvrin nodded. "Three things, My Lord, most recently; though I have others to report at leisure."

"Which I will hear at leisure as well—perhaps tonight, on the Rade."

"As you will, My Lord," Elvrin sighed. "Very well, the first thing is the least, which is simply that while pursuing the task you set us in the Lands of Men, we came upon one of those whose face you showed me in your mind, whose thoughts are to be left alone and their persons, whenever we can, protected—Sandy Fairfax, by name. We watched her for a long while, though we learned very little, for there was much iron about her dwelling. One thing we did learn, however, is that she and others who likewise know of us—including the boy—plan to meet tonight near a certain Track and await our Riding."

Nuada silenced him with a flick of his wrist. "This we know. This they have done for several seasons, and there is no harm in it, for the Borders are sealed and none of them have the art of awakening Tracks. It is a thing they do to affirm the bond of the terrible knowledge they share, for terrible it is to them."

Elvrin frowned. "My Lord, perhaps I have not yet recovered from wearing the stuff of that World, but I do not understand."

"More meat for a longer talk, if you have other messages," Nuada replied. "Suffice to say that most humans who know of us are accounted learned (if not wise) as men, and even many of the Sidhe, account such things; yet what they know of us and our arts and our World does not agree in many parts with what they have been taught about the nature of their own. We inspire them with awe and wonder—and fear. And since Lugh has forbidden them to speak of us to any save those who *do* know, they perforce seek each other out, though some were already friends."

"Comrades bound by common grief."

"In effect," Nuada agreed. "But continue."

Elvrin took a deep breath. "The second thing is that as we were returning to our sanctuary deep in that World's mountains, we chanced on a band of the Sons of Ailill returning from some mischief. Alas, we were weary, and they saw us first, and so were able to arrange an ambush. Two men there were, and one woman—younger than we,

and with the aspect of humans upon them, in dress and
ornament alike, which I will never understand, knowing
how they hate humankind. They harried us with minor
magics, and might have done us actual harm, had I not been
still in human substance, and so able to wield iron. They
were no real threat, yet it reinforces what I have told both
you and Lugh: that many of my age-friends grow reckless,
even lawless; that they respect the king less every year, and
would have their own way regarding the Human World.''

"Ailill's way," Nuada corrected. "His hatred of all humankind is what prompted them to take his name.''

"I know, My Lord," Elvrin replied. "The troubling
thing is that they seemed to know what we were about, and
for the first time had nerve enough to challenge us. And
there was something else, though I caught the thought but
briefly, for I was in human substance and so almost entirely
thought-blind.''

"And . . . ?''

A pause for a sip of wine. "One of them had been playing the changeling game.''

Nuada's hand clamped his goblet so hard the amber
cracked with a snap, but he forced his face to calm. "Lugh
has forbidden that!''

Elvrin shrugged in turn. "Thus more risk, thus more . . .
enjoyment. You were young once. You recall.''

Nuada nodded grimly. "But I never dared defy my king!
I do not suppose you knew these three?''

Elvrin shook his head. "They wore human guise and no
insignia; and there was a taint of glamour about them.''

Nuada leaned back in his chair. "We must inform Lugh
of this at once. You said there was one final thing?''

Another sip of wine, which drained the glass. Then:
"Aye, Lord. And this is most terrible of all, and a thing I
learned but by chance where we passed though, there where
the boy's Gating has worn the Walls thin near the very
heart of this realm.''

"Which none but you and I and Lugh know," Nuada
noted. "What is it you learned there?''

"It was from a human I heard it—overheard it, rather.
And the thing I heard was this. . . .''

As Elvrin told his tale, Nuada's face grew steadily colder, darker, and more grim. When Elvrin finished, he rose. "Bathe, eat, and rest yourself," he commanded. "And meet me again when we begin the Rade. But before you do, find someone you trust and summon Fionchadd. Tell him to meet myself and Lugh as soon as court is over."

"Aye, My Lord, as you will—and thanks unto you, for trusting me with such weighty matters."

"Heavier than you know," Nuada whispered, as the youth departed in a swirl of velvet and leaves. "Perhaps so heavy it will change two worlds forever."

Chapter VI:
Can't Refuse

(Geology-Geography Building,
University of Georgia—
Friday, June 20—midmorning

"So how's the dissertation?"

It was the worst question anyone could have asked Scott, and his friends had long since shied away from it, in terror of their lives—or of scathing glares, anyway. Which, he supposed, as he settled back in Dr. Robert Green's black Volvo wagon and watched Lumpkin Street whisk by, meant that Green wasn't a friend. Except that wasn't true either. They had too much history, for one thing—Scott had first encountered the Great Man during a junior year survey. And no one save a true-blue buddy would've put up with all his crises, delays, procrastinations, and excuses.

But surely Green knew that was a sore spot with him. Surely he had . . . compassion enough not to twist the knife.

"Not what you wanted to hear, is it?" Green chided with a smirk Scott didn't like, as they paused for the light at the foot of the hill where Baxter Street teed in from the left, just past the Tate Student Center. "Makes you wanta scream and yell and call me a heartless creep right? Well, of course the solution to all that is to *finish* the damned thing! I mean, how long can it take, Scott? You've been four-fifths done for months. One trip to the mountains to check stratigraphy. What's that? Four days, max, and I happen to know you like camping. And then transcription: another day; comparison: another two at most, given your aversion to computers. And then you write it up, which shouldn't take more than thirty pages, if you do everything in excruciating detail. Christ, guy, if you wrote one page a day, you'd have it drafted in a month! Let's see, at twenty-seven lines per page, you'd only have to do three lines an hour for nine hours!''

Scott had tuned him out and was praying for the light to change so that Green might possibly have to deal with more imminent concerns than haranguing him—like traffic.

It did—maybe the first thing that had gone right that day. But since he was feeling cranky anyway, and Green *had* fired the first salvo, he felt entitled to counter with one of his own. ''So what have I done to deserve this? Breakfast, I mean?'' He didn't add that Green was a famous miser who never ate out except under extreme duress.

''I'm not paying,'' Green replied cryptically. ''Let's just say I'm more concerned about your future than you appear to be. And since even I, the eternal optimist, have begun to doubt that you'll finish this summer, I—well, you'll see.''

Scott didn't answer. He was still sleepy, to start with. He was also still puzzling over that odd deal with the photos, (both the aberration itself, and what it was that he was supposed to remember about it and couldn't), and likewise wondering if he ought to mention it to Green in either case.

And he was still pondering that when another stop at the top of a long hill also gave him time to ponder a poster someone had tacked to a pole at the corner of Lumpkin and Broad. ''Scarboro Faire,'' it proclaimed, ''East Georgia's Own Renaissance Festival.'' *Crap*, he thought, through a sudden chill; *that was all he needed!* One more ghost from his past to haunt him. One more reminder that alpha reality wasn't at all like most folks imagined: that what he and his youthful adjuncts knew (but didn't begin to understand) about biology, mythology, folklore, magic, religion, and physics, just for starters, was far more than most full professors even suspected. Shoot, one could take a course in Irish myth two blocks away, but David Sullivan, to name one, had talked to Nuada Silverhand face to face! (*Where, he couldn't recall, though he also didn't recall that he was supposed to.*) One could ponder the theory of multiple worlds in a physics class—but he, Scott Gresham, had *been* to one not ten miles away. Somewhere in one of the south campus labs scientists were laboring away decoding fragments of the human genome, with an eye to ending aging, when his own girlfriend had met people who were already effectively immortal. Never mind what those folks might know about real human history should they chose to divulge it. Never mind what that crazy critter Alec McLean and Aikin Daniels had lugged into the newsstand yesterday would do to evolution theory. Or the law of conservation of matter, when it changed shape.

Yeah, Scott concluded, Green might choose to interpret his foot dragging as sullenness, but it was really because he spent a lot of time blanking—simply running on automatic and not thinking—because any alternative could lead in directions that would turn the whole world over.

God knew the entire MacTyrie Gang—Aikin, and McLean, and all that crew—had had theirs turned over for them more than once. (*Where?—he couldn't recall.*) And God also knew that most of *his* friends had experienced a similar . . . epiphany a few years back at that very same Scarboro Faire. He, Piper, LaWanda, and Myra remained of that crew, who actually knew anything—not counting Jay and Dal, who were AWOL in parts unknown. Yet at that, it had taken a couple of years for Myra to ferret out her brother Darrell's connection to certain odd events . . . *somewhere* . . . and then link those events to others she'd experienced herself, at Scarboro Faire.

"Cat got your tongue?" Green teased.

"Ferret almost got my nose," Scott snorted back. And because it was a safe topic, and he'd been an asshole most of the ride, he recounted the tale of his rude awakening. Green was guffawing when he had finished. Indeed, Scott was enjoying his reaction so much he failed to notice they had actually found a parking place downtown. In front of his favorite restaurant, in fact: Harry Bisset's New Orleans Cafe and Oyster Bar. "We're here," Green intoned ominously, flipping down the Volvo's passenger side visor.

"Comb your hair and put your shirttail in. You've got a job interview."

"Job—" Scott gaped. "You *are* joking?"

"Never in my life," Green retorted deadpan. "And even if I was, they're still buying breakfast. Feel free to order whatever you want; these guys are loaded."

"These guys" proved to be one man: a balding fellow of about fifty whose manic manner and constant fidgeting made Scott wonder how on earth he remained as plump as he was—and that in the few seconds it had taken the waiter to escort their little party from Bisset's elegant front bar back to the skylighted courtyard, where they crammed themselves into a booth in one of the arches beneath the mezzanine stair. Somewhere along the way Scott had been told his would-be benefactor's name, which was Ralph Mims. Somewhere, too, they had presumably shaken hands; at least his own hand was clammy when it ought not to have been, and he thought it might still be tingling from an overtight grasp. He assumed that he'd said the right thing, but frankly his head was in a whirl.

Menus appeared. Specials were announced. Drinks were ordered. Scott joined the others in requesting a Bloody Mary, since free alcohol before lunch was one of the world's great decadences. In the meantime, there was coffee: Dancing Goat, if he'd guessed the blend right. While they waited on the cocktails, and Scott tried to decipher the breakfast menu of a place where he only had dinner on special occasions, Mims proceeded to plop a large briefcase on the table, open it, and drag out a handsome faux-leather folder, embossed in gold with a logo that read *Mystic Mountain Properties*.

"Enotah County," Mims announced, without preamble.

Scott blinked at him, stopped immediately, and hoped he didn't look too much like a deer caught in headlights.

"What about it?" he blurted, and could've kicked himself.

Mims was nonplussed. "Ever hear of it?"

"Been there—once. Got a bunch of friends from there. Girlfriend, actually—sort of."

"Sort of from there, or sort-of girlfriend?"

"If you find out," Green chuckled, "tell me, and we'll all three know."

Scott suppressed an urge to bare his teeth at him, and would have, had Mims not, in spite of his twitchy persona, been represented as someone who could get him employed—presumably in his field, or else why was Green along?

"You are a geologist, correct?" Mims continued obliviously.

Scott nodded. "Stratigraphy, mostly. A bit of work with fossils. Geography," he added. "Once."

"You've worked with maps?"

(*Stupid question.*) "Sure," Scott replied, instead. "Actually, I work in the cartography lab right now. It's kind of a holdover from . . . before."

"Landsat?"

"You got it."

Mims reached into the folder and drew out a packet of photographs, which he slid over to Scott. Scott examined them numbly. Basic amateur mountain shots, he determined at once; Myra was an expert photographer and had taught him (tried to, anyway) everything she knew about composition, lighting, and framing. That aside, he supposed he was expected to assess the subject matter, with a probable eye toward commentary on same.

The first had been shot straight down a dirt road, with low forested ridges to either side, looming above fields of broom sedge. A clump of woods ran in from the right in the midground, and behind it, he could make out the shimmer of water, with a bit of mountain rising beyond: a mountain with startling white outcrops crowning its summit.

The next shot showed that same lake, but from the edge, with mountains probing its blue-gray waters and the stone-capped peak dominating the center. A near-perfect cone, he noted: lower than most of the surrounding ridges, but no less impressive—rather like Spirit Island in Crater Lake.

There were several more shots of the mountain, a couple clearly done with a telephoto lens. The next batch depicted the nearby shore, which showed flat shoals of stone shelving down to the water's edge. Those were followed by more of the mountain—double exposures—or something—for the peak had a vaguely nebulous quality, as though it were out of focus, or . . . transparent, or simply not quite there.

At which point he recalled with a shudder the work he had done last night. "Does this place have a name?" he managed, through a sip of coffee he hoped masked his sudden apprehension.

"Locals call it Bloody Bald," Mims admitted offhand. "They seem to have a hard time remembering it."

Scott's heart skipped another beat. *Bloody Bald*—that was the name that had popped into his head earlier that morning. A chill raced over him.

"It'd be hard to forget a sight like that!" Green observed beside him.

"That's what we're hoping," Mims agreed. "See, Mr. Gresham, we at Mystic Mountain Properties have been scouring that area for months in search of the perfect place to build the perfect mountain resort. Something with completely controlled access and completely remote from the rest of the world as well. Something from which there are absolutely no reminders of external civilization except one road and contrails overhead."

"So . . . where do I fit into all this?" Scott finally dared, swallowing hard.

Mims stabbed the topmost photo with a stubby finger. "Would you believe this mountain has never been surveyed?"

Scott took a deep breath. "Actually, yes. As a matter of fact, I was lookin' at the Landsats of this area last night and noticed it in some of them, but couldn't find it on the Geo. Survey master—or anywhere else."

"Here there be dragons," Green commented wryly. "But that's actually not that surprising, not really. That area's damned remote, for one thing; and what with assorted wars, courthouse fires, and so on—that county can't *keep* a courthouse—well, all their records are pretty sketchy. Anyone wants to buy property up there has to chase down the neighbors and take what they say about the corner markers on faith. Only thing you can really count

on is stuff that's been surveyed postwar, and that lake pre-
dates it.''

"How do you know so much?" Scott inquired.

"Went to college up there—didn't you know? MacTyrie
JC, class of 1963. I don't remember that mountain either.''

"Small world," Scott muttered. "But as I was sayin',
where do I fit in?"

Again Mims tapped his photos. "You know how to survey, don't you?"

Scott nodded dubiously. It was grunt work, but you
didn't major in geography (as he had briefly done) and
avoid exposure to that. So was this Mims's big offer? A
summer spent *surveying*?

"I see what you're thinking," Mims said—having
paused to catch the eye of a passing waiter so that food
could actually be ordered. "And yeah, you'd be doing some
surveying. But we also know you like to tromp around in
the woods, so we thought that might sweeten the drudgery
a little. And there's always the small matter of the gemstones.''

"Gemstones?"

"One of the largest star sapphires in the world was found
one county away. Scads of amethyst and other quartz var-
iants from up there, never mind gold. We need you to check
out the whole shoreline a mile to either side of that road in
the picture, which is how much we hope to lease from the
state, which appears to own it. I'd hate to try to build a
resort when I ought to be building a gold mine; on the other
hand, a little recreational prospecting on the side wouldn't
hurt attendance. Needless to say, anything you find on your
own's yours to keep."

"Uh, how long would I be doing this?" Scott ventured.
"I've still got a dissertation, and all."

"Given that these can be construed as extraordinary circumstances," Green broke in, "I can probably get you one
more extension. Frankly, though, I think you ought to take
it. Ralph here tells me they've other projects afoot and
could use a staff geologist."

"We pay well," Mims added helpfully. He wrote down

a figure on the napkin that had just arrived with his Bloody Mary, and turned it around to face Scott.

"Better than Barnett's, anyway," Scott managed, trying hard not to be too impressed—though he was.

Mims stretched a plump arm across the table, offering Scott his hand. "Fine, then; you're on."

Scott shook the hand mechanically, feeling as though these two men had completely hijacked his life, and wondering whether he liked it. (*And what was that gnawing away in the back of his mind, telling him he shouldn't do this?*)

Oh well, it solved some problems and postponed others. It seemed the thing to do—for the nonce. And frankly, he did as well acting on impulse as after careful deliberation, most of the time. "Thanks," he murmured, trying to sound grateful and low key all at once.

Mims cleared his throat. "What're you doing this afternoon?"

Scott glanced at Green. "I, uh, had some stuff I was supposed to turn into you . . . sir."

Green shrugged. "It'll keep."

Mims fairly beamed. "Fine, so you've got time to ride up there with me?"

Scott shrugged in turn. "Have hikin' boots will travel."

"Good!" Mims crowed, slipping him a hundred dollar bill. "Buy yourself a new pair. You're gonna need 'em."

Scott paused before pocketing the cash, but Mims waved it aside. "Now that that's settled," he proclaimed primly. "I think I know what I'd like to order."

"Champagne," Scott told the waiter, who had finally reappeared. "And . . . Oysters Rockefeller."

"That a pun?" from Green.

"Huh?"

"Rockefeller. Rocks. Geology."

Scott felt very foolish, "Oh, right. I see."

"Oysters, hell!" Mims roared, shutting his menu with a snap. "Let's have caviar!"

"But sir," the waiter began. "We don't have—"

"Well, get some!" Mims shot back. "Cost be damned!"

Chapter VII:
Reunion 102

*(Athens, Georgia—
Friday, June 20—midafternoon)*

David wasn't sure what he'd expected when he eased through the door to Myra's studio, with his brain half fried from an anthropology final he'd likely aced, but it wasn't Wainamoinen, Lemminkainen, and Ilmarinen.

Yet there they were: arrayed in perfect tableau on a low pedestal beneath the skylight: three of his buds frozen in place in the guise of the three great Finnish heroes. Actually, identification hadn't been quite that easy—they could've been any number of archetypal macho men. But it happened that Myra had some months back won a very lucrative commission to paint covers for a new edition of classic myths, and had already mentioned several times that the *Kalevala*—the Finnish national epic—was next on the agenda.

He propped himself against the doorjamb, watching.

Myra had certain rules when she worked. One was that though she didn't mind having folks around, they were expected to remain silent unless she instigated conversation; thus Liz (who was a decent artist herself) was curled up on the sofa reading the latest issue of *Graphis*. Another was that she always required music—generally a high-energy film soundtrack, such as *Conan the Barbarian* or *The Last of the Mohicans*, though in this case she'd yielded to the obvious and was shaking the walls with the strains of Sibelius's *Finlandia*.

A final quirk was that she insisted on using her friends

as models. God knew he'd posed enough himself, clothed and sky-clad alike (that was another tendency, though generally only for pencil studies). Most recently Liz herself had stood for the previous volume in the myth series: Queen Maeve of Connaught in the *Tain bo Cuailnge*. His own time was yet to come—there wasn't a ready market for short blond heroes, though he suspected Myra was eyeing him for Sigurd the Volsung.

As for the tableau—well, she was clearly making the best use of available resources. With his impressive muscles and acceptably heroic height, Gary had been the obvious choice for Ilmarinen, the master smith. Stripped to the waist, he loomed behind a cardboard box that she had already transformed in her sketch into an anvil. One brawny arm was upraised, brandishing a very real five pound hammer; "to get the muscle tensions right," was her standard line about such things. The other gripped a pair of salad tongs containing the stereo remote—a very odd Sampo indeed.

Beside him, Darrell had assumed the role of Lemminkainen, the warrior—risky, given Darrell's perpetually foolish mien and spare frame. Or maybe not. Warriors were often fools of a sort, so perhaps she was sending a subtle message; certainly one who went a-venturing in the frozen north could quickly acquire a thin physique. (Besides, she'd draped him in skins, so his prominent ribs didn't show *that* much.) His role in the tableau seemed to be that of anxious client, to judge by the way he was glowering while fingering a sword he might well have brought for repair.

As for Wainamoinen, the shaman-mage, Myra had lived up to her threat of the morning and cast Calvin in that capacity. Like Gary, he was shirtless (and also like him, showing some waistline pudge David hadn't noted earlier); like Darrell, he was contemplating something in his hand. No, actually (as a closer look determined), he was contemplating the hand itself—if you wanted to dignify what far more resembled a cougar's paw with that term.

David frowned at that, and not for the first time that day, either. Cal was a shapeshifter, that was a fact. He had a talisman—a scale from an uktena, a serpent-monster from a nearby World—that let him change form, at certain risk.

David knew he'd been working hard at learning how to shift without it, and to control the change either way—as now, when he'd altered only part of his body.

Still, it made him angry. For one thing, it was using magic frivolously, which wasn't smart in principle, and which David happened to know Calvin's mentor, Uki of Galunlati, had banned in the most explicit terms. And for another thing, if he *was* using the scale to effect the change (you primed it with your own blood, generally by closing your fist around it and wished to be whatever beast whose shape you would assume), he was running a second risk, for each scale carried a finite but nonspecified number of charges, and there was always a chance (especially with an oft-used scale) that you could get stuck in some alternate body. Having a friend with cougar claws permanently attached to his right hand was not a notion David relished, never mind the effect it would have on that friend's musical endeavors.

He'd ignored the matter earlier, first from surprise, then from genuine delight at seeing his friend, and finally from the assumption that apparent frivolity or no, Cal usually knew what he was doing—that last borne out by the way his friend had tried to second-guess him upon arrival, with all that cryptic talk of things having "changed," coupled with a host of warning looks and whatever. And if truth were known, he was a little pissed at himself for having left with the matter unresolved, given the way it had haunted him throughout the final he'd just completed.

But he'd waited long enough, dammit, and had just started to address the situation, in spite of Myra's ban, when she sighed, laid her pencil down, and turned the stereo off with a snap. "Okay, guys: break time. Good job, so far, except Darry you really do have to learn how to scowl— oh, and Cal, you can have your old hand back. I've drawn the paw in special detail, and there're always the photos, just in case."

Gary exhaled expansively and lowered the hammer, reaching up with his other hand to massage what was obviously a very tired shoulder—not that he'd ever complain, not Mr. Testosterone Man. For his part, David grimaced in dismay. What Myra had done was not cool, if she had indeed photographed Cal in mid-shift. Christ, hadn't they all agreed long ago not to risk such things? In paper, print, or paint, alike? The dratted enfield was bad enough (and he suspected Aik was about to make good his threats about enfield X-Rays, if he hadn't already), and now to provide yet more hardcopy . . . !

"You look like a blond stormcloud," Myra informed him calmly—having evidently noted his glare in one of the studio's many mirrors. "A small one," she added with a smirk.

David bit his lip to keep from snapping at her. There was too much chaos circling already; he didn't need to inject more tension. On the other hand, he really had sat on his anger long enough. "Been *practicing*, Cal?" he hissed, as he helped himself to a Guinness from the fridge before flopping down beside a very sleepy Liz.

Calvin shrugged. "Always. And since you seem disinclined to wait until we've got time for the long tale, the short form is that, first of all, it's a new scale, fresh from Galunlati. And second, I've figured out how to keep track of the number of 'charges' left in it, and let me tell you, that one's got plenty." At which point Gary offered him a Guinness of his own—which he refused politely. Some bans, it seemed, Calvin still observed.

David lifted a brow, resisting the urge to ask for elaboration on a matter which Calvin seemed strangely reluctant to discuss. "You been back there?" he asked, instead.

A nod. "Uki was watchin' me in his *ulunsuti* back in February—during the Great Snow—and saw how bummed I was by all that, so he zapped me off for a vacation in— excuse me—Indian Summer."

"Friends in high places," Gary muttered to Darrell, who was already inhaling Guinness number two.

David shook his head. "I dunno, man; still seems risky to me."

Calvin cuffed him on the shoulder. "Can the serious shit, okay? You're supposed to ask how Uki is, or whether I've decided to marry one of the Thunder Sisters, or something, not give me grief about responsibility."

David masked his grimace with another swallow. "Something's goin' on," he burst out. "I can feel it. The chaos beast is loose and something's just waitin' out there to dump on our heads."

"Possibly," Myra agreed with authority. "But don't forget what night it is; don't forget how tuned we are to that kind of thing; and don't forget that everybody we've seen today is tied up with . . . magic somehow. I mean, think, lad; that's bound to skew all our perceptions."

"And speakin' of perceptions," Calvin cried, leaping to his feet, "I've just perceived the sound of a Ford V-8."

"Should've named you Sharp Ears 'stead of He-goes-about," David snorted. *Edahi*—Cherokee for "He-goes-about"—was Calvin's tribal name, which he anglicized as Fargo.

"Shoulda named you Smartass 'Possum, 'stead of White 'Possum," Calvin shot back, already halfway through the door.

Myra lifted a brow at a smirking Liz. Then: "You don't have one of those handles too, do you?"

Liz shook her head. "Missed that particular soirée."

"I've missed 'em all," Myra admitted. "Except one—which was enough, thank you very much."

"Hasn't hurt your paintings," David retorted. "Don't think I don't know you only go Trackin' with us 'cause you hope you'll get to see the real thing."

Myra sighed wistfully. "Well, it'd be *nice* to have the genuine Nuada Silverhand pose for one of my covers. Probably not handsome enough, though."

Liz looked up from her reading. "No danger!"

Myra started to reply, but footsteps had sounded on the stairs: several sets, of various weights and pacings. She sighed again and eyed her refrigerator speculatively. "How did *I* wind up being ground zero?"

"Free beer," David advised—and promptly rose to score another.

Two, rather, a second for himself and one for the voice he'd recognized from the cacophony now assailing the upper landing. An expected voice, as a matter of fact, with whom Cal was conversing animatedly. But there was also a third that sounded suspiciously—and disturbingly—young.

"Sandy!" he yelped, as the door opened to admit a much-encumbered Calvin, followed by a blondish, denim-clad woman roughly Myra's age and size, but with far more striking features of a vaguely (but inaccurately) Native American cast. Like Myra, however, she sported a lithe, athletic build and evinced a similar disdain for makeup. Her hair hung past her waist. Sandy Fairfax—a high school physics teacher whose North Carolina cabin Calvin had been sharing for years—looked confused for the merest moment, then dropped her own load of gear to give David not only the obligatory hug, but also a pair of smooches: one for each cheek. Even as they embraced, David dragged her away from the entrance.

"Dave!" she protested. "What—?"

"Been waylaid in that door too many times today," David confided. "And best I can tell, there oughta be at least one more of you."

Sandy broke free and returned to the landing, to peer down the stairwell. "Gone for the last load," she explained over her shoulder.

David gnawed his lip. "Who . . . ?"

"Brock." Calvin replied beside him, his face a mix of resignation, bemusement, and despair.

David rolled his eyes. "I hope you know what you're doin'."

Calvin rolled his in turn. "Ask Sandy."

"Brock?" Myra called from the door. "Oh, right: the English kid—"

"American," a young male voice corrected from the foot of the stairs. "Savannah, by way of Tampa—"

"Like Piper," Myra mused, joining him. "God, this is becoming Grand Central Station."

By which time the owner of the voice had puffed his way up to the top of the stairs, his breathlessness accountable in large part to the enormous suitcase he was lugging. It was a boy in his early teens; slim and fair-skinned, but with a flag of black hair hanging nearly to his waist—nearly as long as Sandy's in fact—and dyed, to judge by the much lighter roots. He had intense blue eyes and looked, David thought, a little fey—as though he'd seen more than a kid his age ought to have. Not, he hastened to add, that Brock (whom he'd encountered exactly once, at the tail end of one of Calvin's adventures) was much younger than he'd been himself when he'd first met the Sidhe on a July night. The kid was gazing at him oddly, too: as though he knew more about David than David would like for him to know. And there was a bit of what he suspected was adoration present as well, or perhaps hero worship. Calvin, he feared, had been blabbing.

"Hi, guy!" David grinned, relieving the boy of the suitcase. "Welcome to Athens—again."

"Cooler inside," Myra urged from the door. "And if I'm gonna have more guests, I'd kinda like to meet 'em."

It was Calvin's turn to blush. "Oh, right: I forget who knows who, since *I* know all you folks."

"Right," Liz chimed in. "Does everybody know everybody? I mean *really*, not just by reputation?"

"Myra Buchanan," Calvin intoned formally. "Allow me to introduce Brock-the-badger No-name, hot off the boat from Merry-Olde."

"Hot out of the car from Savannah, you mean," Brock corrected, as he shook Myra's hand. "Nice to meet you," he continued politely, with an accent which was an odd mix of British and Southern.

"Hi," Myra beamed. "I've heard a bit about you myself, as a matter of fact."

"Oh, wow!" Brock enthused, blushing.

"That can't be your real name," Gary drawled, as he rose.

Brock froze, as though confronted with an ambulatory mountainside. "Brock's an old term for badger, and badgers are real hard to kill. They also don't have last names."

"His *real* name's Stanley Ar—" Calvin began.

"*No!*" Brock shouted so forcefully everyone stared. "Sorry," he continued, blushing. "Just as soon you didn't, though."

"Sorry," Calvin echoed, ruffling the boy's hair—which provoked a scathing glare. More introductions followed (neither Gary nor Darrell had met Brock before), then a chaos of questions and answers which got everyone sorted out. That concluded, Gary donned his shirt, grabbing Darrell by the ponytail as an afterthought. "Beer," he announced. "We need to get more beer. C'mon, Runnerman; let's do some runnin'."

"Surprised you didn't bring Don Scott while you were at it," David murmured to Calvin as they arrayed themselves around the studio. Brock's eyes, needless to say, were huge. So much for being a jaded city kid. Then again, Myra's collection of knickknacks would've made all but the most ardent pack rat forsake that vocation in despair.

"Actually," Sandy admitted from Calvin's other side, "I asked Don, as a courtesy, but he wasn't interested. Said he really wanted to keep on pretending everything was normal."

"I wish him luck," David snorted. "I've been tryin' to do that ever since I was sixteen"—he regarded Brock curiously. "Uh, how old *are* you these days?"

"Secret," Brock muttered, from where he was methodically working his way around the room. He'd managed about four feet—half a bookcase—and had just reached one of Myra's numerous band posters. "Oh, brilliant!" he crowed. "Eidolon! They're great! I've got all their CDs! Hey . . . they're *from* here, aren't they?"

"Actually," Myra acknowledged drolly, "we know 'em—Morry, anyway: their piper."

Calvin nudged David in the ribs. "We do?"

"Piper—*LaWanda's* Piper," David whispered back. "Morry Murphy's his real name. James Morrison Murphy, if you wanta get technical."

"Brilliant!" Brock repeated numbly. "Brilliant!"

"So," Liz said to Brock, who had just skidded to an awestruck halt at the enormous floor-to-ceiling rack that housed Myra's comic collection, "you're going Tracking with us, I guess?"

Brock nodded absently. "Was stateside anyway, wanted to see Cal, tried to call him to see if we could connect, got Sandy, and we plotted the rest."

Calvin grimaced. Sandy caught the expression. "Probably just as well,'' she advised. ''Haven't heard the news today, have you?''

''No time,'' David supplied. ''Had a final.''

''Ditto.'' From Liz.

''You'd probably have missed it anyway,'' Sandy mused. ''It was Carolina stuff, mostly.''

''And?'' Calvin prompted.

She shifted position in the beanbag chair she'd claimed. ''Short form: kid disappeared from my neck of the woods yesterday afternoon. Eight years old. White trash folks. Older brother who wants desperately to be cool—based on what I could tell from hearing him on the radio. Anyway, like I said: kid vanishes, brother says he was last seen playing hide-and-seek with some''—she made quote marks with her fingers—'' 'really sharp-dressed kids who said they were from the mountain.' ''

David looked up at that, and a chill raced over him. ''Little kid?'' he whispered. ''Jeans? Baseball cap on backward?''

Sandy regarded him sharply. ''So you know . . . ?''

''Depends. Know what?''

''That he was found—this morning—in Athens. On that very street outside this apartment.''

David swallowed hard. ''Did . . . did he say how he got there?''

Myra's face was dead serious. ''He said the pretty kids brought him.''

Liz exhaled sharply. ''Well, that's one less thing to worry about.''

Sandy stared at her. ''How so?''

Liz glanced at David. ''You want to tell her, or shall I?''

''I will,'' David replied. ''I'm the one who saw it.''

And for the third time that day, he related the tale of the boy who'd appeared so suddenly on the sidewalk, and of the troubling Faery youth who'd abandoned him there.

''Figured,'' Sandy grumbled when he'd finished. ''I think they've been hangin' 'round my place too.''

It was Calvin's turn to look alarmed, but Sandy merely shrugged. ''If they want me, they'll get me—but they'll have to pass iron first. But yeah, I'm pretty sure I saw a couple watching the house yesterday; either that, or those were awfully solid shadows. Voices too—maybe. Couldn't be sure; could've been the wind. Almost.''

David gnawed his lip. "Maybe," he said slowly, "we should stay put tonight."

Brock looked stricken. "You mean not . . . go Tracking?"

David shrugged. "Just a feelin', but—I dunno. Forget it."

"Speaking of forgetting," Myra broke in. "Has anyone heard from Scott?"

As if in reply, the phone rang—in the bathroom, where someone had left it.

"Maybe that's him now," Myra sighed, rising.

"Was it?" Liz wondered when she returned.

Myra shook her head. "Piper."

"Piper?" From Calvin.

"The aforementioned James Morrison Murphy. Wannie's car just died out past Crawford and they need a ride."

"I'll go!" Brock volunteered instantly.

"Fine," Myra grunted, already fumbling for her keys. "But since I'm the only one here who won't scare 'em to death, I reckon I'd better go too."

Liz grabbed David by the ear and yanked him to his feet. "C'mon, blond guy," she commanded, "*somebody'd* better start dinner."

Chapter VIII:
Midsummer Night's Team

(Crawford, Georgia—
Friday, June 20—late evening)

James Morrison Murphy—Piper to his friends, which was basically everyone present—lowered the chanter of the bagpipes on which, for ten minutes, he'd been puffing, and wiped his brow expressively, even as the applause began. His sad brown eyes were hopefully bright, his mop of curly dark hair wringing wet with sweat. His wiry body sagged visibly within his trademark Stewart plaid pants and white linen shirt. Beside him, LaWanda Gilmore—Juju Woman (among the other, more sinister, appellations she cultivated)—flashed a toothily wicked grin and laid her black Fender bass atop the nearest amp. A harem's worth of gold bracelets tinkled on the strong, chocolate-colored arms bared by a scarlet tank top. The rehearsal hall—actually, the auditorium of a defunct high school in tiny Crawford, Georgia, twenty miles south of Athens (from which, six hours earlier, the two of them had been rescued from a defunct Pinto)—still reverberated from their last number: Gary Moore's "Over the Hills and Far Away." The rest of the impromptu band—Darrell on vocals and lead guitar and Calvin (after many protests) on drum—smiled expectantly.

"Well?" LaWanda prompted, folding her arms. The tiny gold beads that tipped her myriad braids glittered, but no more than her eyes.

"Great!" David roared, jumping to his feet from the ratty sofa from which, with Liz, he'd been spectating. Alec and Aikin aped his example from the sofa's even scruffier twin. The rest of the tonally challenged (or rhythmically handicapped, as Liz preferred) crew chimed in immediately. "Wow!" was one summarization. "Far out," a deliberately outdated other.

David poked the gawking Brock in the ribs and bent close. "What'd you think, Brit-Boy?"

"Brilliant," Brock retorted. "Brilliant!" David suppressed a far too fatherly urge to ruffle the kid's hair like Calvin had done earlier. He'd been that way himself not long ago: full of flash and fire and energy. His folks thought he still was. In truth . . . he was no longer sure. Brock, however—*he* was like a kid in a candy store; or, more like, a series of candy stores.

Though the boy had grown up middle-class in Florida, fear of an abusive stepfather (who'd raped Brock's older sister, Robyn, right before Calvin met them a few years back, thereby precipitating that encounter) had driven both him and his sibling to seek sanctuary with friends in England. Brock sneaked back stateside occasionally; Robyn didn't. But Brock had been to Athens only once before, and that in haste, and he had nearly overloaded on that small city's wealth of Ameri-pop this second time around: first on food—Liz's patented jambalaya (and dark Atlanta beer he was too young to legally consume)—then on the racks of hip new music in Wuxtry and Ruthless Records alike, next on books and magazines at Barnett's Newsstand and Tennis Bird Shorts, and finally on live music itself.

It had been a damned fine evening. David had had the time of his life, and he *knew* all these folks and had heard most of them perform more times than he could count. Point of fact, he remembered when Darrell had gotten his first guitar, back when the guy was fifteen. And he recalled when his lanky pal had proudly called him up from MacTyrie two days later, to strum a rough but recognizable "House of the Rising Sun" over the phone.

But until he'd come to UGA, Darrell had *been* his musical friend. Oh, he'd known in a general way that Cal played harmonica and guitar, and that drumming was a necessary adjunct to many of the Cherokee rituals Cal had undertaken, but he'd never actually heard the guy sing until three years after their initial meeting. "A man's gotta hold some things in reserve," Calvin had confided. "Otherwise his friends'll take him for granted."

And of course there was Piper and LaWanda, who really *were* musicians. LaWanda had long played in a band called Save the Feet for Last, and had likewise performed the music at Gary's wedding. And Piper—well, wiry, tousle-haired little Piper was a very strange bird indeed: one of the sweetest guys in the world, and spacy as they came. Basically, he lived for rain and LaWanda, his unlikely sweetie. He was also hell-on-wheels on pipes, highland or Uillean, either. And very adaptable.

Which was fortunate, because the assortment of unlikely personnel that evening had also made for some unlikely improvisations and intrumental juxtapositions, if consistently wonderful sounds. Darrell, for instance, had opened with the most obscene blues song David had ever heard, something called "Love Me With a Feelin'." He'd done a couple more solos, whereupon Calvin (who sometimes collaborated with him) had chimed in with a pair of John Denveresque pastiches. That had been followed by Guadalcanal Diary's old "Trail of Tears," which LaWanda had augmented on bass halfway through; and then the Juju Woman herself had ordered the lights reduced to a single candle and treated them to a spooky synthesizer rendition of "Pirate Jenny" (with apologies to Nina Simone), and a rousing rendition of the same singer's "Mississippi Goddamn"— an old civil-rights ditty, whose implications Myra had to explain to Brock, who hadn't a clue.

A beer and snack break had ensued, then assorted jams, while Piper got himself properly psyched. Whereupon, with much ceremony, he'd dived in on a new-and-old Celtic martial medley, consisting of "Brian Boru's March," "Roddy McCorley," and "Foggy Dew" (with LaWanda's eerie vocals), to end with "Green Fields of France." The Gary Moore had been Myra's request.

David checked his watch. They'd have to leave soon; have to shift from artists-and-audience to Trackers. But he certainly wouldn't complain if there were a few more tunes.

Nor, to judge by his rapt expression, would Brock—who, it appeared, would've been just as glad to spend the night worshipping Piper's shadow as waiting by a stretch of leafless ground for an event they had no reason to assume would occur.

Piper raised a brow at LaWanda. "Another?"

She shrugged. "Why not?"

Piper looked straight at Brock. "Requests?"

Brock turned as red as LaWanda's tank-top. "Uh . . ." he choked, but then his jaw hardened and a wicked glint came into his eyes. "How 'bout 'King of the Fairies'?"

LaWanda stiffened abruptly, Myra gasped, and Piper's eyes nearly fell out of his head. An ominous silence filled the room.

Brock looked around in confusion. "Uh, Jeeze," he mumbled. "What'd I say?"

More silence.

"I mean, it's just a song," Brock went on stubbornly. "Isn't it?"

Still silence. Then, from Myra. "Actually, no, it's not—not to Piper."

Brock stood his ground, scowling under his inky forelock. "I don't get it."

Myra gazed about for support, then scowled herself, and dived in. "Well, Brock, the short form is that that particular song played by that particular person, under certain circumstances, isn't . . . just a song. You've heard us talking about Gates before: Gates between the Worlds, and all. And though we've all tried to ignore it 'cause we've wanted to have fun tonight and hang out with our friends, and not deal with serious stuff, the fact is, that when Piper plays 'King of the Fairies' it can sometimes *open* a Gate—or send him through the World Walls, anyway. And since we know that Lugh—he's the local Faery king—is real sensitive about any kind of Gates right now, you can see where we're headed."

Brock nodded sullenly, choosing attitude over embarrassment, which was typical of his age. "Sorry. Didn't know."

David clapped him on the shoulder. "No big deal."

Piper, however, looked almost as sad as Brock—probably because he hated to disappoint such a totally devoted fan.

"Tell you what," Calvin broke in suddenly, gazing at Darrell, "how 'bout something completely different, a lot more fun, and a lot more relevant, if not necessarily as wild or weird or imaginative technically?"

Darrell regarded him quizzically, one brow quirked upward. "You don't mean . . . ?"

Calvin grinned fiendishly, even as he fished out his harmonica. "Ladies and gentlemen," he began, "so to speak"—as he climbing atop a convenient stool—"I give you the 'Werepossum Blues!' "

And with that, Darrell laid down a blues riff, and Calvin started singing.

> *"Oh Lord, my name is Calvin,*
> *   an' Indian Blood run through my veins,*
> *Yeah, my name is Calvin Fargo,*
> *   and Cherokee blood be pulsin' in my veins.*
> *I've had some wild adventures;*
> *   seen an awful lot o' wond'rous things."*

And from that he went on for nearly thirty minutes, detailing in verse after verse and in perfect blues rhyme and meter, the whole long tale of their varied adventures in Faerie, Galunlati, and assorted other realms, starting with what had befallen David that long ago summer night:

> *"You know my buddy David?*
> *   One day he went an' got the Second Sight.*
> *Yeah, you know my good friend David?*
> *   He fooled around and got the Second Sight.*
> *He saw the Faeries ridin'—*
> *   an' that gave him one mighty fright!"*

And so on: first relating David's riddle game with the Seelie Lords Nuada and Ailill, and Ailill's attempts to revenge his defeat on David by assailing his family, ending in Ailill being transformed into a horse. That was followed by Ailill's sister's failed attempt at revenge of her own, for that insult. Next came Cal's initial encounter with David and their subsequent journey, with Alec, to Galunlati, the Cherokee overworld, where Alec had been manipulated into betraying them. Which in turn precipitated a war between Lugh of Tir-Nan-Og and Finvarra of Erenn, during which the sun itself had been used as a weapon and which altercation David and his crew had, beyond hope, defused.

The tale became more personal then, as Calvin recounted his own encounter with a shapechanging Cherokee ogress called Spearfinger, who liked to feast on human livers. Brock brightened as he heard his own name come into the song. That took a number of verses, ending with Spearfinger's dissolution and Calvin's conscience heavy with guilt at the number of deaths he had inadvertently caused, including that of his father. More verses related events one year later, in which Calvin, Brock, and Sandy had helped the last of the not-so-mythical Water-Panthers evade a Cherokee witch who would have enslaved her, during which time Calvin had himself ventured to the Darkening Land to the West: the Cherokee Land of the Dead.

All those verses David had heard—or read—before, and perhaps he alone knew how personal they truly were, for they were part of Calvin's private death song, which he had long ago begun composing at the urging of that same shaman-grandfather who had named him. But there were new verses as well (and David tried not to check his watch as time drew nigh to commence the official Tracking, for some things required their own hour and season), and those new verses told a fresher tale, in which David, Alec, and Aikin had all three dreamed dreams which had led each of them to yet more adventures: Aikin-the-hunter as quarry to the Wild Hunt himself, first in Faerie, then on the Tracks, and finally in downtown Athens; Alec as thwarted rescuer of the Faery woman, Aife, who had betrayed him, then loved him, and who now stayed with him in the guise of a cat-née-enfield; and himself, who'd dared a never-never corner of space—time to win closure with the young martyred uncle for whom he had been named.

And as Calvin's voice trailed off into a whispered hush,

and Darrell's guitar likewise faded, every sound in the room followed them to silence.

As though on cue, the single candle winked out. And someone—David never knew who—whispered an awe-struck, "Wow!"

Silence indeed, then; and breathing. And then LaWanda lit a new taper.

Someone's watch beeped, signaling that it was now eleven, and suddenly they were all bright, creative, healthy (and to various degrees tipsy) young folks again.

Only Myra seemed unable to muster enthusiasm. David noticed how she lagged behind as they filed noisily down the stairs with a jumble of clothes, coolers, and musical instruments. "What. . . ." he began softly, for Myra's ears alone.

She frowned. "Scott. He was supposed to be here and he's not."

David started, though he'd likewise known at some level that Myra's friend and sometime lover had not appeared, and indeed, that more than one person had commented on his absence—generally to be reminded that Scott wasn't very reliable and had been even more spaced than usual of late. "Probably forgot what day it was," Liz assured her. "God knows, he had as recently as yesterday."

"He said he'd meet us there," Myra conceded. "If he didn't make it here, he said he'd meet us there."

"Only one way to find out," David told her with forced cheeriness. And with that he jogged away toward the lov-ingly restored Candyapple Red '66 Mustang he still called the Mustang of Death.

The caravan back to the southern outskirts of Athens consisted of twelve people and a caged cat that was really a Faery woman changed into an enfield; all, now that LaWanda's Pinto had deigned to run again, scattered across four vehicles. David, per tradition, took the lead in the Mus-tang, with Liz, Alec, and Aife along for the ride: the three original Trackers, accompanied, in a sense, by the latest. Then came Myra, with Darrell, Gary, Aikin, and most of the musical gear, in Myra's brand new Dodge minivan.

Piper and LaWanda followed, lest the Pinto suffer another calamity, as seemed likely, given the distinctly yellowish cast of its lights; while Sandy, Calvin, and Brock in Sandy's Ford Explorer brought up the rear. The rest had transport, of course (though not all in town), ranging from Piper's nonfunctioning Harley through Aikin's Chevy S-10 pickup, to Alec's aging Volvo; but in the interest of both simplicity and camaraderie, they always elected to carpool. Nor did it hurt that achieving their goal required invading a place where the presence of too many unfamiliar vehicles after dark might raise more than one set of law-enforcement eyebrows.

In any event, the entire trip from Crawford to Gaines School Road took all of twenty minutes: exactly long enough for Liz to wrest the true tale of his myriad kitty-cat scratches from Alec, and for Alec to promise both Liz and a seething David, *never* to let Aikin talk him into anything that dumb again.

By which time, they were slowing for the railroad tracks where Whitehall Road kinked right, and were themselves preparing to turn sharp left. Alec held his breath (not entirely from tradition) as David braked hard, then swung the Mustang's tail smartly out as they entered the precincts of Whitehall Forest: the University of Georgia Forestry School's sprawling sanctum sanctorum. The Whitehall Mansion itself loomed close on the right: a fantasy of turrets, gables, and towers that was Athens's best surviving example of brick Victorian architecture; and then they were pausing with their lights off long enough for Aikin to dash up and unlock the white pipe gate that barred ingress into the forest proper. A smattering of buildings flashed by on either side, but David could already sense the forest closing in, as the road became narrower, curvier, and rougher by turns. One final sharp uphill left, followed by a trickily abrupt downhill right, and they'd reached Destination One: the combination yard and parking lot of the rustic, log-sheathed cabin Aikin had, for three years, called home. This would be his last week there. Come graduation, he (and the other three forestry jocks with whom he shared space) would have no choice but to vacate in favor of a new batch of underclassmen. Fortunately, none were in residence now, but Aikin was plainly nervous all the same, as he waited for the group to assemble.

Which was odd, David reckoned, given that the Tracking Party itself was Aik's invention: a stubborn romanticization of Faerie when the rest of them had either become scared of it, denied it, or simply become jaded. Aikin, though— he'd known of Faerie and his friends' exploits there long before he'd ever visited that realm himself. And at that, he'd only skimmed the fringe—because Lugh Samildinach had closed the borders again well and proper following their last encounter, two Halloweens back.

Now, however, he took the lead, motioning them to silence as they unloaded small coolers and baskets of food. By agreement—and to humor Aikin's insistence on stealth—they'd every one changed into black: Darrell in Doc Martins and cut-off Levis, for instance; Gary in a mechanic's jumpsuit; and Myra in a thrift store velvet mini-dress, freshly donned tights and ankle-length cloak. Aik simply wore black fatigues and sweatshirt. David was similarly attired, as were Alec and Liz. Another year, David suspected, and that would become the official uniform.

In the meantime, he had custody of the music: a portable Sony CD player with a custom-recorded disc.

Finally, with everyone assembled—still no Scott—Aikin "Mighty Hunter" Daniels slipped into the Georgia night.

He led them first beside the cabin and down a steep trail that ran through a mixture of woods and brush to the gleaming arc of the Oconee River. He paused there to count heads, then pressed onward toward what once had been a mill but was now merely a jumble of concrete ruins towering over the nearside terminus of a narrow dam.

"I recognize this place," Gary whispered to David. "Didn't Myra use it as a background for one of her paintings?"

David nodded. "Alec and me and Aik as elven warriors makin' one desperate final stand."

"Good choice," Gary breathed, gazing about appreciatively.

David agreed. The sky had played hide-and-seek all day,

and there'd been a return of rain during the rehearsal, but now whatever front had been weirding out the weather had largely dissipated, leaving a sky like fresh-dyed black velvet dusted with new-cut gems. The moon, conveniently enough, was full, and by its light the world had gone silver-blue and eerie, transfiguring even the most prosaic-looking of their (mostly attractive) band into beings wild, dangerous, and fey.

"We gonna stand here all night, or we gonna move?" Aikin rasped. "We've still gotta cross the dam, and I'd like to make final landfall well before midnight."

"Why midnight?" Brock asked Calvin. The kid's eyes were feverishly bright, as though they existed solely to drink moonbeams.

Calvin looked at Myra. "I was afraid you'd ask that," she grumbled, gazing at Brock in turn. "And the fact is, that since this is all ceremony anyway, the actual time doesn't really matter, except symbolically. The point is, we come to Whitehall, which is the nearest Straight Track to Athens, on one of the nights we know the Faery Folk ride. We wait by the Track a suitably reverent interval, then we eat. Probably we see nothing—we never have before. We leave token offerings 'cause that's what people used to do. We stay until we get tired, then split. The journey's the thing, not the arrival."

"Cream for the brownies, eh Piper?" LaWanda giggled, elbowing Piper in the ribs.

"Cool it!" Aikin hissed. And with no further ado, he turned and dashed up the ruin's lone functioning flight of stairs. An instant later, he reached the summit, with David right behind. Without bothering to wait for the others (and likely frustrated by their noise, when silence was one of Aikin's deities) they proceeded across the yard-wide top of the dam. It made David giddy—things like that always did, especially bridges, even low, wide ones—but he tried hard not to let his step falter as he reached the middle of the span. The dam stretched each way now, water whooshing and rumbling two yards below his feet, and David couldn't help but recall (as he always did) the sword bridges in all those Arthurian stories: the ones knights had to dare in order to win their ladies. Liz took his hand as he lingered there, and squeezed. "Beautiful, isn't it?" she murmured. "Aye," he acknowledged—and followed his friend to the other side.

The wood that awaited them was not properly part of Whitehall Forest, and in fact abutted a number of suburban backyards not all that far away. Yet somehow it had largely escaped man's attention. Aikin swore there was a small patch of old-growth timber in one hollow, and the fact that a Track lay close upon the Lands of Men there perhaps bore that out. Certainly those woods had a vaguely primeval feel, with denser, lusher foliage than typical, often so thick they had to force their way through. "Aik *does* know where he's goin', doesn't he?" Darrell (who sported the only completely bare legs) complained, as he found his skin assailed.

"Briars," David supplied. "Just look for briars."

"Shit, man, they're fuckin' lookin' for *me*!" Darrell wailed.

Whereupon Aikin curtailed further comment by uttering a low, but very clear, "We're there."

There was nothing special to the ordinary eye; merely a short stretch of relatively open ground close by a bifurcated maple. But David could already feel his eyes starting to itch and tingle, as they did (somewhat unpredictably) in the presence of Faery magic. Especially active Faery magic, as would be the case should the Sidhe choose this particular Track as the route for the Rade, their periodic processional riding to the coast. They might so choose; then again, they might not. The American Southeast was webbed with Straight Tracks, leading not only to and through Tir-Nan-Og, but to a variety of other Worlds, many of which were tiny pocket universes, and only a few of which he knew anything about at all, save that many were, in spite of their size, inhabited. As for Aikin—he was a damned ballsy guy, to return here after the chaos that had transpired when (with Aife's unwitting aid) he'd managed to activate a Track, then get lost upon it, all on a Halloween night.

Would the Wild Hunt be out *this* night? David wondered, with a shudder Liz noted with visible alarm. And why, with so much intellect, creativity, and sheer mental energy among them, was no one talking? For the entire crew had fallen silent and seemed as one to be aping Aik's example and folding themselves down into a ragged double file along a ten-yard stretch of ground distinguished mostly by the uncannily straight growth of blackberry briars along either side, and by the fact that the ground itself, though rugged with moss and grass, did not seem to encourage other growth—nor stray insects or fallen leaves—to accumulate there. Aikin caught David's eye and motioned the three of them forward, to a position at the presumed head of the line—the direction from which the magic had flowed (so Aikin swore) once before.

"Where is it?" Brock muttered, squinting into the gloom. "I don't see a thing."

"Nothing *to* see," Calvin advised him. " 'cept briars growin' in a straighter line than briars have any right to grow."

"Mojo," LaWanda muttered in turn, beside Piper. "Some major mojo here, white boy."

David turned to regard the woman. He didn't know her well, and she tended to make him uneasy. Not because she was black, but because she was just so confidently . . . blatant. LaWanda never did anything by halves, or to suit any pleasure but her own. She was her own woman through and through, said what she thought, and had a knack for cutting through the undergrowth to the heart of the chase. Definitely a lady to have on one's side in a fair fight—or unfair either. You just had to watch your step around her, because if you acted like a fool, she'd be the first to call your bluff.

"Mojo, indeed," David echoed at last. "And I'm mighty glad you're here," he added—because he wanted to, and it was true.

Brock was still squinting madly. "I still don't see it."

"You won't," David replied. "Not likely, unless the Sidhe actually ride on this one—which 'activates' it—or unless you're like a couple of us and have some form of Second Sight. Even then, it helps if they want you to see it."

"But how does it look?" Brock persisted, though David suspected he already knew.

"Like a strip of glowing golden dust just above the ground," Alec said, as he adjusted the cat-cage in his lap. "Ideally, it'll start to glow in the direction from which the Sidhe are riding, and the glow will get stronger, and the dust thicker, and the briars'll diminish, and then you'd better cover your ass and go to ground, 'cause I kid you not, this may be fun to you, but meeting the Sidhe—or anybody from the Worlds—is serious business, and bloody dangerous."

"And, to be honest," David concluded, "I doubt we'd even be out here if we thought there was any real chance of 'em happenin' by. I mean, there are thousands of ways to the coast, so I've heard, and I know the Sidhe like variety."

"I know *I'd* like some silence," Aikin growled from the middle of his line.

"I'd like a beer," Darrell snickered, until an elbow in the ribs from his glowering older sister silenced him.

"I'd like to know where Scott is," that same sister mumbled in turn, twisting round to peer over her shoulder. "He said he'd be late, but still . . . he *could've* phoned."

David shrugged helplessly. "Who knows?" And with that, he unsnapped a CD case and flourished a glimmering disk, which he inserted in his cherished boom box before setting it on the ground on the very fringe of the Track. The strains of Enya's "The Celts" wafted softly through the woods.

As though by unspoken consent, conversation ceased, and the only sound save Enya was that of bottles of Sandy's homemade beer being opened and, per ritual, passed down the line.

"We wait for an hour," Calvin informed Brock, as he handed the boy a brew. "Officially, thirty minutes either side of the witching hour. We try not to think frivolous thoughts. And about the time we've started to feel really stupid and our stomachs all start to growl, we assume nobody's comin', kick back, and stuff ourselves silly."

Brock squinted at the Track again. David, who was enjoying watching him, couldn't help but smile, which he masked by looking down. Even so, he saw Brock start and the boy's eyes grow huge. "Uh," Brock whispered hoarsely, "am I wishing too hard, or isn't this sucker glowing?"

Someone dismissed him with a snort, but David felt his eyes start to burn even more strongly. "No," he corrected, rising. "Brock's right!"

"He is?" From Aikin, who was likewise staring at the ground.

"Yeah," Liz assured him, easing surreptitiously around to guard Aikin's back—which, to judge by the sudden alteration in his expression from romantic expectation to full-out alarm, was a good idea, David reckoned.

Someone gasped. Someone else choked in awe. A bottle fell with a thump and eruption of fizzy foam. And then David's eyes seemed to catch fire, and he saw, sure enough, the Straight Track spring to life a scant yard beyond his sneakered toes.

It was much as he'd seen it before; much as Alec had just described—and yet both mouth and memory provided only dull approximations. There was no truly accurate way to describe what occurred when two Worlds met along what Sandy had speculated might be some odd form of superstring. But that was physics, this was magic: magic that awoke light along a perfectly straight stretch of ground, magic that conjured motes of gold-toned dust from nowhere, magic that made the hard stems and sharp thorns on the nearby briars seem as insubstantial as reflected rainbows, and as drab as day-old mud.

"It's awake!" Brock breathed, incredulously.

"Aye," Calvin sighed. "Which means someone's awakened it. Which mean's somebody's coming. The question is, who?"

David, at the head of the file, wondered that same thing, and found himself more than a little uneasy. The Tracks awoke in the vanguard of the Sidhe, that was a fact. And on the solstices, the equinoxes, and the four cross-quarter days, the Sidhe rode in slow, solemn file—and the Track awoke at that same slow pace ahead of them. But this Track was awakening rapidly—which, as best he could tell, implied that it was being traversed in considerable haste. Trouble was, it didn't bode well when Faeries hurried. They were immortal, after all; had literally all the time in the world.

Liz too seemed to sense a subtle wrongness, and to judge by his companions' stiffened postures and troubled glances, many of them did as well.

And then it didn't matter, because the Track flared to full, glorious flame: a thick yet tenuous carpet of frantically flickering motes that did not quite touch the ground, yet lay at places both over it and in it, and which seemed at once solid and ethereal. His eyes were on fire, and he rubbed them frantically, as tears blurred that miraculous view. By the time he'd regained a modicum of vision, he heard the steady muffled rumble of hooves pressed hard and in anger.

The Track waxed brighter still, lighting every awestruck face with a blaze of gold, and with it that pounding sounded louder yet, but joining it David also now caught the labored hiss of heavy equine breathing.

"Riding hard," Liz noted.

"Yeah," David grunted. "I—"

He didn't finish, because the Track flared up as though it would ignite the world, and out of that nimbus of light that now stretched higher than their heads and ran and expanded for more than thirty yards to either side, appeared the shape of a horse and rider.

Faster they came, and faster yet, with the rider bent low over his mount's neck, and the cloak on his back billowing like clouds in the vanguard of a storm.

And then, with no warning, the rider yanked hard on the reins and leaned back. The horse slowed, then stopped, then rose up on its hind legs in a glory of white mane, gold barding, and wildly flashing eyes.

"Hold!" the rider—a slim but well-built man in high white boots, white hose, and beautifully cut tunic of honey gold—cried, in a voice like bells of crystal ice. And with that, the horse fell back onto all fours. Yet even before that last fore-hoof touched the ground, the rider had dropped his reins and dismounted, all in one deft motion.

"Finno!" David yelped, as the rider pushed back his hood, to reveal a young and incredibly beautiful face, framed with a short mane of thick, silky, gold-blond hair. "Uh, Fionchadd, I mean . . . I guess!"

The Faery youth sketched a hasty bow that, while it obviously included them all, seemed somehow meant for David alone. "Hail to you . . . Dave, I mean David Sullivan . . . I guess—and to all of you veterans of the Tracks. Glad I am to see you all, and in numbers even I dared not hope. Yet the errand I am on is grim, and I fear we have no time for revelry and a very great need for haste."

"Haste?" Liz managed, aghast.

Fionchadd nodded. "Aye, lady, you are summoned this very night to attend the council of Lugh Samildinach, High King of the Daoine Sidhe in Tir-Nan-Og."

PART TWO

Chapter IX:
World Travelers

*(Whitehall Forest—
Friday, June 20—midnight)*

Alec's eyes narrowed dangerously. Already he was backing away from the glittering line of the Track that stretched as far as David could see to either side, and which glowed so brightly the thick-grown trunks that flanked it seemed wrought of molten brass, their leaves of new-cast gold.

David sensed his friend's movement as much as saw it and eased over to steady him with an arm around his shoulders. The guy was trembling—actually *trembling*—his spare, lean muscles taut as bow strings. A sharp, concerned glance at him showed a frightened face awash with tears.

"Jesus, man," David hissed. "Cool it! It can't be *that* big a deal!"

Alec shrugged the arm away and rounded on him savagely, avoiding Aife's cage by the slimmest of knife-thin margins. Leaves rustled under his feet. "Can't it?" he challenged. "*Can't it?*" he repeated, when David didn't reply.

Christ, what had got into the guy? It wasn't as if he hadn't gone Tracking before—stoically, if not energetically. The only difference between this iteration and any other was that this time someone had actually appeared.

Someone with an errand, David amended. A summons he himself distrusted, given its precipitous nature. But if there was going to be another foray into Faerie, apparently with their entire crew, best to nip potential friction in the bud.

"Alec . . ." David began, wishing someone—Liz or

Myra or, better yet, Fionchadd himself—would intercede and calm that most volatile of buddies.

"No!" Alec spat, taking another step back. "I know what you're gonna say, and it's no good. We've been summoned to Faerie. Fine. You go—all of you go! Just don't take me,'cause I've flat had enough! Shoot, the only reason I'm here now is 'cause I keep hoping against hope Lugh or somebody'll ride by and reclaim this fucking . . . cat. And yeah, I know the rationale behind that, but the rest of you don't have to live with it, and Lugh sure as hell doesn't! How'd he like having a former lover around *all the time*—watching, but never reacting?" He spun around to confront the gaping Faery boy. "Well, Finno, tell me? How *would* he like it?"

"He likes it fine," Fionchadd answered amiably. "And I regret that you feel as you do, but with you here, I would much prefer to have your company."

"Of course you would!" Alec raged, and with that, he turned to bolt. He had managed no more than two tentative steps, however, when he uttered a desperate "No," flailed out with both hands, and stumbled backward, to collapse at David's feet in an awkward sprawl.

David's face was grim as he helped him up. He didn't know who to be angrier at: Alec, for acting like such a fool; or Fionchadd, not only for starting all this with his ominous appearance and disturbing message, but also for that subtle movement of his hands just now, which was clearly some sort of barrier spell, close kin to that which had forestalled his own escape when he'd first met the Sidhe behind his house all those years ago.

Fionchadd padded forward, face an odd mix of irritation, amusement, and concern—odd indeed on a usually merry visage. "We have no time for this, Alec," the Faery cautioned, reaching out to lay a slim, gloved hand on his shoulder, gently displacing David's in the process. "No time," Fionchadd emphasized.

Alec swallowed hard and reached up to bat the hand away, but Fionchadd grabbed his wrist and held it firm. Love showed in the Faery's eyes, and compassion. And maybe even real tears, twins to Alec's own. "I don't *like* to hurt my friends,'' Fionchadd gritted. ''And I will swear any oath you like, in any place, before any witnesses you care to name, in this World or any other, that you are indeed my friend! I will not hurt you, nor does anyone in Tir-Nan-Og mean you harm.''

''But . . .'' Alec paused to wipe his face with his free hand. ''Why us? What can Lugh possibly want with us?''

''I am not at liberty to reveal that,'' Fionchadd replied gravely. ''Indeed, I know little more than you, and am eager to be on our way, so that we may both increase our knowledge. Suffice to say that I will be with you at Lugh's council and will learn his full intent even as you do.''

Alec held his breath, swallowed again, and nodded. ''Friendship by coercion is no friendship.''

''And no gift is worth anything that is not freely given.''

Silence.

Fionchadd stared at Alec.

Silence.

The horse whickered impatiently.

Silence.

''Can the rest of you ride?'' Fionchadd called finally, shifting his gaze to survey the uneasy company.

Myra cleared her throat. ''You haven't asked the rest of us if we're *going*,'' she retorted.

Fionchadd regarded her sadly. ''You I do not know, save by repute and rumor. A painter, are you not? Few of my kind practice that art with any true conviction. I am already in awe of you, then; and for other things I have heard of you as well, not the least being the loyalty you have shown your friends.''

Myra lifted her head, gave him challenge for implicit challenge. ''I sense a *but* approaching.''

Fionchadd's eyes flashed fire (Faery pride, David reckoned, in disgust), but his voice, when he spoke, was gentle. ''If you—*any* of you—do not accompany me, I have orders to destroy every memory you have of this meeting. I do not think you would like that, Myra Buchanan. And I *will* tell you this: Lugh will place a ban on whoever does accompany me, and this ban will forbid *any* speech between those who afford Lugh counsel and those who, by remaining here, do not. But those who accompany me will, I am sure, react to whatever awaits them, if not at the time, then later. And the rest of you will be curious, and perhaps they will need your aid, if what Lugh would discuss is what I suspect. But they will be unable to tell you of what transpires. And so, a barrier rises: a barrier of secrets."

"Too many secrets already," Liz growled so softly David knew it was for his ears alone, yet something about the acoustics of the Track (likely abetted by the unseen but evidently quite tangible barrier that had thwarted Alec) amplified her voice.

Fionchadd twisted around to study her. "You will go. Because David goes, you will go, if for no other reason."

Liz shrugged noncommittally, but David could feel the blend of fear and anger in the grip she laid on his arm. "It'll be okay," he assured her. "I—"

"I *want* to go!" another voice announced, its tones muffled by the press of bodies that, David noted, seemed to be crowding closer every second.

"Watch it!" Gary warned, from the front rank—at which point a slim, dark-haired shape wriggled between him and Darrell, and David found himself facing Brock-the-badger No-name.

Fionchadd smiled. "Three, at least—now."

"Four," Alec managed, stepping back to David's side. "I'm trapped. If I go, I know I'll regret it, and if I don't, I'm bound to regret it, too. But"—he looked David square in the eye—"I'll be damned if I'm gonna let anyone—or anything—erect another barrier between us!"

"You are a good man," Fionchadd acknowledged, with more than a hint of smile. "And you others . . . ?"

"Someone's gotta keep 'em outta trouble," Myra sighed. "Which I guess means I'll go . . . I reckon."

"As long as you promise we won't meet the Wild Hunt," Aikin hedged.

"He is elsewhere tonight," Fionchadd informed him darkly. "He thinks he may soon expand his hunting range."

Aikin scowled. "How so?"

"It is for Lugh to say—and now, how say you others?"

"I don't trust Lugh," Calvin said flatly. "And though I doubt you're lyin', you *could* be playin' hopscotch with the truth. But since I've got magic that isn't Faery magic, I suppose I oughta tag along, just in case."

Fionchadd nodded. "And you, Sandy Fairfax, what have you to say?"

"Knowledge is power," she breathed, with a twinkle in her eye. "If Cal goes, so do I—from what I've heard about Faery women, I'd better. Besides, maybe it'll help me straighten out all this chaos I've got myself into trying to puzzle out Faery physics."

"Darrell Buchanan?"

I'm, uh, 'sposed to play music tomorrow night, and really do need to practice."

Myra eyed him askance. "Excuses, excuses, little brother."

"But," Darrell went on quickly, and David was amazed to see that his friend's eyes, like Alec's, were misting, "it ... it may be the last adventure I ever have with the Gang."

"Which means I have to go too," Gary grumbled. "Can you guarantee to have me back by tomorrow? I really would hate to worry my lady."

"Easy as thinking," Fionchadd informed him. "Time is especially flexible on Midsummer's Eve."

"Which leaves us," LaWanda grunted, evidently speaking for both herself and Piper—an affectation that got on David's nerves. "Pipe better follow his own head this time, but ... I'll go, if my only other choice is to have you fool with folks' heads and build barriers between me and my friends." She paused. "See, I don't know why I even think I owe you explanations, Faery Boy, but ... I've been to that place once, and seen the bad side—the scary side, anyhow, and I ... I guess I just wanta see the other."

Which left Piper, who was looking remarkably like a man who'd run off the edge of a cliff and was waiting for gravity to catch him and drag him down to doom. "If I'd known this would happen, I wouldn't have come tonight," he whispered, looking imploringly at LaWanda.

"Yet you *are* here," Fionchadd countered.

Piper's eyes were bright with incipient tears. "If I don't go . . . it won't be good."

"Likely," Fionchadd agreed.

"Promise me one thing, then," Piper pleaded.

Fionchadd folded his arms and eyed him dubiously, gnawing his lip in what David knew was a gesture of fierce impatience. "*What*?" the Faery snapped. "Time flies, and though the Tracks can twist and turn it, Lugh truly did bid me bring you in haste, and yet we tarry. Have your say, Morry Murphy, and be done!"

Piper stared at his feet, shoved a twig aside with a sneakered toe. "The promise."

"Very well—*If it is within my power and a just thing!*"

"A song," Piper stated simply. "I want to learn one new song from Faerie."

"Done!" Fionchadd cried. "And now that is concluded, let us be on our way. . . . You all did say you could ride?"

"Not well," Aikin admitted. "And my butt's gonna hate me if I do. . . ."

"I could get you an . . . Irish elk," Fionchadd offered. "You have ridden one of those before, have you not? With a little help, I seem to recall," he added with a wicked smirk.

"No big deal," Aikin mumbled. "Whatever."

"Anyone else?"

"Nothing special," Piper confessed.

"That will be sufficient," Fionchadd assured him. "And now, let us be on our way." And with that he returned to the Track, patted his steed on the shoulder, and removed a small curved horn from an intricate jeweled mount at the front of the saddle. David shivered when he saw it. Evidently Fionchadd saw him. "Horns it is, again!" he observed. "Horns are indeed part of our history, you and I. Yet this is not the Horn of Annwyn, nor any part of it. It is only a horn of summons."

And with that, he raised the instrument to his all-too-perfect lips and sounded a dozen notes, each subtly different, each of which made the shifting patterns on the Track spark and flare with crimson and azure.

They waited no more than ten heartbeats. Nor, David

suspected, would the clearly impatient Fionchadd dare to wait much longer, given the misgivings their party had expressed. But while everyone present at least loosely deserved the label 'friend,' they were all independent people. Therefore, even if David didn't go, he had neither right, authority, nor strength to prevent anyone else from accepting the Faery's call. And Finno seemed bent on taking as many as he could, which was damned odd. So far they'd managed a unified front, which boded well for a possibly uncertain future. He had to preserve that bond. He wasn't certain why, but—especially in the face of the latest round of incursions from Faerie—he had to keep his friends together.

At which point the clatter of galloping hooves echoed down the Track (such sounds had always disturbed David, given how overtly insubstantial those pathways seemed to be), and an instant later, the first horse thundered into view.

"Motherfucker!" LaWanda yipped, awestruck—and honest in her attitude.

"Not quite," Fionchadd corrected with a smile, "yet well-sired all the same."

Liz lifted a brow. Like most women David knew, she was nuts about horses. Certainly Myra was; and Sandy, in her outdoor-mountain-girl aspect, to judge by her expression, was as well.

"Beautiful!"

"Brilliant!" (That was Brock).

"Not bad." (Was that Gary ... or Aik ... or Runnerman?)

"Epona's get," Fionchadd informed them, as the first pranced to a stop behind him, all in a flurry of silky manes, tails, and forelocks. "By different mates," he appended, with a sly grin at Sandy. "All of them princes of the Sidhe begot when she walked among them."

"As a woman or a horse?" Liz challenged.

"Both," Fionchadd grinned. "As were the sires."

The last of their mounts had arrived by then, and as best David could tell they were mighty fine horseflesh indeed. All had the light builds and slender legs and bodies typical of Faery steeds. And all had narrow heads, glossy coats, dark intelligent eyes; and nostrils that every now and then vented flame. Color alone was the main distinction, for their hides ranged from one as white as Fionchadd's stallion, through every shade of silver-gray he could imagine (some skewed toward what were *not* mammalian colors), to black so dark it glittered.

Aikin, of course, chose the latter.

Somehow, they got themselves sorted out and mounted. At least there were saddles and, more importantly, stirrups. And each saddle, David noted with surprise, as he heaved himself up on the white stallion Fionchadd urged on him, bore embossed atop its high pommel some sigil unique to the rider. His was a yinyang symbol. Calvin, who rode nearest for the nonce, sported a stooping Falcon. Alec's, to his surprise, was a printed circuit; Aikin's was a stag at gaze.

When the last leg had been flung across supple leather, Fionchadd studied them for a long moment, then stalked up and down the file, checking seats and cinches. "No one has ever fallen from a Faery steed," he told them. "At least not of their own will. But as things stand now in Tir-Nan-Og, tonight could witness . . . many changes."

And with that, he strode toward where his own mount waited at the head of the line and in one fluid motion leapt astride. "No need for spurs," he advised, "these beasts know their destination. *And*," he continued an instant later, "it occurs to me that we have means to speed this journey."

Before anyone could respond, he swung around and looked Piper straight in the eye. "You, Morry Murphy: play for us! Play for me, if no other, for I have not heard your skill. Play, O James Morrison Murphy, that tune called 'The King of the Fairies'!"

Piper turned pale as his platinum mare, but before he could protest further, LaWanda thrust a hand into the jumble of musical gear that had somehow become attached to his saddle and passed him his Uillean pipes. Piper was sweating, David noticed, though his balance seemed fine. But already his fingers sought the chanter.

* * *

It was like no Riding David had ever essayed—though most of those journeys had been under duress, and not necessarily on what he suspected was a High Road favored by the Sidhe. Some things didn't change, however: the way reality shifted as soon as they'd taken more than a dozen steps down that shimmering golden road. The way the blackberry briars that flanked it in their own World immediately began to whorl and twist and swell in size, so that they quickly formed a tube maybe five yards across completely encircling the Track. The way the Track itself grew brighter and dimmer by turns, as the motes that both comprised it and drifted above its surface ebbed, flowed, and sometimes vanished altogether.

Yet some things were different as well. David could've sworn that the last time he'd fared this way the briars had held off, that theirs had been a more gradual transition: a simple walk in the woods, save that the trees had grown larger, taller, older, and eventually more exotic as he'd progressed. And of course he'd had different company. Shoot, he'd ridden with the Queen of Battles herself: the Morrigu, though at the time she'd turned herself into a mare. And though Liz had also been with him then, they'd been on a much more—to him—urgent quest, namely locating Aikin, who, having captured Aife (in enfield guise) when first she'd entered their World (back when they had no idea she was other than what she seemed), had used the power innate in the beast to activate the Track whose location he had dreamed, and so venture into the webwork of Worlds so long denied him.

Yeah, it was different this time, all right, and for other reasons as well. *This* time there was the security of having his closest friends along; *this* time there would be no secrets. Never mind the assurance of having Finno in the lead, who actually knew how to navigate such places. But the main change was the haste with which the journey was accomplished.

It *had* to be the music, and surely Piper had never played so well. They rode in procession, solemnly, almost as though they were themselves on a Rade. And while "King of the Fairies" was properly a fiddle tune and meant to be played ever-faster (every version he'd heard had been rendered thus, at any rate), Piper played it slowly, almost as a lament. Indeed, a sort of sadness seemed to pervade their band. Certainly there was little levity, even from those from whom he would've expected it, like Brock and Darrell. Yet there was no real gloom either, in spite of their somber clothing, the shadow tones of their mounts, and the golden half-light that lit their faces from beneath far more often than distant, filtered suns lit them from on high.

"I feel it too," Fionchadd acknowledged at last, falling back to pace David and Liz, who rode second in line. "You have not said it, but I feel it: the melancholy. As if we were at the end of all things."

"Are we?" David dared. "*Something* sure has changed."

"The edges fray," Fionchadd admitted. "That which was clear and certain has become muddled and vague. *Here* and *there* are no longer separate entities."

"Never were, I thought," David retorted. "According to some philosophy."

Fionchadd smiled wanly. "Some day I will put on mortal flesh and spend some useful time in your World. Though we are older than you, and wiser in the ways of Power, yet there are many things in your Lands we but vaguely comprehend."

"I wonder," David mused, "if there's really any need for all these barriers."

Fionchadd blinked at him. "What do you mean?"

A shrug. "The World Walls, I guess. Is there any real reason they have to be? Couldn't we, like, all live together in one World? Couldn't we learn from each other? I know it'd be hard at first, 'cause our science would certainly turn upside down; but you folks—"

"You are forgetting iron."

"You could put on the substance of our World," David countered. "And if there was only one World. . . ."

Fionchadd shook his head. "You forget. The World Walls were not wrought by us; we only reinforce them—sometimes. You could no more destroy them than you could . . . destroy the attraction between the sun and moon.''

"But you folks could live in either—and if you put on our substance, like I said—''

"We would still be drawn back to Faerie. If we did not return, we would go mad. And I doubt you want a host of insane Danaans dwelling in your midst!''

"Oh well,'' David conceded. ''It's something to think about, anyway.''

"Aye,'' Fionchadd sighed, ''and though you have not noticed it, we are almost there.''

David started, not realizing how all that thought—all that internalization—had caused him to lose track of the external world entirely. He focused on it now, and focused hard. There were trees beyond the briars—when had they appeared?—and occasionally, beyond them, he glimpsed meadows or flat plains or deserts of odd-colored sand, from which strange glassy forms erupted like dancers frozen into crystal or stone.

"Play faster!'' Fionchadd demanded. ''Play twice as fast again—and see what we shall see.''

Piper did. With the utter seamlessness of a master musician, he picked up the tune as it came around and began to increase the tempo. LaWanda co-opted Calvin's drum, and with it, she contrived an ever-faster cadence, which Piper never failed to match perfectly. And suddenly all the world became fast music and the slow, steady tread of the horse beneath David's seat. And then the music waxed faster yet, and the motes of the Track began to rise higher, and higher still; first to the horses' hocks, then to their withers, and finally over their heads. As the cloud reached his chin, David had the awful sense he was about to drown, and found himself taking deep ragged breaths, straining to keep his head above what felt most like a blood-warm sea that was at once effervescent and charged with electricity.

"Relax,'' Fionchadd urged. ''Do not resist. Let it become, instead, a pleasure.''

David started to reply that such was easy for him to say, but then Liz leaned toward him. ''Close your eyes,'' she advised. ''It makes it easier.''

A final deep breath—and David found himself in the most profoundly peaceful state he'd ever experienced. He could stay this way forever, wafting along as though he truly had no body. It was like his lone encounter with a sensory deprivation tank—save that there was still Piper's music, and the light beyond his closed eyelids was golden.

"Halt!" Fionchadd commanded abruptly, his voice oddly thin and distant, as though the mist sucked away its very volume.

David hated to hear that word—indeed, he did not immediately recognize it.

But there was no more music; that had ended in mid-note.

And with it, like water running from a sieve, the drifting golden motes ebbed away, so that a moment later David found himself between a pair of rough granite trilithons twice as high as his head, gazing down a grassy, sunlit slope across no more than a mile of open plains to a perilously steep-sided mountain girt with walls and terraces and gardens, atop which glimmered what he recalled from more than one sighting: the twelve-towered palace of Lugh Samildinach.

"Wow!" Brock gasped, riding up beside David, mouth agape. "I'm sorry I keep saying that," the boy added. "But sometimes—well, sometimes the right word really is 'wow.'"

"I know," David acknowledged. "I remember the first time I saw it. It was dusk, and Alec and I were campin' up on Lookout Rock back in my home county, and I'd just got the Sight the night before, only I didn't know it, and I saw what I thought was just plain old Bloody Bald—that's what it's called in our World. And then I saw that mountain rise higher, and show—well, I don't have to describe it, you can see it for yourself."

"Wow!" Brock repeated, and grinned. And for a moment David too surrendered himself to the view.

A thousand feet—two thousand—who knew how tall those towers rose? And how far around were those walls? Geometry might tell, in theory; but David suspected that anyone assaying them with ruler or tape would find his efforts thwarted. Yet the place was not insubstantial, not ethereal, not ever-shifting. Rather, it was far *too* real, yet impossible in its intricacy. The overall impression was of relentless verticality, determined straining for height, so that the towers sported flutes and subsidiary turrets and buttresses and arches and ornate crenelations and rank upon rank of tall, narrow stained glass windows.

It was Gothic, yet it was not, for it was too spontaneous and organic. It was Celtic in its whorling complexity and the fluidity of its shapes, yet without that culture's pervasive earthiness. It was Moorish in the delicate intricacy of its ornament, yet almost Art Nouveau where those ornaments were allowed to meld and merge and flow free.

"And you say you have no artists," Myra snorted, joining them. "I could spend a year studying a square yard of that—and we're still miles away."

"Miles to go before you sleep, too," Fionchadd reminded her, "and I did not say we were the builders."

Myra's eyes widened, her brows shot almost to her hairline. But Fionchadd preempted any reply. "Nuada told me that," the Faery explained. "The line about sleeping, I mean. A line from one of your poets he liked very much—because it said exactly what it ought. It means something different, too, when one is immortal."

"Someone's coming!" Alec announced—precisely as Gary, LaWanda, and Sandy shouted the same. They no longer rode in file, but had fanned out across the fringe of the stone-crowned hill atop which they had emerged; yet now they crowded closer, gazes probing the landscape anxiously. By following Alec's pointing finger, David could barely make out a cloud of pale dust emerging from the eaves of a dark-leaved forest halfway between the palace and their party. Even as he watched, the dust clarified into riders: a whole host of mounted men, with the glint of armor about them and long gold-and-white banners snapping above them in no obvious wind.

"We must meet them!" Fionchadd called—and set heel to his steed and galloped down the hill. David had no choice but to follow, not when he noted his more foolhardy friends (notably Darrell and Brock) getting a head up on him. "Hold, guys!" he hollered. "These folks probably know Finno, but if they know any of the rest of us, it's—uh—probably gonna be me, so I guess I oughta take the lead—if nobody minds."

Alec grimaced sourly. "My friend the hero."

"Reluctant hero," David shot back. "A man's gotta do what a man's gotta do." And with that, he kicked his own mount in the ribs and raced Fionchadd mac Ailill down the hill.

They met on a road of golden stone inset with interlaced spirals one shade darker, surrounded by a plain of knee-high grass that could have been waving strands of silver. "Lugh honors you indeed," Fionchadd confided as they approached the other party, who had halted in double rows a short way ahead, naked swords set crossways across their saddles, silken banners waving. "He has sent his personal guard."

David tried to look grim and noble as the parties paced toward each other. They were identical, those Faery knights, and like a dream from another age. White horses carried them, with white velvet barding dripping golden fringe almost to the ground; and silver armor clad them: rings of fine-wrought mail casing arms and legs and throats beneath white velvet surcoats. High-crowned helms covered their heads like caps, the long ear pieces and nasals all worked with impossible swirls and spirals. Shields they bore, too, though set at rest, each bearing Lugh's device: *argent, a sun in splendor, Or*—so a human herald would blazon it. And that device was repeated on the breast of their surcoats and on the long cloaks that fell from their shoulders on either side, to merge their own fringes with those of the horses' accouterments.

Fionchadd leaned toward David and grinned. "Come with me—my friend," he said, then twisted further around. "The rest of you form into file in the order you first trod other Worlds."

A few mumbled comments followed, and more than a few uncertain glances flitted about, but Liz quickly took charge and got things sorted out—the main problem being what to do about Myra, Piper, and LaWanda, who, though they'd clearly been to at least one other World, weren't sure how certain events qualified. In the end, they decided that if they'd wound up in a place that weirded them and later discovered that place was connected to some other reality, that counted. The upshot was that Alec came right after David, and that Aikin brought up the rear.

That accomplished, Fionchadd began to walk his horse forward, with David right behind. When the two groups were within maybe ten yards of each other, the two closest knights separated from their ranks and moved out to meet them. They alone wore visored helms, and not until the nearer was directly opposite him, did David note the subtle difference in the armor along that man's right arm. And then he recognized the glitter of those cold, dark blue eyes. He was gazing not on a mere Faery captain, Lugh's household guard or no, but on Nuada Airgetlam himself: Lugh's warlord, counselor, and—no pun intended—right hand man.

Nuada did not remove his visor, but David thought he saw the corners of that one's eyes crinkle, as though, beneath all that complexity of metal, he were smiling.

As for the other... David didn't know him, though Fionchadd obviously did. They stared at each other a moment, and Fionchadd actually looked nervous—anxious, anyway. "Have you brought the ones Lugh summoned?" that one demanded.

"I have," Fionchadd replied. "I have brought them *all*."

"All *you* were sent for," that one corrected. "And long enough it took you! Now follow me . . . and quickly!"

And with that, the Faery jerked his steed around and galloped off down the golden stone road between the long file of mounted knights.

Nuada—if that indeed were he—did likewise. Fionchadd mirrored them. David came next, and heard the rest of his companions fall in behind, then a louder clatter as the knights closed ranks in their wake.

It was a wild ride that ensued, in contrast to the stately pace they had maintained along the Track or the confused jumble of their cross-country gallop to the road. This was simply speed. A mad race down arrow-straight pavement that led through forests and fields and across at least one river, until, very suddenly, they emerged from one final (and very dark) wood comprised of what seemed to be giant sequoias, and found themselves confronting a shining white wall twice as high as any of those trees. At first glimpse that wall seemed unadorned, as it swept off into unguessable distance to either side, but a closer inspection showed that it was in fact thick with patterns: more of the ubiquitous spirals set in wide bands of inlaid stone at man height as far as David could see—except for straight ahead, where the pattern rose in higher relief and stronger color to frame a slender, arched recess ten times as high as the nearest banner pole.

David's breath caught—as, by the sound, did most of his companions'. He gazed at Fionchadd expectantly, seeking some cue as to how to proceed.

"Watch," the Faery murmured. "Wait."

David did, scarcely breathing as lights awoke on the panel framed by that arch; lights that became a pattern of a thousand colors, like stained glass lit from within, save that *these* patterns moved.

The captain—or perhaps it was Nuada, David couldn't tell from the rear—rode forward, to halt directly before the center of that vast glowing portal. Dead silence came with him. And then suddenly that one uttered a—well, *maybe* it was an actual word, but it was more like the sound of command itself: absolute desire made manifest, whereupon the panel slowly split down the middle and folded outward to either side.

"Dismount," that one ordered, in what David was still not certain was either heard with the ear *or* in English.

Another glance at Fionchadd showed him already down from his saddle, and David took the hint and also dismounted. Someone was there beside him as soon as his feet touched the ground: one of the guard—and *not* Nuada. "Follow," the knight said, and before David could so much as blink, another had joined the first on the other side, and he was being escorted into the palace of Lugh Samildinach. Fionchadd was up ahead, he saw with relief, as his eyes adjusted to the surprising gloom of what proved to be a hallway barely wide enough for three grown men—or Faeries—to march abreast, but with vaults too high for light-dazed eyes to discern. The dominant impression was of piers of silver-toned marble marching endlessly away, the spaces between filled with wide stone panels carved with yet more whorls and spirals.

For a long time they trooped along—so long David actually began to tire—but just as he was about to voice that complaint, their hallway suddenly teed into a far wider one at least as tall. For a wonder, this one was carpeted—in burgundy, red, and black—and even better, it was brightly lit, with what looked amazingly like Georgia sunlight, save that this gleamed from complex gilded globes set at ten-step intervals twice their height along both walls.

Another door loomed ahead, with two more guards flanking it, and as Fionchadd walked toward it, the two knights who had accompanied David fell back to either side. "After you," Fionchadd offered, with a sad smile. "And welcome to Tir-Nan-Og."

David could only grunt and roll his eyes. Impulsively, he spun around—protocol be damned—and located Liz and Alec. Their faces were unreadable, so much emotion registered there: fear and awe most obviously. Without further ado, he slid between them and threw his arms across their shoulders.

So it was then, that with his best friend on his left and his girlfriend on his right, David Kevin Sullivan, of rural Enotah County in the wilds of extreme north Georgia, squared his shoulders, took a deep breath, and strode through that final portal.

Chapter X:
Revelations

(Tir-Nan-Og—high summer)

David's first impression as the massive doorjamb fell away behind him and he stepped into the space beyond was of surprising intimacy, almost—dared he think it?—homey disarray.

Certainly the room he entered, that the rest of his comrades were now crowding into, forcing him further forward, was not the vast chamber he'd have expected from such an imposing portal. Though high-vaulted, with simple round arches of rough-cut stone, the space itself was small when compared to the scale of the rest of the palace: thirty feet wide, perhaps, and no more than half again as long: the size of a small house, say.

And filled with light. For the walls between the piers opposite were almost entirely glazed: panes of honey-toned glass interspersed with white or clear, all frosted with more of those interlace designs; while the plain granite blocks of the other walls were brightened by tapestries depicting wildly romantic landscapes and vivid hunting scenes that would not have been out of place in a French Renaissance chateau. The pale limestone floor was piled thick with oriental rugs—human work, by the look of them, and priceless. A fireplace dominated the right hand end, carved of ruddy stone in the shape of a slightly whimsical hell-mouth. Real flame reddened that rocky gullet, while ranks of metal goblets steamed on the raised hearth that served as the leering sculpture's tongue. The smell was wonderful: wine, herbs, and delicate spices. David's stomach rumbled.

As for furniture—they'd been summoned to a council, and the room was set up as a council chamber—sort of. The rugs were strewn with comfortable-looking seats of every kind, interspersed with diverse small tables, all facing inward toward a larger trestle table, behind which a pair of what could only be described as thrones were set—empty, for the nonce, save for the dozen or so enfields that dozed or padded or stretched lazily about them. Lugh's pets, if David recalled right.

Those were the *only* empty places however—save a quarter arc of seats directly in front of them, into one of which Fionchadd had already settled, motioning him and his companions to do likewise. David chose a low sofa-loveseat thing upholstered in nubby green, but he did so mechanically, for his gaze swept wildly about the room as he took in all those people who had turned to stare at him, like schoolmates sizing up the new kid in class.

That was the second thing that had startled him: *all those people*. There were fifty of them if not more; enough to fill the place, yet not to make it feel crowded. But the thing that charged him with absolute awe was that they truly were people. *Human* people. His kind, not the strange grim beings who claimed this World. Not the Sidhe, the Seelie Court, or the Tuatha de Danaan.

No, these were just regular folks. Some old enough to be termed ancient, some—a few—clearly younger than he. Most had an American look to them, and most, though not all, were caucasian. As for dress, that too was southeastern standard: jeans or fatigues, a lot of T-shirts, one or two folks in what he thought of as church attire. A couple in bathrobes. Though he knew it was impolite to stare, and seriously uncool to gape, he couldn't help doing either, gaze flitting from face to face around the room. He was searching for someone, he realized, anyone . . . any face at all that looked familiar. He half expected to see his Uncle Dale somewhere, or even his brother, Little Billy. Certainly both of them had experienced Faerie firsthand more than once, and not in the most pleasant contexts, either.

In spite of his care, however, he almost missed the lanky, middle-sized man lounging in a juncture of pier and wall,

for the man's denim jacket was the faded blue of the ocean
worked on the tapestry behind him, and his shortish hair
nigh the same auburn-brown as the cliffs above those woven waves. The face, however—angularly bland, but basically good-looking, thirtyish and worn by experience and a
life outside—he'd seen before. A glance at the man's hands
confirmed it. The right was bare and tanned, the left gloved
in tight black leather.

David's heart leapt. *John Devlin!* That was John Devlin!
A man he'd met exactly once, though they'd spoken on the
phone a score of times. But more to the point, a man who'd
befriended his namesake uncle in the weeks before that uncle's untimely death in Lebanon. Devlin knew some *stuff*,
David reckoned, though he'd been unable to determine exactly what, save that the man seemed to have arcane knowledge, arcane power, and—apparently—arcane connections.
He'd never managed to ferret out the specifics, but he suspected from certain objects he'd observed the one time he'd
visited the guy's north Georgia cabin, that he practiced cer-
emonial magic; and from what little else he'd managed to
discover, it was magic from a different . . . tradition than
that which empowered the Sidhe. That he was present now
was more than a surprise. Christ, the man had never let on
a thing, though David had revealed as much of his own
outré adventures as he absolutely dared.

At which point his reverie was cut short because Devlin
had caught him staring. A brow quirked up, a sly half-smile
curled Devlin's lips. He raised a hand—that hand—minutely, in subtle acknowledgement.

"Close your mouth," Myra muttered behind him, prodding him with a well-placed finger. "You're starting to
drool."

David turned half around. "All these people. . . ."

Fionchadd shot him a wicked grin. "You didn't think
you were the only one, did you?"

"Son of a bitch knew all along!" David growled, nodding toward the smirking Devlin.

"Who did?" from Liz, who had joined him.

David nodded again. "Him. John Devlin. You know, the

poet? *Where Youth and Laughter Go. That* John Devlin. David-the-Elder's friend.''

"Oh, right. Wonder what he's doing here.''

"The same thing we are, obviously,'' David drawled, then finally managed to tear his gaze from that lone familiar face that had not accompanied him, to check on the rest of his party. They'd taken care of themselves, apparently, and claimed the remaining places—an even mix of sofas, cushions, and well-padded chairs. Alec alone remained hesitant, but when he saw David scowling, he scowled back and eased around to a cushion on the floor, scrunched up between David and Liz's legs. David reached out to pet him on the head. "Don't worry, big guy; I think we're safe. This doesn't look like a dangerous crowd.''

"It looks like a *scared* crowd, though,'' Alec retorted. "Or haven't you noticed.''

In spite of himself, David glanced around again. A few of that host did look apprehensive. But most merely looked tired or sleepy, which made sense, if they'd been roused from their beds for what he feared was an emergency meeting. He started to query Fionchadd, but at that moment his stomach gurgled again.

Fionchadd lifted a brow, then motioned to one of the white-liveried figures who had just entered and were now ranging themselves around the walls. One nodded in turn, and slipped toward the fireplace, where he retrieved a pair of goblets from the hearth. Others mirrored his example, and with them came still others bearing trays of food. The room became a flurry of motion, as food and drink were dispersed. A particularly full and mounded plate of meat, bread, and melon was set on a small stone table between David and Fionchadd, even as one of the—did you call anyone who was obviously Faery a servant?—well, whatever they were, one handed him a steaming goblet of gemencrusted gold that would've made the Ardagh Chalice seem like foamware from Burger King.

He examined it warily, then shifted his gaze to Fionchadd. "Last time I heard, it wasn't safe to eat Faery food.''

"Why, whoever told you that?'' Fionchadd teased, eyes

wide above a far-too innocent mouth, as he helped himself
to half a small glazed fowl. "Besides, what makes you
think this is from Faerie?"

Liz poked him in the ribs. (Did everyone have to do
that?) "Just eat, Davy! I did before I caught myself, and if
I'm gonna be stuck here forever, you'd better be too."

"Humans!" Fionchadd chuckled, as he lifted his goblet.
"Do you trust no one at all?"

"No," Alec grunted from the floor. But his hands, too,
were laden—with a long slice of crusty bread piled high
with sauced meats and mushrooms.

"Makin' yourself at home, are you?" David chided.

A weary shrug. "Might as well, seein' how we're stuck
here. God, I wish Lugh'd put his ass in gear and get things
going."

"Cool it!" David warned anxiously. "These folks have
got mighty sharp ears."

"Doesn't matter," Liz reminded them, eyeing Fionchadd
speculatively. "They're also telepathic—some of 'em, anyway."

"Wish *we* were," David grumbled. "Then we could get
some idea of what's goin' on."

"You are about to find out," Fionchadd murmured.
"Watch."

And indeed the room was falling quiet, as what David
had taken for a window overlooking a sunlit garden suddenly opened, and with far less fanfare than had attended
their own arrival, two tall figures strolled in.

One was Nuada Airgetlam, called Silverhand: no longer
in armor and thus instantly recognizable by his long blond
hair and the intricate silver vambrace and gauntlet that replaced his missing right arm—what of it showed beneath
a robe of thick-napped velvet, gold on one side and white
on the other, and open down the front like a dressing gown.
Nuada nodded to someone as he took a seat, and David
followed that gaze, surprised to see that this great lord of
Faerie had acknowledged John Devlin.

Why . . . ? But then he knew. Devlin too was down a
hand. The left had been shot off trying to save a friend in
some "police action" or other, back when the guy had been

an army Ranger. The glove he always wore covered the prosthesis that replaced it.

"Is that Lugh?" Sandy whispered behind him, elbows braced on the sofa.

"Yeah," David acknowledged, inspecting the other figure who had accompanied Nuada.

He didn't look much like a great lord of Faerie at the moment (though David suspected that was a deliberate ploy, designed to put them at ease). Though tall, strong, and handsome, he had entered casually—his tread steady, but no regal stride. He'd eschewed a crown too, or any other symbol of rank. Instead, his black hair flowed unbound past his shoulders, a spill of ink down a long plain robe of gold and scarlet.

His mustache flowed as well, the long ends brushing his collarbones. Neither he nor Nuada were smiling. They conferred briefly, then scooted their thrones closer together. A further pause ensued, while each received a goblet from a lingering server, then another for a pair of savory swallows and a clinking of vessels, as if to say, "okay, comrade, here we go. . . ."

At times, David thought, they were all too human. If only he didn't fear this was all for show, all a carefully contrived PR event.

Lugh cleared his throat, then tapped his goblet gently with a nail. It rang bright as a gong, but far more piercing. The servants sketched deep bows and departed in haste through the door by which Lugh and Silverhand had arrived.

As the last fragment of conversation rumbled into silence, Lugh sat down. A leader among equals, he was, yet clearly in command, though trying very hard (it seemed) to appear nonthreatening. He surveyed the room for a long moment, examining every face—and, David feared, every mind—then puffed his cheeks and spoke.

"I welcome you here," he said formally, in a voice like low soft chimes. "Some of you I know; some I do not, yet all of you have heard of me—though even now there are those among you who think me a myth or a dream or a demon or a fiend from some child's play. Yet I thank you;

and thank you again for my friend Nuada, beside me; and a third time for my kingdom, Tir-Nan-Og, Land of the Ever-young.''

He paused for a sip of wine—and only then did David realize he hadn't tasted his own. He did so hastily, finding it sweet and smooth yet with more than a hint of effervescence, vaguely like pine needles mixed with tarragon and zinfandel.

Lugh took another sip, not rushing anything, then went on. "Friends, I call you, and truly you must be friends, to rise, many of you, from your beds to answer a summons you in no wise expected, delivered in so much haste at such, to you, odd hours. Yet I have summoned you, and you have come: those among mortals who by diverse means have learned of us: of the Tracks and the Worlds and the Daoine Sidhe. Some we have sought out, some have made your way here by wit alone, or, sometimes, unfortunate luck. One bond you share, however, and that is knowledge. Dangerous knowledge, often. Knowledge that you dare not share in turn, lest you be judged . . . odd, if not truly insane. Knowledge that brands you different, that builds walls between you and your kith and kin; that makes you distrust the very world around you.

"And yet, you are special in that knowledge," Lugh continued. "Elite you are, and elect, and there is not one of you but is here by my express will. All of you I have watched from afar, all of you I have studied. With some I have had converse for years. A few I have met but once, and that scarce longer ago than yesterday. Few of you know each other—the exceptions were the last to arrive''—he nodded toward where David and his companions sat—"and you, in particular I would greet and wish well, whose lives my kind have so disrupted, and whose acts in turn have so disrupted mine!''

David knew from the wash of heat flooding up his face that he was blushing—he hated being the center of attention, for all that—too often—he found himself the leader of the band. Certainly of the MacTyrie Gang, all of whom—as Darrell had noted—were present. At least Runnerman was getting *his* wish. This was one fine send off to their youthful brotherhood.

They were looking at him too, David realized, every eye in the room had turned to stare straight at him. He gazed elsewhere—not accidentally toward John Devlin, who hadn't moved, but was regarding him with absent interest. David tried to distract himself by decoding the black T-shirt visible beneath the man's jacket. He could just make it out. *Widdershins*. That was a band. Louisiana, he thought. Celtic. He'd never heard them. But widdershins had other implications as well. One walked nine times widdershins around this or that, and odd things sometimes occurred. He wondered if that was how Devlin had come here. Had he walked nine times widdershins . . . ?

Lugh cleared his throat softly, and David felt the pressure of all those eyes diminish, replaced by Lugh's alone, which still bored straight into him. "I am immortal," he intoned. "You are not. Time matters to you, and so I would not waste it. Therefore it is best that I address the matter at hand, that which has caused me to summon so many humans from so many beds for the first time since we came out of the Air and the High Air to Ireland."

Lady Gregory, David identified. The first line of her book *Gods and Fighting Men*, which had been his introduction to the no-longer-so-mythical Sidhe all those years ago.

"To get to the point," Lugh went on, "the King is the Land, and the Land is the King, and the Land and I have a problem. Some of you may know this. Those of you who are astute have seen the clues, though Nuada seeks with equal vigor to veil them as they appear. Yet he and his cannot be everywhere, nor observe everything that chances. More and more your World intrudes on ours, and ours on yours, with equally unpleasant results: a . . . *car* breaching a bodach's hold here; a child stolen from your World there, and bestowed some other place: these events are no longer uncommon."

Another sip of wine, and Lugh's voice quickened. "There is a reason for all this, however, one that should be clear to the clever or learned among you, and the reason is simply this: the World Walls, which have, since we came to this World, divided our Lands from yours, are failing. We are unsure of the cause, and we know that some of it is simply the way of things, the way stars grow old and die, or moons slow in their circles. Yet some is not. The World Walls can be pierced, and there have long been places where they are so thin they can be made to dissolve entirely. And we too have been guilty, for more and more we have bored through the Walls directly, eschewing the safety of the Tracks, which does them far less harm. And before accusations are leveled—before any one of you assumes guilt that is not your own, and I mean *you*, David Sullivan—be aware that at worst, you have but speeded the inevitable. And while you have undoubtedly done our lands harm, your intentions were honorable, and I, at least, bear you no malice.

Another pause. "Still, the worst has happened. For reasons that are yet unclear, the glamour with which I reinforce the World Walls here is failing along with the Walls themselves. Those of you who dwell in certain parts of the Lands of Men—the name you use is Enotah County—know of a peak named Bloody Bald. Once it stood alone in a secluded valley, crowned by cliffs of solid white stone that shone like blood when the sun of that World struck them at dusk and dawn. We likewise saw it, when we came to this Land from across the Seas Between, from Erenn. We saw it in that World and we loved it; and we saw it in this as well, and knew we had found what we sought: a heart for the realm we would build. Tir-Nan-Og, we called it, diverse parts of which you have seen today. Certainly you have seen a mountain, and a palace on that mountain; but what some of you may not know is that this palace lies atop that wonderful peak that so ornaments that other World. I made it the center of my realm: two mountains atop each other, with my citadel upon the higher, yet the lesser provides its core, for though our World is not fully round, it depends for its shape and strength on yours."

("Wish I had a notebook," Sandy—ever the physics teacher—muttered. "Better yet, a tape recorder.")

"Eventually mortals came," Lugh resumed. "Red men, the fathers of Calvin McIntosh's folk, and they regarded that peak with wonder. Bloody Bald they called it, in their own tongue. And to protect ourselves from them, we raised a glamour. Time passed, more men arrived: white men. The glamour held, save at Dusk and Dawn, and to all but the Sighted, even then. Yet white men were curious, and asked questions, so we augmented our glamour with enchantment, so that any who chanced to view either mountain would forget it as soon as they moved on. That helped, yet people settled nearby—Sullivans, by name—with the blood of Er-enn in their veins. Them we could not fool so easily, when the first of that clan built his cabin on the very foot of Bloody Bald. Still, we maintained peace. We clouded what sights we could and cloaked what memories we might. And more time passed. More men came, and a lake was built, which would surround that mountain, and so we relaxed our vigilance, for surely no one could set foot there unseen.

"And now we have reached the present. The Sullivans we have learned to trust, more than they know. And we have learned to trust those they trust in turn. Did you never wonder, David Sullivan, why you never spoke of Bloody Bald beyond your kin and closest friends? You have seen it every day, have often swum in the waters thereabout; you have spoken of it to Alec McLean and Aikin Daniels and Gary Hudson and Darrell and Myra Buchanan and Liz Hughes. They likewise have named it to their friends. But ask yourselves: has anyone ever named it back to you? Have *any* others you have brought there ever named it? Have you ever named it beyond your trusted clan? You have not! I have forbidden it, and a ban from me can be very, very subtle indeed."

David's gut knotted at that, at once from anger and awe. God, Lugh was a sneaky bastard! How dare he confess to something like that! Messing with his friends' minds! Messing with his own, for all he knew. He was a clever asshole, too: mixing the good and the bad, sugar-coating his connivance. Well, Mr. Lugh'd best be careful now, 'cause Mad Davy Sullivan was onto him, and would no longer drop his guard!

"At any rate," Lugh concluded, "all this is history. The problem is now. And the problem, simply stated, is this.

The glamour has all but failed. Humans have seen Bloody Bald, and retained that memory. They have eluded our grasp, and too many now know of the mountain's existence for us to seek them out before they in turn tell others. Images have also been made and distributed far and wide. And before you ask why we cannot change those memories anyway, I would reply that with the glamour failing, some of those men will return, or others like them. And before you ask can the glamour not be reinforced, I tell you we have done as much as we dare. Even I cannot maintain it forever—not were I to stab a dagger through my hand and join myself by blood and Power entirely to the Land, as already once of late I have done—and the effort to preserve what remains grows stronger day by day. Eventually the glamour *will* fail utterly. Therefore, we must act while something can yet be done, while choices still remain among both humans and Sidhe."

There was a rumble of voices at that, not all of it sounding pleased. David definitely wasn't, and he imagined Aikin in particular (who was the most woodsy of the Gang, and the biggest romantic) was absolutely livid.

Lugh cleared his throat again. "A council, I have called this, though all you have heard is discourse from me, yet there is one more thing I would tell you, which is what has, to use your term, forced my hand, and that is this. Men have learned of this place, as I have said. But these men are not like you. They have no magic in their souls, only love of riches, pleasure, and power. These men have formed a plan—I learned of it but today, to my regret. They have acquired territory in what is known in the Lands of Men as Sullivan Cove. They have likewise acquired rights to the lake in which this Mountain stands, and thereby to this mountain itself. They would build there—many buildings they would build—to entertain themselves and others and so win more riches. More to the point, they would build structures of iron—iron which can damage the World Walls. Iron which, we very much fear, could *dissolve* the World Walls here, in the very heart of my realm. This I will not allow. I will not give up Tir-Nan-Og. I will not give up this mountain. I will not give up this palace that stands upon it, nor the rooms I keep therein, nor the bed in which I sleep, nor the chair in which I study, nor the throne in which I hold court! It is mine, by ancient rite, and the blood I gave to link myself to it with unbreakable bonds. The King is the Land, I have said. The Land is the King. And my land—my *self*—I am determined to defend!''

Silence then—stunned silence, for Lugh's voice had hardened as he spoke, from careful amiability to oratory of skill and power. He'd played them like harps, too: had made them relax, then dropped the big one. And the trouble was, he was clearly far from finished.

And then it hit David: delayed reaction, like when the space shuttle had exploded, which someone had told him about in passing, and which had only struck him with full force two hours later. A *resort*: that was what Lugh meant. Someone was going to build a resort that threatened Tir-Nan-Og.

A resort in Sullivan Cove!

"No!" he gasped. This couldn't be happening! No way! No way! No way! Surely someone up home would've heard and told him, or moved to head off such a stupid thing. Surely they couldn't do anything that big without his folks' permission, which he'd see they never gave—as though such a thing were possible!

He made to rise at that, to stomp up to Lugh and demand details. Screw Tir-Nan-Og! He had to know about Sullivan Cove and he had to know it now!

"No, David!" Liz hissed, reaching up to restrain him. He glared at her, nearly snarled, but Alec was there too, gazing at him sadly. Oddly calm, for all his earlier storm and fury. "Wait," he urged softly. "Listen. That's what you'd tell me. You'll gain nothing by rash action now."

"Your friend speaks true," Fionchadd agreed, handing him a cup of some mint-smelling liquid. "Lugh would not have called you here had he not sought your advice."

David flopped back into his seat, looking sullen. His protest had taken the merest instant; had all been lost in the furor that filled the chamber.

"Why are you telling us this?" a woman demanded,

from the opposite corner. She was old enough to have white hair and withered skin, and wore the look of a scholar. David was glad she'd spoken up. He didn't dare, not now, not here; not when he, though a guest and probably under some sort of protection, was totally outgunned and out-manned.

"I tell you this," Lugh replied simply, "first because it is something you should know, for affairs in my Land affect affairs in yours. I have not lied, nor will I. I will protect my land. Your Land, has in effect, invaded. Invasion is tantamount to war. Think what that implies. War between the Lands of Men and Tir-Nan-Og."

"You said *first*," the woman reminded him coldly. "What is second?"

Lugh managed a thin, grim smile. "I have also told you this because I would know my enemy. I do not ask you to betray your kind, for surely I would not betray mine—as indeed I would do, should I let this situation persist. I ask you, in short, for advice. How do I deal with this? I do not want war between our Worlds; such a thing is unthinkable. Yet I refuse to relinquish my Land."

"In other words," Sandy called, "you want us to come up with a nonconfrontational solution that won't betray the existence of Faerie."

Lugh's smile warmed at that, and Nuada added one of his own. David himself was pleased, first that one of his comrades had spoken so eloquently, concisely, and coolly, and second because he hadn't had to—which might've been a mistake, consumed as he was with anger and fear and dismay. Only pure strength of will kept him from thinking about that now—and he wasn't so sure Fionchadd wasn't fooling with his mind; steering it from that far-too-dangerous course. One more account to be settled later—whenever later was.

"You have the gift of words, Sandy Fairfax," Lugh laughed. "I could not have put it plainer. And you are exactly correct. The problem began in your World. It would be best if your World resolved it—and there is time, a little, during which that may be accomplished."

"How *much* time?" Aikin called.

A tiny frown flickered across Lugh's brow. "Until iron bites the stone of Bloody Bald."

"You can't . . . just keep that from happening?" Liz yelled back.

Lugh shook his head. "We cannot touch iron—as you should know."

"Not even by—I dunno—suicide attack?" That was Gary.

"I mean, you guys *are* immortal, right?"

"Not where iron is concerned. I will not—cannot—explain further, save to say that *that* mountain is *this* mountain, and *this* mountain is also *me*."

"Will iron on the mountain kill you, then?" That was Alec.

Lugh's face was like ice. "It will never get the chance."

David took a deep breath. He started to speak, to ask one question, then changed his mind and tried to frame another. Yet all around, his friends were tossing out cogent comments right and left. Debate was raging. People he didn't know were joining in. Lugh was dancing a razor edge, he decided: warning of potential attack, yet hinting at his own vulnerabilities—which in turn implied he wasn't truly worried, which in turn worried the hell out of David. He drank the last of his wine, though he knew it was stupid to seek answers in the bottom of a glass—or fabulous goblet, either.

He was getting sleepy too, which was damned irritating when now of all times he needed to be attentive and alert. He wished the wine were coffee. And realized, to his dismay, that he'd actually tuned out the last two questions—which meant none of his companions had asked them.

The tide of debate was changing, though; shifting away from queries about Lugh's acts and options, toward what could actually be attempted in the Lands of Men to forestall that new construction. One of his fellow human advocates was clearly a lawyer and was tossing around the phrase "environmental impact statement."

Which *could* delay things, David conceded. But might be a problem, someone else pointed out, given that the potential developers had high-level political support—though not as high as the current, pro-environment, governor.

But at the very least, someone noted, there would still be surveying. And if a single surveyor drove an iron piton into the wrong place—well, according to Lugh, even that could spell disaster.

And then someone suggested a class-action lawsuit, which someone else observed would have to involve the Sullivans as principal litigants—was David willing to pursue that?

He found himself saying yes, without much conviction. No way in hell he had the patience to deal with something like that, but if someone else was willing to get the ball rolling, he'd certainly go through the motions.

He hoped it didn't come to that. Surely there was some quicker, less cumbersome, and more reliable alternative.

"So why don't you guys just kill 'em?" the youngest person there save Brock—the girl couldn't be sixteen— hollered.

"Because," Lugh explained patiently, "you cannot kill a . . . corporation."

"You could run it out of business."

"Which we intend, through our agents, to pursue. But as I said: time is of the essence."

"Crash their computers?" someone else suggested. "I'll be glad to try."

"I give you my permission to make the attempt," Lugh chuckled. "But if you accomplish that, what happens? They will seek you out. They may find you. If they do, there will be a trial and they will surely convict you. Will you seek asylum here? I will grant it. But you, I know, have a complex life and a large family. Will you uproot them? Can you live without them?"

The man retreated into thoughtful silence.

"It seems then," Lugh declared finally, "that little can be settled now. Very well. As I have told you, we have time—a little. I would ask you to use that time turning all your thought and energy to this. For though this problem affects but a small part of your World, at present, in the end it could consume it all. My folk grow anxious. They grow fearful. They grow angry. They grow desperate. And some, I know, grow impatient. And though I am king, I cannot control them all. A fortnight—your time—we have, so I have been informed. Use it well. I will summon you all again then."

And with that, Lugh Samildinach rose from his throne and strode from the hall. Nuada followed after.

"And I doubt it will do either of us any good," David growled at their shadows.

"Come," Fionchadd urged, as the room dissolved into chaos. "I will show you to your quarters."

David glared at him, shook off the hand that sought to steer him toward the door. He strained on tiptoe, seeking . . . seeking John Devlin, he supposed. Someone, *anyone*, who was older, wiser, better versed in the ways of the world than he. God knew *he* was out of his depth! Shoot, what had he ever done? Grown up in Enotah County, made decent grades, goofed off with his buddies, then gone to college and repeated those last two rites ad nauseam. What he needed now was experience, and more to the point, objectivity. And, dammit, he needed it from another guy, not from Myra or Sandy. For them this was simply one more crisis: regrettable, but ultimately remote. For mountain-born Devlin, David somehow knew, it was a thing he lived.

But Devlin was gone.

Doors had opened where doors had no right to be, and a veritable phalanx of Lugh's servitors were escorting that whole vast assembly away.

"Come," Fionchadd murmured again, his face a mask of concern. "Lugh does not wish you to speak among each other."

Again David thrust the Faery's hand aside. "Great! Lugh calls us here, but then he won't hear what we have to say! He tempts us with knowledge, then jerks that knowledge away. What's he afraid of? That we'll compare notes and find out more than he wants us to?"

Fionchadd's face went hard and still. "That, my friend, is *exactly* what he fears. He walks a sword's edge, does our king. He asks—nay, *needs*—your support, yet he fears you may precipitate his fall."

"Shit!" David snorted, gazing fixedly at the floor. In

spite of the presence of his friends, he had never felt so alone. It was too much. Too much responsibility. Too much chaos. Too many competing problems. Lugh was concerned for Tir-Nan-Og, and David had no choice but to fret over it as well—but only because what occurred in Tir-Nan-Og affected his own place. *His* heart and center. The place that he could no more rip from his soul than Lugh could his own bright realm.

He shivered at that. Without intending too, he'd reasoned himself around to an understanding of how the High King felt.

"Come," Fionchadd pleaded a third time. "Your quarters await. And I will tell you this, if it helps: Lugh has never quartered mortals in this number in his palace before. Saving Oisin, every mortal here has either been a slave, a prisoner, or a lover."

David's frown shifted to a wry half-smile. "And which are we, I wonder? Still . . . gotta make the best of a bad situation. Okay, Finno. You lead, we'll follow."

Chapter XI:
Floor Fight

(Tir-Nan-Og—high summer)

"God!" David spat viciously, as he slumped against the massive ornate door he'd just sought unsuccessfully to slam. "I thought we'd *never* get anywhere!" Without waiting for reply, he stomped into the room to which Fionchadd had escorted them, sparing the barest glance at the splendor of their surroundings, caring not the least for the honor Lugh had bestowed by offering them lodging there. Though not the first night some of them had spent in Tir-Nan-Og, it was undeniably the first any had been housed in Lugh's own citadel.

David didn't trust it. It was too good to be true. Lugh was being too up and up—too solicitous. And the terrible thing was, there was nothing he could do. He was trapped. How had he put it earlier? Totally outgunned and outmanned.

Or maybe not. He still had his friends, none of whom had spoken since his tirade, and all of whom were ranked around the room gazing at him speculatively. He glared back, trying to read their faces. Trying, more to the point, not to reveal too much of his own indecision. He was their leader, dammit; for good or ill, it was him. Oh, Myra and Sandy might be older, Calvin more world-wise, Alec and Liz equipped with more common sense, Gary more practical. But he was their . . . their own pocket Lugh Samildinach. The man skilled in every art.

Ha!

The only art he was skilled in now was sulking. Or worrying. Or being pissed. Or simply feeling sorry for himself. The only good thing, he concluded, was that he was no longer even the tiniest bit tired. Which pissed him all over again. It was in the wine. Or the food. Or the air itself. It wasn't real, wasn't natural. It was more of Lugh's goddamn magic—magic that seemed fair set to destroy every single thing he held dear.

Still not looking at anyone, he stalked over to the nearest chair, flopped down in it, and kicked off his sneakers with a noisy flourish before helping himself to a long draught from the frosted copper tumbler on the black lacquer table at his side. His hair fell into his eyes—when had he lost the tie that bound it? He batted it savagely away. Only then did he take stock of the environs.

They were in a lounge of some kind: a salon. Vaguely Arabic, somewhat Byzantine, more than a little Moorish, with festoons of delicate arches and filigree balancing a blessedly low ceiling inlaid with calligraphic designs, and walls that seemed wrought as much of drifting skeins of sea-toned silk, as of stone, wood, or metal. The far side was open, revealing an arcade of more delicate pillars surrounding a garden which in turn curved around a sparkling azure pool maybe ten yards across. It was night, (Hadn't it been daylight when they arrived, by this World's time?), and stars sparkled above intricate crenelations that blocked all other view. As for the rest of the palace, the famous twelve towers: none showed. Presumably they were massed behind this place. This *suite*, to use Fionchadd's term. The place where they were free to sleep where they would until break of day.

And that was a laugh, wasn't it? David doubted he'd ever sleep again.

Others, however . . . Gary was yawning, and Darrell likewise looked crispy if not fully fried. They'd had long days, though, to have arrived so early in the morning with Myra.

Someone cleared a throat.

"Well," he charged. "What do *you* guys think?"

"Do you really want to know?" Liz retorted, coming over to sit by him.

"It's a crock, is what it is," Alec volunteered at last, as

silence stretched and lingered. He dragged up a cushion and sank down on it, not far from David's feet. He still had the cat-cage. Still had Aife. David found himself wondering what effect the iron bars in that prison might have here, where iron supposedly never cooled. As though reading his mind, Alec grimaced. "Guess I'd better let her out. She's been stuck in there a bloody long time. I was gonna free her soon as we got back from Tracking."

"If not sooner," Aikin hinted, cuffing him. "I kinda figured you'd free her on the Track."

"Thought about it," Alec admitted, as he opened the cage. "But the fact is, she really is Aife. We only see the cat, and sometimes the enfield, but we forget there's consciousness in there too. I don't like mistreating animals; I *won't* mistreat a—uh, essentially a person. It'd be like torturing my poor old senile granny. She might not know it, but I would."

"Spoken like a true humanist," Myra remarked from a nearby sofa, where she was concocting a snack of some impossible seafood delicacies from a cache she'd found on the arcade. Aife was intrigued too, judging by her twitching nose and whiskers, but was taking her own sweet time investigating. Alec lost interest in her but left the cage door open.

"Right," Sandy agreed, busy with a sandwich of her own.

"But the fact is, folks: we're evading the question."

David lifted a brow. "You brought it up; you answer. What do you think?"

Sandy gnawed her lip. "I think we are honestly too tired and too . . . shell-shocked to think anything rational right now. I know I'm not at the top of my form, and I doubt anyone else is either. Oh, there's energy around; you can feel it in the air, and the food was great, and a lot of little things that were bugging me physically seem to have gone bye-bye. But brains don't work like that, and emotions certainly don't, and tonight both have taken some damned solid hits. I know you folks from Georgia must be about to lose it. Never mind all that crap Lugh laid on us about his troubles; there's a major threat to a place you've loved from birth and, for all practical purposes, held sacred.''

David nodded, and Gary uttered a weak, ''Here! Here!''

LaWanda was pacing back and forth like a caged leopardess. ''If I wanted to be snotty, I'd say it serves you right. That's if I wanted to be snotty. I'd say it's time white folks knew what it was like when somebody marches into their land with power and knowledge they can't stand against and takes command. I'd say that, but the fact is, I don't believe it. And whether or not I do, I'm still human; and whatever happens up here, sooner or later it's gonna touch me wherever I am. Shit, folks, Sullivan Cove's a little place; ain't nothin', really, just the pretty ass-end of a grungy little redneck county. But it's all the world to some of you. It's your heart, it's your gut, it's your center. I got my own. But if things don't change, which is to say, if we don't try our own dead-level best to fix things, my own heart and gut and center may be next. I don't know what those folks are plannin' if the bulldozers start to roll, but they're gonna have to be damned careful or they'll blow their own cover all to hell. A place like these developer folks're talkin' about, it costs money. Lots of money. And when folks start throwin' that much cash around, other folks start watchin'. I'm not sure Mr. Lugh Samildinach knows how *many* folks start watchin', but one slip, and it's history. He can't spin doctor *Time* or *Newsweek*. And he sure as hell can't spin the *National Enquirer*! And, folks,'' she finished with a wicked glint in her eye. ''Mr. Magic Man may have mojo, but we got steel!''

David giggled; couldn't help it. Couldn't resist. Which was all he needed. First to get mad as hell, then to get punchy. He squinted at the tumbler curiously, wondering how it had gotten so empty. And yawned.

No, dammit! He'd been almost feverishly alert bare seconds before; he had to stay functional now. Had to coordinate their council of war.

''It occurs to me,'' Liz observed, ''that we're probably not smart to talk about this stuff here. I mean, think, folks: look at the situation. Lugh springs a big one on us out of the clear blue. He asks us to talk about it and report back. Then he asks us to spend the night—which he's never done.

Now maybe he's simply being Mr. Nice Guy. He *is*—sort of—Irish, after all, and also, if I may say, Southern. Hospitality's a big thing with both of 'em. But maybe he's got a hidden agenda. Maybe he *wants* us to talk. Maybe he's got this room bugged. Maybe he doesn't *have* to; they're telepathic, after all. Maybe he's left us here close at hand so he can eavesdrop, hear what we really think, what we really plan."

David gnawed his lip. "Yeah," he acknowledged. "You may be right. I'm mad as hell too, but that's not gonna help my thinkin'. Nope, what I'm gonna do"—he sat up abruptly, gazing beyond the arcade to the softly glimmering pool—"what I'm gonna do is go swimmin'. Anybody wants to can come along."

And with that he leapt to his feet and sauntered toward the garden. Alec looked briefly stunned, then sighed and likewise rose. He padded over to poke the dozing Darrell with a toe. "You want M-Gang history, Runnerman? You want the Gang to have one last hurrah? Get your fuzzy butt up and out there. You too, G-Man. 'Dippin's the oldest ritual we've got—'cept for the Vow."

"Vow?" Brock echoed, puzzled. "What . . . ? *Yiiiii!*"

For Aikin had grabbed him around the waist and in one deft sweep (he was surprisingly strong for his size) flung the boy across his shoulder. "Vow!" Brock insisted stubbornly, through a veil of hair. "Vow!"

"Never to lie to another member of the Gang," Aikin recited. "Always to give straight answers to questions sincerely asked."

"But only to other members of the wretched Gang," Myra grumbled, in their wake. She eyed Darrell speculatively. "Is it incest to skinny-dip with your baby brother?"

"Long as you don't pee in the water," he retorted, then looked puzzled, as though he wasn't at all certain that what he'd said made any sense, which, in large part, it hadn't.

David, meanwhile, had reached the pool. It was beautiful out there: warm, but with a silky wind that brought precisely the right amount of welcomed coolness. The water was dark and inviting, the only light coming from the stars and a series of piercework balls set on slender silver columns around the rim. The pool itself was round. A pile of white robes were stacked nearby—obviously someone, probably Finno, had anticipated them. Not caring who saw—most of 'em had anyway—he shucked his clothes: fatigues, sweatshirt, and the tightie-whities he ruthlessly retained in spite of fashion.

He was in the water before anyone else arrived.

It was wonderful. Like that final few minutes on the Tracks, and the wine he'd consumed during Lugh's rant, the pool seemed to hold a subtle effervescence, as though a million unseen bubbles popped against his skin. And God, but it was relaxing! How long had it been, anyway, since he'd gone swimming in any form, never mind skinny-dipping? UGA had all kinds of pools, but folks raised their eyebrows there if you dropped your drawers. Shoot, the last time he'd actually 'dipped must've been back in October, after his and Aikin's ritual hunt.

Without thinking about it, he dived, seeking a bottom that seemed long in coming, out near the middle, where he'd wound up. Once his toes finally brushed stone, though, he lingered, poised in stasis just above the . . . *mosaic*, he suspected, by the way it felt when he probed it with a foot. Perhaps, since this was Faerie, he could remain there forever. Then he wouldn't have to deal—again—with all this Faery bullshit, nor suspend his life to protect his friends, and now, it seemed, the very land that had begot him.

He drifted in place twenty feet down until flashes seared his eyes and his lungs felt nigh on bursting. When at last he broke surface again, it was just in time to receive a face full of spray that had to be someone cannonballing. An instant later, Gary emerged beside him. David was waiting. He set one hand firmly atop his brawny buddy's head and forced him under, then slipped casually sideways to avoid the wrestling hold he knew without doubt would follow. And dived, and rose again, closer to the shallows. Hair streamed in his eyes; he flung it back as he felt his feet touch bottom. Eventually his vision cleared enough to determine that every one of his comrades had joined him, and most had shed every stitch. It was no big deal with the guys; he'd 'dipped with 'em all before, save Piper, who was, by report, even less body shy than he. Women were usually more coy. Only . . . Sandy, and to his surprise, LaWanda, were both calmly undressing on the edge. In spite of her earlier comment, Myra also had a rep as being prudish—odd, when one considered how much she liked to paint nudes—yet there she was as well, shapely breasts floating in the water. Liz had always been the most modest, though, and had never shucked out around any guy but him. She had now; he wondered if that was significant.

"Don't say a word," she warned, as she swam up behind him and wrapped her arms around his chest. "You've been bugging me about this as long as we've been together; now you get your wish."

"I'm not gonna ask." He twisted around to nuzzle her cheek. "But don't you think Finno was right, back there on the Track? Doesn't this. . . . Don't you feel kinda melancholy? As if we all know everything'll be different after this, no matter what? Myra's had a sense of foreboding for days."

"Maybe," Liz murmured. "But frankly I don't wanta think about it now. In fact, I'm *done* thinking!" And with that she released him, sank to her neck, and glided away.

"Dave?" someone ventured from the other side. He shifted around to find himself confronting a thoroughly sodden Brock, whose flag of hair was plastered to his back. Really long hair, he noted absently, when the kid lost his balance and fell; it went clear down to the cleft of his buttocks. No tan lines, either. Odd, for someone fresh from England.

"Dave?" Brock repeated, when he righted himself. "I, uh, wanted to catch you solo but never got the chance, and now . . . who knows? Anyway, I . . . I wanted to give you something."

And with that he reached to his throat and lifted the fine silver chain that lay there, and with it the quarter-sized disk of bright metal that had rested between the boy's scanty pecs.

David had seen the chain before but never truly noticed it. The rest had been obscured first by clothes, then by distance. But as Brock wriggled out of it (it required navigating quite a lot of hair), David got a closer look. It was a medallion, wrought of stainless steel or something similar, with the chain running through a loop cast into the top. A boar's head showed on either side, worked in high relief.

"The Sullivan crest," Brock explained. "I found it in an antique store in York and thought—uh, somebody told me I oughta buy it. Didn't cost much, so I did."

David accepted the medallion with a grin but resisted another urge to ruffle the kid's hair. He probably got more than enough of that, and surely didn't need it from—he feared—one of his heroes. "Thanks," he replied instead, checking the chain for a catch, finding none, and sliding it over his head and around his neck. It thumped against his chest: bright metal against dark-tanned skin. Almost, he thought, it glowed with its own light. Oh well, the kid *had* reportedly had a couple of sessions with Uki in Galunlati. Maybe he'd picked up some mojo there. Not wise to ask, though. Not now, where maybe even water had ears. Besides, he'd had enough magic.

"Sure," Brock grunted after an expectant pause, then executed a neat backflip and stroked toward the edge, where he heaved himself out, retrieved a robe, and padded nonchalantly toward the softly gleaming arcade. Only then did David realize that there were still no towers visible—from any direction. They'd climbed stairs, true, to reach the suite, but nowhere near enough to have gained the top of one of those skyscraper pinnacles. And all of them had pointed tops, not the open ones a spread like this implied.

But did it really matter? All he cared about now was getting himself out of here before he zoned out in the water (when had he gotten so sleepy?) and locating a nice soft bed.

"Coming?" he queried Liz, as others likewise began to depart. He waited a moment longer, then waded toward the steps at the shallow end, close enough behind Calvin to observe, yet again, the faded stooping falcon tattoo that adorned his friend's right "cheek." "Hand me a robe," Liz called from the lowest step. "Please."

David rolled his eyes, but complied. An instant later, he'd claimed a robe of his own, retrieved his civvies, and was following Brock's soggy footprints toward the suite.

It didn't completely encircle the garden as he'd first surmised. Rather, smaller chambers flanked the entry salon, two to a side, which meant they'd have to double up. Sandy and Calvin already had. Alec and the rest of the Gang were batching it next door—conveniently in a room with four narrow pads that looked remarkably like futons. Piper and LaWanda would surely prefer some privacy, but likely be willing to share with Myra, who'd known them nearly as long as he'd known Alec, Aikin, and Liz. Which assumed Piper and LaWanda actually *went* to bed; last he'd seen of 'em, they were locked in an embrace, waist deep in water. If LaWanda was as bold and opportunistic as she projected, he doubted they'd sleep much tonight. After all, when would she get another chance to do the wild thing in Tir-Nan-Og?

As for him, Liz, and that possibility . . . it seemed unlikely, given that the one remaining room was occupied by a large empty bed—and Brock, curled up on something between a futon and a sofa, fast asleep like a loyal puppy.

David dropped his civvies atop a fabulously thick rug patterned with interlaced winged serpents—how odd the worn black cotton looked against that elaborate richness—flung off the robe, and leapt onto the bed. Liz joined him. Together, they tunneled beneath an enormous fur coverlet striped in black, gold, and gray. And before they could do more than stroke each other wistfully and utter dreamy goodnights, they slept.

David awoke abruptly, to the sound of a nerve-wrenching yowl—

—Loud, protracted, and at fearfully close range.

There was also a rattly hiss.

He sat up, every nerve tautly alive and tingly, as the sour taste of adrenaline flooded his mouth. Before he even knew he'd so chosen, he flung himself out of bed, squinting into the half-light of the shrouded room. A wind had picked up, stirring the silk hangings into phantoms and false shadows—which didn't help. He was still peering vainly about in search of the uproar when it thrust itself upon him in the

form of a fighting, spitting cat rolling across the floor to
tumble across his bare feet, then move on, even as he
skipped aside.

A cat locked in desperate battle with something he
couldn't make out, save that it had the long sensuous body
of a snake and leathery wings like a bat. *Quetzalcoatl*, he
concluded automatically, *without the feathers*. And then
had no more time to gawk, because the serpent-thing managed to free itself from Aife's determined grasp long
enough to launch itself at him like a striking diamond-
back. He danced backward, slammed into the bed before
he expected to, and sat down abruptly. By which time Liz
was scrambling across the cover toward him. "David,
what—?" she mumbled through a yawn.

"Hell if *I* know," he panted, regaining his feet and fumbling about for something with which to swat the serpent—
which was clearly up to no good—without damaging the
vulnerable kitty.

Silk grazed his hand, and he grabbed the topmost swath
of bedding and heaved the wad toward the rolling, hissing
mass of fur, wings, and scales.

It missed—or the target moved—but he had no time to
locate more, for the serpent-thing tore itself free again and
once more lunged toward him. He batted at it from pure
reflex, but connected badly. The thing sailed by, then
swung around, flying quickly but clumsily with what might
be a damaged wing. David backed away, ducking frantically—felt something dense and furry tangle with his feet,
and fell—hard—winding himself on the floor.

The thing was on him in an instant—he had barely time to
register a gaping red mouth and a thousand fine white teeth
before it hit. He beat at it again, twisting wildly, but that only
served to skew the impact. And then suddenly, it was no
quasi-reptile there, but a man—man-shaped, anyway: a
naked Faery male crouching over him with a wickedly
gleaming dagger poised in one upraised fist. "Die—
human!" that one shrieked. And stabbed—straight at David's heart.

David flinched and closed his eyes, even as he tried to
wrench away from an impossibly complex grip that pris-

oned both his legs and shoulder. This was it. He was gonna die. He was gonna—

"David!"

Liz . . . ? Or someone else? He opened his eyes just in time to see the blade flash down—and his would-be assassin dragged back by a furious, black-haired shape that flung itself atop him from the rear.

Not fast enough, however, or with sufficient force to divert the blow.

The dagger hit—

—And the world exploded into light.

David felt a wash of heat across his chest, and closed his eyes, but even so saw afterimages. He also felt the weight that pinned him shift away, and rolled in the opposite direction, to fetch up short against the bed—which sent lights of a different kind exploding through his skull. Awkwardly, dizzily, he tried to rise.

"David, what happened?" Liz breathed, scrambling up beside him.

He stared dazedly around the room, still half in shock. "I dunno—'cept I think Aife intercepted that snake-thing in here—that's what it *was*, anyway." He pointed to what sprawled motionless on the floor: a young Faery male; dead, evidently, or dying—flat on his back, with one knee raised and a shocked expression on his far-too-perfect features. That latter surely was due in part to the fact that his right arm no longer existed below the elbow, nor, as far as David could tell, did the dagger it had held to work its near-fatal mischief. There was no blood.

"He tried to kill you!" Brock gaped from where he'd landed after his part in thwarting the attack.

"Yeah," David panted, "he did."

"But why?"

"Didn't like me, I guess." David fumbled for the robe he'd discarded upon retiring and found his fatigues instead, which were better.

"Go get the others," Liz directed, searching for her own clothes.

"It worked!" Brock crowed, for no obvious reason.

David blinked at him. "What did?"

"The medallion. Iron. Woman who sold it to me said it had a charm of protection on it: protection against the Sidhe. I thought she was lying. Guess she wasn't."

"Good thing, too," David added, though something told him the boy had not told all the truth.

"The others," Liz repeated. "Surprised they're not here already, what with all that racket and the fact that these rooms are open on one side."

"Faery soundproofing?" David offered absently. "Good a guess as any. And—Oh shit!" He sprang up from the bed.

"What?"

"What's to say we were the only ones bein' attacked? Oh, Christ, we gotta hurry!"

He had taken two steps of the ten needed to cross the room when something moved before him. Light on the rug, he assumed: a flicker of firelight on an impossibly intricate design.

But then the rug came alive. A coil of interlace spiraled out of it, altering as it rose into another bat-winged serpent, this one much larger than the other—easily ten feet long: the size of a good-sized boa or python. Even as its tail was still unwinding, the winged forepart hurled itself at David. He tried to dodge, but found escape blocked by an outthrust coil, which then whipped suddenly toward him and knocked him down. "Shit!" he gasped, as he tried to roll away.

"Fucker!" someone roared in turn, and for the second time in less than a minute, David saw battle joined, this time by Calvin, who stood framed in the entrance for a fraction of a second—a swarthy blot against an inky sky— then, like Brock before him, hurled himself into the fray. He was Calvin when he lunged, anyway; when he landed he was a tawny Florida panther. Cougar. Catamount. *Felis concolor*. Whatever. The important thing was that he was holding his own against his scaled opponent. Even now claws had pinned the forepart, while fanged jaws sought to get a grip behind the monster's head.

That head snapped wildly, too; each bite narrowly missing, but nevertheless growing closer, as Calvin found his hundred-sixty pounds of black clawed, white fanged mass unequal to easily that much sharp-tipped scale and squirming muscle. Somehow David managed to regain his feet, saw Brock scampering past—hopefully to warn the others—but could find no way to assist. A wrong blow could injure his friend—or put himself back in peril of fangs and who knew what else? Or—

"Cal! Watch out!" Brock shrieked. The tail had finally freed itself from the carpet in which it had hidden and arched above the knotted combatants. Something gleamed there, at the end of the spine. Something that dripped a viscous, steaming liquid.

"Stinger!" David shouted in turn.

Calvin's human reflexes were already fast, and in cat shape they were equivalently quicker. With one twisting heave, he wrested himself free of the coils that sought to bind him and rolled away. The stinger struck the floor—and dug in.

The serpent-thing wasted the merest instant trying to extricate itself, before its shape began to waver. For a heartbeat it became a man—Faery male, anyway: young as the other, and similarly dark-haired—and then it altered again. Not to any living shape, however; rather, it seemed to lapse back into the woven pattern in which it had lain in wait—save that it now lay upon bare stone floor, no thicker than the other shadows there.

"Get it!" David bellowed. But the thing was faster in that form than he could ever have expected, and shimmer-slither-slid into the arcade and thence into the salon, aiming for the suite's single door.

David ran. Calvin loped in a tawny blur. Liz and Brock were slower shapes behind them.

"Shit!" Brock yelped, for the thing was accelerating—had become a shadow in truth—and moving fast as a shadow in shifting light had managed to gain the entrance. Calvin chased it desperately; indeed, ran so hard he slammed into that unyielding portal. Too late.

David skidded to a halt beside him. The thing was gone, but had not escaped entirely. A rag of black hung from Calvin's claws. A rag that, as they stared in mute amazement, slowly became a long shard of what looked sickeningly like the thick red muscles of a human thigh.

"Fuck!" David gasped, swallowing hard, leaning on the door. *"Fuck!"*

Liz was there beside him, holding him, or bracing him. He could've used either just then. And then Calvin rose up beside him: human again, and furious. He shook his hand as though he had seized something utterly foul, even as the other released the *uktena* scale with which he'd effected the change. "Check the others," he told Brock. "I'm goin' after that asshole!"

"The others're fine," LaWanda assured him, from behind. "Wait a second, I'm goin' with you."

"Me too," Aikin echoed. "Let's travel."

Chapter XII:
Wising Up

(Tir-Nan-Og—high summer—night)

"We can't *all* go," David protested, gazing wildly around the hard-eyed group ranged before the suite's imposing door—the door beneath which whoever—or whatever—it was that had just attacked him had seconds before made good its slithery escape.

LaWanda's eyes blazed defiance. "You wanta take time to stop me?"

David was already framing a scathing reply when Calvin laid a hand on his shoulder. "She's right, Dave. Every second we waste, that fucker gets further away. I oughta be able to track 'im—assuming he leaves a blood trail. But we don't have time to argue."

David tried the door—massive cast-bronze pulls in the shape of leering demons. "Doesn't matter anyway; can't get through."

Calvin grinned triumphantly. "Watch me!" And with that, he grabbed the scale and clenched his fist around it. His eyelids closed. He took a pair of deep breaths, exhaled another—and *changed*. One minute he was a middle-sized, well-muscled young man; the next, a blot of shadow sliding down the door and through the hair-fine crack at its base.

LaWanda's eyes were big as saucers. "How'd he—?"

David couldn't resist a grin of his own. "Short form? The scale's got mojo. With it, he can turn into anything he's eaten."

"He's *eaten* one of them things?"

A shrug. "Prob'ly got a nip in durin' the fight. Or—"

He had no time to elaborate, for something snapped in the latch, and the door eased inward. Calvin was standing there, grinning like a fool. And stark naked. "Here, Cal," Brock hissed, and tossed him David's discarded robe. LaWanda, David noted, wore another; but Aikin, like himself, was back in fatigues, though shirtless; and everyone—due to the haste with which they'd assembled—was unshod.

Liz fidgeted at the door, looking far more angry than frightened. "I want to go," she complained, "but somebody's gotta keep an eye on stuff here—wake everybody up, and tie up that other guy, just in case. Brock—"

The boy scowled. "I was gonna go too!"

David shook his head. "You've already been more help than most folks, and frankly I owe you my life twice over. But we can't afford to argue. The trail's gettin' cold."

"Right," Calvin agreed. "Us three guys are the stealthiest folks I know, and I've got more sense than to fuss with LaWanda. You've got some good folks here. My advice? Arm yourselves with whatever steel you've got on you, tie that other asshole up proper, and stay in one place where you can see each other."

"I'm on it," Brock announced—and fled.

"We'll knock the old M-Gang cadence," Aikin advised, as he joined the others in the corridor outside. "That way nobody can sneak up on you. Alec'll know it. If not, get G-Man or Darrell."

And with that the panel snicked closed, and lest anyone have seconds thoughts about following them, David bolted it. He gazed at Calvin expectantly. "Neat trick there, my man."

A grim chuckle. "Sometimes I amaze myself. God, but that thing tasted awful! And *bein'* it . . . I dunno, Dave. . . . I'm not sure I'd do that again if I had it to do over. I mean, I've felt some strange instincts in my time, and worked with some screwed-up senses, but that—! Faugh! Gag! Let's just say it was disgustin'."

"Any sense of whether it was originally human—Faery, or whatever—or if one of those other forms was its main one?"

A shrug. "Faery—I think."

"Which means, if you wanted to, you could become a duplicate of our assailant?"

Aikin's mouth dropped open. "You could?"

Another shrug, this time with a sour grimace. "Probably. I've done that *once*. Don't recommend it, either. Memories tend to come with it, and instincts. Trouble is, it's hard enough just bein' me; I don't need competition in my own head. And now," he concluded irritably, "if you don't *mind.* . . ."

David paused to check out the corridor. Nothing remarkable, really, beyond the fact that it was windowless and curved to the right—and down, describing a gradual spiral around their suite. Otherwise. . . . Groined arches of black marble supported the ceiling, their piers interspersed with panels of repousséed silver. The floor was beige stone, smooth but unpolished. Against it, the trail showed unmistakably in a steady splatter of glistening red, leading to the right.

As quietly as they could, they followed it. Calvin led. Aikin, who hunted a lot and was nearly as quiet as Calvin, went second, ahead of David. LaWanda brought up the rear. David caught an occasional soft ping or clink as her braid-beads struck each other. He wondered what Cal thought about such noisy accoutrements. He also wondered if it wouldn't be wise to keep an eye on the ceiling. After all, their assailants could easily have had accomplices. And even if they were only pursuing *one*, there was no good reason the guy couldn't shift again and lurk in the vaults' many shadows—or, barring that, simply sprout wings and fly away in the shape he'd worn earlier, or another.

Unless there were rules about such things. Cal had wounded this one. And that other guy had remained in his own shape when he died. Maybe injury precluded shifting. Or maybe not. It didn't work that way with Cal. In fact, shapeshifting healed him. Cal now sported a foreskin he hadn't had when David met him—because the genetic blueprint locked in his cells rebuilt him *as designed* after he changed. That was also why his tattoo was fading. It didn't happen all at once, though, so it was still possible that they might be able to identify the culprit by locating a Faery youth with a limp, or an odd depression in his leg.

Which presupposed they reported this, which didn't necessarily seem wise.

All at once it struck David like a blow—more of that delayed reaction effect, like the shuttle. *Someone had tried to kill him!* Abruptly, he was shaking—which made it damned hard to stealth. To calm himself, he inventoried his pockets for potential weapons. Slim pickings: car keys, a few bits of change, and a Swiss Army Knife. He slid out the later and opened the longest, thickest blade. Not much, but it was steel. And steel had saved him earlier.

Steel? Or enchantment? His fingers sought the medallion Brock had given him. He preferred the former, but the latter was a better guess—the kid was a pretty straight shooter. Still, something bugged him about the boy. It was just too convenient, dammit. He'd only had the medallion a few hours, and already it had saved his life.

Of course there *were* things that shielded one from the Sidhe—he'd had a ring like that once, until Liz had sacrificed it to resurrect Fionchadd. She wore it now—unmagicked.

And then the thought ambushed him again. *Someone really had tried to kill him!*

Which raised the question of who? Lugh's faction? Well, he didn't trust them worth a hoot, but it seemed unlikely Lugh would've either resorted to such extreme measures or singled him out. Which left the clearly disloyal opposition, who could have any number of motives. God knew Lugh had pointed him out in council as one around whom a storm of options circled. Ridding the world—Worlds, rather—of him would definitely solve a number of problems, if one favored certain alternatives.

Trouble was, that last line of reasoning implied a traitor somewhere: someone who'd attended the council. And since Lugh, Nuada, and Fionchadd had been the only Faeries present, and he preferred to trust them all, as far as this situation went, that implied a human double-crosser. Or that someone was masquerading as human but really wasn't. All at once David found himself wishing he had someone else to bounce this theory off of. Someone sufficiently remote from it to retain a modicum of objectivity.

Someone like John Devlin.

Where *was* Devlin, anyway? Shoot, where was anybody? Likely not together, that was for sure. They'd dispersed when the council had ended, with no time for one-on-one interaction—which (as Finno had admitted) had to be a deliberate ploy. Divide and conquer. So why did Lugh let him and his friends bunk together?

It was all too confusing. And probably not worth debating now, when they were in hot pursuit of someone, who, if apprehended, might possibly provide real answers.

"Shit!" Calvin spat abruptly. He stumbled to a despondent halt and slumped against the wall. David joined him, directed his gaze toward where his friend was pointing.

The trail ended on the sill of a narrow window—one far too narrow for any of the Trackers to squeeze through. Calvin studied it thoughtfully. "Looks like our friend shifted again—or something. I could go after him as a bird, I guess. But that'd leave you guys in the lurch, and I'm not so sure even this little trek was smart, now that my brain's workin', 'stead of my adrenal glands."

Aikin slid down the wall to slouch on the floor, tired-eyed and slack-jawed. "Well, *I* sure can't change shape!"

"Me neither," LaWanda echoed. "I ain't got *that* much mojo."

David gnawed his lip, looking around anxiously. He feared to speak, yet was desperate to share the notion that had just popped into his head. Fought its way to his lips, rather, given that his mind was threatening to explode with competing speculations.

"Talk, Sullivan," Aikin ordered, poking him in the ribs. "Your chin's gonna get dirty on the floor."

David took a deep breath. "One thing. I don't know what you guys've been thinkin', but I'd bet money that whoever jumped me wasn't workin' for the big guns—anyone important, anyway."

LaWanda lifted a brow. "How so?"

" 'Cause they didn't know diddly-squat about us. I mean, think, folks: they attacked me, presumably 'cause

I'm either the leader of our group, or 'cause I'm from Sullivan Cove—which implies they *want* this resort to be started, so they can go to war with us, which implies they expect to win. Only, they missed a bunch of things. To start with, they knew we were all human, so they underestimated us in general. Number two, they either missed Aife altogether—maybe 'cause of the iron on her cage—or else they just figured she was a regular cat. But either way, the fact that she was able to slip up on 'em implies they hadn't seen us until we got to the suite, maybe even until after we got to our rooms—my sense is they were hidin' there ahead of us.''

Calvin nodded slowly. "Could be. But they didn't know I was a shape-shifter, either—which I'm positive took that last guy off guard.''

"And I doubt they knew about this," LaWanda added, prodding David's medallion with a two-inch-long, gold-lacquered nail. "Shit, *I* didn't notice it 'til just now. I—" She broke off, eyeing the disc suspiciously. "That thing's got mojo. I don't know what kind or how much, but it's there.''

David nodded in turn. "Figured. But we can talk about that later. For now, we need to get back to the folks. The longer we're gone, the more I think there might be more of those sneaks around; that we might've beat feet way too soon.''

Aikin puffed his cheeks. "I'm afraid you're right. I also agree that those folks didn't do their homework worth a damn. In *fact*," he continued, "now that I think about it, we're not exactly your normal bunch of . . . humans. Like, we know a shitload of magical theory. Cal's a shape-shifter. You've shifted shape, and so have Brock and Sandy, back when you guys had scales. I have too—once, with Aife's help. But the point is, everybody could if Cal'd let us use his scale or could get hold of more. You've also got the Sight, Dave; and Myra says she's got it sometimes, and Liz can scry. LaWanda claims she's got 'feelin's, and who knows what other kind of mojo? Piper's music's got *something*, or we couldn't have got here so fast, and Alec's got magical trinkets out the wazoo. The point is, we're a lot more than we seem to be. Shoot, Gary and Runnerman are the only normal guys here.''

"Don't think too hard about them, either," David cautioned, rising to his feet and giving Aikin a hand-up on the fly.

Calvin cast one doubtful look at the too-narrow casement and began retracing their steps. They were halfway back—by guess—when Calvin brought them up short. Aikin nearly bumped into him, and David did bump into Aikin. "What's the deal, Red Man?" LaWanda hissed.

"Never mind," Calvin mumbled. "It'll keep."

"Better hurry, then," David urged. "Way things are goin', there may not *be* a later. I'm not at all convinced we're gonna get out of here with anything like accurate memories. I wouldn't be surprised if we just woke up by the Track with empty bottles around us, thinkin' we'd all passed out."

"Aife'd know," Aikin countered. "She may look like a cat, but the woman's awake in there. Point of fact, I suspect the woman's a lot *more* awake, now that we're back on her home turf. I doubt it was a coincidence that she saved you. Not just a kitty on the prowl, anyway."

"Maybe," David grunted. "But I don't like talkin' out here—or anywhere else, for that matter."

"Back in the room, then," Calvin conceded. "I promise."

David was more than a little surprised that they actually made it back to the glittering portal unassailed. God, but he was jumpy! He actually found himself holding his breath as he, not Aikin, gave the requisite MacTyrie Gang secret knock before shooting the bolt again.

The door cracked open instantly, to reveal the suspicious, if sleepy-eyed, gaze of Alec McLean, who pulled back the panel as little as possible and ushered them in. "How'd it go?" he yawned. Then, "Christ, Dave, are you okay? Liz told me—"

David shushed him with a spontaneous hug, which surprised both of them. "I nearly lost it," he choked into Alec's neck, as he found his eyes awash with tears. "I nearly lost . . . *you* guys. I nearly lost . . . *everything.* I—What if I'd died?''

"You'd know something we don't," Myra drawled. "Or else you'd know nothing at all, and either way you'd have more peace of mind than you do now."

Sandy ambled up to join them, sandwich in hand. She saw David peering at her latest fanciful concoction. "Eat when I get nervous," she confessed. "Better than smoking, cheaper than drinking. More productive than sleeping. I—" She gazed about frantically. "Where's Cal?"

David blinked at her. "He was with us a second ago. Did anybody—"

A sound reached them from without: the soft metallic snap of the door being bolted. David stiffened in alarm, but before he could do more than push at the panel, a tide of darkness flowed under it from outside. He backed away instinctively, dragging Alec with him. And was still back-peddling frantically when that darkness rose up before them: a man-shaped shadow in three dimensions—whereupon it began to blur, stretch, and acquire a modicum of color. For an instant it clarified into what was clearly the second Faery youth who'd assailed them—the one whose face David had glimpsed before he'd gone shadow and fled. But then that form likewise collapsed back into the initial pool of darkness, which immediately altered again; but this time when it solidified, it was Calvin.

"Shot the bolt," he explained, scooping his jeans off the floor by the door. "Didn't want somebody to happen by and wonder."

"Can't hurt," Alec agreed, reaching down to scoop up Aife, who'd been rubbing against his legs and purring. "Besides, *they're* the ones who owe us explanations."

"I've got some," Calvin volunteered breathlessly. "But folks . . . I think you'd better sit down."

David frowned, but reclaimed the chair he'd sprawled in earlier, along with the same copper tumbler. It was still frosted, still held that delicious liquid. Exactly as *much* of that delicious liquid. The rest crowded round, lolling on the floor or collapsing into pillows. Only Calvin remained afoot, looking pale, wary, and extremely thoughtful. Finally he too sat. "It's like this," he began. "You folks know

I'm a shapeshifter—and if you didn't know before, you do now. Those of you who've seen me do it, or who've done it yourselves, know that in order to change, I have to prime the uktena scale with my blood''—he held out the scale for all to see.

"But anyway," he went on, "it's easiest when I shift to something my own mass, and a lot more pleasant when I shift to something with a decent-sized brain. Otherwise instinct starts to squeeze out memory, and if you're not careful, your *self* will get squeezed out too. But what I'm gettin' at is that to shift into any shape, I have to have eaten whatever it was—a drop of blood in my mouth's enough. Just now I fought that shadow-thing. I bit it, and I tasted its blood. But that wasn't its real shape; it was really one of the Sidhe—and that made me wonder. So when I went shadow a minute ago, I tried something I hadn't tried before—had the idea while we were gone, Dave. See, Faeries shift with some power besides a scale; but since I, in shadow form, wore a shape *wrought* by that other power, I figured I might also *have* that power when in that shape. And guess what? Once I was in shadow-shape, I *could* draw on its power to assume the shadow's original form. It wasn't a lot of fun," he continued, "but the point is, I basically became that last guy who attacked Dave—which means I could access that guy's memories. It's scary as hell in somebody else's head, never mind someone who's both . . . magical and immortal; there must be a zillion zillion memories in there, and I could only risk a couple seconds before I fried my own brain. But anyway, what I was *tryin'* to do was find out who attacked us, but I missed that and . . . learned something a whole lot worse."

"Enough suspense," Liz snapped. "If I'm gonna freak, I'd as soon get it over with."

"You won't like it."

"I already don't."

Calvin took a deep breath. "Lugh lied to us . . . I think. As best I can tell, the guy who attacked us is some kind of double agent. And while I truly don't think he was workin' for Lugh when he jumped Dave, he's definitely party to privileged information. And to make a long story short,

Lugh's got a plan already in place. The instant—the *instant*—any construction begins at either the Cove or, God forbid, Bloody Bald, he's gonna raise the level of the lake—*your* lake, Dave—and force the developers out that way."

David's mouth popped open. For the thousandth time since reaching Tir-Nan-Og, his heart flip-flopped and his emotions neared overload. Not without difficulty did he regain a modicum of control. "That son-of-a-bitch," he gritted.

Calvin grimaced helplessly. "There was no easy way to tell you."

"Smart, though," LaWanda mused. "He don't have to hurt nobody, and he gets his way without either revealin' himself directly or raisin' questions that could lead to him by a crooked path."

"It really is a backup plan, too," Calvin emphasized. "I think."

"So much for that council," David groaned. "I knew it was too good to be true."

"No," Myra countered. "It was sincere. I don't know how I know that, but . . . it just felt right. Any good leader's gonna have contingencies, though, and Lugh's had centuries to plot and plan. Christ, he's probably had millennia. This is no different. He's given us time—basically a burning fuse, I guess it is now. But it really is clever—and I'm sure, based on what I've heard, that he can not only do what he says, but has figured out a way to make it seem like a natural occurrence—natural as we define it in the Lands of Men, anyway."

"So the Cove gets flooded," David spat. "And Lugh gets to keep his palace and his crown."

"Was there any doubt about the latter?" Alec snorted.

David shrugged. "Maybe. Just a guess, but my feelin' is that Lugh's throne isn't as secure as he'd like us to think it is. For one thing, where were the other Sidhe? Just Nuada and Finno—unless those other folks were bogus too, and set up for our benefit: shapeshifted Sidhe or plain old illusions, maybe."

"But not Finno," Alec pointed out. "Or if that wasn't

him, it was someone enough like him to activate the Track.''

"And violate the Ban," Liz appended. "Which means that whoever summoned us was acting on Lugh's orders."

"So we distrust Finno too?" Alec sighed. "Great! So, who *can* we trust?"

"Nobody," David muttered. "Nobody here, except—well, maybe just nobody." He paused thoughtfully. "One thing I can do when we get home—assumin' we do—is to call John Devlin—that guy in the corner with the glove on his left hand, for those of you who don't know him. I don't know Dev real well myself, though I've been up to his place one time and we've talked a bunch. But I can phone him, and if he was actually here tonight, I'm pretty sure he'd tell me."

"Unless he's been one of theirs all along," Alec cautioned.

David was already formulating a reply when he froze. "God, you're right!" he gasped. "We really can't trust anybody. Shoot, since I didn't see most of you guys until you showed up today, I'm not even sure I can trust all of you!"

"We could check," Alec ventured. "We could all hold something iron."

David shook his head. "Wouldn't help. We could be human and ensorceled; God knows the Sidhe don't have any qualms about fuckin' with our minds. Or we could be Faeries in human substance, which lets 'em touch iron."

All at once LaWanda chuckled, then laughed out loud. "Conspiracy theory," she chortled. "That's what this sounds like: the world's ultimate kick-ass conspiracy theory!"

"Which doesn't change one thing," David replied. "There's still at least an even chance that two weeks from now, *if* we're lucky and it takes that long, the place I grew up in, where my folks and my favorite uncle and my kid brother live, will be underwater. I've gotta stop that. And there's only two ways to do that: stop Lugh, which I *can't* imagine doin', or stop the resort from bein' built, which I can *barely* imagine doin'."

"I dunno, Davy," Liz began, but at that exact moment a firm knock sounded on the door. An image promptly formed in his mind. *Nuada.*

"Bad time for company," David grumbled. "But I reckon we'd better answer it." Without waiting for reply, he rose and padded toward the door. It was unbolted. He pulled it aside. And sure enough, the figure on the threshold was Lugh's second-in-command. The Faery's face was hard and grim. Unreadable. But his eyes spoke eloquently of anger: flashing like summer lightning.

Yet Nuada made no move to enter. "It would be good if you let me in," he said, in a voice like low, rolling thunder. "I cannot enter otherwise, though some evidently preceded me, even as they evaded me just now."

"You knew about that?" David blurted. "What the hell—"

"*Learned* about it," Nuada snarled back, as angry as David had ever seen him. "Never imagine that one such as I thinks remotely the same as you!"

David was taken aback, but stepped numbly aside to motion the Faery in. Nuada strode straight toward the prostrate—and bound—body of the captive assassin. "Dead, by his own foolishness and his own will," he declared. "By the time he lives again this will all be over, one way or another. He is both clever and a coward: clever enough to spy on his betters, and brave enough to risk the consequences of attacking you. More than that, I would be a fool to suggest until I have more knowledge. For now"—he spun around in place—"I must get you out of here. In fact you must leave *now*. Collect your gear at once."

"Aife too?" Alec dared, as the rest dispersed in frantic haste.

"Of course," Nuada snapped. "She saved David's life. She nevertheless cost many others. It is for Lugh to release her, not I."

"Good thing we had her, though," David noted, trying desperately to relieve tensions he sensed reaching critical mass among everybody present. Which was just as well. Acting meant not thinking, and thinking was too close to worrying, and he had more than enough to worry about right now.

"You are all stronger than you know," Nuada admitted. "That makes you valuable friends. It also makes you dangerous foes. I would prefer the former, but I may not have that choice much longer—and in any case, you must depart at once. The fewer who know about this the better. Come with me! Quickly! *Now!*"

And without further ado, he turned and marched, not toward the door and the hall and the rest of the palace, but toward the garden in the center of their suite.

David stared at him stupidly, there being no obvious escape route there save the sky. Then again, this was Faerie, where anything could happen; God knew it had before. A pause to retrieve his scanty baggage—the rest of his clothes, the boom box, and a backpack full of snacks—and he followed his one-time mentor. Liz was by his side in a flash, and for some odd reason, Piper, for a wonder trailing LaWanda.

"Don't like this place," Piper confided. "Hate it, really. Freaks me. I was here once before, see; and they . . . they weren't nice to me. Not even your friend"—he fairly spat out the word—"Lugh."

"Why?" Brock wondered (obviously eavesdropping), as they reached the garden.

"He won't tell you," LaWanda broke in. "They made him play for them. They made him play and play and play. They'd have made him play forever—or until he died—if a friend of ours hadn't accidentally . . . called him away."

"Other days, other magic," Piper proclaimed. "Thought I was through with that crap."

"Not when you play as well as you do," Nuada informed him, from where he had halted by the near edge of the pool. His face was as hard as David had ever seen it; a dangerous, almost maniacal, glint lit his dark blue eyes. "In fact," Nuada went on, stroking his elegant chin. "It is well you mentioned that, for it will aid me."

The rest had arrived by then, and David did a quick body count. Everyone was accounted for, even Aife, back in her plastic cell. Alec was taking no chances.

Nuada too surveyed them, and sadness joined the harsher emotions on his face. "I am sorry your visit ends on so foul a note," he sighed. "I truly had no idea affairs had fallen so far as to violate Lugh's peace in his very citadel, and when we find those who have, friend or foe, they will die the Death of Iron.

"But that is for another time," he continued, gaze once again sweeping over them, to fix at last on Piper. Piper flinched, as though the Faery's stare actually hurt him.

"Not for this palace would I harm one such as you," Nuada vowed, and it was as if he spoke to Piper alone. "But time dissolves, and with it hope, and with it also options. Therefore . . . play for me, Morry Murphy, that tune whose name you dread."

Piper blanched, then frowned, then grimaced wearily. He slid the bellows that powered his pipes under his arm and began very quietly, to play "The King of the Fairies."

"Faster," Nuada commanded. "And when I give the word, all of you, close your eyes and . . . jump."

David knew better than to argue, and was far too eager to see an end to all this chaos to conjure up the energy to dread. Instead, he simply gripped Liz's hand with his right and felt for someone else's with the other. The flesh he found was rough and male—probably Aikin. But then it didn't matter, for as the tune increased in tempo at the start of the second round, Nuada shouted, "Now!"

Startled as much as anything with the force of the Faery lord's shout, David leapt. Forward . . . forward, and then down . . . and down . . . and down.

It was taking longer than it ought to impact, though; and his body had gone utterly numb. How else explain how he could no longer feel anyone's fingers, how the air was neither hot nor cold, how his very senses themselves had dissipated—how he seemed to have drawn in upon himself, save that his arms could still move a little fore and aft, and his torso still twist from side to side.

He knew without doubt that he was falling, but then some odd new sense that had nothing to do with his inner ear did something screwy to his balance, and another urgency entirely bade him be aware of what transpired before his newly opened eyes.

He saw water flashing up at him from a pair of preposterous angles, then struck it, and continued down. He gasped for breath, watched a bubble escape his mouth, chased it, and before he could stop himself inhaled again, through his . . . gills!

For it had hit him all in an instant that he was no longer an efficiency-sized tweenaged boy, but some kind of fish. A salmon would be most appropriate. The Salmon of Wisdom, say, or given his propensity for stumbling into World-sized trouble, the Salmon of Terminal Ineptitude.

Right . . . and wrong, came a thought into his brain—Nuada's, he assumed.

Follow, that one demanded in turn. *Do not think, for that way lies danger.*

That last injunction proved even more difficult than usual for David to heed, thanks to the new distrust of all things Faery that all but overwhelmed him. Still, he was able to do as commanded and chase the tail flipping ahead of him. Down and down it swam, and some part of him determined that they were making for some secret bolt-hole in the bottom of the pool, for a deeper blackness than the surrounding ink-dark waters loomed there. Beside him—around him—he was aware of the others; and, uncannily, of a continuing ghost of Piper's melody.

And then that darkness reached up to enfold them, and it was like being sucked into a maelstrom.

It seemed forever that journey lasted, but just as he began to feel real concern, that voice once more entered his mind. Two words only it spoke. The first was *upward*; the second was *farewell*.

Upward sounded a fine idea, and David swam that way. The water was growing colder, he realized, and he was tiring. His body felt thick and heavy. His tail had lost its strength and a muffled ringing clogged his ears.

His ears!

He had ears again! And feet! And full-length arms. And . . . apparently, clothes.

Waterlogged clothes.

And a backpack.

He couldn't breathe water, though; and drowning was already lapping at the gates of his nose and mouth. Summoning all the strength he possessed, he forced himself to rise, angling toward that bare glimmer of light he desperately hoped marked the surface.

Closer and closer—and he broke through. Air flooded his lungs. He drank it down hungrily, breath after thankful breath, treading water.

Other heads appeared: Aikin's first, then Alec's, then Gary's, then Myra's, and finally, at long last, Liz's. More followed, but he had eyes only for his lady. She swam over to him. "Welcome home," she sputtered.

"Home . . . ?"

She raised a dripping hand from the dark water and pointed to the sky. Moonlight gleamed there. Their own moon, exactly as it had appeared when they'd crossed the dam at Whitehall all those hours back. Which was typical. One never knew how time ran in Faerie. Not that it mattered now.

What *mattered* was reaching shore, getting dry, and contriving a battle plan. (When had he made *that* decision?)

Only . . . where was the dam? Silverhand had spirited them from the pool in Tir-Nan-Og back to the Oconee River, but where exactly in the Oconee had they arrived?

"Shit!" Darrell sputtered. "Where are we? No, don't tell me—Oh crap!"

David twisted around to look at his friend, but then he saw what had lain unseen behind him and shock escaped in a startled gasp. They would find no dam because they were nowhere near Athens. Athens was on the Piedmont; this place was surrounded by mountains. Nor were they in a river; this was a lake—a most particular lake. For behind Darrell, gleaming like a beacon in the bright moonlight, rose the perfect stone cone of Bloody Bald—Silver Bald they should call it now, or Icy Bald, or Bone-White Bald.

"Christ," Alec breathed beside him. "We're back in Enotah County!"

"Better'n where we were," Calvin coughed, then motioned to his left. "Shore's that way. I say we get there pronto."

No one argued. Fortunately, they were all decent swimmers—even, as they discovered, Aife, the no-longer imprisoned cat.

"This is BA Cove," David informed them, as he stroked along. "In case any of you missed that."

"The heart of the trouble," Aikin appended. "And the question I have right now is how the hell do we get back to Athens?"

"That's the least of our worries," David snorted. "We'll check in on Uncle Dale. He's got a pickup and something that passes for a car. Between the two, we'll manage."

And on they swam.

More than long enough, too, encumbered in clothes as they were. Eventually, David shed his pack, and was strongly considering shucking sweatshirt and sneakers as well, when he felt mud beneath his feet. An instant later, he tripped on a submerged stump, and by then the water was shallow enough for them to wade ashore. It took him a moment to get his bearings—they'd made landfall a fair way south of the place they usually based their swimming parties. Evidently, there'd been a strong current tonight— or something.

At any rate, they were back on dry ground. His favorite uncle—great uncle, actually—lived less than a mile away, shorter than that if they went overland.

Something about closed-in spaces with short sightlines spooked him, though. Therefore, as de facto leader of the expedition, he chose to escort the whole bedraggled band along the shore. Before long, a thick patch of wood appeared, riding a small peninsula that shielded any view of the more open land beyond, in the middle of which (so David told them) lay the turnaround and the road to Sullivan Cove.

They didn't see the small tent pitched just north of that low ridge's spine until Brock literally stumbled upon it. And David truly didn't see the man lying in a sleeping bag alongside, until he'd tripped over him. Someone swore. A head appeared. David stared at the moonlit face astounded.

''You!'' they yelped as one.

''You, indeed,'' Scott Gresham grumbled. ''Christ, Dave, get off me! I—What the fuck are *you* guys doin' here?''

PART THREE

PART FOUR

Chapter XIII:
Homerun

*(Sullivan Cove, Georgia—
Saturday, June 21—the wee hours)*

"I could ask *you* the same question," David gasped, as he braced himself against the nearest tree—a pine, as it turned out; rough bark sticky with resin. He wiped his hands on his fatigues, which reminded him of how wet he was. Waves slapped against the shore of the nearby lake, reminding him again. A chill breeze found him—too cold for what was already an eerily cool June—and he shivered, wondering if that were some after-effect of their precipitous escape from Tir-Nan-Og.

Scott wriggled half out of his sleeping bag and squinted up at him, then started—twice—in bleary-eyed double-take. "Christ, Sullivan, there's a zillion of you guys! What the hell?"

"Twelve," David corrected, "if everybody made it through."

"I repeat," Scott yawned. "What're you guys doin' here?" Then: "*Myra* . . . ? What?"

Myra shouldered through the crowd and crouched down on the sleeping bag beside her sometime lover. "We've got a long story; yours *oughta* be short. We're wet; you're dry. So how 'bout you go first?"

"Actually," David inserted, "you've got a point. We're wet . . . and it's not exactly ninety degrees out here, in case you haven't noticed. So I tell y'all what: my Uncle Dale lives a little ways up the road. He's safe. We can debrief up there."

Scott eyed his sparse campsite. David followed his gaze. Everything looked new: the tent, the sleeping bag, the backpack, the cooler. The expensive hiking boots Scott was fumbling around for. Myra found a dry towel hanging from a nearby limb and swabbed it across her face and hands. "Anybody?" she offered, extending it like a trophy. Liz claimed it, and while Scott scrambled into jeans and plaid flannel shirt, and laced up those preposterous clodhoppers, everyone else took a stab at drying off.

David, who was more used to being cold and wet than most of his compatriots, waited until last, though he skinned off his sweatshirt and tried to wring it out. He also surveyed the lake. It gleamed serenely, the waters bright under the full moon, the rocks atop Bloody Bald flaring like a lighthouse further out. *A beacon . . . or a warning?* He doubted he'd ever be able to look at it without flinching again. "Fuck," he grunted, mostly to himself. "Phoney fucker."

"Okay," Scott announced, "let's travel."

"I can't help observing," Myra murmured, easing up beside Scott to stride squishily along, "that you're nowhere near Whitehall Forest."

"Neither are you!"

"We also established that it's a *long* story."

Scott sighed wearily. "You want the lowdown *now*?"

"We'll burst if we don't know something, Scotto," Aikin urged. "Go for it."

A tired sigh. "Well, the short form is that . . . I've got a job."

"A job?" From Myra and Alec at once.

Scott nodded. "Sorta stumbled into it, actually. It all started this mornin'. . . ."

And for the next quarter mile he told them about breakfast with Ralph Mims and the man's unexpected offer.

For a wonder, most of the crew remained silent as they slogged along the moonlight gravel of the Sullivan Cove road. And for a bigger wonder, none embarked on any discussion of what had occurred back in Tir-Nan-Og. *Shellshocked*, David supposed—not that he blamed 'em, after all that had occurred during the last—hour, he reckoned it was. Shoot, most folks spent their whole lives without ever seeing a shape-shifter, much less two dangerous ones and a third who was also a friend, never mind having their own skins rearranged without warning. He very much doubted LaWanda had headed to Athens intending to spend the wee hours as a fish.

Or maybe they were all deferring to him, waiting for him to begin. Though Myra, as Scott's lady, seemed to have taken temporary charge, he was their implicit leader, if for no other reason than because he knew the most about this particular situation.

What he *didn't* know, however, was where Scott fit into the pattern. And so, like the rest, he listened—and waited.

"So why didn't you call?" Myra demanded, when Scott reached the point where Mims had suggested a day-trip to Enotah County.

Scott looked chagrined. "Thought it didn't matter. Mims was in a Godawful hurry, see—was after breakfast, anyway—so I basically had to shop on the fly and wing it. I thought we'd be back in time for me to go Trackin' with you guys. Shoot, I *thought* I'd get to show up and spring the good news: surprise bombshell, and all. I thought," he admitted sheepishly, peering at Myra askance, "you might actually be proud of me."

Myra's face clouded; she gnawed her lip. "I don't know," she murmured. "We'll see. I'm not sure *what* all this means yet."

Scott regarded her curiously. "I presume *this* refers to your, uh, precipitous arrival?"

"Tracking kinda got the best of us," Myra acknowledged. "But we'd better not get into that yet." She cast a furtive glance around the darkened valley.

Just hills and fields and mountains, David tallied, as he followed her gaze. *Hills and fields and mountains I figured I could count on staying here.*

Scott studied Myra a moment longer, then squared his shoulders and resumed his narrative. "Anyway . . . we made it to the cove, and Mims gave me the nickel tour. We were just fixin' to leave when he got a call on his cell phone. Big meetin' over in MacTyrie. Money folks had decided to get together at some fancy new restaurant there. I could come if I wanted, but he could tell I wasn't crazy about the idea. 'No big deal,' he says—but it might take a while. I told him I had to get back to Athens. He asked why, and I couldn't give him a reason that didn't sound silly against an offer of a for-real good-payin' job—I was tryin' to do the good impression thing, see. Anyway, we compromised. I'd camp here—I wanted to get off by myself anyway, so I could really puzzle this thing out; I kinda felt like I'd been carried off on a whirlwind or something— and while I did that, he'd do his meetin', then run me back to Athens in the mornin'. In the meantime, we raided a sportin' goods store—God, but that man throws around cash—and here I am.''

"And here we are, too," David echoed, pointing toward the file of ragged cedars that fronted a dark, decrepit-looking turn-of-the century farmhouse, parts of which were quickly falling to ruin. A newish house trailer perched on a low hill beside it, pale behind a long wooden deck David hadn't seen before. Lights burned in the nearer end, promising someone still up and stirring in the living room.

"Every time I see this place, I think about *that* night," Liz confided, drawing close.

"Don't remind me," Alec grumbled through a shiver that was not entirely born of another sudden blast of cool air. "That's the worst night I ever spent. We nearly lost Dave, and . . . that's when I found out about Aife."

"Oh Christ," Aikin groaned, smacking himself in the forehead. "Where *is* she?"

"Shit!" Alec moaned in turn. "Good question. She was in the water. But the cage. . . ."

"Too much iron, I bet," David mused. "Magic has trouble with that stuff." He patted his pockets in quest of his knife, and found no sign of it.

"We'll find 'er," Aikin assured Alec. "Soon as we dry off, we'll go back to the lake and look."

David expected Alec to protest, but he simply shrugged. "Whatever. I just don't have enough energy to care right now."

David inspected the environs. "For those of you who

haven't been here before, this is my Uncle Dale's place. Not the house," he amended, nodding toward the ruined dwelling, "the trailer. I, uh, kinda messed up his old place, so we had to get him a new one. Might be a little crowded in there, too. My folks live on up the road, by the way, but . . . let's just say we're a lot better off here. Uncle Dale's cool."

"He'd better be," Liz chuckled, though her face was grim. "He's about to have a lot more on his mind than Jay Leno."

David took a deep breath. "No offense, folks, and I guarantee there'll be no problem, but I'd better go up solo— break the news gently, and all. You guys can hang out at the old place. I'll retrieve you soon as the coast is clear."

The coast cleared soon enough, but David's favorite uncle (who, blessedly, had asked no questions—yet) quickly determined that the trailer was far too small for so expansive a gathering, so their impromptu council reconvened in the living room of his former dwelling. While Dale strove to get a fire going in the fieldstone hearth, David distributed the blankets, towels, and odd lots of clothing they'd scavenged from assorted trunks, chests, and closets of both the old man's residences. Guys dried off in one decaying bedroom, women in its slightly more intact twin. At least the walls kept the wind out, the roof was relatively solid, and there was glass in most of the windows. When David returned to the main room a short while later, it was to find a merry blaze popping and crackling, and Dale already contriving a pot of his patented coffee-an'-'shine.

He couldn't help smiling at the comfortable familiarity of that tableau. Dale Sullivan was in his eighties, thin and brittle-looking, with long white hair tied back in a tail. But he was ageless too, and, in a great many ways, as young as anyone present. Certainly he retained a progressive outlook and, more important at the moment, an open mind. David was desperately glad he was here; couldn't imagine the world without him, in fact.

But he couldn't imagine a world without Sullivan Cove, either, and that could be underwater a month from now—

or worse. It was funny, really, how he'd always pictured Dale going on forever; outlasting them all, as he'd outlasted one wife and a much-beloved nephew he'd all but raised. And now, it seemed, he'd even outlast his birthplace.

If displacement didn't kill him, as it had effectively claimed David's great-grandpa, when the lake had drowned the original family farm.

Where had the Sidhe been then? he wondered. Probably up in their castle cheering on the TVA, since the lake meant even more protection than glamour—for them.

At which point a thought surfaced, on which he knew he had to act promptly or it'd gnaw at him the rest of the night. And since he already had too many things gnawing on him, one less would help a lot. "Back in a flash," he told Dale and Liz, who were wiping the dust from a kitchen's worth of abandoned coffee mugs. "Don't say anything important without me."

And with that he dashed outside and jogged up the ragged bit of yard to the trailer. It was unlocked—always was—and he zipped inside. It was the first time he'd been alone in what seemed like centuries, and the silence embraced him like a lover. It was warm in there, too, and homey, and things had vibrant colors, not moonlight-eerie blue/black-gold/silver hues. If he let himself go, he could fall asleep in an instant. And maybe when he awoke he'd discover this had all been a dream.

Ha!

What he was seeking up here was proof, even the tiniest bit, that what he'd experienced tonight had actually occurred. And more to the point, that there were still options—and resources—available beyond the ones he knew. Forcing himself to resist the siren call of Uncle Dale's worn plaid rocker, he found the phone. A check of his sodden wallet produced an even more sodden address list. Fortunately, the one he needed was still legible. Snugging the receiver between his head and shoulder he dialed a number in Clayton, Georgia.

The phone rang. Once. Twice. Four times.

Someone picked up. No, dammit, it was an answering machine; David could hear the soft electric whir.

"You have reached John Devlin's residence," the recording intoned, in a soft north Georgia drawl. *"I can't come to the phone right now, but if you'll leave your name and number, I'll get back to you when I remember to check this thing."*

David waited a whole minute longer to be sure, then hung up in disgust. It had been a long shot anyway, and he truly didn't know what he'd have told the man if he'd got him. Maybe just sought confirmation that the person he'd glimpsed at Lugh's council really had been there; that the "convenient illusion" theory, at least, was inviable. Of course that would also be proof that everything else Lugh had said was true—most of it, anyway.

As for Devlin's absence—likely he was abed in Tir-Nan-Og.

Or—the thought struck David like a blow—dead! There'd been one attack, after all; no reason there couldn't have been others. Maybe Lugh's palace had been alive with assassins tonight. Or maybe they hadn't *been* assassins; maybe they were in Lugh's employ. Or maybe, even now, Nuada was turning other surprised sleepy humans into fish, and waters all over the country were vomiting up shell-shocked, soaking wet people.

A knock on the door startled him. He glared at it even as it opened. It was Gary. "Just lookin' for you, man," he ventured with a lopsided smile. "Dale said to corral you so we could get this show on the road."

David nodded wearily and joined his friend. Gary flopped an arm around his shoulders and left it there as the two of them trudged across Dale's new deck and back down the hill. "Don't tell a soul I said this," Gary confided, "but I'm scared shitless by all this stuff."

"Me too," David confessed. And by then they'd reached the cabin.

Dale met him at the door and thrust a steaming, chipped-china mug into his hands. David almost dropped it, it was so hot, but after all the cold he'd endured lately, that was actually a relief in a way. Certainly the pain perked him up a bit, and the scent was heavenly. Dale always bought the best coffee money could buy, and the moonshine he ran off in a still whose location even David didn't know was the best in a dozen counties. Both aromas merged in the heady steam, and David could already feel his mind clearing, even as the alcohol calmed his nerves—conditioning, he knew; he'd not even sipped the potion, though he remedied that at once.

At which point he noticed that every eye in the room was fixed on him. He grimaced and slumped down on the hearth. A skeletal sofa was the only furniture worthy of the name still in place, but a pair of mattresses had been recruited from the adjoining bedrooms, as well as a collection of cobwebby cushions. Dale cleared his throat in anticipation, and Scott looked like he was doing his best not to fidget.

"Well, Uncle Dale," David began, "you too, Scotto— Actually, I'm not sure where all this started, but the best I can figure, it was like this. . . ."

His cup was empty when he concluded—which surprised him, given that he scarcely recalled more than that first blessed taste. Not all of his companions had completed the story with him, however, and Gary and Darrell were all but snoring. Sandy likewise looked tired and kept jerking herself awake, where she sat neatly in a corner, resting her head on one hand. *Longer day than you figured, my girl*, David reckoned. *Bloody whole lot longer!*

He took a deep breath, followed by a bogus swallow, then surveyed the assembly expectantly. "So . . . now that we're all back on a level playin' field, what do we do?"

"We—" Liz commenced, then faltered. "We see who that is on the porch," she finished sourly, rising and padding toward it, closer than the rest.

David intercepted her—amazing, given how tired he was.

She whirled on him. "Davy, why—?"

" 'Cause it could be one of them," he snapped. "They've come into this World before, no reason they can't again, good guys or bad guys, either. But they can't get inside unless we let 'em. Screens on the door—*iron* screens. And—"

"Actually," a tired voice called from without, "it is

more that we are conditioned by our own hospitality."

"Finno!" David cried, as much to Liz as to the slight figure who, now that he'd wrenched the door open, was sure enough lurking on the shattered front porch. "Come *in*," he appended, when the Faery hesitated.

Fionchadd actually looked . . . old as he slumped into the room, and his plain gray tunic bore more than its share of suspicious stains. But before David could register more than that, the Faery unfolded his arms. Something leapt from them to the dusty floor.

A cat. A very *soggy* cat, that made a beeline for Alec.

"Aife . . . ?" Alec yawned, having dozed off, to awaken to a lapful of dripping fur. "Sorry, old gal! I—Shit, I thought I'd lost you, but I was just too tired—" He stopped in mid-apology and looked around, blushing. "Sorry," he informed his companions. "Too much goin' on too fast; I'm not handling this very well."

"Nobody is," Myra assured him. "And I'd bet money Finno's got another tale."

David raised a quizzical brow, then, when the Faery didn't move, motioned him to a seat on the hearth and thrust a cup of coffee into his hands as he sank down beside him.

"Hell's broken loose in the palace," Fionchadd announced after a long, deep swallow. "That is how you would put it, is it not?" He took another draught. "Nuada sent me," he went on. "He said for me to protect you. He said some of our folk might come into this World and try to kill you, and for me to guard you with my life."

David regarded him warily. "You really are *you*, right?"

Fionchadd first stared, then glared at him. "Who else would I be? What right—?"

"No," Liz cautioned. "Don't mind him. He's tired. We all are. We've had a long day and an awful night, and it's still a long way from over. We're glad to have you here. But you'll have to excuse us if we're a little bit paranoid."

"Sorry," David apologized, slapping the Faery on one high-booted knee. "We could spend the next hour provin' you're who you say you are, or we could spend it learnin' something useful, and then figurin' out what to do."

Fionchadd managed a tired smile. "I know less myself than I would like. What I do know is this: I left you at your chambers and sought my own, Lugh having warned me not to linger with you until you had had time to consider among yourselves what he had revealed. I sought diversion. And then Nuada found me, told me what had transpired in your suite, and sent me here. I was opposed. There were attacks on other of Lugh's guests. At least one succeeded. Beyond that—I know Lugh would make every effort to protect his counselors, though I doubt many humans awakened in the palace at their leisure."

"Devlin," David broke in. "John Devlin: is he okay?"

Fionchadd shrugged. "I know him but slightly, mostly by sight and reputation. From that I assume that he had little to fear—but I heard nothing of him myself."

"Didn't have time to hear much, though, did you?" Uncle Dale noted pointedly.

Fionchadd shook his head. "It—I cannot imagine such a thing: Lugh's hospitality so thoroughly violated."

"Who were those fuckers?" Gary yawned. "The ones in our rooms, an' all?"

"We are not certain," Fionchadd replied. "There are many factions who would cause many different kinds of strife for many diverse reasons. Myself, I suspect the Sons of Ailill. They are the most reckless, the most militant, the most open in defiance of Lugh."

"And because they're immortal, they can risk a lot," David concluded. "Like Nuada said earlier: by the time they rebuild bodies, this may all be over."

"Which," LaWanda observed, "don't bode well for Mister Lugh."

"Why not?" Brock wondered through a yawn even bigger than Gary's.

" 'Cause it means they don't expect him to be around to punish 'em when they reincarnate, or whatever it is they do," LaWanda told him. "Shoot, for all we know they've gone after him too."

"No," Fionchadd countered. "That cannot be possible. I—" He broke off, face a mask of perplexed incredulity. "They are young—younger than I, even. They are rash.

They cannot have thought this thing through." He paused again, shook his head. "It is chaos for chaos's sake. Action to stave off boredom. They stir up wasps merely to see who they sting."

"Russian roulette," Darrell mumbled, having just awakened. He sat up and poked the inert Gary in the side.

"Perhaps," Fionchadd murmured in turn. "I do not know."

"Well," Myra declared, with what David knew was forced enthusiasm, "I hate to bring this up again, but . . . what do *we* do now?"

"Go back to Athens, I hope," Darrell urged. "I mean, as far as the . . . real world's concerned, I've still got the Earth Rights festival to play."

"It *is* Saturday, isn't it?" Alec broke in.

Dale nodded. "June twenty-first—in case you had another Saturday in mind."

David chuckled in spite of himself. "Yeah, that seems to be the question all the time, doesn't it? What *are* we gonna do? Short term—and I hate to mention it, but the sooner we get goin' on it the better—*and* long term? Two weeks long, anyway."

"I can get you all back to Athens," Dale volunteered. "If a bunch of you don't mind ridin' in the bed of a rattly old pickup truck. I'll drive it. David can take my new car."

David almost missed the reference, then started. "You've got a new car?"

Dale grinned smugly. "Was gonna surprise you when you come up. Bought me a Lincoln Town Car."

David rolled his eyes. "Better'n some, I guess—for what we need right now."

"Got it in Bill's garage," Dale beamed. "That's why you didn't see."

Liz cleared her throat. "Uh, I hate to mention this folks, but Myra's right: We really do have to figure out some kind of battle plan."

Sandy counted on her fingers. "Way I see it, we've got two options. *We* either figure out how to stop this resort from being built, or we figure out how to stop *Lugh* from stopping it."

"What?" Fionchadd and Scott bellowed as one. It was impossible to say who looked more alarmed.

"You are mad if you think you can stop Lugh," Fionchadd spat, abruptly all anger and ice. "I—"

"Shut the fuck up!" Scott roared, rounding on the Faery, face flushed with a fury of his own. Fionchadd was not the only focus of that wrath, though, and the force of it made David shiver as it came to rest on him. "Goddamn it! Shut the fuck up, all of you! In case you haven't noticed, this isn't just about you! I've sat here like a good little boy and listened to you spout the same old party line, but now I'm gonna have my say! And—*And*," he continued more loudly, glaring at Fionchadd again, "I'm *not* gonna take second seat to any goddamn Faery!"

Fionchadd's eyes all but shot sparks. His hand slid to the small dagger David had just noted at his hip. David was quicker, though, and caught that strong slim wrist before it could work any mischief. "There's time for us all to have our say," he gritted. "Unless we talk for two weeks."

Scott puffed his cheeks; his eyes still showed anger's embers, but no longer the fierceness of irrationality. "This isn't just about you guys," he repeated through clenched teeth. "In case you haven't noticed, you're talkin' about my job! More to the point, you're talkin' about my fuckin' future—the only future I may have if I don't get myself straightened out in a fuckin' hurry. These aren't great folks to work for, but they offered me something that was mine, which is more than any of *you* cared to do. Sorry, but that includes you, Myra; you've listened, but you've not helped much otherwise, 'cept to say what you didn't like, what you didn't want me to do. But I don't want a fight now. I'm like the rest of you: half-crazy about all this . . . this Faery jerkin' around. But the fact is, I *have* to have this job. And it looks like I've wound up on the side of the enemy, but—Oh, hell . . . !" His conviction dissolved into a strangled sob, and he buried his face in his hands. "I— Shit, guys, you've put me in the fuckin' middle here, and I just don't know what to do!"

Silence then, while Scott wept into his knuckles, and the rest exchanged troubled glances. "Here," David whispered into that tense, strained lull, passing Scott a fresh mug. "It'll calm you down."

"Make me crazier'n I am already," Scott snorted back, but drank the coffee to the grounds. "Sorry."

"Probably," Myra agreed. "But actually, things may not be as bad as you think. For one thing, whether you know it or not, you may be able to help."

Scott blinked up at her, looking puzzled. "See," she went on quickly, "what we've got now is . . . is access to more information than we had before. Basically, we've got somebody—you—who's on the inside. You can help us get a better idea of this entire situation."

Scott glared at her. "The *situation* is that they want to build a resort here and you don't want 'em to, and that the best thing for me isn't the best thing for you!"

"Best thing for you in the short term, maybe," Sandy returned. "I don't know you very well, but from what I've heard from all these folks, this doesn't sound like the real you. Frankly I don't see you as the earth-raping type, and that's what's going on here."

"They just want me to survey," Scott protested. "They want me to look for potential . . . mining options."

"Fuckin' great!" David groaned, rolling his eyes. "Double rape, then: rape the land with a resort, and rape the land with tourist gold mines!"

"Sapphires," Scott corrected absently. "And amethyst. And I don't want to rape the land. I *hate* that kinda shit. But I've seen the plans, and they're actually not that bad. Mims says they're gonna try to be real low-impact. You won't even be able to see much of it until you actually get there."

"Just a hotel on top of Bloody Bald!" David growled.

Scott shook his head. "Inside Bloody Bald. They're gonna hollow it out; use the natural fissures for windows. Only thing you'll see from the land's the boat dock."

"*Inside* the mountain?" Fionchadd gasped. "That is even worse than I had imagined!"

Scott shrugged helplessly.

Silence.

"You could play two possible roles," the Faery offered

at last. "You could be a friend, or you could be a foe. If you choose the latter—if you continue as you seem to be inclined—you risk these friends, who would be your friends forever, in exchange for fickle gold."

Scott's eyes flashed dangerously, but Myra covered his mouth before he could reply. "Let him finish," she hissed. "He talks sense."

"Thank you, Lady," Fionchadd murmured, with a little bow. "You could be a foe," he repeated. "Or you could be a friend. You could be a—"

"A spy!" Brock finished for him. "Sure! It's brilliant. You're our inside man! You tell us what's going on; you hold up progress, you—if nothing else, you buy us time until we can figure out what else to do."

Scott's face clouded. "Damn you!" he growled. "I hate you!"

"Why?" Myra shot back. " 'Cause you know it's what you really oughta do?"

Fionchadd toyed with the dagger David had stopped trying to deny him. "Gold," the Faery whispered, as though to himself. "It all reduces to gold."

Scott's glare could have melted stone. "If you mean money, yes it does."

Myra shook her head. "I'm disappointed in you, Scott. I thought you'd have a higher price."

"I'm tired of worryin'," Scott retorted. "This could set me up for the rest of my life."

"At the price of your soul?"

"I can't worry about that. I—Haven't you ever done something that was good for you but not for somebody else? It all boils down to what you want to worry about."

"I thought you were a hero," Myra spat. "I guess I was pretty damned wrong."

More silence. Scott stared at the floor, stirring the thick dust with a shard of kindling stick. The fire popped. The coffee cooled.

"Okay," he breathed at last. "I'll . . . I'll do it—what I can. I'll be your goddamn mole. *But*," he added bitterly, "if this falls out like I think it will, you guys have gotta be there for me. You've gotta help me build some other future, 'cause I sure as bloody hell ain't gonna have anything left of the one I've got right now!''

"Deal!" Myra cried at once.

"Deal," Scott echoed with far less enthusiasm, but with the ghost of what David was certain was a sincere, if rather wan, smile.

To David's surprise, Fionchadd was grinning. "Okay, Finno, spill it," he commanded. "You look like the cat that ate the—never mind."

Fionchadd raised an elegant arching brow. "Gold," he repeated softly. "No gift is worth anything that is not freely given—and since Scott has just offered up his future, I feel free to offer a gift of my own."

Scott scowled at him distrustfully. "What?"

Fionchadd's grin widened. "When this is over, should this beautiful land remain intact, I will see that you find far more riches hereabout than those others would ever have paid you."

"Not . . . all at once, please," Scott objected. "If I don't work for it, it, uh, won't be good for me."

"I intend you to work for it," Fionchadd assured him. "But there is still one problem."

David took a deep breath. "Right, Finno—and thanks by the way, for holdin' your tongue when we had no right to expect you to—but the fact is, there's something *you* may not know about."

Fionchadd frowned. "And what is that?"

David told him about Lugh's plan to flood Sullivan Cove.

The Faery's eyes were like granite when he had finished. "This . . . could change many things," he rasped. "And I now see why you are so consumed with the need for haste!"

"Glad you understand," David drawled. "Now—do you have any suggestions?"

"About how to stop Lugh?" Fionchadd replied with a bitter laugh. "As soon try to stop the winter."

A resigned shrug. "Another point of view never hurt."

Fionchadd shrugged in turn. His smooth brow furrowed in thought. "No," he cautioned after a pause, "do not dismiss me so easily. You simply caught me . . . off guard. But I am thinking, and what I think is this.''

David leaned forward eagerly. ''What?''

Fionchadd took a deep breath, then stood and began pacing around the tight-packed room. ''One thing,'' he informed them, ''Lugh is not the only Lord of Faerie. There are others, though mostly they look to him because of the way our Realms lie in space and time—and please do not ask me to explain *that* now. Finvarra warred with him but lately, and has little cause to love him now, so we might find an ally there, though I doubt it, for even bitter enemies may join to combat a foe that would destroy both—and whatever else you say, sooner or later, the Lands of Men *will* destroy Faerie, or render it uninhabitable. Finvarra has time, however; Lugh does not.''

Another deep breath, and he went on. ''Arawn of Annwyn is even more removed. He will watch Lugh and Finvarra. So will Rhiannon of Ys. But''—and here Fionchadd's face brightened—''there are others who might take a larger view.''

David shook his head in confusion. ''Who?''

''The Powersmiths!'' Fionchadd declared triumphantly. ''They are as far beyond the Sidhe as—forgive my arrogance, but this is true—as the Sidhe are beyond you. They have arts no one in Tir-Nan-Og, or Erenn, or Annwyn, or Ys, either, could begin to understand.''

Liz ventured a smile. ''And if I remember right, you are yourself related to the Powersmiths.''

Fionchadd nodded. ''If I had not thought of this, you would have; thus, I risk nothing in the long cold sweep of time. But you are correct. My mother's mother is of that line.''

''Would she help us?'' Aikin inquired.

''She would—*might*—get us a hearing with those who could.''

''Assuming we could get there.'' From Calvin.

Another nod. ''Assuming. But I think that might indeed be possible.''

David eyed him askance. ''In two weeks? No—less than that; we've got two weeks *max*.''

It was Scott's turn to scowl. "Two weeks? I don't understand. How—?"

"That's where you come in!" David chided, slapping him on the leg, having figured out where Fionchadd's logic was leading—he thought. "You keep 'em busy here with a holdin' action while we go off and bring in the big guns."

"Maybe," LaWanda amended. "You folks are mighty big on *maybes* and *mights*."

Myra took a long draught of coffee. "It's all we've got right now. I'm open to suggestions."

"I'll give you one when I got one," LaWanda returned. "Right now, I'm just thinkin'."

Alec stroked Aife absently. "So what you're saying here is that we've basically got two goals. Scott slows things down here however he can, and somebody goes off and tries to convince the Powersmiths to talk sense into Lugh?"

David looked around helplessly. "Any other ideas? Or are we all agreed in theory?"

Liz shrugged. "Makes as much sense as anything we can come up with on the fly. Uncle Dale, what do you think?"

Dale took a leisurely swig of coffee-an'-'shine, and studied each one in turn. "I think there's a lot of thinkin' been goin' on here, and most of you folk're a heap lot smarter'n me, but . . . basically it makes sense—as a frame. But you can't do any of this by yourselves, by which I mean you can't send any one of you off to do this stuff alone. And since this is my land you're talkin' 'bout here, even more than it is Davy's—'cause I've lived here longer, boy—I'll help Scott however I can. I'll be a haven, if nothing else, 'cause I don't think we need to involve Bill and JoAnne 'less we have to."

"And please God, don't let Little Billy get wind of it," David appended. "Please, Uncle Dale, I truly do beg that of you."

"Do what I can," Dale grunted. "But as I was sayin', you folks are gonna have to work together."

Gary coughed nervously, looking, David thought, very, very unhappy. "I—uh, God, but I hate to say this," he began, "but . . . I don't think I can; not much anyway. I've got a wife, see, and a kid, and a job. And the wife and the

kid don't know about all this stuff, and I don't want 'em
to. I'm not closing any doors, or anything, but whatever I
do will have to be inside . . . inside the context of my real
life. I'll help, but only when *I* can.''

David flopped an arm across his shoulders and gave him
a brotherly hug. ''Actually, G-Man, I understand. And,''
he continued to the group at large, ''anybody says different's gonna have to deal with me.''

Sandy had not spoken for a good long while, but now
she cleared her throat in turn. ''Folks, what do you think
of *this*?''

And for the next ten minutes she told them.

''Not bad,'' Fionchadd acknowledged when she had finished.

And, David agreed, it truly did seem to be a well-thought
out plan.

Basically, they would form two main groups, with assorted subsidiaries. One would be based in Enotah County
and try to delay construction of the resort. Scott would be
in this group, of course, and Uncle Dale, though not ac-
tively. Calvin would join them as well, because he had a
lot of woodcraft and other less common but potentially
more useful skills. To David's surprise, LaWanda also
asked to be included, but gave no explanation. Since Gary
lived nearby, he'd do what he could, but they'd try very
hard not to involve him. Darrell had musical commitments
he couldn't break, and—as he admitted himself, no other
talents save being silly—so he was out of the loop but on
call if anyone thought of a way he could be utilized. Of the
other ''woodsy'' folk, neither Sandy nor Aikin (who had
summer school and one final quarter respectively) dared
sacrifice academics, but both agreed to run interference at
their institutions—Western Carolina and the University of
Georgia—and, perhaps more importantly, on the Internet.
They would also provide hands-on aid on weekends whenever viable, and possibly at night as well. David had also
suggested they try their damnedest to locate the enigmatic
John Devlin.

That took care of one group, and even Liz agreed that it
contained a useful mix of skills.

The other group were what Sandy called the Envoys. This band would dare the Seas Between and try to contact the Powersmiths, whose land, Fionchadd reminded them, was primarily accessible through Annwyn, which might not give them a warm reception. Fionchadd would be point man, and David had no choice but to accompany him, because he was uniquely qualified to explain the human side of the crisis while still maintaining some small grasp of the complex subtle workings of Faery politics. Liz and Alec would also be part of this expedition, basically because Sandy said they were used to working together and it would be bad karma for them to be separated. It would blow hell out of graduation, but all three agreed to worry about that later.

Which left Myra, Brock, and Piper.

"I'll do anything you need me to," Myra offered. "But I'll tell you what I'd do if I had my druthers."

"What?" Sandy asked curiously.

"I'm an artist, what do you think?"

"Painting vacation in Faerie, huh?" Liz teased, with the first real laugh anyone had dared all night.

"Wish I still had my camera," Myra replied wistfully.

"What about me?" Brock demanded. "I mean, I know I'm just a kid—kind of—but I actually do know some . . . magical stuff."

"I'm afraid he does," Calvin confessed. "And since I know him too well to expect him to stay put, and we don't have time to lock him up—actually, I think we oughta send him off to Annwyn. Most of what mojo he knows is Cherokee tradition, and it might be smart to have somebody on hand that's used to thinkin' about power some other way than the rest of you guys do."

Brock fairly glowed, but Piper, who'd sat silently in the corner all this time, simply looked sad and doleful, as all eyes turned to him.

Fionchadd strode over and knelt by him. "I promised you a song," the Faery reminded him. "There was no time to give you one this evening, but if you will join me on this one journey, I guarantee you *five* new tunes every night."

Piper stared him straight in the eye, but his face was tight with dread. "If you will promise."

"I do," Fionchadd affirmed. "But I must be truthful, Morry Murphy, if we are to get where we must in time, I will also have need of you."

David sauntered over to join them and nudged Fionchadd in the side with a toe. "Uh, I hate to ask this, but I'm about to keel over on my feet, and I'd rather not hit the hay tryin' to work out even one more thing I don't have to, but . . . how the hell *are* we gonna get there?"

Fionchadd smiled cryptically and did something complex with his fingers. "With Morry Murphy's aid, we will leave from here at dawn—by boat."

"Piper . . . ?" David began, through a sudden yawn. But Piper, like everyone else, was dreaming.

Chapter XIV:
All at Sea

(Sullivan Cove, Georgia—
Saturday, June 21—dawn)

The last thing David recalled seeing before sleep ambushed him entirely was the sad, wistful look in Fionchadd's inhumanly beautiful eyes. The first things he saw when he regained bleary-visioned consciousness were Piper's soulful brown ones staring at him across a foot of dirty floor. Utterly disoriented, he blinked in alarm and sat up abruptly, almost frantically; yawning, feeling hungry, tired, and sore all three—and likely a number of other unpleasant things endemic to staying up late, drinking too much, and sleeping on raw pine boards. Piper remained where he was: scrunched up along one wall of Dale Sullivan's abandoned farmhouse—watching.

David wondered how long the little guy had lain there like that. God knew *he* did it often enough; it was the only safe time to really look at your friends: when you awoke beside them and they were still asleep. Things showed on sleepers' faces that were lost in the clear light of day. He wondered what Piper had seen in his.

A soft movement was Fionchadd crouching beside him, with—wonder of wonders—a cup of coffee in his hand. "I am not sure I prepared this properly," he confessed, "but I tried to watch last night. It seems I may be in this Land awhile, so I thought it wise to learn its ways and wonders."

David yawned again and scooted up against the wall—the same one against which he'd slumped when sleep had claimed him. It was not quite dawn, he reckoned, by the warm glow visible beyond the grimy windows: sunrise edging the mountains with scarlet and gold. Three hours, at best, by extremely approximate guess: that was how long he'd slept. Everyone else still did—save Piper, who was now 'possuming. And Fionchadd.

"You hoodooed me!" he accused, as he accepted the brew; too muddleheaded to do more than gripe and tease at once. The former was appropriate, the latter an indulgence: proof he was back in what he laughingly called the real world. Teasing was something real people—human people—did.

"You needed sleep, and there was too much in your mind to allow it," Fionchadd returned. His face was tight with anxiety—probably, David surmised, because he was in a hurry.

"Shit," David grumbled, mostly to himself, and tried to rise without making too much noise. "Guess we need to roust the rest of these sluggards and get our butts in gear."

Fionchadd shook his head. The room filled up with silence—almost with peace. "If we wake too many, we will talk all day. Better those of us who must travel the Tracks and the Seas seek those ways alone. You should be the one to rouse them—*only* them—for they trust you as they could never trust me. The others will awaken when we are safe away. I will leave word with them so that they do not fear."

David nodded solemnly and nudged Piper with his toe. "C'mon, Music-man, rise and—well, I don't expect anybody to *shine* this early, but do what you can."

"Coffee," Piper mumbled through a yawn, as he rolled onto his back. His expression hadn't changed from earlier. Still shell-shocked. Still . . . fated—or wyrded—or maybe simply doomed. All at once David hated himself for the part he'd played—and was yet to play—in upsetting the life of this sweet, flaky, unassuming guy.

"Coffee," Fionchadd echoed, and knelt to pass Piper a steaming cup.

While Piper drank, David busied himself waking the others—those he assumed would respond to the effort. Liz first (he couldn't resist stealing a kiss), then Alec, Myra, and finally, because he didn't trust him not to be disruptive,

Brock. To his surprise, the merest tap on the shoulder roused the boy. Even more surprising, the kid stretched twice—full and languidly, like a cat—then rose gracefully and padded onto the porch. An all-too-familiar sound ensued. David raised a brow at Piper and smirked. Piper smirked back—and stood. David eyed the door and lifted the other brow. Piper nodded.

David felt much better when he returned a short while later with a comfortably lighter bladder and a fidgety Brock in tow. The others were up by then—Alec, Liz, and Myra— and were all sipping at assorted cups and mugs. Myra scowled at hers. "There's something in this besides coffee—or moonshine," she announced accusingly, gaze fixed on Fionchadd.

"It will make you alert and help you—what is your word?—*focus*. You may need to be alert as we begin this journey, for our route may be a queer one until we win the coast. You may also need courage. You do not need to dilute that courage with fear."

Alec's reply was a grumpy grunt, followed by a gasp of sheer panic as he glanced around the room. "Oh, God— where's Aife?"

"At present, she is an enfield," Fionchadd informed him. "Soon enough that will change. Have no fear, I can speak to her mind-to-mind. She will journey with us."

"Speakin' of which," David murmured through his second cup. "Actually, speakin' of a number of things—uh, what about food? And travelin' gear? Clothes, and all? And weapons and stuff? I mean, I've got all kinds of weapons and whatnot I've picked up on my forays to other Worlds. Trouble is, it's all back in Athens—but oughtn't I to take it? Or what about weapons from our World? Guns, or . . . iron?"

"You would be a fool to carry iron where we are going," Fionchadd snapped. "Enough to be useful would proclaim our presence like a torch, and we must move in stealth. As to the rest: there will be food. There will be clothing. The other gear might serve us, but time would serve us more—as you know."

"Yeah," Brock broke in impatiently, "but exactly

how're we going? Shoot, *where're* we going, for that matter; I don't even know that much, really.''

Fionchadd took a deep breath. ''The Land of the Powersmiths lies beyond Annwyn, which lies . . . atop the country you call Wales the same way Tir-Nan-Og lies across the southeast part of this Land. But it does not lie across Wales at the same point in time.''

Brock gaped at him incredulously. *''Huh?''*

Fionchadd grimaced. ''This is not the place to lesson you about such things. Suffice to say that the Realms of Faerie overlap the Lands of Men one way in space and another in time. One way is . . . level; the other is . . . at a slant. Ask no more of this, for truly I tell you, we must hasten.''

It was a wary-eyed crew who assembled on the ruins of Dale Sullivan's front porch, and David, for one, felt wildly unprepared. If not for Alec's compulsive neatness, he couldn't even have combed his hair. His friend had come through, however, with the proper implement—and probably had a horde of other useful articles tucked in his fanny pack. David wished he hadn't dumped his own backpack, and wondered which of its contents he'd miss a week, or a month, from now—

—if he was fretting over such trivialities at all. For now, he had to worry about larger problems. About these friends—all back in their mysteriously cleaned and dried Tracking garb—who were venturing with him into the unknown. And those others who might face equal, if different, perils here behind.

At which point the sun lifted full above the horizon and, as though that were a sign, Fionchadd pointed to the left, toward the lake. David wasn't surprised to find their path leading there. Nor was he taken aback when Fionchadd steered them past Scott's camp, to a secluded cove maybe a quarter mile around the southern curve of one glassy finger.

He could see Bloody Bald from there, but only dimly, for a froth of oak leaves on a peninsula further north laid a veil of darkness across the view. He had deliberately refrained from seeking it earlier, for fear of what he might find—like a phantom palace consumed in raging flames.

"Well," Brock huffed, when they finally halted on a relatively clear stretch of sandy marge, where a small stream ran in from the mountains to the south, "I don't see no boat."

Fionchadd smiled cryptically, then ambled over to where a rotten stump braced a fallen limb, leaving a dark hollow beneath. He squatted there briefly, only to rise again with something in his hand. Brock's face lit up when he saw it, and David too felt a thrill of wonder—and recognition.

"We're going in a . . . *toy* boat?" Myra choked.

"Not if that's what I think it is," David giggled.

"One like it," Fionchadd admitted. "I retrieved it from a secret place while you slept." He held out the object for inspection.

It *was* a toy boat, or appeared to be. More properly, it was a model. An exact replica of what most resembled a Viking longship with a small central cabin, the whole thing no more than a foot in length. It was made mostly of wood, and every detail was depicted, from the incredible delicate carving on the dragon-head that graced the prow and the spiraling tail at the high-curved stern, through the thread-fine rigging, to the line of tiny shields along either side.

"No oars," Piper remarked, to David's astonishment. Even more amazing, Piper's eyes were dancing.

"That is where *you* come in," Fionchadd replied. "But not yet."

"I'm not gonna ask!" Myra muttered. She whipped her black cloak around herself with a theatrical flourish and slumped down on a stump, sipping from the coffee she alone had had sense enough to bring along.

"You have seen this like before," Fionchadd told David and Liz, as he slipped down to the water's edge and set the boat gently in the shallows. "You have seen a ring much like these two as well," he added, raising his hands to display matching bands on each fourth finger: a silver Our-obouros with blue eyes on the left; a golden, red-eyed one on the right. He scratched the gold one affectionately, then extended it toward the boat. Brock hissed in alarm, and Myra too cried out, as the tiny head opened its jaws and vented a spark of flame. The fire promptly ignited the miniature rigging, and an instant later the entire vessel was ablaze. "No!" Myra groaned, reaching forward. "If you didn't want it—"

David caught her before she could do anything rash. "Watch!" he urged with a smirk. "I did exactly the same thing first time I saw it."

"If you say so. . . ."

"Oh, Jesus, man!" Piper breathed behind them. "It's . . . *stretching*!"

And so it was. As the model burned, so it expanded, growing larger and larger by the second, so that less than a minute later it was the size of an actual vessel—a hundred feet or more end to end, and fifteen at least across the beam. The mast brushed the overhanging treetops. It had also drifted further from shore, so that it now rode high and proud fifty or so feet out.

"Son of a bitch!" Piper mouthed.

"Not what I'd have said," Myra retorted. "But I know what you mean."

Brock's eyes were big as saucers. "How—?"

Fionchadd's face knotted in a resigned scowl. "I see I am going to spend this entire voyage fielding questions, but the simple answer is that the ship was made mostly of Fire, and in order to make it smaller, that Fire was removed. When I relit it, the flame was restored. It is quite simple, really."

"Right," Brock snorted. "Yeah, sure."

"Think freeze-drying," David suggested absently, turning his gaze toward Liz. "You're remembering, aren't you?" he continued, more quietly. "The way you and I first did it on a ship like this—place like this too, actually."

Liz responded by blushing.

He kissed her impulsively.

"Uh, I hate to mention this," Brock broke in, "but . . . I thought we were going to the coast."

"We are," Fionchadd assured him.

"This is a long way from there," Brock persisted. "And that's a mighty big boat, and I don't think there's a river big enough to hold it up here. . . ."

"Not here," Fionchadd agreed. "But somewhere *be-*

tween here and Faerie. It is for that I require Piper's aid.''

Piper started. ''Me?''

A nod. ''You have your pipes, have you not?''

Piper first looked shocked, then stricken, then despondent. He shook his head.

Fionchadd scowled at him. ''But how do you propose to learn tunes if you do not have your pipes?''

Piper studied the ground.

''Never mind,'' Fionchadd sighed, with a wink at David. And with that he returned to the place from which he'd retrieved the ship and drew out something far less wieldy than a toy boat, and far, far larger. It sprawled across the Faery's arms like a nerveless octopus. A set of pipes. *New* pipes, to judge by the gloss on the wooden drones and chanter, and the bright plaid fabric those pipes were set into. Uillean pipes, too: for there was also a shiny new bellows.

Piper's mouth dropped open. ''These—'' he began, then faltered. ''These are fit for a—''

''A king,'' Fionchadd finished. ''Which is convenient, for it was a king who wrought them.''

''But. . . .''

Fionchadd peered up at the sky. ''Not now. We must hasten. I have talked too long and the Worlds draw apart. If I would set us on our path aright we must hasten.''

Alec gazed about anxiously. ''Aife. . . .''

Fionchadd puffed his cheeks, then closed his eyes. An instant later, a familiar yellow shape darted toward them through the bracken. Alec picked her up and stroked her. She purred.

''Seems to me,'' Liz drawled, ''that you and that cat, which you claim to hate, are getting along better and better.''

Alec bared his teeth.

Fionchadd cleared his throat. ''Come, oh talkative ones, our vessel awaits.'' And with that he strode into the lake.

David followed. So did the rest. The water had almost reached David's chest (it was cold, too, and he wondered what they were going to do about dry clothes) before he was able to snare the rope ladder hanging down the side halfway back. He eased left to let Liz and Myra ascend before him, with Fionchadd assisting them aboard, then clambered up himself, ahead of Alec and Piper. Alec handed up Aife. Piper handed up his fine new pipes. A moment later they were all on deck.

Fionchadd slapped his hands against his gray-clad thighs—which were already, David noted sourly, dry. "Now, Piper," the Faery said. "I will whistle a tune, and that is the tune you should play."

Piper eyed him warily. "I'm not that good."

"The hell you're not!" Myra cried. "I've heard you reconstruct songs you heard weeks before note for note."

"I have faith in you," Fionchadd acknowledged. "Now listen."

And with that he pursed his lips and whistled a slow, plaintive air. Twice he repeated that melody, and by the time he had begun a third round, the new bellows were pumping, the bag was full, and Piper's fingers were dancing along the chanter.

And the ship was moving. Slowly, at first, and then more rapidly, it swung around in that narrow, hidden cove and eased into open water. David's heart sank, for surely this would put them in plain view of anyone watching through the glamour that shrouded Lugh's palace, and the last thing he wanted was for anyone there to know what they were about. Yet when they finally cleared the cove, Bloody Bald was gone.

So were the rest of the mountains.

A mist had risen around them, appearing so stealthily it was as though it had congealed from the very air. That air was glowing—or the lake was—and when David hurried up to the prow to determine which, it was to see the unmistakable glitter of a Straight Track lying upon sun-gilt water. An upward glance showed blue sky; a downward glance, the light of an unseen sun glittering on oddly transparent ripples. But all around was mist: mist that looped and whorled like certain all-too-familiar briars. And all the while, Piper kept on playing.

* * *

The interval that followed had the quality of a dream. The sky never gained a sun, but was otherwise unchanging. The ship glided smoothly. The fog showed no sign of dissipating, though sometimes the whorls and spirals roiling through it took on a different cast than at others. Piper no longer played—Fionchadd had told him to stop as soon as they came fully onto the Track, and had cautioned him not to amuse himself with trying to repeat that melody, and absolutely not to attempt themes and variations. As best David could tell, it had something to do with the Tracks having a certain resonance, and matching that resonance with the pipes. Magic was also involved, of course— Power, as the Sidhe would say—but whether that magic was born of the Tracks, the pipes, the ship, the tune, or Piper's artistry, David had no way of knowing. For himself, he was content to relax while they waited for their mundane clothes to dry—Fionchadd had found them loose tunics in the tiny central cabin. Liz had queried that, but the Faery had only smiled and informed her that he had far less Power than some of his tribe, had used it lavishly of late, and would rather the sky assumed the task of leaching water from fabric than his own poor humble self.

They'd also eaten: leftovers from the council, if David wasn't mistaken. And now, warm, dry, full, and relatively unharried, they followed Fionchadd's advice and slept, strewn in a comfortable pile in the bow; everyone—probably by design—in partial contact with someone else, as though to affirm their reality in the face of pervasive strangeness.

Fionchadd stood in the prow, watching. Once Brock joined him. Once, as well, did a yawning David, though he could think of nothing useful to say. And then, again, he slept.

Myra was in heaven. David could see that by the way her lips curved as her pencil raced over the pad of what was not quite paper Fionchadd had produced from the cabin-of-many-wonders. She looked incredibly content, too: curled by the gunwale atop a sprawl of thick, green-hued fur. She had long since relinquished her Tracking togs (the cloak and minidress had been a mistake, she'd been first to admit) in favor of a plain loose tunic of blue-grey velvet that had likewise come from the cabin.

David strained to peer over her shoulder—which always bugged her, though by now she ought to be used to it. "Looks just like 'em," he opined.

It did too. Fionchadd stood in the narrow angle behind the ship's prow, gazing forward intently, his profile like chiseled marble. Brock stood right beside him in precisely the same pose, long hair whipping behind, but little different otherwise, save for a stubbier nose. Myra had captured them exactly: two fine young men of two Worlds, both displayed in profile, both posed identically, with the intricately carved curve of the prow curling up and around and eventually out of frame. It was not the first sketch she'd assayed since the voyage began, nor would it be the last. Even with no landscape visible beyond the pervasive fog, she hadn't lacked subject matter.

"With a face like that," she confided, nodding toward Fionchadd, "I could fill up a thousand pages."

"Actually," the Faery replied with a troubled scowl, "I thought I was rather plain."

Myra snorted derisively and flipped the sheet over. David wondered what her next subject would be—Liz playing catch-the-string with Aife, perhaps (would the enchanted Faery woman admit to such frivolity should she ever wear her proper shape again?); or Piper polishing his brand new pipes; or Alec sunbathing in his skivvies when there was in fact no sun.

Instead, Myra rose, stretched, and sauntered over to stand beside Fionchadd. "One complaint, oh tour guide," she remarked with a wary chuckle, "not a lot of background 'round here."

"Soon enough," Fionchadd assured her, turning back to the Track ahead, then straining forward abruptly, as though he'd finally seen something there besides fog. "In fact, sooner than that," he amended, "if you do not object to drawing more ships."

Brock, who'd let himself be distracted from sentry duty by Myra's arrival, uttered a startled yip and clambered halfway up the carved figurehead—a dangerous perch for certain. "Brilliant!" the boy enthused. "Oh wow!"

"Wow's right!" Myra agreed. Then: "You! Dave! Fetch my pad!" As soon as he delivered it, her hand was back in motion.

David didn't blame her.

The fog had thinned before them, though it still loomed heavily alongside and aft, and the Track still glittered across the waves. David wasn't sure what he'd expected, but it wasn't a rugged semitropical coast crowned with more of the milky haze, below which, as in a harbor, a half-dozen ships similar to their own rode at anchor. Their sails were furled, but seemed to be white; and white-and-gold pennants snapped from their single central masts.

"Jeeze," Brock blurted, even more enthusiastically. "They're . . . hovering!"

And so they were: their keels fully exposed a bare hands breadth above breakers that seemed not one whit affected by what hung like silent leaves in the spray-filled air overhead.

Fionchadd squinted into the unaccustomed glare. "So are we," he told the boy, "but you are correct, and I am a fool not to have noted as much myself. I saw what I expected, not what I feared."

Liz squeezed in to David's right, likewise squinting at the vista that drew ever nearer. "Something wrong, Finno? You look tense as . . . as Aife when she's surrounded by iron."

Fionchadd's face was grim. "I feared this," he repeated through his teeth. "This Track does not emerge into the Seas at Lugh's coastal haven, which I went to more lengths than you know to avoid, lest we be detained there and questioned. I knew, however, that he was seeking other havens less subject to the vagaries of the Seas, which, like the Lands, are being eaten away by your World. I thought these were merely scout ships, but our sharp-eyed friend here says those ships hover above the water, which only ships made by the Powersmiths can do."

David frowned. "Is that a problem."

The Faery scowled in turn. "Lugh has few such ships,

and I one only because of certain . . . connections and certain kin. But those *are* Lugh's ships, and such ships always carry warriors. These are surely charged with guarding this new coast.''

Alec ambled up to join them. ''What gives?''

Fionchadd's scowl deepened as he turned back around, shading his eyes. Myra kept on sketching. ''Nothing, maybe, or maybe much, depending on whether they see us. But—Wait, they *have* seen us! Those on watch point this way.''

Alec yawned. ''So . . . ?''

''If they see us they will detain us. This is no warship and we are no warriors, not against those who crew those vessels. I—''

''—They're coming this way,'' Brock interrupted.

''Bloody Hell!'' Fionchadd spat.

David raised a brow and started to say something about the Faery having been around humans too long, but then he saw his face, which was growing darker and more worried by the second.

''We cannot let ourselves be stopped,'' Fionchadd gritted. ''Yet how can we elude them? Those are ships of Powersmith making, to cleave the air as well as the water, and such ships are swift indeed.''

''Great,'' Alec grunted. ''We've barely started, and already we gotta go back.''

''Or be captured,'' Liz countered ominously.

Fionchadd's brow furrowed in thought. Clearly he was thinking hard. Myra turned a page, having already filled one with drawings of the small fleet. She began another—unfortunately in far more detail, for the ships were much, much closer. Wind rattled the paper.

Fionchadd glanced down at it reflexively, then away—then back at the parchment again. His eyes grew large; a wicked smile curled his lips. ''Keep drawing,'' he commanded. ''Draw *every* ship; draw as though your life depended on it—for it may, and if not your life, your freedom!''

Myra gaped at him.

''Draw!''

"Fine!" And with that she returned to her sketching.

Fionchadd closed his eyes. He took a deep breath, then two more. His shape began to waver, then to contract and expand in odd directions, as he quickly became a totally different creature. An erne, it appeared: a sea-eagle; the largest David had ever seen. Before David could do more than utter a gasp of protest, wind filled the Faery's wings and he was aloft, his clothes a shimmering gray pile on the planking. David followed his flight until he was a mere dark blot wending his way toward the approaching vessels—which seemed to be approaching more slowly now: very small comfort indeed. Probably that was a function of moving against the predominant flow of the Track. Maybe.

Christ, what did *he* know? All he knew was that their guide had deserted them, and unless the Faery was over there parleying, they were in very deep shit indeed.

Myra filled another sheet and kept on drawing.

David shaded his eyes but could make out little more than intensifying glare. The sun—*a* sun, anyway—had just burned through the mist and set the waves a-blazing as though they were strewn with powdered gems. "What's he doin'?" he asked Brock, even as he tried vainly to get his own eyes to focus, to recall that he did, in fact, have the Sight, and sometimes it was useful in situations like this.

Maybe it was, or maybe the air simply grew clearer. All David knew was that he located the erne flying toward the mast of the nearest vessel. Abruptly it swooped down, incredibly fast, then banked up again as quickly—but not before it had grazed the banner that whipped and snapped atop the mast. Men swore on the deck; he could hear them even at this range, and knew they uttered curses, though he didn't understand a word of their dialect. But by then the erne had moved on. Another banner suffered attack—which made absolutely no sense—and then another and another. By the time Fionchadd had strafed the fifth vessel, however, its crew was ready. Arrows flew, but none found purchase in their friend. Only one ship remained unassailed now, and Fionchadd was winging toward it.

But a whole phalanx of arrows greeted his arrival, and

he barely had time to wheel about and flee before they sliced the ether.

"I don't understand," Alec muttered, looking at David. "I absolutely do not understand."

"Magic," Brock replied. "Has to be."

Myra merely grimaced. "Wish I could freeze-frame some of this; that last would've made a great painting."

"Know what you mean," David acknowledged—just as Fionchadd touched down on the deck.

Something glittered in the eagle's talons. Several somethings, as it evolved: shards of thick bright cloth torn from those longships' banners.

"What—?" From Liz.

A whoosh of air was the Faery reclaiming his proper form; naked, save for the Ourobouros rings. "Give me those drawings—now!" he ordered, even as he found his cloak and fanned it across the planking.

Myra blinked once, then complied.

"Well done; oh, very well done," Fionchadd approved, as he sorted through the pile. There were four of them. "I am sorry to do this," he added, as he tore the depictions of the ships from the pad and arranged them in a certain pattern atop the cloak. "This is all I can think of—and we can only hope that those folk do not likewise employ painters."

Myra scowled her confusion, then shifted to a full-fledged frown as Fionchadd scattered the strips of fabric atop the drawings, connecting one to another. "Oh, *I* see!" David murmured, as the Faery rubbed the silver Ourobouros ring and brought the tiny dragon-head near one scrap of banner. A flicker of flame flashed out. The fragment ignited, as did the next and the next. The drawings beneath them soon did likewise, though not the Faery's cloak. An instant later, the deck sported a good-sized conflagration. White smoke billowed skyward. Fionchadd spoke a word that made no sense in any language David had ever heard, and glanced up apprehensively. Brock beat him to the prow by bare seconds. "Oh wow!" the boy cried. "They're on fire! And shrinking as they burn!"

David joined them, not daring to believe the boy's description. But Brock had been correct. The fleet, sure enough, was blazing—all but one vessel—and the rest really were contracting as those flames consumed them to the keels.

"Leaving one intact is a risk," Fionchadd grumbled. "I wish I could have claimed part of that one as well, but perhaps they will be busy enough saving their fellows."

"They don't shrink with the ship?" Alec wondered.

The Faery shook his head.

"And they can't just shapeshift like you did?" Liz added in turn. "Become fish, or birds, or whatever?"

"Some can, but that art is not as common among our kind as you seem to believe," Fionchadd returned. "Nor is Powersmith magic . . . compatible with that of Faerie on all occasions. Also, we are not precisely *in* Faerie, but rather in a realm nearby, and Power can vary with distance from one's native World. The rules do not always work the same from World to World, either. After all, you cannot shapeshift without assistance, but I can."

"And since none of your kind can draw," Liz chimed in, "it never occurred to them that you could bespell them that way."

"Well," Myra concluded flatly. "I'm glad to have been of service. Now if I can only remember how those ships looked, I can try to duplicate those sketches."

Alec gnawed his lip, then tapped Fionchadd on one bare shoulder. "Now let me get this straight," he began, "best I can figure, you used contagious magic, or whatever you guys call it, to hoodoo those guys. Those were Powersmith ships, right? So you used some kind of screwy Powersmith fire to . . . dehydrate 'em by remote control."

"Deflame 'em!" Brock corrected.

Fionchadd merely nodded and continued watching the fleet dissolve. "It was a risk," he repeated. "Not all risks end as fortunately."

"We're movin', though," David noted, "headin' out to sea. And the fog's back."

"Good," Fionchadd retorted. "That will hide us." He

whirled around, gaze fixed straight at Piper, who hadn't moved throughout the entire encounter. "Morry, my friend," he continued. "Forgive me, but it is time for another music lesson."

Chapter XV:
Weathering the Week

(Sullivan Cove, Georgia—
Saturday, June 21—morning)

"Le' me 'lone, Marshall," Scott mumbled into whatever mildew-smelling mess was draped across his face. "Le' me th' fuck alone!" Something was poking him in the ribs—poking with extreme vigor, too. He batted at it clumsily, one part of what passed for consciousness expecting to impact Marsh the ferret, even as a slightly more alert aspect rejected that hypothesis on the grounds that Marsh was too small to muster that much thrust, never mind direct it—again—into his ribs at that specific angle.

"Wake up, White Boy," someone giggled, followed by another, more forceful, assault.

"What th' fuck?" Scott sputtered, as he flung away the cover (it proved be a moth-eaten sweater, sufficient only for his face) and sat up groggily. "Oh shit!"

"Name's LaWanda, actually," LaWanda drawled, deadpan. Whereupon she squatted beside him and latched hold of his left ear, by which handle she proceeded to haul him to his feet.

"Do you *mind*?" Scott protested, applying pressure to her wrist, even as he sought to twist away. She fought him—it was an ancient game between them, but one he didn't feel like indulging just now, what with all kinds of bizarre foolishness flooding back into his brain. "I'm not in the mood for this, okay?"

"Just keepin' you humble," LaWanda advised, releasing him.

Scott massaged his injured appendage—and only then ventured to take true stock of his surroundings.

"Fuck," he yawned, "kinda hoped I'd dreamed all that."

"If I'm gonna be in *anything*," LaWanda informed him, "it'd be somebody's nightmare."

Scott yawned again and took quick inventory of the inert forms scattered across the floor. It didn't take long. He yawned once more. "Started out as twelve," LaWanda volunteered, "plus you, Dave's uncle, the Faery boy—and that cat, or whatever it is. Seven left, countin' us."

She seemed to be right, though it was difficult to distinguish people from piles of clothes, bedding, and miscellaneous defunct fabric. Calvin McIntosh, he determined finally, was the dark-haired lump beside the front door; Aikin Daniels, a surprisingly similar, though smaller, one by the back. "Looks like we've been well guarded."

LaWanda snorted. "Not and have eight more hightail it in the middle of the night without nobody knowin'."

Scott scratched his butt absently, and followed his nose to a large aluminum percolator sitting close by the freshly tended fire. It smelled sublime. "*Somebody's* got their head on straight, anyway."

"Not them two, though," LaWanda countered, pointing toward the less intact of the adjoining bedrooms. "Gary and Darrell in there, sawin' some *serious* lumber."

Scott managed a smile—which brightened considerably when he tasted the coffee. "And what's 'er name? Sandy?"

"Bathtub."

"And . . . the rest?"

A shrug. "Gone, like I said. Don't surprise me, really. Faery left a note."

Scott raised a brow. "Wanta show me?"

"Can't. I found it. I read it. It vanished."

"V-vanished?"

"Dissolved. Turned into glittery dust and sweet-smellin' air."

"Better'n the way this place smells," Scott sniffed, gazing once again at the grimy chaos of Dale Sullivan's abandoned living room. "So, what'd this note say, anyway?"

"That they were gone. That they'd *be* gone at least a week. That they wished us luck."

Scott scowled into his mug. Something pattered against the roof. He glanced up, then scowled more deeply. "Doesn't give 'em much time."

"Don't give any of us much time," LaWanda amended. "I—" She cocked an ear heavenward. "Is that *rain*?"

"If we're lucky," Scott mumbled. "I—Oh, shit!"

"What?"

"My stuff. My bag's still down by the lake. And all that other crap."

"So buy more. Tell that Mims guy your dog ate it."

Scott glared at her and stumbled to the nearest window. He just hadn't had enough sleep, absolutely not even slightly enough to keep somebody as wired as he usually was going.

He braced himself against a splintered window frame, set his cup on the flaking sill. And gazed out into Dale Sullivan's former backyard. The patter on the tin roof became more insistent. He loved that sound—normally. But not now, not when he had outdoorsy things to do. He squinted through the grime that patterned the cracked pane. This was a fine one—if you like showers: a good, solid all-day soaker, if he read the omens right.

"Piper loved rain," LaWanda murmured, beside him.

"No accountin' for taste," Scott chuckled. "Remember that time—"

"—He went out in the backyard in a goddamn downpour, got nekkid, and started soapin' himself and singin'? And we heard, and all got umbrellas and flashlights and snuck out there and surrounded him and then turned 'em on, with him in the spotlight?"

Scott couldn't help but laugh. "Those were the days."

"Piper . . . loved rain," LaWanda repeated. But this time there was a catch in her voice. Scott gave her impulsive hug. "Not *loved*, Wannie; *loves*. Don't worry 'fore you got to."

"Everything changes," LaWanda whispered, and turned away.

It rained harder; thunder rumbled with it, like distant ar-

mies on the march. "Startin' to think like Sullivan"—Scott
grumbled, not moving—"damn it."

The rattle on the roof muffled a series of clumsy thumps
by the front door. "Cal's up," LaWanda announced. She
cast one final wistful glance out the window, and departed.
Calvin had made it to the hearth and was sorting through
the amazing array of crockery scattered there, in quest of
a cup that didn't look too grungy. "What's the matter, Red
Man?" LaWanda chided. "Don't like roughin' it?"

Calvin rolled his eyes. "There *are* advantages to civilization."

LaWanda nodded. "Dishwashers. Coffee grinders. Fax
machines."

"I was thinkin' hot-and-cold runnin' water."

"We got *cold* right outside, Red Man."

"How 'bout hot biscuits, though?" someone challenged
from the back porch, right on cue.

For a wonder, Scott beat Calvin to the door, though he
had to step over the tight, black-clad knot that was Aikin
in order to open what passed for a back door screen. He
prodded the kid with a toe for good measure, in memory
of a certain interlude involving a certain Barnett's Newsstand and a certain enfield. God, but it seemed like ages
since then!

"Here," LaWanda grunted, shouldering between both
Scott and Calvin to relieve Dale Sullivan of the foil-covered
tray that filled both his hands. The smell tickled Scott's
nostrils, for the nonce more enticing than coffee.

"Biscuits," Aikin mumbled from the floor.

"Sorry I'm late," Dale apologized, as he deftly avoided
the slowly uncoiling doormat to join them inside. "Power
went out for a spell while these were cookin'. Hope it didn't
ruin 'em."

"Happens in the mountains," Calvin sighed. "I know."

"What does?" Sandy yawned from the door to the bathroom. She stretched languidly, and combed absently at her
preposterous fall of hair.

"Storms," Dale replied, handing her a biscuit (ham, by
the slab of pink-red meat hanging out on every side) and a
steaming mug. "Power's never been real reliable up here,"

he added, shucking a well-used raincoat. "Lines gotta cross lots of mountains, for one thing. And in spite of all these dams, *our* power comes out of Knoxville, so if anything happens along the way, out go the lights down here, more 'n likely."

Aikin was up by then—and so, at a minimal level, were Darrell and Gary. Food was already being consumed in heroic portions. There was plenty of yawning, blinking, and scratching of assorted body parts. And a *lot* of complaining about the weather.

LaWanda had returned to the window and was gazing out again. It was raining harder. Sandy joined her there. Scott was getting restless. But just as he started to insist they consider their situation, Sandy spun around abruptly.

"We've got this wrong," she proclaimed with conviction. "Bitchin' about the rain, I mean."

Scott stared at her as though she'd just turned purple. "It's a damned inconvenience, is what it is! You don't have to be out in it!"

"That's debatable," Sandy retorted. "But you're right about the other. It *is* an inconvenience."

Calvin's face lit up, as though he'd followed her thought, but had now raced ahead of her. "Oh, right! When it rains, it's hard to survey. It's also hard to work construction."

"And you can't run power tools without power," Aikin added brightly.

Calvin peered at Dale. "What's the forecast, anyway?"

Dale grinned back. "Rain for the next two days. *Hard* rain."

Sandy stroked her chin. "And what happens if it rains hard for two days? To the lake, I mean?"

A shrug. "Water rises—'less they open up the gates of the dam and let it out."

Sandy poked Scott in the ribs—he was getting damned sick of that, too. "Can you survey in the rain?"

"Not . . . well," Scott admitted. "And you really kind of have to have a crew. Other guy's supposed to be up here tomorrow—Monday, I mean."

"And what were you gonna do 'til then?" LaWanda purred.

"I was *gonna* go back to Athens, feed my pet ferret, and tell my friends I had this neat job workin' outside in the mountains. That was before I made a certain stupid promise."

"What *about* your job? Didn't you say something 'bout . . . prospectin'? Lookin' for gold, or whatever?''

Scott nodded. "Gotta pace the shore a mile either way and check out the stratigraphy."

"Can't pace no shore if the shore's underwater," LaWanda laughed, through the widest grin Scott had ever seen.

He gaped at her in confusion. "What, dare I ask, are you talkin' about?"

"Rain!" LaWanda chortled. "Rain here. Rain in Knoxville. Rain in all them places in between. Rain on the dams and the power lines. Rain on Ralph Mims and his fancy notions. Rain on two miles of lakefront property!"

"Oh hell yes!" Calvin chimed in. "Goddamn, girl, you're a genius!"

Scott stared at his mug stupidly, wondering if his batch of brew lacked some crucial additive that was making his companions think so bloody quickly. Himself, he didn't *start* hitting his stride until noon. Which was probably why Mims had been able to con him so easily.

Evidently Calvin noticed his confusion. "You don't get it, do you?"

Scott shook his head. "Fraid not."

"Rain!" Calvin echoed LaWanda. "It's rainin' now. When it rains, you can't get much outside work done, and neither can anybody else."

"And when it ends?"

Calvin's face split virtually from ear to ear. "That's just the point! It ain't *gonna* end—not as long as I have anything to do with it!"

"Oh, gimme a break!" Scott growled. "You can't make it rain!"

"Oh yes he can!" Sandy countered. "If he's thinkin' what I'm thinkin' he's thinkin'."

"And," LaWanda added with a thoroughly nervewracking cackle, "I'll bet I can help out too—but first I gotta call up my granny!"

(near MacTyrie, Georgia— Monday, June 23—early evening)

The Explorer's door slammed with the satisfyingly solid thunk of something new, expensive, and well-made. Calvin barely noticed it, so attuned was he to other noises—*natural* noises—like wind and rain and thunder. Next to them, the sloshy crunch of big all-terrain tires and the muttery growl of a healthy Ford V-8 merited no acknowledgment. White noise. Like the slap of windshield wipers. Like—almost—the sound of someone slogging across the muddy yard of Aikin Daniels's family's mountainside cabin to keep him company he wasn't sure he needed.

He'd never tell Sandy as much, however. Besides, she wanted to help; and, he very much feared, he—and everyone else he knew who'd gotten mired in this sorry enterprise—needed all the assistance they could muster.

"Hi!" she sang out with clearly forced cheeriness, as she ambled up behind him, where he perched on a chair-height maple stump on the north side of the cabin. He was gazing north, too—hadn't turned around. And he was frowning.

He reached up to grasp the hand she laid on his shoulder, but didn't otherwise acknowledge her. She was used to it. It was a necessary adjunct to psyching for the ritual.

"Have a good trip?" he murmured, to be polite.

"Not bad. Rained—of course. Otherwise . . . school was school. I begged off that self-study meeting and came on over. Figured we could find someplace to eat out when you're done."

"I'll need it. Fasting's not my favorite occupation."

She stroked his back. It was bare—all of him was, save where the white deerskin breechclout covered his loins, the garment a war-naming gift presented to him by Uki, his mentor in Galunlati. The hand halted shy of his waist-thong. Sandy knew better. Sex was a distraction. Women themselves could be, when a man was about . . . certain business. A mensing woman was anathema, because women's power was stronger than men's to start with, and with the bleeding came the need to replace that blood— figuratively, of course. Sandy was safe, as far as *that* went; they'd learned their lesson a couple of years back.

"What's the forecast?" he inquired, gazing once more at the sky. It was still raining, as it had since Saturday. Still, the storms hadn't lasted as long as predicted—damn it. He hadn't planned to come out here until tomorrow.

"Front's moving in," Sandy supplied, easing around so that he could barely glimpse her from the corner of his eye: a tall blond fire limned by sunset against the darker pines. "Clear weather behind, and cooler."

"How's the lake?"

"Up two feet, according to Scott. Nearly in the trees."

"He gettin' anything done?"

"Is he *supposed* to? No, seriously, he's being real careful to wander around outside a lot, be seen doing it, and be very wet when Mims's crowd happens by—thank God they gave him a pager. He's scribbled some stuff on maps to keep 'em happy, and he spends a lot of time showing 'em ore samples—which are really handfuls of dirt, since they basically don't know *anything* about geology. He's not giving 'em encouraging news."

"They takin' it okay?"

"Gettin' frustrated by the rain and the power-thing, but they're not giving Scott grief about it . . . yet."

"What about that other surveyor?"

"Scott told Mims to tell him to wait 'til the weather cleared up. Guy didn't seem to mind."

"Better and better."

"One problem, though . . . maybe."

"What?"

"They say that if they can't trust the power here, they may install their own generator."

"We'll have to see what we can do about that, then," Calvin replied, slapping his thighs. "Now, since you've gone to all the trouble to get here, I guess we'd best get started."

"Only as an observer," Sandy emphasized. "Seeing Newtonian physics debunked before my eyes isn't exactly *my* favorite occupation."

"Sorry 'bout that."

She pinched his butt. "No big deal."

Calvin took a deep breath and inspected the sky.

It was true, as he'd sensed was the case: the weather really was turning. And, he supposed, most folks hereabouts would be glad to see that happen, seeing how the rain had come down in absolute buckets for one day solid, and in nasty, wind-blown sheets for a day and a half since then. The lake was full. Streams were starting to finger their banks, while rivers reassessed their courses. The lowest-lying land was already flooding—including a field that belonged to David Sullivan's folks. Calvin regretted that—for all their narrow-minded, redneck ways, Bill and JoAnne were good solid people, and Little Billy was going to grow up to be exactly like David—but that was the price you paid. A little rain now could stave off a flood further down the road.

His job was to make sure that road was a whole lot longer.

In spite of his initial confidence, it would take considerable doing—if for no other reason than because he was going to attempt something no one he'd ever heard of had tried before. Being kin to who he was at Qualla, and knowing who he knew in Galunlati, he'd picked up more than a smattering of Cherokee—well, white folks called it magic, but he'd never liked that term, because it implied something unnatural, when it fact it was the centermost part *of* the natural world, as much a function of being alive as breathing. It was only when those forces were used for ill that there was trouble. And God—or somebody—knew he was acquainted with that aspect as well.

Still, he hoped recalling old things and refining them into new was more than the arrogance of youth, or the last ditch fumblings of the truly desperate.

Practically the first thing he'd learned from his grandfather was the formula his people used to turn aside a storm. He knew that formula worked, because he'd used it more than once himself *and* seen it used by others, and the way it worked was simple. Everything in the world was alive on some level, to some degree. And everything also, at some level, had human emotions and reactions to those emotions. Therefore, to turn a storm, you personified it. You told it that its spouse was fooling around somewhere else and it had better go set the matter straight.

That was if you wanted to *turn* a storm. What he wanted to do was to *bring* a storm—better yet, a bunch of storms— and tie them all together—in one place—for a good long while. Unfortunately the old Cherokee homeland—the southern end of the Appalachians—was the second rainiest spot in the lower forty-eight (after the Pacific northwest), and while it was possible the formula he needed existed, he'd never heard of one. He'd therefore spent the last two days designing what he prayed would be a workable alternative.

And now, at sunset (which was a Power time because it was a *between* time, which meant it partook of the essential essence of more than one agency), he was ready to to test his skill.

He'd already constructed his Power Wheel. It had taken some doing, actually. One usually drew them, or inscribed them on the ground, but that hadn't been viable this time for the simple reason that anything so rendered would quickly be washed away. He'd therefore dug one instead: a circular trench a foot deep and wide and ten feet across, with four equal spokes meeting in the center and oriented toward the cardinal points. It was full to the brim now, and running over, the water nigh as red as blood, courtesy of good old Georgia red clay. He'd placed sticks at the ends of those lines, too: staves from a graveyard cedar tree that had lately been blasted by lightning. Each stick also wore its designated color: red to the east (fresh deer blood for that, and no one had better ask how he got it); blue to the north (the juice of the year's first blueberries); black to the west (charcoal from the fire at Dale's house: *dead* fire to honor Tsusginai the Ghost Country, which lay in the west); and white to the south (white ashes mixed with bear fat). It would all wash away if he was successful, but that would merely transfer the power to the earth, and the power of the earth was one of the things he needed.

Taking another deep breath, he squared his shoulders and turned toward the east, whence came victory. Then, raising his head, so that his long hair tickled the middle of his back, he pointed one hand heavenward and addressed the sky. And though he'd carefully rendered the words in Cherokee, he'd first puzzled them out in English, which was still the way he thought them:

Yuhahi, yuhahi, yuhahi, yuhahi, yuhahi
Yuhahi, yuhahi, yuhahi, yuhahi, yuhahi—Yu!

(That *wasn't* English, or any other tongue, but it was necessary to attract the storm's attention.)

Listen! You have drawn near to hear me, O great storm, oh most magnificent ruler of the sky. It is a fine storm, you are: the very finest—so fine I would have you remain here so I may admire you. I have tricked you before, but I swear that I speak truth to-day. You act as though you would leave now, would follow the lies of some other shaman, but I say you should stay here. Your wife will be here soon, and she will bring her sisters! You should call your brothers and meet them and have a dance. Oh how the sky should dance! We will see how mighty you are! How magnificent! The Red Dog of the East will see you and know your might! He will see the red blood of the land which washes from your sweat, and lap it up like the blood of the hunt and be grateful. The Black Bird of the West will also see you, and be flattered by the blackness of the cloak you cast across the sun, dark as that Black Bird's wings. The Blue Fish of the North will see you and be pleased that you make more cold blue places for him to swim. And the White Tree of the South will see you and welcome the hot white trees of your lightnings and they will dance together. Hear me, O storm, and heed me. Hear me, O storm, for I welcome you and all your

*brothers here to these mountains, where I would have
you dwell as long as you like and dance!*

And so he repeated thrice more: once in each direction.
And at every quarter he pointed to the clouds that roiled
and rippled through the fitful air, and gestured them in a
long, slow circle, back to the center of the sky. And every
time, too, he exhaled a puff of his own breath, and stirred
it with the wind that was already whipping through his hair.

Twice he repeated that circuit, and then once more; and
every time he completed a rotation, the sky drew darker
and darker and the clouds piled thicker yet. Abruptly, the
rain returned, falling in sheets that slashed at Calvin's
streaming flesh like silver knives. Thunder roared, and
lightning seeded the clouds with naked electric pines. And
when that storm was fully involved in its fury, Calvin
stretched both hands as far above his head as he could and
swung them around in a circle, as though he would gather
the forces conjoined there—and with one final downward
sweep, pointed them southeast. *"Dance,"* he screamed, in
Cherokee, "Dance in Sullivan Cove!"

Three hours passed before Sandy could see well enough
to drive. They passed that time in Aikin's cabin putting an
end to all that fasting.

(Sullivan Cove, Georgia—
Tuesday, June 24—sunset)

Dale looked pretty damned funny, LaWanda reckoned,
with all those cobwebs in his hair. Shoot, the old guy
looked kinda like a spider himself, thin and kinked and
knobby as he was, and with his shoulders all humped over
like a spider's little head hung in front of that great big
lumpy body. He even had the eyes—spiders had lots of
'em, eight sometimes, or more. Except these were just
round designs in the bandanna he'd bound around all that
nice white hair.

Not that she looked one whit better, except she supposed
she oughta be a black widow, what with her black jeans

and black leather jacket and the screaming red tanktop she
wore beneath 'em; with her hair all done up in tight braids
just like a big mamma webster sittin' right up there on top.
Or maybe, she amended, like the scared little mate the big
mama 'widows were supposed to chow down on when they
finished fuckin'.

"If I'd known I'd be spendin' half the day slippin'
'round under buildin's," the old man chuckled wryly, "I'd
have wore me a hat."

He wiped at his hair for emphasis, then, for good measure, slapped gloved hands against the sodden gray walls
of his derelict woodshed. Dust flew, absorbed instantly into
air and soil that could scarcely become any wetter. The
ground squished in the space between them: as much mud
there as grass.

She supposed she shouldn't complain, as she joined Dale
in a mad dash to the superior shelter of the nearby smoke-
house. They needed rain, after all, and Cal had made it rain,
and now it was her turn. Besides, rain was a tribute to Piper.
She wondered how he was doing, never mind where he
was doing it. The point was, he'd gotten himself all caught
up in magic, and she knew he hated that stuff. It was a
tribute to *him* that he endured it anyway. But Piper would
do a lot for a friend—or a young, good-lookin', south Georgia JuJu woman—who was the grandchild of a JuJu woman
ten times over.

As Granny had reminded her on the phone, before she'd
told LaWanda what she needed.

"Get any?" LaWanda demanded, forced to talk louder
than she liked in order to be heard above the raindrop-rattle
on the roof. It made her voice go harsh and shrill: irritating
when she cultivated a low smooth rumble, half molasses
and half river grit.

Dale lifted a brow mysteriously, then smiled like a worn
gate creaking open and reached under his shapeless khaki
jacket to remove a large dusty jar with a screw-on lid.
Something moved in there: *many* somethings. Dark ones,
too.

It was full of spiders.

Hundreds and hundreds of spiders.

"Reckon that'll be enough?" Dale beamed, fumbling around in his pockets—which produced an odd-looking, extravagantly curved bowl-pipe and attendant matches. "If not, I reckon we can go on up to Bill and JoAnne's."

LaWanda accepted the jar and inspected it critically. Legs danced across the glass. The patterns they made in the dust there reminded her of those Celtic interlaces she'd seen so many of up at Lugh's. Tiny eyes gleamed like evil beads. Watching.

"Where'd you get all these?" she gasped. "Widows, too! Lots of 'em." She regarded him skeptically. "You didn't get *bit*, did you?"

Dale laughed: a sound like wood splintering. "Too smart for that—or my skin's too thick, one. Or maybe I ain't got enough juice in me to go to the trouble of suckin' it out."

"More like they could smell all that 'shine in you and didn't wanta get pre-pickled."

Dale eyed her warily. "What you gonna do with all these?"

LaWanda shook her head. "Can't say. That's part of the mojo. Granny says I can't tell."

"Guess it's what happens that matters," Dale mused. "Not the way you get there."

"I'll tell you if it works," LaWanda conceded, looking speculatively at the door. The rain had slackened. She thought she even saw a sunbeam out there. That would make Scott as happy as it would've dismayed Piper all to hell. Because that was one point nobody—including Scott, she was proud to note—had bothered making: that Scott thoroughly detested bad weather. Still, he was doing his part—or so he said. "Best way I know to make it rain," he'd confided last time they'd got together, which was that morning, "is for me to go campin' in a tent."

That's where he was now: scrunched up in that two-man out on the point south of the Sullivan Cove turnaround, watching the lake waters rise up above the naked rocky shelves that lined the shore.

Poor Scott.

Dale lit his pipe. "You don't need me, I'd best be goin'".

Gotta check up on the rest of you younguns. See what Aikin's learned on the Internet.''

"What was he tryin' to learn?"

"Anything he can 'bout Ralph Mims and Mystic Mountain Properties. And I think he was lookin' for something called *The Anarchist Cookbook*.''

"God," LaWanda snorted, "that boy really *is* serious."

"Rain's let up," Dale observed. "Don't know about you, but I'm ready to get outta here."

LaWanda slapped her hand down on a rickety shelf beside her, but cupped it in lieu of laying it flat, then curled her fingers around something that moved. "Got another one!" she grinned. Then: "You do what you gotta do; I gotta do my thing too!"

"No you don't, you little eight-legged motherfucker!" LaWanda warned thirty minutes later. She swatted at the inky mess of angles and baggy body that had just sent one of those legs probing toward the rim of the cast-iron bathtub in Dale's abandoned house, and knocked it back down inside.

And sighed.

Was she really ready for this? She'd put up the front, but now was time to pay the . . . the piper, she finished with a lump in her throat, as tears unbidden burned into her eyes.

Fuck this! she chided herself right back, and set the last of the half-dozen Mason jars on what remained of the linoleum floor.

Took another deep breath, and peered into the tub.

The bottom was alive: crawling with arachnids of every shape and size, from tiny little guys not as big as the end of her pinky finger to those godawful big wood spiders that looked like they could saunter right out of the kindlin'-pile and carry you off for dinner. There were black widows, too: lots of 'em, most of which had lived under this very house, and which all the others seemed to be respecting, to judge by the distance they kept from those hard, glossy legs and those evilly gleaming bodies, black as her brother's new Camaro.

There were flat spiders, too, and leggy ones, and spiders

that were all round abdomen; spiders that were naked, spiders that were furry, and spiders in between. There were
garden spiders in black and yellow livery, and fiddle-blacks
in sensible brown and gray. She'd even—wonder of wonders—found a comatose tarantula, which Dale opined was
one Little Billy claimed to have lost, that he knew JoAnne
had flushed down the john. Some of these fuckers could
sure hold their breath!

Rain rattled the roof again, and a leak jingled into the
corner, to establish a new puddle there.

Which reminded LaWanda of what she was about, which
was also what she'd been dreading. But Granny had told
her this was how it had to be. And Granny was always
right when it came to mojo.

Taking a deep breath, and muttering a short prayer to a
God whose attentions she generally preferred to avoid,
LaWanda Gilmore took off her muddy black shoes and
grimy white socks, rolled up her soggy britches to the
knee—and stuck her neat brown feet into that squirming
tub.

"Step on a spider, make it rain," she chanted, gazing at
nothing save her own grim reflection in a grimy mirror,
even as she felt things crunch and squish beneath her heels
and toes. "Step on a spider, make it rain," she repeated
over and over, still not looking down. Still trying, very
hard, to convince herself that this wasn't much different
than stomping grapes, save that these oozed the wine of
mojo out of their shattered shells.

Pain stabbed into her once or twice (but there was no
power without pain, Granny had advised); and she felt her
stomach give a nasty heave as her heel came down on what
had to be the panicked tarantula.

But it was already raining harder. And in honor of Piper,
LaWanda Gilmore smiled.

Chapter XVI:
Moebius Ship

(the Seas Between—no time)

David was getting royally sick of bagpipes.

He hadn't the vaguest notion how much time had elapsed since they'd hoodooed Lugh's vessels—six hours perhaps, or six dozen—but he hadn't expected to have practically every single spare instant since then soundtracked by caterwauling. He really *didn't* know how long that performance had lasted, either, because there was either no sun by which to determine such things, or the sun was *wrong*: too large, too small, or an odd color—like lime green. And while he knew it was all *one* sun viewed from the diverse Worlds that layered around the Track, still, the effect was damned disturbing. Never mind what those screwy light-dark alterations did to his circadian rhythms, which were clearly plotting serious rebellion.

He was pondering mutiny of his own. It wasn't that the music was bad—normally he loved the pipes, highland or Uillean either. But normally he wasn't stuck on the deck of a boat with a set being played nonstop—and a hundred feet was actually far too close when Piper really started wailing, nevermind that the relentless fog that shrouded every sight save sky, Track, and (close in) water seemed to amplify rather than inhibit. Shoot, he wouldn't have been surprised to see some vast leviathan rise out of the deep, drawn to what it mistook for a mating call. Hadn't Bradbury written a story like that, involving a lighthouse and a dinosaur? And hadn't the lighthouse suffered dire consequences when it failed to respond to that Jurassic hormonal urge? Or was he confusing the story with the movie based on it: *Beast From 20,000 Fathoms*, or whatever?

Misery, however, appeared to be loving company; certainly everyone else seemed to have sought the same solution he had, which was to cram into the stern and pray the sail screened out the worst of the noise.

Noise. . . .

Actually, it was pretty decent music, if you didn't have to hear it all the time. At least Liz and Myra had distractions: they liked to draw—which they were doing. Brock could evidently sleep through a Who concert. Alec had Aife—and cotton stuffed into his ears. Fionchadd was forward, listening raptly to Piper's playing. Which left David to sit and stew.

Dammit!

Eventually he could stand it no longer. He reached over to stop Liz's pencil in mid-line. "Remind me," he muttered, "to make Piper vet his promises through me next time."

Liz looked up from her drawing: Brock's bare feet rendered in excruciating detail. And scowled. "Thought you liked the pipes."

"I do! It's just . . . I dunno. It's like too much chocolate, or something. I think I've OD'd on it."

Whereupon the music ceased abruptly.

Liz started, then twisted her head down at an awkward angle, to peer beneath the sail Fionchadd had unfurled a short while back—mostly for appearances he said. It was red and wrought of a canvaslike material far coarser than most Faery sails. A silver chameleon was limned upon it in thick silver cord: an homage to the name Fionchadd had received in Galunlati: *Dagantu*, in reference to the way the Faery moved, all quick and deft and flickery—like a lizard.

"Oh, Christ!" Liz moaned. "He's passing the pipes to Finno. Please tell me he knows how to play."

David rolled his eyes. "I hope so, but I fear not. I think it's that art thing again: the one thing we're better at than they are."

Liz regarded him askance. "What about the so-called

Faery musicians that are always enchanting us poor mortals?''

"Stolen humans, I reckon. Hey, maybe that's what happened to Hendrix and Morrison. They're not really dead, and those were just sticks of wood left in their place.''

Myra's eyebrows lifted delicately. "Interesting theory, anyway.''

Liz nibbled her pencil. "All that stuff Pipe's been playing is *safe*, right? It's not supposed to do anything weird, like pierce the World Walls, or sort through Tracks, or anything.''

David traced designs on the deck with his fingers. "Finno promised him songs. I assume he meant songs he could actually use and enjoy. Therefore, safe songs.''

"He'll be the hit of the 40 Watt if he ever gets back to Athens,'' Myra drawled. "*If.*''

David pinched her leg. "I thought you were the eternal optimist—and here we are at the bare ragged start of what Finno says oughta take three days Faery time this time of year, and already you're complainin'.''

"You were too,'' Liz protested. "I—''

The rest of her words were drowned out by the most godawful screeching David had ever heard.

"Jesus Lord-and-Savior!'' David yelped, gazing around imploringly.

Brock still slept—though he *had* flopped over and folded his arms around his head. Alec grinned and forced the cotton further into his ears. Myra calmly reached into Alec's fannypack, secured the remainder of the wad, and proceeded to mirror his precaution.

David and Liz exchanged resigned glances. David had a sudden idea.

"C'mon,'' he hissed, grabbing Liz's hand. "Something I've been meanin' to ask you—''

Liz grimaced irritably. "Now?''

David gestured down the deck. "Would you rather listen to that?''

"I . . . see what you mean.'' Fionchadd was clearly not a very quick study.

"Don't do anything I wouldn't,'' Alec called too loudly,

as David and Liz sprinted for the tiny cabin that projected waist-high amidships, just behind the mast. The cabin-of-many-wonders, they'd termed it, for its ability to produce anything needed, from food, to clothing, to drawing materials, to—well, not sunblock, if Alec's fresh new burn were any indication.

David led the way down the short flight of steps and pushed through the thick carved door into the lushly carpeted space beyond. Silence enfolded them there, as complete as any tomb.

"Thank God!" David sighed, as he sank down against the nearest of the dark wooden cabinets that framed the low-ceilinged chamber. Liz joined him there, sitting opposite in lieu of beside. Which generally meant she was pissed but indulging him.

"Need a favor," he blurted out, before she had time to berate him for distracting her from her drawing. Evidently he had the most sensitive ears on the whole frigging vessel.

Liz's brow furrowed cautiously. "What?"

David fished into the neck of the belted tunic he'd adopted like everyone else but Alec, and drew out the medallion Brock had given him. It gleamed even in the dim light admitted by the thick frosted glass windows that lined the cabin's walls for a foot below the rafters. Impulsively, he raised it to his face and inspected it more closely. It seemed to have suffered no damage from having turned— or simply blasted—a Faery assassin's knife. And it really wasn't anything special to look at, bar an occasional hint of glow that was so subtle it might've been a trick of light. The boar relief on both sides was workmanlike, if vaguely Celtic in execution. Someday he'd have to find out why the Sullivans had claimed that for their emblem.

"What do you make of this?" he demanded.

"What do you?"

A shrug. "Kid gave it to me in the pool back at the castle. Said he bought it in England. Said somebody told him it was magic, and that it was supposed to offer protection against the Sidhe. It's my family crest," he added.

Liz frowned. "Odd coincidence, huh? Protection against the Sidhe *and* it's your family crest."

David nodded. "I thought so. And I can't say why I think this, but . . . it just seems like Brock's not bein' quite straight with me about it."

Liz's frown deepened, though she made no move to touch the medallion. David had removed the piece and cupped it in the palm of his hand, which rested on his thigh. "Would you like to elaborate?"

A long sigh. "Hell if I know. I mean, I know the kid's basically a straight shooter. Cal wouldn't put up with him if he wasn't, never mind Sandy, and sure as hell not Uki—and before we get off this boat, remind me to find out what he's been up to out there—or up there—or in there, or wherever Galunlati is from here. But anyway, I just thought I'd ask you as a favor, since I know you don't like to do this, if you could, you know, do a scryin' on it."

Liz exhaled wearily, but held out her hand. "I'm not very good at this, you know. It tends to come when it wants to, not when I do."

"So you've said," David returned. "Still, anything'd help. I don't want to accuse Brock of sneakin' 'round on me, but I don't want mojo around I don't know about, either."

"Ha!" Liz snorted. "Would that there was mojo we *did* know about! Now hand it over."

David was not entirely surprised to feel an odd reluctance thrill through him as he let the disc fall into Liz's palm and coiled the chain atop it. That accomplished, she closed her eyes and took three deep breaths.

David watched avidly—a little frightened. He hated to do this to her, but he also hated not knowing. Yet he also feared what he might find—

The door burst open. Light flooded in. Alec stood there, dark against the glare, and preposterously wild-eyed. "Dave!" he yelled. "On deck. *Now!*"

David started to protest—but then he saw the sky. "Oh shit!" he choked. "Forget that, Liz: come on!"

Liz blinked in startled confusion, like someone who'd barely awakened.

"Come on!" David repeated, as he grabbed her hand.

"Davy, what—?"

"Come on!"

"Davy, I—Oh shit!"

For Liz had seen it too.

He froze there, at the base of the stairs, shivering uncontrollably and staring at the sky—at the entire *world* beyond the gunwales, which had clearly gone totally, utterly bonkers.

It was black. It was white. It was gray. It was clear, it was cloudy. It was still, it was giddily awhirl. It looked like a TV screen trying to show dead air, a test pattern, and a kaleidoscope at once, save that all those hues were dark and grim and muddy.

Liz pressed against him, shaking; he clasped her back, and didn't mind a bit when Alec clutched him from the other side. Myra was also there now, face pale and drawn, fluffy hair flailing wildly in a wind that had roared in from nowhere with the force of a hurricane. Brock wedged in as well. A moment later, Piper likewise squeezed in beside them.

"What's goin' on?" David shouted.

Piper's face had gone completely blank—from surprise, or unadulterated terror, David didn't want to know. He still had his pipes, however; David doubted he'd ever let them out of his sight again.

"Piper?" David all but screamed through the still-rising wind. "What's up? Where the hell is Finno?"

"Trying to save your skins!" the Faery called from above and behind them. "Trying to atone for not attending to what I should have."

David twisted around. Fionchadd was braced atop the cabin, striving mightily to lower the sail. It didn't seem to be working. "Need some help?" David hollered, because that was what you were supposed to say.

"Nothing can help us now!" Fionchadd yelled back, releasing the line he'd been holding, which sent the sail crashing onto the deck, where it draped across the forepart of the cabin, revealing the dragon prow—and what lay beyond.

David's blood turned to ice when he saw it.

Nothingness! He was gazing at absolute *nothingness!*

A nothingness they were sailing into.

"Finno!" he shrieked one last time, though the Faery's face was less than three yards from his own. "What the fuck?"

"A Hole!" the Faery screamed, even louder than before—from necessity. "A Hole in the Seas where your World has eaten through!"

And then everything beyond the gunwale turned white.

"We aren't *anywhere*," Fionchadd groaned, when he reentered the dragonship's cabin. With seven of them sheltering there, it was approaching cramped, even with everyone being fairly slender, Brock being small for his age, and David somewhat less than average height. Alec, at five-ten and one-fifty, was by a slight margin the largest.

Still, however tight the quarters were, it was better than being on deck, where there was neither zenith nor horizon; neither right nor left nor up nor down visible beyond that hard arc of deep-carved oak and the graceful curve of the dragon prow.

"We can't be nowhere," Liz shot back—being practical because it kept her sane, David reckoned. He wondered how long they'd last—or how long they'd lasted already, given that time itself seemed oddly protracted, so that some words took whole minutes to complete, followed by entire sentences compressed to one quick, wavery burst.

Fortunately that didn't happen often, but David wasn't so sure they hadn't slept, or passed out, or . . . died. Certainly it seemed an eon since Fionchadd had explained their situation, and another since he'd gone back on deck to make certain. At least things had calmed down out there. At least the sky was no longer crazy—because there was no sky. No water beneath them either. And no Track.

But maybe the worst thing was Aife. Lugh's curse was that she be a cat in the substance of the Lands of Men for most of the time, only returning to enfield form briefly at dusk and dawn. But where there *was* no dusk or dawn, nor never was, apparently—whatever drove Lugh's magic had clearly slipped the bounds of control. One moment she was a cat, the next, an enfield, then the cat once more, and at times a bit of both, in the most outlandish combinations, and all the while venting the most ungodly screams, yowls, and whistles David had ever heard. He had a good idea what was prompting them too, given that his own experiences with shapechanging were nothing to write home about, comfortwise; in short, it hurt like hell. And to have that happening all the time, with no control, and with instincts winking in and out, and senses playing realignment games, and knowing somewhere at the heart of all that chaos a sentient intellect lurked—well, he hoped, if they ever got out of this, Lugh would consider this punishment enough and lift the curse.

Alec would probably go for that, too—assuming Alec, or anyone else, ever went for anything again.

At which point the whole of reality gave one final twisted lurch and stabilized. " 'Once upon a midnight dreary,' " David dared, in hopes sound was working as it should, which it presently seemed to be.

"We can't be nowhere," Myra objected, belatedly. "In all of space-time there has to be . . . *somewhere* we can be."

"You sound like Sandy," Brock snorted. "She'd eat this up with a spoon."

Liz snorted in turn. "She'd be scared as shitless as the rest of us, you mean. I don't think it's sunk in on you yet, Brock . . . but we can't get out of here—can we?" She gazed at Fionchadd imploringly.

The Faery's face was grim; his shoulders slumped. "I should have been watching," he reiterated. "Yet the last time I sailed this way, there were no Holes. And there has never been one so large so close to shore."

Alec glared at him. "You knew about those things and didn't warn us to look out for them?"

"Do *you* worry about krakens when you go to the beach?"

Brock scowled in confusion. "Krakens?"

"Giant squid," David supplied impatiently. "He means that you don't look for things where you don't expect to find 'em. And while I'm certainly not happy about bein' here, I don't think there's anything to be gained by pointin' fingers."

Fionchadd spared him a wary smile. "I suppose if I am to die, I could do worse than the six of you for company."

Piper, who'd withdrawn into a corner with his pipes, twitched at that and peered out from beneath his tangle of hair. "Die?"

"Eventually. It happens."

David shook his head. "No, I won't accept that. For any problem, there's a solution. We got into this thing from a physical place, therefore that place still exists, therefore the juncture between that place and this likewise exists. *Therefore*, we should be able to find it."

Fionchadd shook his head in turn. "You amaze me," he confessed. "In the face of all this, you still retain hope."

"I've got things to do," David sighed. "Folks're dependin' on me. I've got a kid brother I'd like to see grow up and go to college. I want to swim in the Cove again before whatever happens, happens. I don't want poor Scott and Aik and Calvin to spend the rest of their lives wonderin' what became of a bunch of their buddies."

"What do you propose?" Fionchadd challenged. "My power comes from my World. The further from my World I go, the less Power I can call upon. And here, I must tell you, the cord is stretched very thin indeed."

"I thought we weren't *in* a World," Myra countered.

"Stick a knife through an onion," Fionchadd replied. "Which layer is the blade in?"

Liz slapped her fist against the floor. "This isn't doing any good! We can sit here for what might be a pretty odd forever making neat little similes, but that won't help us get out of here. I'd prefer to come up with a solution before we all go apeshit from despair."

Fionchadd shrugged helplessly. "I have no Power that would do us any good."

"What about Piper's music?" Liz retorted. "Surely there's a song somewhere that'll get us—"

"They resonate with the Tracks, but there *are* no Tracks in a Hole—or else *everything* is a Track, as one of my mother's kin once implied," Fionchadd explained. "But

even if that last were true, it could take longer than you
have to live to locate the right set of tones.''

"Best we get started, then," David advised, looking at
Piper.

Piper shuddered and clutched himself more tightly.

Myra studied him for a moment; then: "Maybe sometime, but not now. No, folks, there has to be something
else, some other means of finding our way out of here.''

Silence.

Breathing.

Aife, who'd stabilized as an enfield, vented a pitiful
whistle that ended on a disturbingly human note.

"Finding," Brock blurted abruptly.

David gaped at him. "What?"

The boy's face was all but glowing. "Finding. Myra said
we had to *find* our way out of here.''

"So?"

"So . . . I know a charm for finding.''

David's eyebrows invaded his hairline. "A charm . . . ?"

"Cherokee.''

David felt as though a vast weight had lifted from his
soul, though another part knew it was far too early to raise
hopes as faint as these. Still, it had worked before, if the
boy was suggesting what he supposed. Shoot, it had even
worked on *him*—had drawn his consciousness back to his
body when he lay dying in Uncle Dale's house, the same
night the house had been trashed beyond repair. "You got
a stone?" he found himself asking.

Brock promptly pillaged his pockets.

Fionchadd, meanwhile, was gaping like a fool—odd indeed on Faery features. David shot him a hopeful grin.
"That's what we brought him for, remember? Magic from
a different tradition than any of us are used to.''

Myra looked easily as confused as Fionchadd, but Piper
actually seemed marginally intrigued. Certainly the ball he
had contracted himself into had loosened.

Brock's face fell. "No go.''

"What're you looking for?" Myra wondered. "Maybe
I—''

"No," David broke in triumphantly, "I've got it! And

with that he removed the medallion he'd replaced around his throat, all that vague time ago. "Will this do?" he added, to Brock.

Brock reached for it, but David snatched it back. "I'll respect your privacy for now—such as it is, or is ever like to be—but someday you and me are gonna talk about this thing."

"Someday . . . we will," Brock agreed, as David relinquished his hold.

"I learned this from Cal," Brock confided, folding his fingers around the talisman. "He learned it—I think—from Uki, or his grandpa. I had to fake it one time, but that scared me a bunch, so I learned how to do it right."

"It?" Alec queried impatiently.

"The finding ritual. The *Cherokee* finding ritual. I mean, I know it's a long shot, since we're the ones who're lost, but—Oh, crap, I forgot something! This may not work!" He gazed expectantly at Fionchadd. "It's safe on deck now, right? If you don't go all vertigo, or something?"

The Faery nodded.

"And you can still steer this thing?"

Another nod.

"And . . . *are* we moving?"

"We were moving when we entered the Hole. All rules I know say that we should continue to do so until something stops us."

"So you should be able to steer this thing? To make it go where we want?"

Fionchadd wrinkled his nose. "I should—assuming I *had* a direction."

"And where was it we were going to start with?" Brock persisted.

"Annwyn—first."

"Why not back where we were?" Alec countered.

"If we're going anywhere," Brock replied with exaggerated patience, "It might as well be where we want to go, instead of back where we've already been."

"And," Fionchadd amended carefully. "It is possible we might actually gain time in the bargain."

Brock frowned for an instant, then set his mouth. "Okay

. . . everybody cool it for a minute and let me think. And—I don't know if it'll do any good, but maybe you guys oughta all hold hands or something.''

"Wish I had my ulunsuti," Alec grumbled, as he scooted in to complete the rough ring they were forming around the boy. He was referring to the magical seeing-stone he'd seen destroyed two autumns back—at the cost of one very important Faery life sacrificed to save him and David and Liz and Aikin.

David suppressed a giggle. "I thought I'd never hear you say that."

Alec didn't reply—possibly because Brock had glared at him. "Quiet!" the boy snapped. And with that, they all fell silent. David took Liz's hand in his left, Fionchadd's in his right. They were equally smooth, which in no wise surprised him. The Faery's, though, was stronger.

Brock, meanwhile, inhaled deeply and let the medallion slip through his fingers, then closed his eyes and began to chant softly in a language David had heard before but couldn't even vaguely claim to understand, bar the odd word or phrase here and there—plus some English Brock had been compelled to slip in. As the boy continued, he began to swing the medallion in a slow, wide circle.

Sge! Ha-nagwa hatunganiga Nunya . . . bright medal, ga-husti tsuts-kadi nigesunna. Ha-nagwa dungihyali. Agiyahusa . . . my way, ha-ga tsun-nu iyunta datsi-waktuhi. Tla-ke aya akwatseliga. Stanley Arthur Bridges digwadaita.

He repeated that thrice, then started over, this time in English:

Listen! Ha! Now you have drawn near to hearken, oh bright medal! You never lie about anything! Ha! Now I am about to seek for it. I have lost my way, and now tell me where I shall find it. For is it not mine? My name is Stanley Arthur Bridges.

That too he repeated thrice, before returning to bastard Cherokee. David held his breath, watching intently. He was also, at some level, trying to ease into a trance himself, even as he wished, very hard, for the desired effect to occur. Fionchadd, he realized, was sweating.

Brock had recommenced the English version, but nothing seemed to be happening: the disc still swung in the same wide circle.

Or did it? Wasn't the trajectory shifting the merest fraction? Wasn't it becoming more oval?

It was! Beside him, he heard Liz's soft gasp. She'd seen it too. And it really was altering, the oval narrowing into an ellipse, tending in one direction, as though unseen forces drew it there.

Fionchadd's face had also brightened as he stared at the disc with rapt interest. Hope showed there for the first time in . . . however long it had been. And if Finno was optimistic, they surely had cause for celebration.

Whereupon Brock broke off abruptly and opened his eyes.

The medal no longer moved, but neither did it hang straight down. Rather, it slanted slightly, but clearly, toward the cabin's aft port corner.

Fionchadd rose at once and opened the door, then closed it quickly behind him—just as well, because David still couldn't stand to look at that vast . . . nothingness out there.

No one moved for a long time—not until the cabin gave the tiniest of lurches and slowly began to realign itself along the axis indicated by the medallion.

Brock remained where he was, staring fixedly at what he had wrought. He was barely breathing and clearly trying hard neither to speak nor move. David felt very sorry for him. This was something they hadn't considered. The boy had shown them the way out—maybe. But who was to say how long that journey would last? And if anything disturbed their . . . finder, would he be able to repeat the procedure? Or had that been the Galunlati equivalent of a magical one-shot deal?

But then footsteps pounded on the stair, and Fionchadd thrust his head through the doorway, face alive with joy.

"I have lashed the rudder," he proclaimed. "Unless that medal lies, we should be free of here anon."

It was only then that David realized what had saved them. Cherokee magic. And iron—which was anathema in Faerie.

"Land ho!" Fionchadd shouted.

David roused himself from where he'd been napping in the cabin, wedged between Alec and Liz, with Brock at his feet like a puppy. (Why did that image keep recurring, along with that infuriating urge to pet him?) Myra sprawled behind Alec. Piper was as far from the stairs as possible. And snoring. Aife was a cat again.

"Wha—?" Alec mumbled. "Huh?"—as David jostled him on his way to his feet. David squinted into the half-opened doorway, still fearing what might lurk beyond. Fortunately, Fionchadd filled most of it, but the Faery was grinning like a fiend.

When David finally summoned up nerve to peek around him, it was to see what could only be night sky. That woke the need to press forward, leaving his companions to respond as they wished. Fionchadd gave him a hand up the stair.

"Son of a bitch!" David yipped, "you weren't lyin'!"

Nor had he been. Not only had they returned to tangible reality—waves, clouds, and the line of the Track between—but they had arrived within sight of land: an unbroken range of ominous, blood-dark cliffs that marched off to haze to either side, beneath roiling, night-lit heavens the color of tarnished steel. Even close at hand, the surrounding seas were black as ink.

"Do not look behind you," Fionchadd cautioned as they strode toward the prow. "The Hole—or *a* Hole—still gapes there. But already it grows smaller."

David needed no second warning. If he never saw anything like that again, it would be too soon. "Is that . . . Annwyn?" he ventured, wondering why he felt compelled to speak so softly.

Fionchadd nodded. "Arawn's realm. The Lord of the Dead, some of your folk call him, though they are wrong.

But Annwyn *is* a dark land, compared to Tir-Nan-Og. The sun shines there but dimly, and the light is often tinged with red. Grim land breeds grim thoughts.''

David folded his arms. ''So now that we're here . . . ?''

''—We seek landfall at a place where I hope Arawn will not find us. I do not fear him, precisely, but I fear what he might have to say about our mission. He—like most of our kind—would prefer the Powersmiths kept to themselves. The last time they interfered, he was not pleased.''

''I remember,'' David acknowledged. ''I don't blame him.''

Fionchadd started to reply, then caught his breath. His eyes narrowed. He thrust David roughly aside and dashed to the fore-port gunwale, scanning the coast intently.

''What the f—?'' David commenced. But then he too saw. ''Ships!'' he groaned, as he joined the Faery. ''I guess it's too much to hope it's the good guys bringin' the welcome wagon?''

Fionchadd did not respond, but his shoulders were taut with tension. ''Those are Lugh's ships,'' he gritted, ''which alone would not delight me. But,'' he continued shakily, ''the nearest is the one we escaped when we began this voyage.''

''That's impossible!''

The Faery looked him straight in the eye. ''It is not. Who knows how much time passed in this World while we were caught . . . Between?''

''So they got here ahead of us?''

A resigned nod. ''And surely alerted Arawn. Even now they turn toward us.''

David suppressed a shudder. ''Will they take us captive, do you reckon?''

''No,'' Fionchadd spat. ''This time, I am certain, they will kill us.''

''*Kill us?*'' another voice screeched: Alec stumbling across the deck, face white with alarm.

Fionchadd drew himself up very straight, though he was still slightly shorter than Alec. ''We can fight,'' he declared. ''Or we can run. Which way would you have it?''

"Death now or later? Huh?" David muttered. "Be nice to have another choice."

"Tell me about it," Alec panted, as he skidded to an awkward halt. "Guess I oughta go get the others. It'll give me something to do."

David gaped in disbelief as Alec spun around in place and retreated across the deck. He would've shouted something scathing in his wake, too, had not Fionchadd restrained him with a firm grip on his shoulder. "Any action is better than none, and we have spent much time of late pondering impossible options."

David rolled his eyes. "I noticed."

Fionchadd regarded him levelly. "So what *do* we do? Run, or fight?"

"*Can* we fight?"

"They outnumber us."

"Then we run."

"Fine. Now . . . *where* do we run?"

"What do you mean?"

"They may very well catch us on the Track. But we have another choice; one they dare not make."

David's mouth popped open. "Not—"

The Faery nodded. "The Hole."

David had to brace himself to keep from shaking. But then he saw the confident, almost triumphant light that filled Fionchadd's eyes. "It means aborting our mission."

"It means . . . *redirecting* our mission," the Faery corrected. "There are still ways to contact the Powersmiths. The one I chose was only easiest."

"Galunlati!" David breathed.

Again Fionchadd nodded.

David braved another glance at that dark coast. And the ships—which had clearly grown closer.

"If Lugh's ships are here ahead of us, that means it's . . . it's several days after we left, though it doesn't feel like it. Which means that by the time we get back, we'll have lost a whole fucking week!"

"True. And our friends will be expecting us."

"But we can't reach Galunlati from here?"

A shrug. "I think not. For that, we must go through your World."

"Not even with the Hole?"

"I would not risk it."

David thought for a long, cold moment, during which the ships grew closer still. "Well," he announced at last. "I'll keep everybody belowdecks. You just . . . do it."

And with that, he strode back to the cabin.

Chapter XVII:
Secrets Squirreled Away

(Sullivan Cove, Georgia—
Wednesday, June 25—midday)

"Yo! Scott Gresham here!" Scott sang into the receiver, trying to sound cheerier than he felt. Actually he ought to sound fairly decent, since he was dry for a change, and the incessant rain was barely a distant patter here in the Enotah Arms Motel, where Mims had thoughtfully relocated him when the tent (along with the peninsula on which it was situated) had succumbed to a surfeit of water. Langford Lake was three feet higher than it had been four days ago. Which was enough to utterly drown the shoreline; which was enough, period, if Scott had any say.

"Mr. Gresham!" Ralph Mims returned, through a very uneven connection—likely a function of the ongoing deluge, as was practically every other electrical or electronic glitch that had plagued north Georgia since certain friends of Scott's had started doing things that weren't possible with the weather.

The phone staticked again—Scott had to thrust it away from his ear to hear. Marsh the (illegal in a motel room) ferret nipped at his bare toes. "Scott?" Mims barked. "You there?"

"Right as . . . rain," Scott responded. "Uh, sorry."

"Not your fault." Mims didn't sound happy, though. Nor should he.

"So, what's happenin' down in the Classic City?" Scott inquired with politeness as forced as his salutation.

"As far as things that concern you immediately, not a

lot. It's raining—no surprise there—this is Athens, after all.''

"Right," Scott agreed sagely. "You know what they say? Skies of gray: rain's on its way; skies of black: rain on your back; skies of red: rain on your head; skies of yellow: rain on a fellow—''

"Etcetera, etcetera," Mims finished irritably. "So, I take it there's no progress?"

Scott shifted his weight to his other foot and took a sip of the lone Sam Adams Porter that remained from the stash Aikin had spirited up from Athens on his last supply run. "Uh, not as much as either of us would like, I'm afraid. Lake's up another six inches since the last time you checked in, and the bank—by which I mean everything that was exposed rock, dirt, or sand when you and I first got here—is completely covered. Locals say that's not too unusual, and they're not complainin' much, 'cause they know how dry it can get up here. They say the lake's been a lot further down than when we saw it, too. This just balances out."

"Shitty timing, though."

Scott started to nod, then realized how stupid that would be. "Uh, yeah," he mumbled. "No way I can do any prospectin' in this, either. Never mind get out to the mountain itself. What little shore was accessible is gone now; it'd be like tryin' to dock with a glass-brick wall. Shoot, you'd fall off if you weren't careful—if you didn't wash away. *If* you could find somebody willin' to take you out there in the first place. Apparently folks *value* their boats up here."

"May have to buy one, then," Mims retorted. "If worse comes to worse, we could always write it off."

(*And would you write me off too?* Scott wondered. *If I went down with that goddamn write-off boat?*)

"Scott . . . ?"

"Sorry. Got distracted."

"Anything else?"

Scott shifted his weight again. "Well," he began carefully, "I've been tryin' to figure out some good we can get out of all this delay, and one thing that occurs to me is that it might help the . . . the prospectin'."

"How do you mean?"

"I was supposed to check the shore for potential gem-stone nodes, right? Well, I happen to know that those big sapphires you were talkin' about were found in places where lakes like Langford have gone down after flooding. I won't bore you with the technical BS, but basically . . . they wash out of the ground."

"What about amethysts?"

"That's a different matter—not that they don't wash out too, but the good ones you usually gotta dig for. I'm gonna keep checkin', though. Gonna raid the local library."

"Gotta get you on the Net, boy."

"Any time."

"Got some news down here, too," Mims volunteered after another round of pops and crackles.

"Oh?"

"Real progress, actually. Architects called today and said they'd finished a revised set of blueprints for the marina and landside facility. Had 'em already started, actually—that was the set you saw. Just have to adapt 'em to what's really there. In the meantime, they blew up some Landsats to get the shoreline and scale, then scanned that plus those photos we took into a computer along with those plans, and *voila*: instant 3-D resort. Except for the Mountain Lodge, I mean."

"They look good?"

"I dunno. They're up there, I'm down here. And unfortunately, they're scared to download a copy to me 'cause of these frigging power fluctuations."

Scott's eyebrows lifted slyly. "Oh, so it's all on disc then?"

"Plus a model and a couple of printouts. But essentially . . . yes. You oughta run over there and see 'em if you get the chance."

Scott coughed in lieu of reply.

"Anything else?" Mims prompted. "This was mostly a check-in call. I'll be back up tomorrow. If it clears, I'll meet you in town and we can zip out to the lake together."

"I'll look forward to it," Scott lied.

"Anything else?" Mims repeated. "Beer, maybe? *Good* beer?"

"I'd take some of that," Scott acknowledged, with a wicked grin. "Bye."

He was still grinning, if somewhat ambivalently, when Calvin ambled out of the bathroom where he'd been showering. "Cal, m'man," he called with far more enthusiasm than that stiff, awkward conversation with Ralph Mims, "have I got some news for you!"

"You gonna nurse that soldier all night?"

Aikin bared his teeth at Scott from across the cheap lamp table upon which the two of them, for the last hour, had been playing five card stud, and raised the bottle of freshly-imported Sam Adams to his lips with casual deliberation, eyes never leaving Scott's face. Not a good poker face, either. Aikin had won every hand. The motel TV showed ESPN with the sound turned down. Calvin was sprawled barefoot and shirtless on the king-sized bed, maybe watching almost-local boy Bill Elliott silently lap Dale Earnhardt: an event that would've set dyed-in-the-wool Ford man David Sullivan jumping around and cheering. Or maybe Cal was snoozing. Or getting himself psyched for his latest round of mojo-making. Certainly Cal hadn't eaten (so he'd said) since that morning. But what Cal didn't know was that Aikin hadn't either. Or slept, or engaged in anything even vaguely sexual (mostly five-finger Mary these days), or done anything else Cherokee ritual claimed was proscribed.

Yep, he was officially here to bring Calvin certain botanical supplies. But that wasn't the only reason. And he supposed it was time he got to it.

"Four nines," he announced, and laid down his hand.

"Fuck me!" Scott spat, and dumped his three eights in the trash can by his feet, pushing the pile of pennies that had been the pot straight off the table and into Aikin's lap—and the ugly green shag carpet.

Aikin made a point of ignoring them. He cleared his throat. "Cal," he called, stretching over to rap their third conspirator on the ankle. "I've been thinkin'."

Calvin didn't move, save that his eyelids twitched, and his irises shifted sideways beneath them. "Dangerous thing, in one so young."

"You got me by two, last time I noticed—*old* man—but seriously. . . ."

Calvin lifted a brow.

Aikin leaned back in his chair and puffed his cheeks. "I've been thinkin'," he repeated. "And it occurs to me that you may not be the best man for what we were plannin'."

The brow didn't move.

"Yeah," Aikin went on uncomfortably; he didn't know Calvin well, and if the truth were known, was a touch in awe of him—anybody who was quieter in the woods than he was deserved a certain measure of respect. Which didn't change raw facts when you had 'em on your side. "Uh, yeah. See, I think the basic idea's fine—in fact, I know it is. But . . . I think I oughta be the one to execute it."

Calvin's lips barely moved. "You?"

A nod. "Uh, yeah. See, folks don't know you up here—not many, anyway. And most of the ones who do know you, even to sight, live over 'round Davy's folks' place. Plus, I, uh, hate to say it, but you're pretty distinctive lookin', which means folks are likely to remember you, and the last thing we need is for anybody to draw attention to themselves, 'specially where you'd need to be."

"So?"

"So . . . I'm local. I grew up in MacTyrie. I'm over there all the time, even now. And folks're used to me sneakin' 'round. They wouldn't think anything about it if I was prowlin' through a graveyard or something. You, they'd—"

"—Arrest," Scott concluded, cooping Aikin's beer in lieu of retrieving a fresh one of his own from the tiny 'fridge in the corner. "Actually, Aik may be right. After all, the hard part's not the doin', it's the gettin' in and out."

"Or there and back," Aikin supplied. "You'd be conspicuous as hell on your bike."

"A bitch in the rain, too," Scott noted.

A shrug. ''So Aik can drive me over in his truck, let me out, then circle back to get me.''

''Score one for the Red Man,'' Scott remarked.

Aikin glared at him. ''But Cal—''

Calvin fingered the uktena scale on his bare chest reflectively. ''No.''

Aikin felt a surge of anger, which he quickly suppressed. The last person he wanted to lose his cool around was Calvin. He chewed his lip for a moment, then took a deep breath. ''Give me one *good* reason.''

''It's dangerous.''

''So was drivin' up here in your famous rain.''

Scott looked up from rummaging through the trash can in quest of the cards he'd forsaken. ''He's got you there.''

Calvin scowled. ''I know why you really want to do this.''

'' 'Cause I'm the best person,'' Aikin shot back instantly. He'd anticipated that one.

Calvin shook his head. '' 'Cause you're magic-obsessed, but you've only done it that one time, when the Wild Hunt got after you, and you didn't get to enjoy it then; whereas me and Dave have done it a lot. It's something me and him share that you and him don't. Part of that chip-on-the-shoulder, I-was-the-last-to-get-to-Faerie bullshit thing.''

Aikin felt his anger striving to return, this time far more forcefully. He swallowed hard, refusing to be baited. ''I was a fish too,'' he growled instead.

''Did you enjoy it?''

''Didn't have time!''

Calvin snorted.

Another deep breath, and Aikin tried a different tact. ''Look at it as furtherin' my education. I'm a forestry major—''

''—Another point for the Aikster,'' Scott put in.

Calvin eyed him warily. ''Whose side are you on?''

''The angels, of course,'' Scott smirked.

Calvin lifted the scale and ran a speculative finger delicately along one milky-clear edge. It looked, Aikin thought, like a palm-sized fish scale cast in semitransparent resin, bar that red inclusion at the root. ''I shouldn't,'' Calvin muttered, "and I'm probably stupid if I do, but . . . okay. I mean, I wouldn't want you to *cry*, or anything—and it really would be a pain if I went over solo on my bike—conspicuous to park, awkward to change, and bitchy weather all. But," he added archly, "*I'm* gonna drive the getaway car."

It was Aikin's turn to protest. "Nobody drives my truck!"

Calvin slipped the thong that secured the scale from around his neck. "No pain," he grinned, "no gain."

"I feel for you both," Scott giggled. And fell silent.

"Twenty minutes, max," Aikin emphasized an hour later, as Calvin eased Aikin's pickup to a crawl beside the parking lot of the MacTyrie Tastee Freeze. It was midnight, and the lot had been deserted since eleven—not that it would've mattered; Aikin had tinted every window in his S-10 absolutely to the legal limit. And Calvin, at the wheel, could've been his twin—when you glimpsed them in the dark through a layer of smoke-colored film. Cal was taller, of course (so was everybody else—including David—Aikin admitted sourly), but that didn't show sitting down; and with his hair pulled back in a tail, their 'dos were nearly identical—especially since Calvin also wore one of Aikin's trademark black sweatshirts and the floppy khaki hat his friends, to a man, fairly loathed.

Aikin wasn't wearing much at all—Calvin had advised him not to—just black sweatpants and shirt, and cheap Chinese slippers. Stuff he could doff or don in a hurry.

Calvin was watching him too, with a mixture of amusement and irritation and . . . genuine concern, as best Aikin could determine. "Any time," Calvin prompted. " 'Less you've changed your mind. . . ."

Aikin didn't answer. Rather, he closed his eyes and felt for the scale that now lay oddly warm against his chest. A deep breath, and he clamped his fist around it—hard. Per Calvin's instructions, he tried to ignore the fine clear pain building there, where the edge sliced into the heel of his thumb; and focus instead, first on his breathing, then on the beast he would become.

They'd discussed a number of options, but in the end had settled on something both obvious and easy—with the caveat Calvin had already stressed three times on the trip down MacTyrie's main drag.

He had to have eaten the target beast, of course; but he was a wildlife major, and had actually tasted quite a number of unlikely critters, furred, winged, and scaled alike. And while it was best if the prototype had roughly one's own mass, Aikin didn't think your garden-variety Georgia whitetail would be the optimum choice for the middle of a very small town, while 'gator and German shepherd had too many other limitations. Unlike Calvin, he hadn't sampled cougar or bear; but either would've been completely over the top anyway.

Instead, he thought small: soft gray fur, white belly, and tiny bright black eyes; ears like folds of velvet, and nimble paws, thick strong haunches, and a tail like a twitchy plume erupting from the end of his spine.

For a long moment nothing happened, and he was on the verge of opening his eyes when he felt a wash of heat spread up his arm from the scale—a rush that was followed by a conflagration and far more pain than he'd ever experienced, in far more places than he'd ever imagined he possessed. Calvin had warned him about that too, so he tried not to think about it; tried, instead, to focus not on the process, but the result: on what a very fine squirrel he would be.

If he ever finished changing. Maybe—

The pain intensified, threatening to drown thought—and Aikin suddenly felt *everything* collapsing upon itself, as though his skin were shrinking across muscle and bone, forcing them to compress along with it. Except that parts were being forced out too, at odd places like the base of his spine. Weird notions awoke in his brain and started nagging, and it was suddenly hard to think like a man at all, because trees had become important all at once, and nuts, and—God? what was that awful smell? Was it *Calvin*? Or synthetic velvet upholstery, or motor oil, or Oreos, or what?

And then reality clarified abruptly, and he dared open his

eyes (and wasn't that weird: to have eyes on the side of such a preposterous honker?), and inventoried those odd new senses.

And would've probably spent the next hour doing the same, had Calvin not powered the passenger window down and reached over to give him a solid tug on that elegant flag of a tail.

Reflex sent him to the window sill before decision did, and the quickest of backward glances showed his clothes slumped in the seat, with the scale gleaming approximately where his own human hands instants before had been.

And then the night seduced him, with an orgy of sensory overload he'd in no wise expected, and before he knew it, he'd leapt from the car to the soggy parking lot tarmac.

For a miracle, it wasn't raining. (Cal had wondered about that too: whether his and LaWanda's workings were running down, or if the forces they commanded were only off regrouping.) And for a bigger and more fortunate wonder, there were no stray dogs hanging around the dumpster behind the restaurant.

But Aikin scampered swiftly anyway, across the Tastee Freeze lot and into that of the building next door: a brand-new prefab cedar-shingled A-frame someone had trucked in the previous Friday, above the door of which a sand-blasted wooden sigh proclaimed *Mystic Mountain Properties*. Perhaps, Aikin considered, it should've read *ground zero*.

A mechanized roar behind him made him scurry toward the nearest tree before he realized it was only Calvin, per plan, driving away. Which gave him twenty—twenty what?—Oh: minutes. Yeah. Sure.

Aikin felt a chill at that, for he could already feel his humanity slipping, as those instincts necessary for rodent survival kicked in major-league and threatened to overwhelm his own, more subtle, ones. And since reflex was on the ascendent anyway, courtesy of Cal's little yank, he had to work to remember who he was and, more importantly, his mission.

Mission . . . ?

Right. He studied the darkened A-frame critically, con-

firming what Cal had told him from his own afternoon re-
connoiter. The roof beams angled close to the ground on
two sides: an easy leap for a squirrel (and awkward for
your average derelict hound, which was also a considera-
tion); a ventilation stack showed up top, of the sort that in
working hours spun leisurely, but this time of night was
stationary.

Aikin was amazed at how quickly he arrived. Shoot, getting around in this shape was virtually the same as thinking!
No way his clumsy human bod could've navigated an
equivalent slope and surface so rapidly, with so much facility.

The vent was another matter; mostly, he realized, because the squirrel wasn't all that fond of touching bare
metal. He overrode those instincts, though, and poked his
nose inside (Gosh, but whiskers were useful!), then his
sharp-nailed paws, after which the rest of him followed
without volition.

Disorientation lasted but an instant (he was, after all, upside down), before he let those clever new reflexes carry
him a couple of feet further, then twist him sideways to
emerge in the A-frame's rafters. The rest was a piece of
cake, and before he knew it, he was crouching on the
thick (and rather tacky) shag carpet taking stock of Mystic
Mountain's portable two-room office-cum-showroom-cum-
architecture lab. The front was clearly a reception-and-
display area: richly but sparsely furnished, with a plethora
of posters and brochures on the walls depicting other Mystic developments.

His goal, however, was in the back: the office proper.
And fortunately the door wasn't fully closed—a good thing
too, because he'd just realized he hadn't brought the scale.

A pair of leaps took him there, and his human aspect
uttered a satisfied, silent "Bingo!"

Cables, cables, everywhere, and also a right nice fax, he
chanted to himself, amazed on one level at how playing
stupid doggerel through his mind helped keep the human
part of that mind ascendant. Which was a good thing, because there was a bloody lot of stuff in that room that made
him mad as hell (never mind what it would've done to

David)—and emotion was anathema to intellect. It was hard to keep your cool, though, when you were confronted with things like photographs of Sullivan Cove overlaid with corporate trademark graphics. Like maps of the place all over the walls, with color-coded push-pins stabbed through 'em. Like an incomplete but perfectly executed scale model of what had to be the marina. Like an official-looking checkbook protruding from beneath an expensive leather ledger. Like the bloody blueprints themselves.

It was an embarrassment of riches. And he had less than twenty minutes in which to mine it.

Okay, then: first things first. He'd start with maximum damage, then work his way down to the peripheral stuff.

And that means you, Mr. . . . whatever brand you are. (*Expensive*, is what they were—though neither of the machines bore any obvious logo.) And with that, Aikin checked to see if the computers were connected to a UPS (both were—smart, given the incessant thunderstorms, but a slight complication to his still-evolving plan), then leapt for the nearest such accessory and neatly flipped it OFF. That accomplished, he slipped around to the keyboard and took quick stock of his situation.

The machine was on but in SLEEP mode. Good: Now he wouldn't have to fiddle around with passwords and such. It was also pretty stupid, he had to admit. Then again, he doubted Mystic's pet architects expected what amounted to industrial sabotage to be effected in what they surely regarded as an ignorant little backwater town. *Trusting fools! Probably figured making a couple of backups was enough!* Which wasn't getting anything actual accomplished. Sooo . . .

Aikin studied the keyboard—difficult, given it was roughly twice his own size—but had little trouble turning on the monitor: a nice big presentation type, worth about $2,000. *Even better!* It was a program he knew—already up and running. Obviously these folks used these machines for one purpose only. It was therefore short work to call up the main menu, determine which was the primary CAD program, move from there to what he presumed were the architecture files, then the project folders—and delete the lot. Piece of cake, actually—except for the fact that it took most of the force he could muster to mash the keys (squirrel arms were apparently about as strong as human fingers), and hitting the SHIFT key with a foot while stretching for others with his paws took a bit of ingenuity. Too, the screen seemed the size of a movie screen—from his point of view. But it worked pretty damned well, all things considered.

Except that it was just too easy. Until he recalled something he'd heard in class one time and promptly stashed in his "interesting information not to be acted upon" file. Something he'd never actually considered doing. Still . . . a man (or a squirrel) learned from experience. Had he been human, he would've grinned fiendishly. As it was his lips barely moved (though that certainly didn't hold for the rest of him) as he hopped and stretched and skipped across the keyboard. Various prompts appeared, and then the one he wanted. FORMAT C:, he told the machine, and answered YES to the assorted queries as to whether that was what he *really* wanted to do.

And then it was simply a matter of watching in smug (if somewhat guilty) awe, as the main hard drive erased itself.

Trusting fools! he thought again as he repeated the operation on the second machine. Teach them to underestimate mountaineers! Still, he didn't quite trust his own efforts. Plus, who knew what sort of backups might be around? Therefore, he proceeded to first gnaw through every power cord in sight, eject all disks from the various drives, then chew the hell out of each one with his fine new incisors, before knocking it to the floor.

And then he found what was surely rainbow's end indeed: a plastic box completely full of tapes. A squirrel wouldn't know what to make of such things, but Aikin was rather more than your basic .22 fodder, and it was thus but a few seconds' work to flip that container open, then thoroughly unwind, gnaw *and* scratch *and* excrete upon the entirety of its contents.

That accomplished, he chased the awful plastic taste from his mouth by chowing down on a good chunk of the top two sheets of the ledger, then clawing the rest for good measure. Ditto the checkbook and blueprints, which he also knocked to the floor beneath the computers.

Finally, he played Godzilla vs. Tokyo with that nice little balsa wood model—tasted better than paper, anyway.

And just as he was departing, he noted something that made him doubt even his own remarkable luck.

The computers rested on a narrow counter set against a wall, adjoining the larger one that held the ledger and the thoroughly splintered model. But the model-builder's supplies were conveniently stored nearby: on metal shelves hung from the wall above the various components. And those supplies included a pair of squeeze bottles of Elmer's glue along with a number of plastic jars of acrylic enamel.

Teeth made tidy little holes near the bottom of each container, and a tad of main force-plus-dexterity, with more than a little gravity thrown in, put all those viscous substances to leaking directly atop those much-abused keyboards—and the main drive units. He even tipped a jar of Insignia Red into the fax machine, whence it dripped neatly onto the scattered blueprints like thick electronic gore. With any luck the combination would gum up enough of the works to cause Mystic Mountain a good couple of days delay—replacing equipment and programs, if nothing else. And while they might still have backups—well, any delay was better than none.

Yeah, Mystic Mountain Properties would be in for a surprise come morning.

And, as best he could tell, it was time to get going. A quick scamper brought him back into the front room, and a glance at the clock there (not as easy to read as he'd hoped, courtesy of that weird-ass nonbinocular vision) told him he was in fact dead on time.

It was more than a little disconcerting running straight up the A-frame's vertical front wall, but that was easier than trying to manage the slanting sides. Even better was the fact that there was a ventilator screen up in the point he hadn't noticed before, which made getting out far less problematical than getting in. And since he was now accustomed to those strong new choppers and knew that any damage done them here, short of actually breaking one, would be repaired when he shifted back to human form, he made short work of chewing through the thin metal mesh.

And was outside a minute later.

Not a minute too soon either, because the set of headlights that had just blazed into view from where the driver had been circling a small town's worth of blocks belonged to a certain black Chevy S-10 with heavily tinted windows. It slowed as it approached the Tastee Freeze but didn't turn into the lot. Aikin plotted an intercept course across Mystic's skimpy yard and onto the sidewalk beyond, but deliberately held off on the final run for home and let the S-10 pace him. That was also part of the plan. Though there was obviously no evidence of human involvement in the Mystic Mountain vandalism (He'd been careful to leave a nice selection of rodent tracks, and how many squirrels had fingerprints on file anyway?) there was still an element of risk in letting his truck be seen cruising by a crime scene twice in one evening when he was supposed to be a hundred miles to the south. On the other hand, it wasn't really safe for a squirrel to go frisking down a semi-rural sidewall by his toothsome lonesome late at night. The solution was for Calvin to tail him half a block, thereby affording a modicum of insurance, then let him in.

That block was ending right now.

Calvin stopped for the red light there, and Aikin availed himself of that additional run of good fortune to scramble up the running board and through the passenger door Calvin reached across the seat to open. As soon as Aikin made landfall in the right-hand bucket, he commenced digging through his scrambled clothes, questing for the scale.

"Lookin' for this?" Calvin teased, just as the light changed again, and the truck moved on. Something vitreously bright dangled from the fingers of his right hand.

Aikin's heart rate doubled, and before he could stop himself, he'd leapt up and sunk those fine strong incisors of his into Calvin's nearside pinky.

"Son of a bitch!" Calvin yipped, and dropped the scale to the floorboards. Aikin grabbed it there, drew blood from both front paws, remembered how pissed he was about Cal's bullshitting and having to surrender his truck—and with those emotions as guide, swiftly reverted to short, compact, dark-haired normality. Before they'd reached the middle of the block, he was fumbling back into his britches.

"Mission accomplished?" Calvin inquired casually, reaching into his jacket.

Aikin nodded smugly, too full of himself to continue being pissed. "Mission accomplished."

Calvin merely grunted—and tossed something small and round in Aikin's direction.

It was a year-old walnut.

Chapter XVIII:
When the Ship Comes In

(the Seas Between—no time)

David's fingers had barely brushed the heavy gold filigree handle of the half-open cabin door when he heard a hard, dull thump, followed by a sharp hiss from Fionchadd. He froze, trapped in mental stasis, wondering whether to proceed as he'd intended, which was to warn the rest of his comrades that their oh-so heroic embassy to the Powersmiths had just been aborted before they'd even made landfall in Annwyn, or to pivot back around and determine what could possibly make someone as jaded as Fionchadd mac Ailill gasp in what had sounded, the more he considered it, like alarm.

One affected his fate potentially more than the other, and so he turned.

And saw nothing that could've prompted that reaction: only the prow of the dragonship riding high on a dark Faery ocean, with a line of barely paler cliffs bobbing up and down beyond, beneath ominous red-gray clouds. "Finno, what—?" he demanded, his tread fearfully loud on the broad oak boards as he pounded back to the prow.

As David had been himself bare seconds earlier, Fionchadd likewise seemed locked in uncertainty. He'd clearly intended to hasten to the tiller in the stern, so as to ease the ship around and flee—retreat rather say—back down the Track toward the Hole that had so recently coughed them forth. But something had caught his attention in midstride, and so he remained in place: torso facing half-aft, head twisted left, to peer back over his shoulder.

"What—?" David repeated. But then he saw.

An arrow protruded from the arc of rail heretofore obscured by the bulk of the Faery's body: a slim white bolt that had pinned Fionchadd's slender hand firmly to the dark, unyielding wood. David ducked instinctively, even as he crossed those last few yards, fearing that arrow might be vanguard of others—he knew better than to underrate Faery archers. Yet even as he risked one quick glance over the side—toward that troublesome fleet that had just forced them to alter their plans—Fionchadd vented an agonized groan and tumbled to the deck, the bolt now free, but torn halfway through his palm.

"Oh, God, Finno, *no!*" David wailed, as he scooted around beside his injured friend. He reached reflexively for the arrow—then paused, lest he do more damage. The tiller then? Could he steer this craft back into the Hole? Another peek over the rail gave neither hope nor comfort. The fleet was still out there, making no move toward them, yet showing no sign of preparing to depart. On the other hand, somebody over there had just shot this ship's captain. And if Lugh's folks knew who else crewed this vessel—like a bunch of inept humans—they'd have no reason for haste: could reel them in at their leisure.

A final check showed someone hauling at what David supposed were anchor lines; still, no one seemed inclined to rush. Christ, only one person was even looking their way! David could make him out but barely: a tiny shape with an even more minuscule bow.

A moan from Fionchadd jerked him back to that far more imminent matter. "Finno . . . ?"

"The . . . arrow," the Faery rasped, face tight with pain. "Help me . . . pull it out!"

"I'll have to break it!" David warned, as he reached for the thin white shaft. It looked like bone, he noted absently. And the bloody head seemed one with the rest of it—as, now he checked more closely, did the fletching.

Fionchadd's other hand flashed up to stop David's, even as he brushed the bolt. "No!"

"But—"

The Faery's eyes were huge, though whether with pain,

fear, or possibly some other emotion, David couldn't determine.

"It'll hurt more," David cautioned.

"I accept the pain, but . . . this is important."

"Whatever you say." And with that, David knelt down across Fionchadd's wrist just above the injured hand, and thus braced; took the shaft in both fists—and pulled.

The Faery's already pale face turned paler yet, and David actually heard Fionchadd's teeth grind together as that arrow slid slowly through flesh. Raw bone grated against what *looked* like wrought bone, and blood spurted around that juncture in tentative gouts. It didn't smell like human blood, though; it was far too . . . sweet.

And then all that remained was the fletching. "Hold on just one more second," he admonished through clenched teeth of his own—and using most of his strength, jerked the shaft the rest of the way through.

Fionchadd relaxed immediately and vented a long, soft sigh. Already his face was clearing: lines of tension that had made his features look almost human swiftly blurring away. David sat back on his haunches, staring at the arrow in disgust. It was covered with blood. *Faery* blood. The blood of his most loyal friend from all that strange, troubled World. Sick with anger at . . . at all this incessant chaos and violence, he supposed, he twisted around to fling the bolt overboard like the tainted thing it was.

A hand restrained him even as he rose: Fionchadd's hand—the good one. The Faery's eyes were bright with shock.

"No!"

David let him drag his arm back down, staring at his friend in dumb amazement as Fionchadd slowly freed the arrow from his fingers and laid it on the deck. "Watch!" Fionchadd whispered.

David did—wondering what he was supposed to see. Wondering, more to the point, if they had this much time to burn. "The fleet—" he prompted anxiously.

"Will wait . . . I think. Long enough, anyway. I—"

A noise from beside them drew their attention. Something was up with the arrow. The blood was gone, for one thing—and it was moving: writhing and twisting gently upon the deck, like a snake seeking to shed its skin.

More and more like that, in fact, for as David watched incredulously, the arrow split down its whole length; something . . . disturbing happened to the air around it—and before David could voice even the shortest yip of alarm, a young Faery man lay there: naked, blond, and—even for a Faery—thin. The man blinked for a moment, uttered a terse "thank you," to the two of them in general, then turned his attention fully on Fionchadd.

"I have little time," that one gasped, "if I am to maintain the deception I have just employed, yet there are things I must tell you in that brief span." He took a deep ragged breath, then another, and seemed by his expression to be in more than a little pain himself. A final breath, as though he drank strength from the very air, and he spoke again. "The first thing you should know is that Arawn of Annwyn has sided with the Sons of Ailill in firm opposition to humankind—this I have learned since our fleet arrived at sunrise. His precise plans remain unclear, though I know that he considers Lugh's throne at risk and Tir-Nan-Og . . . ripe for picking—as your human allies would say," he added to David. But then his face darkened again. "I am certain Arawn will sail soon. I am not certain when he will arrive, for he distrusts the Seas. Ys watches. The Powersmiths stir, but no one knows their thinking nor dares to ask."

"I dare," Fionchadd challenged. "We were on our way there."

"You would never have arrived. Arawn had already set guard upon his borders."

Fionchadd raised a brow. "His throne is unsteady too? If there are those who plot against him, surely I would have known."

A wry smirk. "You trust too many, my friend; even as you trust too few. You are a true son of Ailill's body, yet you side with those who shamed him. You are half a Powersmith, yet you do not seek their arts or their Power. You choose humans as your allies, yet you support the mighty in Tir-Nan-Og."

"Wait a minute," David broke in. "How do we know we can trust *you*? Who are you, anyway?"

"You can trust him," Fionchadd assured him. "Names do not matter, but he has gambled much coming here, and his blood and my blood have mingled before, as they did in the arrow now. He is loyal to Lugh—and to me—in full degree, and he is cunning and clever but not strong in Power. He drained all his strength effecting that first change. He needed mine to recover."

David studied the stranger skeptically. "He . . . changed to an . . . arrow, and had someone shoot him over . . . ?"

"Someone else loyal to Lugh," the stranger acknowledged, "someone the Sons, should they learn of this, will deem a traitor."

"As they will you, my friend," Fionchadd noted softly.

A tense smile. "If we are clever they will not know of our deception. They will think the bolt that should have slain you failed"—he grabbed Fionchadd by the arm and stared him hard in the face—"but you must leave *now*! Let this vessel float a time, as though it were aimless; then, when you will, turn and flee. Take the Tracks. Dare the Hole—I care not. I had lost hope of even seeing you here, yet you came. I have risked much in helping you; do not let that risk have been in vain! I—No, I will not say it. No more time remains!"

And with that, he scrambled on hands and knees across the deck, and—after one brief check above the rail on the seaward side, rose like a spring uncoiling and leapt overboard.

David flopped back against the gunwale, gaze fixed firmly on his Faery friend. "What the *hell* is goin' on?"

"More than I knew, apparently. But it seems I have friends where I did not expect them—or at least they are not foes."

"If they're on Lugh's side, they're not on mine," David retorted.

"Some sides . . . face two ways," Fionchadd sighed wearily. "Sometimes even there . . . or four . . . or five."

"Strange bedfellows. . . ."

Fionchadd regarded him strangely. "Sometimes."

"So—can we trust him?"

A shrug. "He bought us time. He told us things we might find useful. He risked himself."

David surveyed the coast. "From what he says, though, those ships, that you said were piloted by Lugh's folks . . . were really crewed by the Sons of Ailill?"

"So it would seem. Whether that means mutiny, or treason in the ranks, I have no way of knowing."

"And that guy . . . ?"

Another shrug. "He will swim in secret back to that ship. He will regain his own shape—presumably with the aid of his friend, the trusted bowman. If both are fortunate, no one will be the wiser."

"And if someone finds out?"

"The Death of Iron, I suppose. That is the normal doom of traitors, and Arawn would certainly style them thus. I—"

"What're you guys *doing*?" Alec hissed from the top of the cabin stair.

"Wasting precious time," Fionchadd grumbled—and made his way, still hunched over below rail-level, toward the stern, where the tiller was.

David watched him go, even as Alec approached. Other faces showed behind, but David waved them back, then grabbed Alec by the leg and yanked him down. "Go get everybody," David ordered, "and tell 'em to run out here all crazy, like Finno's just been killed!"

Alec gaped for a startled moment longer, then complied. Myra, it evolved, proved especially apt at keening.

"I can't believe that worked," Alec breathed what seemed like hours later. "I absolutely cannot believe it!"

David gazed pointedly at the deck—better that than the chaos that had swallowed all view of the shore and the fleet behind them, or the nothingness that loomed ahead: there, in what he'd come to call the event horizon. Fionchadd was still at the tiller, which he could maneuver from below the rail—and would linger there a brief while longer. Annwyn was a tiny blot at the end of the Hole (odd that those things didn't necessarily lie flat upon/within the water, as David had always assumed they would, the few times he'd heard them mentioned). The Track was a glitter in their wake, save that closer in it had dissolved into a sort of crooked spiral that twisted around the sky before vanishing entirely. "Luck," David offered eventually. "Of which we seem to have more than our share, both good and bad."

Alec nodded glumly as he ambled across the deck. David joined him, laid a comradely arm across his shoulders and gave them an impulsive squeeze. It was the first time he'd done that in ages. He wondered, suddenly, how much they had drifted apart: victims of larger events; flashier, more demanding friends; inconsistent priorities and interests. He'd always counted on Alec's absolute loyalty, the same way he relied on breathing. But maybe he shouldn't take it so much for granted.

"Love you, man," he murmured.

Alec smiled wanly. "Just in case."

"What?"

"We don't get out of this."

"That's not what I was thinkin'."

"Doesn't matter," Alec whispered. "Love you too."

Silence.

And then, quietly, but clearly from Fionchadd. "It would be wise if you went below."

"If we weren't up to our butts in alligators," David informed Brock, "I'd make you answer those questions before I pass this over. I haven't forgotten your promise," he added, pointedly.

Brock snatched the medallion from David's fingers, smiling smugly, even as he composed his face to innocence. "Thank God for 'gators, then."

" 'Gators," Liz snorted from the cabin's corner. "This all started with one of them."

"There's one thing good about all this, though," Myra mused, with a sly grin at Piper, who was polishing his pipes in the opposite corner. She paused expectantly.

Piper evidently caught that cue and glanced up curiously, less wired than any time lately. "What?"

"We didn't have to stage a burial at sea for Finno."

Piper looked perplexed. "That would have been . . . very bad."

"Yeah," Myra gave back smugly. "I couldn't have stood another reprise of *Amazing Grace*."

Piper threw a drone at her—then looked appalled, scrambled after it, and kissed it in desperate apology. It was good, David reckoned, to see even that much sign of the pre-voyage Piper.

"Cool it," Brock snapped from the middle of the cabin, "you may think this finding-thing's easy, but it's not; I need your help if we're gonna get outta here."

David nodded. "Good point." And scooted over to join him.

"And a good *question*," Liz appended, "is where, exactly, are we going, anyway?"

"That could be a problem," Fionchadd admitted from the door behind them—beyond which David could once again see that awful colorless sky. He quickly turned away.

"How so?" Liz inquired.

The Faery shifted his weight. "I am not certain how our young friend's Power functions," he began. "But before, he had a name for the place he sought. The place from which we came—by which we entered the Hole, I mean—*has* no name I have ever heard. It is not Tir-Nan-Og, but a realm that lies . . . above it."

Brock fidgeted with a stray lock of hair, face tight with nervous anxiety. "Names have power, Cal says, but . . . that last time, I mostly just asked for the way out."

"Worked, too," Myra drawled.

Fionchadd ignored her. "I have been pondering that, however; and it now seems to me that it might be wisest to simply seek out Tir-Nan-Og. If we are fortunate, we will arrive well beyond sight of that coast. Perhaps if we then sought some other landfall than the traditional southern haven. . . ."

David frowned. "In that case, why don't we just return to our World and be done with it?"

Fionchadd frowned in turn. "We cannot—from here. The Hole began there . . . yet it has not burned *through* there. It is the same as . . . as swinging that medallion through the air. You can pass your finger through the places it has been, but not through the medallion itself.''

''Ah,'' Alec said. ''Like it's the laser beam that cuts, not the machine that makes the beam, only you can't have the beam *without* the machine.''

The Faery gnawed his lips, then nodded. ''I think so.''

''Yeah,'' David mused. ''But what about the Powersmiths? Couldn't it take us straight to them, without bothering with Annwyn?''

Fionchadd shook his head. ''To tell you true, I know little about Holes—none of us do. But one thing I do know is that they *cannot* take one everywhere, at least not directly. Were it not for Brock, we would be lost entirely, and even so, we have taken more risks than you know— and been luckier than you can imagine. As for this Hole, it is a Hole through *one part* of the Seas Between, yet as best I know, such Holes only touch the seas of Worlds close about them. The Land of the Powersmiths touches this World only in Annwyn, rather as Tir-Nan-Og touches your World; its seas touch other Worlds entirely. It—'' He broke off, shook his head. ''There are no words for these things in your tongue.''

''Well then,'' Myra told him sweetly. ''Someday you and Sandy'll have to invent 'em.''

''And there's not gonna be any someday,'' Brock warned, ''if you guys don't form a circle over here so we can get goin'.''

''Coast is clear!'' Fionchadd called from the deck. ''Come on up!''

''More you hang around us, more you sound like us,'' David chuckled, as he scrambled toward the cabin door. Liz was right behind. Lord, but she was good woman, to put up with so much . . . crap. They'd just escaped from a situation that didn't bear thinking about by the razor edge skin of their teeth—a situation that had him quaking in his boots, and nearly made him shit his britches, had he been wearing any. (They were all still slumming around in knee-length Faery tunics.) Yet she'd stayed cool throughout. Maybe it was a woman thing: strength under fire—grace under pressure, or whatever. Or perhaps it was just that Liz was a lot more sure of herself and of what she really wanted than he was. She lived in the present and found what pleasure she could there. He still lived, he feared, in his boyhood "someday" and "tomorrow" and "whenever." Not that he couldn't function in the real world, he hastened to add. It was just that there was so much he wanted to do, or had to do, or was looking forward to, or regretting, or dreading, that he rarely had time to afford *any* of those myriad possibilities the absolute conviction they deserved. He was like Alec and Scott, he realized, with a sick little twist in his gut: just some self-absorbed little brain-fried space cadet, going through the motions.

Whereupon Liz pinched his butt, which set him in motion of another kind.

The air, when a sudden breeze found its way into the stairwell, smelled like heaven. It was sheer bliss to be back topside, too; after another enforced, temporally-ill-defined incarceration in the dragonship's ever-more-claustrophobic cabin. Before he could stop himself, David had ducked between Liz's legs, hoisted her up on his shoulders, and was running laps with her around the deck. Alec joined in at once, grabbing Brock on the fly as they embarked on another lap. Myra snickered tolerantly. Fionchadd gawked in bemused disbelief. Piper grabbed his pipes and pumped up a jaunty reel.

David skidded to a clumsy halt and sank down, laughing. Liz tumbled off his back, laughing even louder. The ship rang with it: clear Faery air thrumming with human joy.

"Are we back?" Brock burst out. Sweat sheened his face.

Fionchadd rubbed his chin. "We are away from the Hole. I *think* we are where I desired, which is to say this is Faerie. Beyond that"—he shifted his weight—"truly I hate to disrupt all this levity, but . . . we are still in danger."

David froze on the verge of jumping atop Alec and giving him the thorough tickling his far-too-serious buddy clearly needed. He looked up, scowling.

Fionchadd's brow likewise furrowed. "These are the seas of Faerie. The shores of Tir-Nan-Og cannot be far off, for I smell that strand. But—There is no easy way to say it: I fear ambush."

"Ambush?" David countered. "Or interception?"

The furrows deepened. "Both, perhaps. Lugh still commands this coast, or did when we departed. The coast in the next World . . . up has apparently fallen to the Sons of Ailill. Lugh may know this, or he may not. There are circles within circles in this, and I cannot see them from far enough off to see them clear."

" 'Specially as you may be a circle yourself," David remarked.

"A very small one," Fionchadd returned. "You have far more true friends than I."

"It would seem, then," Liz said slowly, "that the smart thing to do is get the hell out of Faerie entirely and back . . . wherever."

"Our own world, I hope," Alec urged.

Fionchadd clapped him on the shoulder. "It would certainly be an attractive option."

"Okay," David declared, "let's do it."

Fionchadd caught his arm as he made to leave. "It is not so easy. I knew the tunes that took us on the journey we just assayed, but I had taken time before to learn them. From here . . . One *could* return to the Lands of Men from here, but no place useful. And then we would be bound by distances there, for the Tracks, as you know, do not lie everywhere."

"So where's the nearest?"

"The nearest that would be *helpful* would be the one where I found your company."

"The one out at Whitehall?"

"Aye."

David puffed his cheeks. "And we can't get there from here?"

"Not unless we go somewhere else first."

"Which would take time." David inhaled sharply, feeling suddenly very uncertain in his stomach. "What time is it, anyway? What day?"

Fionchadd studied the sky—though what he saw in all

that green-blue blankness, David had no idea. "Five days since we left."

"Five days! But we lost three days in the Hole!"

"And no time at all returning."

"So we're actually . . . ahead of schedule?"

"We have none to waste, if what we learned in Annwyn is true, but yes."

David grimaced sourly. "So basically what you're sayin' is that we've got time, but we've gotta hurry."

"I am saying that it is not wise to remain here long."

"Therefore we need to reach, optimally, the Track at Whitehall."

Brock gaped at them incredulously. "By *boat*?"

"Of course," Fionchadd acknowledged with a cryptic grin. "Do you doubt me?"

Brock shrugged.

David eyed Fionchadd askance. "And there's *no* way to get there from here? I mean, I'm *not* doubtin' you, or anything," he went on instantly. "It's just that I've noticed you tend to think a certain way—have to, I guess—and sometimes you ignore what to the rest of us seems pretty obvious."

"Other traditions," Brock summarized. "I could always use the medallion again."

"You could," Fionchadd agreed. "But"—once more he stroked his chin—"Actually, there may be something simpler—in this World, anyway."

David raised a brow. "Wanta tell us?"

Fionchadd turned toward Alec. "You are the only one here who brought anything beyond the cloths on your back from your World, correct?"

Alec's brow furrowed. "I've got my fannypack, if that's what you mean?"

"Well, then," Fionchadd prompted, "go get it!"

Alec regarded the Faery sullenly when he returned a moment later with the green nylon object in hand. Fionchadd pondered it as distrustfully. "Metal tape—zipper, I mean. Iron. Would you mind . . . ?"

Alec bared his teeth as he unzipped the pack and emptied the contents onto the deck. David was amazed at the diversity Alec had managed to secret in there—everything from a tiny pocket calculator through three packs of sugar to a bright orange condom, still in its (slightly mildewed) wrapper. Alec blushed but made no move to hide it. Fionchadd merely sorted through the pile. ''A-ha!'' he cried at last. ''I have found what we need.'' And with that, he held up what David took for a dark shard of broken glass.

Alec stared at him as though he'd just grown another head. ''*That*? That's just a point I made in an outdoor skills class.''

''Precisely! Something you made—presumably in or near Athens.''

Alec nodded dubiously. ''So?''

''There are several means by which Powersmith vessels navigate,'' Fionchadd explained. ''One is by music; one is simply by the tiller. There are some of which I may not speak, but one of which I can is that a weapon made by hands and placed in the dragon's mouth will lead the dragon to the place where that weapon was wrought—or close by.''

''So,'' Alec ventured, brightening, ''that edge I made two years ago might actually take us back to Athens?''

Fionchadd nodded. ''The Track at Whitehall, at any rate.''

Alec turned to study the dragonhead, then snatched the stone from Fionchadd's fingers and passed it to the startled Brock. ''Here, kiddo,'' he purred, nodding toward the carved prow. ''This is a job for a young man.''

The fog was back. Which was just as well, David reckoned. Magical landscape was fine if you had nothing better to do than watch it drift past a carved oak railing. But those landscapes were not always to be trusted, and more to the point, the very fact of their existence held alarmingly dark implications. Shoot, back home in Enotah County chubby redneck housewives were lolling in red plastic loungers, eating pork rinds and reading romances, while holding Camel cigarettes between fingers bright with cheap diamonds and red lacquered nails. Street kids in Athens were squatting atop garbage cans in front of Barnett's Newsstand, reading *Flagpole* and trying to panhandle enough cash for the day's first Mello Yello and Jolly Rancher. Lawyers were litigating over nothing. Legislators were trying to determine what constituted marriage.

And there was about to be war in Faerie.

War that *could* slop into the Lands of Men.

David wondered if Jesse Helms was ready.

He shifted in place, sparing the dragonship yet another cursory inspection, while wondering, not for the first time since they'd begun this (hopefully) final leg of their odd tour, if this was a good time to conclude a certain bit of business concerning Brock and an iron medallion. Or Liz and that medallion, for that matter—if he could get either of them alone long enough for serious discussion—*or* for serious scrying. Oh well, he conceded, maybe someday.

He sighed, inhaled deeply—and coughed.

Another breath, a sniff, and he noted the odors this time. Sure enough it bore the unmistakable scent of pine trees, diesel fumes, and (faintly) sewage. "Liz!" he bellowed. "We're back!"

Back, however, was surprisingly slow arriving, and day became night before the fog cleared entirely. There was at least one sunset-or-dawn in there too, to judge by Aife's brief transformation. Yet by the time the last wisp of clinging damp whiteness fell away from the vessel's flanks, and the ship itself began to slow, there was no doubt about it: they were sailing down the Middle Oconee—probably (and hopefully) near Whitehall Forest, to judge by the heavily wooded banks slipping silently by on either hand.

Fionchadd padded up beside him in the prow, even as they others likewise gathered round. "What happened to the Track?" David demanded, pointing across the river to the night-wrapped woods on the right. "Isn't it somewhere over there?"

The Faery grinned. "This close, in this vessel, we could . . . do a little sidestep."

"Hope nobody sees us," Liz grumbled.

"Silverhand's got spin doctors if they do," Alec snorted, but even he was smiling. In point of fact, he looked as

relieved as David had ever seen him. Piper wasn't the only
one who hated forays into Faerie.

"Far shore," Fionchadd advised, and trotted back to the
tiller. An instant later, the ship began to angle toward the
bank opposite that upon which, among other, more public
facilities, Aikin's cabin stood. Soon enough, it navigated
one final curve, and the dam hove into view: a low bar of
white beneath what was clearly a waning moon. And then,
before anyone truly expected it, the keel nosed into a sand-
bar a bare ten yards shy of the terminus of the dam, and
they were back in the Lands of Men.

David wasted no time climbing atop the rail in the shoulder of the dragonhead, from which he leapt down to the
warm, soft sand. He couldn't resist rolling in it. "Here!"
Alec called from the deck. "Catch." He tossed down a
large floppy bundle. His clothes, David realized, as he
sought to right himself; he'd forgotten to change out of the
far more comfortable Faery togs. "Thanks!" he grunted,
as Brock hit the ground beside him, followed by Liz, then
Piper, then Myra. Alec came last, bar Fionchadd.

No sooner had the Faery touched ground than he strode
toward the ship's prow, stroking his silver ring. The ensuing spark glimmered like a lost star in the night. An instant
later, the ship was aflame—

—and shrinking quickly indeed, as whatever odd Fire
bound it together dispersed, its eerie blue flickers barely
brightening the looming woods. In no more than ten breaths
time, Fionchadd stooped down to retrieve their former craft.
He passed it to Brock with a grin. "Here," he teased.
"You're the only one here who looks as though he ought
to play with toys."

Brock bared his teeth at him, but accepted the prize.

David was first back in mundane dress, first on the dam,
first off it, first up the steep brushy bank between the river
and the road, and first to the parking lot in front of Aikin's
cabin.

He halted there, out of breath and shaken. This was
weird—a little *too* weird, actually. It was as if time had
coiled around itself and restored them to where this latest
round of weirdness had begun. It was the same place, the

same moon—the expected cars in the parking lot (and a good thing, too, that latter).

Only . . . something had changed. The moon had waned: he'd already noted that. And—right: Sandy's Explorer was gone entirely, and Aik's truck wasn't where he'd left it when they'd picked him up before the Tracking Party. Which in turn reminded him, not for the first time, that Piper, LaWanda, and Cal were surely on somebody's shit list, given that at least one of them had clearly been elsewhere than Athens when they were supposed to be performing at the Earth Rights Festival there.

Which damned sure wasn't his problem. His most imminent concern at present was getting Aikin's attention without rousing his other roomies—two of whom, by their trademark vehicles, were still in residence, probably anticipating imminent graduation.

Alec, for a wonder, seemed to read his mind. "Aife," he adjured the cat meandering through the bushes behind them, "go find Aikin."

The cat blinked yellow eyes at him—then trotted back down the bank to where the rear deck of the cabin jutted into space. She melted among the shadows beneath that overhang, only to reemerge soon after atop it. Fortunately, one of Aikin's windows faced the back. A light was on in there.

Which meant he was likely up; odd, now David considered it, given the probable hour. Even so, it took three plaintive yowls and a set of meows to lure their friend outside—in full woodman's kit: cammo fatigues, khaki vest, and purposeful-looking boots—but minus his glasses, which made him squint into the gloom. "Aik!" David hissed. "Down here!"

Aikin eased over to the rail and knelt, peering through the uprights like a newly awakened mole. "Dave?"

"Among others. What gives?"

"Plenty," Aikin panted without preamble. "Scott called five minutes ago. All hell's breakin' loose up there."

Chapter XIX:
Storm Wrack

(Sullivan Cove, Georgia—
Friday, June 26—dawn)

"How much longer?" Alec inquired with absolute sincerity, leaning forward from the Mustang's back seat, in which, for nearly two hours, he, along with Aikin, had been ensconced. He sounded anxious too, and frightened.

David didn't reply—and not only because he was too tired to respond with the requisite snappy comeback and too worried about both the situation that had prevailed when they'd left the Lands of Men and that into which they were returning.

No, at the moment, he was simply concerned about keeping a thirty-year-old car with dubious tires and a light back end on the road in what was surely the world's ultimate downpour. The wipers weren't up to even half this much precipitation, nor were the headlights; and he wasn't sure his nerves were either, when the odds weren't anywhere near his preference regarding what this monsoon-from-hell portended.

"Oughta know by now," Aikin chided Alec. "You've come this way a thousand times," he went on relentlessly, with more sarcasm than David deemed necessary, but also venting the frustration he was still trying hard to keep in check.

"David! Slow down!" Liz gasped from the front passenger seat. She grabbed at the dash pad with one hand and the side of her seat with the other, as the Mustang plowed into a particularly long, deep puddle.

David felt the steering go numb and held his breath, fighting the urge to apply the brakes, which could spell disaster. As it was, the rocky bank to their right loomed alarmingly nearer. Any closer, and—Well, that would solve several problems and create dozens of others.

"Dammit!" David snapped, when traction returned. "Will you guys just shut up? One of you wants me to hurry; one wants me to slow down. I . . . just wanta arrive."

Liz nodded mutely. David tried to regain control. It hadn't been that bad a trip, so far—until the rain had kicked in, and that had only been at Helen, ten miles back down the road. They didn't have that much further to go, either, to Sullivan Cove; and, as Aikin had observed, he could drive that road blindfolded or in his sleep. Presuming, of course, there was still actual pavement beneath that solid sheet of water.

"I know what you're thinkin'," Aikin dared, in defiance of David's ban. "You're wonderin' whether this is Cal's doing or LaWanda's or Lugh's."

"I'd *prefer* it was natural," David growled, downshifting as the Mustang found the first hairpin of the several that heralded the approach to Franks Gap. Once over that, he was home free—or in it.

"Feel better, don't you?" Aikin persisted. "Now that somebody's actually named what you fear."

"What I wish," David retorted, "is that Scott'd had more to say."

Aikin rolled his eyes—barely visible in the Mustang's mirror. "I told you what I knew—I mean, gimme a break, man, it's not hard to remember four lines. *'Aik! Thank God! Hell's broke loose up here. I don't know what good you can do, but get your ass up here. I'm at Dale's. Something's—'* And that was it. I never got to find out what *something* was 'cause the phone went out. Tried to call back and couldn't get anybody. Called my folks in MacTyrie, just to see if it was all over up there, or only at the Cove. Couldn't get them either."

"All of which we knew," Alec remarked. "All of which you're repeating just to hear your head rattle."

Aikin bared his teeth at him and retreated to the seat's

farthest corner. David was sorry for him—he was generally a quiet, unassuming guy. Easy to underestimate. He only ran on at the mouth when he was nervous. He only repeated himself when he was scared out of his skin.

The road steepened. Water slid across his lane in thick black runnels, but the sky ahead showed the first hints of a dull and soggy dawn. More rock flashed by to the right, and he glimpsed the gleam of headlights in his mirror. Good: Myra had caught up again, and was soldiering right along in her new minivan. And with her were Piper, Brock, and Fionchadd.

That last still freaked him too. The decision to head north immediately, in response to Scott's summons, had not been difficult, but posed certain problems nonetheless, principal among them being the fact that Fionchadd still wore the substance of Faerie, which would render it impossible for him to ride in a car.

Trouble was, his assorted exertions of the last few days, plus his loss of blood—and attendant Power—during his mysterious friend's arrow-ploy, had left him—he admitted under pressure—very weak indeed, and certainly frail for his kind. Clearly too weak to face what he might encounter should he brave the Tracks again and return to Tir-Nan-Og. He had enough strength left to change substance, but that was all. Until he could rest for a time, he was scarcely more powerful than an ordinary human, and that both galled him and frightened him half to death. "I do not wish to be weak among mortals," he'd confided to David. That he'd risked that handicap anyway was proof of how fried he was. Or how loyal. Nuada, David recalled, had told the Faery youth to guard them with his life. He hoped Finno didn't take that pledge too literally.

A sudden pitiful yowl from the back seat made David jump—and almost wreck the car in the process, as a reflexive tug on the wheel set the back wheels sliding for the shoulder. Another tortured scream ensued, and though David recognized the source, it still chilled him to the bone. No creature should sound like that, mortal *or* Faery.

"Sorry," Alec murmured. "That's why I was asking

about the time. It's, like, dawn; and you know what happens then. And we're in a car—''

David bit his lip—hard. "Yeah, I know," he acknowledged, "but we don't have time to stop so she can get out, and there's nowhere *to* stop anyway, for—*What the hell?*''

Something had just struck his neck, where it rose above the seatback. And close on that initial impact came teeth and claws, as a suddenly panicked Aife sought to claw her way out of the car by the straightest route, which lay through David's head.

He braked frantically—stupidly, part of him advised—but managed to navigate the latest switchback, just as the enfield—for so she mostly was now—scratched/kicked/pushed her way into the space between his left shoulder, the window, and the armrest. And lodged there, screaming like she was being skinned alive. David tried to extract her with his nonsteering hand, but got raked raw for his trouble, and swore vividly when a second attempt got him raked again. "Aife, fuck it—!" he spat, as he tried to subdue her. "Alec, can't you get your effing—''

"Stuck," Alec and Aikin chorused as one.

"Damn!"

David had almost got the car stopped by then, and still had sufficient presence of mind to pray that Myra would see his erratic driving and slow herself. Being rear-ended by a Caravan with a carload of friends on the way to a World-shaking emergency on a rainy night was not his idea of a gay old time.

Fortunately, the enfield had untangled herself.

If only she'd calm down! David grabbed for her again—only to find her in his lap and questing for his throat with a mouthful of teeth that were really quite alarming viewed at such intimate range. He snatched clumsily for her muzzle, missed, and got vague impressions of three sets of hands not his own flapping every which way around his chest and head, and then something grabbed his neck and tugged.

Not his *neck*, he corrected an instant later: the medallion that hung around his neck: the one Brock had given him.

"God, Davy, don't let her—'' Liz shrieked.

But it was too late. With a surprisingly audible *ping* the chain parted beneath David's ponytail, and with a sort of gagging gulp, the enfield swallowed the attached iron disc. Liz managed to drag the chain free of the jaws, but nothing any longer dangled from it.

By which time David had got the car halted, and the enfield was docile once more.

"Sorry, man! Oh, man, I am so sorry!" Alec wailed, as he reached around to retrieve his pet. "Oh, Jesus, man—"

"Never mind," David grunted, as he put the car in first and started off again—slowly, since it was raining harder yet. "God, what got into her?"

"Steel around her," Aikin opined.

David rubbed his throat with his less-injured hand. "Yeah, well, if steel freaks her so much, why'd she swallow my medal?"

"Blind reflex?" Alec offered. "Panic? I dunno. I mean, if she'd wanted to swallow it, she could've done it back on the boat. 'Least she's in the substance of this World; otherwise we'd *really* be in deep shit."

David didn't reply, and neither did anyone else, and two minutes later they crested Franks Gap and entered Enotah County. By the time they were halfway down the mountain, Aife was calmly grooming her cat-self as though nothing untoward had occurred.

Sullivan Cove was essentially underwater, and all that in only five days' time. David's heart sank as he swung the Mustang onto the long straight that unwound through his folks' front-forty. A high bank reared above and to the left. Somewhere up there was where he'd first seen the Sidhe on that long-ago summer night. And the cornpatch was up ahead, filling bottomland to left and right—and easily knee-deep in water. The creek was out as well (no surprise), but had not yet invaded the road, and the new culvert seemed likely to remain in place. Which was fortunate, because he had to cross it to enter Sullivan Cove.

More desolation greeted him there. His folks' drive was a virtual river of mud, and the sorghum patch across the way looked even worse than the cornfield. If this kept up, Lugh would have his way. Unless—awful thought—Lugh really had jumped the gun and was drowning the cove already.

"Cal better *hope* this isn't his," David grumbled, as he accelerated past his ancestral home—Big Billy was a famous earlier riser, and it'd be just like him to glance down the hill on his way to the morning chores. As if in reply, water splashed the windshield—muddy water this time, through which he could barely see. A glimmer of headlights showed that Myra had made the turn behind him.

A quarter mile later, they met the wind. It almost stopped the Mustang in its tracks, it was blowing so hard; driving sheets of rain into the windshield like rack after rack of wicked, steel-edged knives. David half expected to see the paint stripped right off, never mind the howling that filled his ears: thunder—and air forced in odd directions with far more fury than was—or could be—normal. Scott had been right: all hell had broken loose, and *that* call had come nearly three hours earlier.

So David was forced to creep along at a nerve-wracking crawl, through ruts that hadn't been present the last time he'd been that way, through places where he flat out couldn't see *at all* and had to rely on faith alone. Once through a patch of water so high the alternator light awoke and flickered ominously. A trip into neutral and lots of gas solved that, and first gear put them back on higher ground before the car completely drowned out. A check—risky— out the window showed the sorghum bent absolutely over like medieval supplicants, and the pines up on the ridge curved like ranks of drawn bows. Even as he watched, one broke. He started at that—and jumped again, as he wrenched the wheel to avoid an oak limb that crashed into the road ahead.

Somehow, far too many minutes later, they splashed into the wide muddy torrent that might've been Dale Sullivan's drive.

Dale's pickup was there; so was Scott's old Monarch (evidence there of at least one run to Athens), Calvin's BMW bike, and Sandy's muddy Explorer—LaWanda's suspect Pinto was still where she'd left it: back at Aikin's place in Athens.

Lights were on at both the house and the trailer, dim in both places too, which implied a power-outage being staved off with kerosene lamps.

David parked as close to the house as he could, and told his friends to stay put while he reconnoitered. Without waiting for reply, he forced the car door open—even here, with the house to break the wind's full fury, he had to exert a fair bit of muscle—and almost fell, so fierce was the force brought to bear there. A cracking pop behind him made him jump nigh out of his skin for the ten-millionth time that day. But it was only the cedars in the yard, whipping about like rags from some giants' washing.

He had to use the back steps because the fronts no longer existed, and was more than a little disappointed—as well as being soaked to the skin—to find the place deserted. A quick search produced a note, however. It was Scott's hand, and very shaky, and simply read, *"Couldn't stand not knowing any longer. Gone to the lake to check out the lay of the land (sic). Join us there if you find this."* There was a time notation too: fifteen minutes prior.

A further inspection showed sign of recent habitation, a number of troublesome leaks, something truly appalling in the bathtub, and no sign of Uncle Dale, except for a pot of coffee still warm on a hearth that showed less fire than embers.

David thought of checking the trailer, but a dozen steps up the hill proved the error of that idea, when he slipped and sprawled on all fours in the mud. He was thoroughly soaked—but no longer muddy: the rain came down that hard—when he staggered into the side of the Mustang over a minute later.

Blessedly, he'd had the sense to leave it running, and more blessedly, Myra'd had the sense to remain in her own vehicle as well, but he motioned to her anyway: pointing toward the lake over and over until the shadow-shape in the driver's seat gave him a thumbs-up and nodded.

Back in the car again, he dabbed at his face with the towel Liz handed him, then reversed out of the drive.

If the first part of the cove had been bad, this last half mile was ten times worse, and he actually had to creep along at slow walking speed to make any progress at all. The road was more water than land now, and most of that land was jagged rocks washed free of gravel: rocks that could do a major number on an unsuspecting Mustang oil pan.

Lightning seared his eyes. Another flash followed in its wake. Another. He had to halt entirely until his vision cleared, and even then could only inch forward, plagued with afterimages. One more curve and they should be there—almost.

More lightning, but they made that turn, and the land opened out before them, and for the first time, they could see Bloody Bald.

See where it was, anyway, for the entire horizon was smoky-dark with roiling clouds, fractured with jagged silver lightning. The world went black, then white, then black again, limning the mountain in eerie high relief, before shrouding it utterly. For an instant David thought a Hole was actually burning through there, for the effect was not unlike that which accompanied them. But then he recalled that Holes were born of his World—more to the point, of concentrations of iron in his World—and that, for the moment, he hoped, they were still in their own place.

No one spoke. Even Aife had fallen silent. The rains came harder yet, and with them, likewise, the wind, which actually shook the car, though it was heavily laden. More lightning, too: flash after flash. David could scarcely see to drive, and yet he pressed slowly onward.

But then something dark loomed ahead, even as the land opened out at the turnaround that marked the southern arc of BA Beach, and they were there. "Town Car," Alec noted.

David eased in close beside the big sedan, and was relieved to see Myra flanking it on the other. When their front doors were side by side and no more than six inches apart, Liz rolled down the window. The adjoining one likewise whirred down, to reveal a wild-eyed Calvin at the wheel, with everyone else accounted for. "So what's the deal?" David yelled across Liz's lap.

In reply, Calvin merely pointed. His face was tight with fear.

"Jesus!" Aikin whispered behind him.

Something new was happening—something besides wind and rain and lightning; besides things that had no color at all of themselves, and washed away all other color save those that arrived with the grim and faded dawn.

This was yellow. Pale at first, and then gaining intensity and strength and going gold. A line—a flickering line, true, but real—blazing to life above the waters of the lake.

"A Track," Aikin breathed. "Oh, Jesus!"

"There's no Track there," David protested.

"Oh yes there is—now!" Liz retorted. "But—Oh, my God, it's . . . it just flared once, and now it's gone!"

David blinked into the sudden color vacuum.

And blinked again an instant later, for out of the silver-steel darkness that was lake and sky and horizon alike, a figure was manifesting: tall and racing toward them, surrounded by a trembling nimbus of light. Headlights flashed across fabric and metal, as that figure continued its erratic approach.

"Oh, fuck!" David groaned. "Oh, Christ-in-a-Chevy motherfucker!"

More rain then, and more lightning, and something slapped against the window—and screamed. David caught a flash of startled male features—*Faery* features. And then the figure vanished: pounding—staggering rather—into the gloom that swallowed the road down which they'd come.

For a long moment David could do nothing but sit and gape, and it took a longer pause to realize that words—*a* word, anyway—had just flared into his mind.

"Follow!" David managed at last. "He wants us to follow him!"

"Back," Liz shouted desperately, across the gap to Calvin.

Calvin nodded and mouthed a silent "yes." David saw him put the Lincoln in gear. He only hoped Myra also got the message or had sense enough to follow. With Finno in there, she might.

The only good thing about the trip back up the hollow was that the wind was at their backs, as was the rain, which meant the windshield was marginally clearer.

David drove as fast as his frazzled nerves allowed, which was barely fast enough to keep pace with that fleeing figure. As best he could tell, the guy was a warrior—wore partial armor anyway, and he thought there was a sword and metal vambraces. But he bore no helm or shield, and all he could tell about the tattered surcoat was that it might once have been snow white.

No, *was* white, he confirmed a short while later, as a stretch of reasonably clear road allowed him to gain ground on the runner. And then his heart sank again. White with a gold sun-in-splendor. Lugh Samildinach's livery.

"Shit!" Alec swore behind him. Then: "He's going up to Uncle Dale's place!"

David had no choice but to follow. With everyone finally accounted for, he'd do anything to get indoors, mysterious Faery notwithstanding.

That one reached the house ahead of them, though—and leapt straight up on the porch, blond hair flailing wildly in the wind, surcoat beating at him savagely. Yet when David finally wrenched his door open, it was to enter an island of calm. *Hurry*, came that thought again. Without pausing to question his own wisdom, he scrambled onto the chest-high porch. Other doors slammed behind him. Voices yelled or swore or yammered, but they were all white noise now, lost in the greater cacophony of the storm.

The Faery met him on those rough, worn, half-rotten boards, and gave him a hand up when he slipped, even as others joined them and more yet angled around to the more accessible back. But the stranger made no move to enter. David scowled in confusion, then realized that the man was waiting for him to bid him welcome. "Bloody hell," David muttered, even as he grabbed what remained of the door and motioned that tall figure in.

Everyone else, he was relieved to see, either followed or was already there.

As for the stranger—he was gazing around as though in shock, dark eyes wild and feral, elegant nostrils flaring. Aife hissed at him, then uttered an inhuman screech and bolted for the adjoining kitchen. For a wonder, Alec didn't pursue her, content for the nonce to slump down on a torn, brown leather cushion between the hearth and the window.

"Faery—?" David dared, because he could no longer stand the suspense and had no strength for propriety.

The man stared at him, then rubbed his eyes and stared again, his eyes slightly out of focus. David was vaguely aware of Fionchadd standing in the doorway, frowning.

The stranger's face tensed abruptly. He started, then shivered and sank down—nearly fell—onto the hearth, where he buried his face in his hands. "Awful," he choked, his English so oddly accented David guessed he rarely spoke it—if he spoke often at all; not all Faeries did. Obviously this one had had little contact with humans.

Fionchadd slid down by him, did something odd to the cooling percolator, filled a cup, and passed it to the man. The Faery's hands were actually shaking. "Awful," he repeated. "Awful, but . . . someone had to tell you."

"Tell us what?" David demanded, as the man once more fell silent.

"The worst that could happen," the man returned, face now as wet with tears as the water running like molten silver into his eyes.

"*What?*" Fionchadd insisted. Then said a word in a language David didn't know.

The man's face grew minutely sterner, as though he had drawn strength from that injunction. When he spoke again, his accent was clearer, though he still stared at the floor. "Lugh no longer reigns in Tir-Nan-Og," the man declared. "I was one of his guard. I fought to the last. He . . . he said you would want to know."

David's eyes were huge, but no larger than Fionchadd's. "You . . . must explain," he heard himself reply.

The Faery shook his head. "It was the Sons of Ailill. They have not slain him, for even they dare not slay a king—not until they have made good use of him. But . . . he *will* die. They have already chosen his successor. When the Bright Season reaches its center at what we call now the Feast of Lugh, Lugh Samildinach will be . . . murdered. It must be then, for only on that one day will the Land accept a new king, and the Land, as you have seen tonight, already rebels at the loss of its ancient master.''

Fionchadd looked as though everyone he'd ever known or loved or cared about had just died. "This cannot be!" he roared.

The stranger grabbed his hand. Both hands, David saw, were shaking. Tears had started in Fionchadd's eyes.

"It is true, though," the stranger stated. "Lugh no longer reigns, nor yet does his successor. *No one* truly reigns in Tir-Nan-Og, but soon enough one will. And this new king they would raise up, I will tell you now, will be absolutely no friend to humans. Indeed, as soon as he is confirmed in his power, the flooding—the *real* flooding, not this which you have seen here—will commence."

"Sullivan Cove?" David had to ask.

Again the man shook his head. "No," he countered, "*every* place where Tir-Nan-Og touches the Lands of Men."

"Oh, my God," David gulped. "That's most of Georgia!"

A weary nod. "And not only that," the Faery continued, "should *any* iron bite the flesh of the sacred mountain, those who wield it will taste iron themselves soon after."

Footsteps made David glance up, to see Scott stomp across the room, then kneel at the Faery's feet. It was impossible to read Scott's emotions, but he looked wired enough to explode. David held his breath.

"Now let me get this straight," Scott began, in an oddly calm, slow voice. "No matter what happens, they're gonna flood—"

"Everything," Fionchadd finished for the stranger.

"Resort or no?"

"Apparently."

"And if any construction begins . . . ?"

"They'll kill the developers."

"And flood things anyway?"

"Apparently."

"Shit!"

"Great!" LaWanda growled. "Now we gotta look out for the bad guys too."

"So it would seem," Fionchadd agreed.

"Or," Uncle Dale rasped, from his place near the back of that tired, dripping, and now-incredulous company, "we *could* try to set things straight."

David gaped at him. "You don't mean—"

Dale nodded so vigorously his goatee waggled. "Makes as much sense as anything else, and it sure looks like there's gonna be risk any which way. But yeah: we've gotta put Lugh back on his throne."

David gazed back at the floor, at the puddle slowly forming there. And thought of a North Carolina kid ripped from his play, toyed with in some unknown manner, then released in an alien town a hundred miles away in the midst of a storm. "And how do we do that?" he challenged. "I have no idea."

"No," said a female voice from the kitchen door, in oddly accented tones. "No," it repeated, when it had their attention: "but *I* do."

"A-aife!" Alec stammered through a strangled gasp. "You're—"

He didn't get to finish, for she said it for him. "Yes, my Alec, I seem once more to be a woman."

No one spoke then but the thunder.